R P CARRUTHERS

R P Carruthers is the nom de plume of Rupert Copping, a writer and visual artist living on the west coast of Scotland. He was born in London but grew up in South America. With his Scottish wife and their children he lived for fifteen years in Spain. He has had a previous novel, Before the Dawn, published by Skylight Press. His paintings are exhibited and collected worldwide. For more information visit www.flamebooks.net or follow Flame Books on Facebook.

THE TIDE ALSO TAKES

A Historical Novel

R P CARRUTHERS

FLAME BOOKS

First published in the United Kingdom by Flame Books
Torrin, Isle of Skye, IV49 9BA
www.flamebooks.net

Cover template by www.thatdesignguy.co
Formatting by Sohail Liaqat

Printed and bound in Great Britain by lightning Source.

ISBN 978-1-7399164-9-7

For my wife, Jemima

Constraints I found impossible to avoid in the story here told have obliged me to manipulate the topography, in particular on the Isle of Skye and some small areas around Loch Duich. Had I not done so I could not have stitched the narrative together. Apart from this and a certain liberty with names, incidents, and descriptions of historical characters, I have tried to keep everything as accurate as I know how. If I have failed either on the Scottish/Gaelic or Spanish side the fault is entirely mine. The Author.

Triùir a thig gun iarraidh – gaol, eud is eagal.

Three things come uninvited – love, jealousy and fear.

caminante, no hay camino / se hace camino al andar

pilgrim, there is no path / the path is made as one walks

Antonio Machado

ONE

The Arisaig MacDonalds, along with Shona's younger sister, were crowded into a twelve oar birlinn that was already rowing away from the shore and towards the open sea beyond the sound.

Shona's smaller boat was also about to leave the Isle of Skye. As it was being pushed by men into deeper water, Shona, clutching her shoes, turned to the group standing with her on the white sand. Behind them, amid rocks and pungent seaweed, were gathered the two hundred or so men, women, and children who made up the Glas sept.

All who could were dressed in whatever scraps of finery they had available. But the funeral had started three days before and after the feasting and drinking their clothes were bedraggled. Morag alone, Shona's childhood friend, somehow managed to look dainty as ever. The same could not be said for Shona's male cousins, or her fatigued sister-in-law, or her brother, who was red eyed, still drunk, and without his blue bonnet. As for Shona's aunt, now a widow, she appeared not to know where she was; hunched over, silent, face vacant under the hood of her arisaid.

There was little talk. All that could be expressed had already been sung, danced, or spoken. After short farewells, Shona placed her shoes under her armpit, hitched her two petticoats and striped blue and white wool skirt up to her strong thighs, and stepped into the shallow water. As she did so a lone piper lifted his bagpipes, put the reed to his mouth and, inebriated though he was, managed to blow a pibroch for his departing kin.

Beneath the transparent surface tiny flatfish scurried away from Shona's toes as she trod in the sand. When she reached the boat, the water above her knees, she dropped her shoes over the side and grabbed the rim of the wooden hull. One of the men might have helped her, but Shona had known boats all her life and she swung aboard with careless ease.

The boat had a square sail and six oars. Being one man short, Shona sat on a bench beside Old John and took hold of an oar herself. She was not the only woman on board. Neil's wife, Elsbeth, was also one of the rowers. Elsbeth was short and strong; around the same age as Shona, in her twenties, but her clothes and adornments were less fine, for she was a servant. As they rowed out to sea Shona paused to look up. Beyond the rock and sand where her clan stood watching her departure the ground rose in a low broken bluff before levelling out. Here turf dwellings – some of stone – with thatched roofs were visible among hilly patches of green pasture or recently ploughed fields. But it was not such a large area before, on one side at least, it became enclosed by steep slopes of dense woodland, and whose trees were starting, just now, after the long winter, to put out leaves.

Shona was sad to be leaving her birth home, but almost as this feeling manifested itself a contrary one of confused resentment against her departed uncle rose up. The softness then vanished from her green eyes and she hunched forward, raising her voice to join the others in the rowing song and pulling on the oar with abrupt vigour.

Still, her thoughts continued to bother her. Had she not herself, years ago, agreed to the handfasting? So why then did she blame her uncle, even now when he was returned to dust? As if when alive he had owned the second sight, she told herself. But that was clearly one gift her uncle had not owned. So why was she thinking uncharitably of him? Had her uncle not been right to believe, in good faith, that she and Hector would make a happy match?

They had not been strangers to each other after all. She had met Hector as a child when her father sold Hector's father the brandy he was taking from that no good factor of Donald of the War. Shona would always recall as a child going down to the cove with other children to wait for her father's return. It would be dark, cold, and often raining, but there would be shelter under the entrance of the cave, where she would huddle, out of reach of the waves thundering on rocks. Beyond the rocks the sea would be shrouded in darkness, but at such times of the year her father went out it was rarely so dark as in the night-days of midwinter. Mostly there was a glimmer from the sky somewhere; enough for her to spot her father's boat emerging from the dimness, silent, sails furled, broad and low on the water. No sooner was the boat seen than one of the other children – usually a fleet footed boy – would run off to alert the clan. Meanwhile, further to the side of the cave was a space of shore less disturbed by rocks and here the boat would be grounded and men in rough shirts and breeches would jump out and stand to receive the barrels that were passed to them. Presently more men from the clan would arrive to help transport the merchandise into the cave. Her father was one of only a few people in the clan to own a pencil and a ledger. Under the yellow glow of a lantern, sitting on a barrel, her father – red bearded, tall and strong – would stubbornly record and double check against the ledger every item that came into the cave.

Shona's father, Douglas Glas, known as Red Douglas, was a freebooter and the chieftain of all that endured of the sept. That they endured at all, with any degree of independence, was due to the activities of Douglas and his brother, William. Were it not for the hijackings at sea the sept might not have endured. The land did not produce enough in timber, cattle or grain to sustain them. Had the MacDonald of Sleat been able they would have deprived them of every last acre. That they had not was in part due to the feeble character of their chiefs and factors, and to the confusion of the times; but more so, Shona believed, it had been due to her father's ability in hijacking the brandy and rum that was destined for the MacDonald factor. It was theft, but not of the grievous kind. Land taken by fire and sword, that *was* theft. But not long before she was born her parents had known the 'ill years' when early droughts and summers of rain had spoiled the crops and sheep and cows had died of plague. People had lived on nettles, berries, fish, seaware, birds, sheep and goats, but it had not sufficed and in the winters many had starved to death. Even in good years the land did not always provide abundance. After Shona's father became chieftain the burden he felt for the sept weighed on him. So he became a freebooter. Through selling timber he was already acquainted with boats and their trade. In a few years he and his brother had fast and capacious boats of their own as well as a network of informants all the way to Glasgow and even Liverpool. On several occasions Red Douglas and his brother had taken with them men of the clan and hijacked boats plying the sound. The crews of those boats had been threatened and merchandise seized by force, which is how Red Douglas had come by his repute. But Shona knew that her father had been averse to this practice. He had qualms. He considered the risk to himself and the clan too high. Hijacking brandy and rum with the connivance of the transporting vessel was, on the other hand, both honourable and safer. No one was coerced. And the MacDonald factor was obliged to pay only on receipt, so his consignments were lost but his outlay spared. As for the crew of the transporting vessel, they received their cut, so they had more to gain than to lose. The merchants in Glasgow or Liverpool would fare less well, though some would have their business underwritten. Others to lose would be persons in charge of excise duty, but like everyone else Red Douglas gave them no thought. But the coin he made from selling on the rum and brandy — that he did care about. In a poor year grain could be bought, and oats, and cattle. And he could keep at bay the MacDonald factor who was not only angered by the seizures of brandy and rum intended for himself but who wanted to destroy the Glas sept altogether and acquire their land.

One of Red Douglas' customers was Hector's father, Hector Matheson, The Experimenter. They named him thus because he was a learned man who spoke Latin and French and was intent on trying out new ways of doing things. He was a laird with land in his own name, but as well he was a tacksman for the Earls of Seaforth, the dynastic chiefs in that region of Scotland. The Experimenter lived on the mainland, a voyage of several hours from the Glas stronghold on the Isle of Skye. Red Douglas was keen to teach his son, also named Douglas, the ways of the sea; but it was Shona who showed a real passion for boats. To her father's amusement, as a child, always if her brother was going, she demanded to be taken as well. Red Douglas was reluctant, for space was limited and the sea not to be trusted. He did not want to put both lives of his children at risk at the one time. But Shona was so forceful that on occasions he succumbed or at others her brother would not go and she would take his place. The first time Shona met Hector was when at the age of eight she went with her father to sell The Experimenter brandy and claret at prices lower than he could have agreed elsewhere. On the voyage over Red Douglas allowed Shona to hold the tiller and, young as she was, he taught her how to sail with the wind. They were greeted on the shore by The Experimenter himself and his wife, Margaret. The Experimenter was very tall, taller than her father, and Margaret so slight that she barely came up to his chest. Shona thought she was bonnie. Over a fine linen damask shirt and a wool skirt she wore a soft multicoloured arisaid, which was pinned to her shirt by a big circular silver broach. The arisaid then rose over her shoulders and up over her head. Unlike Shona's own mother she wore no kertch. Under the hood her long hair was bound in a plait, the ribboned end of which twisted around the frilled neck of her shirt and over her shoulder. Shona was entranced. She thought Margaret, dressed as she was and with her sparkling blue eyes, looked more like a fairy princess than her own mother ever did.

The house where the family lived, that first time Shona saw it, seemed to her wondrous. It stood on its own a little way in from the broad curve of the shore. Around it was grass, where hens, ducks, and hobbled goats were grazing. There were sundry outhouses too, and a few trees along the edge of a burn further out. Beyond the burn and behind the trees were fields and just a glimpse of a settlement. But what struck Shona at once was the commanding size of the house and its whiteness. The houses where she lived, her own included, and be they of turf or stone, were all dark and rough. This one, by contrast, was pale, nearly white, like she had seen on the manse in Camus Cross. The roof was thatched, the same as hers, but altogether the house was, if not much longer, considerably wider. Inside, when she went in with Margaret, she was spellbound by its opulence. In her own house the partitions were made of wood or wicker work and, with the exception of the byre, did not reach the roof; but here there were rooms with walls that were thick, smooth, painted white, and went all the way up to a flat ceiling of planks. And at home they had a floor made mostly of rough loose stones but here the stone was all close fitting, shiny and flat. There was more furniture, too, and two pictures on the walls and more things that seemed to shine or show colour. And although there were hens about they were not sitting up on the planks, because there were no planks where they could sit. Instead, on one side of the common room, near a large table, was a case with rows of books behind leaded glass doors. So many books that Shona lost count, whereas in her own home there were only ten or twelve books plus her father's ledgers. Their biggest book was the bible; the book from which Shona and her brother, though not her baby sister, were just starting to learn English.

Red Douglas and The Experimenter stayed outside while the boat was unloaded. Shona joined Margaret at the hearth, which again was all different. At home the hearth was placed in the centre of their common room and had only a hole in the ceiling for the smoke to escape; Margaret's hearth was built against the gable wall and had a chimney and a roof of its own large enough to sit under.

An infant was asleep in a rocking crib near the hearth, and a servant came and went from the room. Shona was made to sit on a stool to one side of the cauldron hanging on its chain over the embers of a peat fire while Margaret sat close by in a low, high backed chair teasing wool onto a hand held spindle and asking Shona, who, from a pocket sown to her skirt, had removed the knitting she had brought with her, questions about her and her mother.

Shona, glancing about, wondered where the byre was located. Some of the houses in her settlement had hardly any kind of wall at all dividing the common room from the animals. Her own house had a wall made of thick wooden planks to separate the byre from their common room. Shona liked having their animals close by. In winter it made her house warm and comforting. Here, there was no sight of animals, although a waft of manure did come from a doorway near her. She was preparing to ask Margaret about it when there appeared through the doorway at the other end of the common room a boy. He was barefoot and wore little more than rough breeches and a dirty linen shirt.

Hector was tall and thin. He had his mother's upturned nose but his father's grey eyes and long face. Shona had the impression he was older than her and she felt herself withdrawing when he stared at her and said nothing. Margaret got Hector to greet Shona, which he did reluctantly. Then the infant, Hector's sister, woke up and Margaret put down the spindle and lifted her from the crib. Hector said he was done with school for the day and now he was off to mend a broken handle. Margaret obliged Hector to take Shona with him. Hector did not appear keen and Shona wanted to stay in the house but they had to do as Margaret bid.

The first two rooms at the main entrance of the house, past the front door, were general storerooms. They contained barrels of salted meat, seed, grain, boxes, tools, weapons, iron ore, nets, hair and hemp rope, halters, hides, nails, and much else. Only the back room had a small window, so in order to see better Hector left the front door open and after a little searching he found a bundle of long alder sticks for handles in a corner behind wooden boxes. He chose three and got a small axe and carried them outside to the back of the house, where Shona's bare feet squelched in the mud as she followed behind him.

Hector measured the sticks against the hole in the croman. He chose one, picked up the axe, and setting the stick down on a rock was about to taper the end when he had another thought.

'I will show you swordplay,' he said, holding the stick up. 'Do you want me to show you?'

All boys knew swordplay. He was only trying to impress her; but Shona was suddenly defiant. 'My father is teaching me to sail,' she answered.

Hector was momentarily silenced. But he recovered and went on to show off his knowledge of the seven cuts, seven guards, and three thrusts. He made Shona hold up one of the sticks while he took up martial stances and moved in and out slicing air and prodding her with his own stick. Shona's stick became heavy on her arm, which began to ache, but she was not going to let him know. When she could no longer hold the stick up, she dropped it, saying, 'I wish not to play any more.' Then she ran off around the side of the house to go and stand by the burn that was not so far away.

It had not been the best of starts. Yet Shona wanted to believe that even in that first prickly childhood encounter she and Hector had, at some indefinable level, recognized each other. Were it not so it would appear to her that, in marrying Hector, she had made the wrong choice. It suffocated her to think that she was destined to pass the rest of her married life in a situation that was often disagreeable to her, with a man she would cease to know. "The handfasting is what your father would have wanted," her uncle William had insisted, to encourage her, in the year before she married. And her aunt had nodded and said it was so. If Shona entertained any doubt she had not been able to consult her parents, for both were dead by the time she was sixteen.

Shona's mother died of the fever. She took ill one day and fell to the ground. Father had her put to bed and called Iseabal. The old woman recited incantations, rubbed her mother's body with a healing stone, and gave her potions of brandy mixed with goat droppings and herbs whose names Shona did not know. But her father, in distress, had then changed his mind and sent for one Beaton, a physician of fame. He arrived four days later on the back of a pony and wearing a big black hat. Behind him came a servant with a pack horse. At once Beaton threw out the old woman's potions and sent her away and made up a potion of his own from some powders he had brought with him. The next day the physician left. But mother did not improve. She lay in her boxed bed, on a mattress of heather, eyes closed, complaining of cold even though she was soaked in sweat. Iseabal stopped Shona outside the house and said she should go to the yellow spring with her brother and they should walk in a circle sun-wise three times, then drink from the spring and bring back some water in a flagon for their mother to drink. Shona asked father and he, despairing, gave his consent. When they brought the water back mother was too weak to swallow. It dribbled back out of her mouth. A little later a rattling sound came from her throat and she died.

Father was never the same after mother died. From night to morning the red in his beard and hair turned grey. He stopped smiling and walked hunched over, without vigour, like a man no longer desirous of life. Shona kept waiting to see father return to himself, but all that happened is that one day he went out fishing in the sound for mackerel with three others and the boat was struck by a whale. The boat turned over, two were drowned, father and young James. James' body was washed ashore days later but father's never appeared. The clan searched all along the shore this side of the sound and the other but there was no sign of him. Without a body they could not have a funeral for him. Shona suffered even now, eight years later, for not being able to grieve for her father as custom allowed. There were some in the clan who claimed to have seen the ghost of Red Douglas walking up and down on the shore, in the company of the fairy folk, and intent on looking for what, some said, must be his bones. Shona had not seen his ghost herself but she was ready to believe the sightings true because it was said that without a proper burial a person's soul could not easily depart.

Her uncle's funeral, on the other hand, had taken place as it should. There could have been more people, it was true, but there were sufficient in any case. MacDonalds, one of whom was married to her younger sister, had come from far and wide. Even representatives of the MacDonald of Sleat had come, and some others too, in spite of their maybe having reason to have held a grudge against her father and her uncle for their freebooter ways. That she herself had come without her husband was due to him being on business in Edinburgh. And while it did occur to her to fill a second boat with others related to her husband, and who had known her uncle, she had decided against it for everybody was occupied with spring work. Now was not the best time to deprive people of their livelihood.

For three days Shona had taken part in the wake in her uncle's house along with her relatives and the intermittent procession of visitors who came to pay their respects. As was the custom upon entering the house every mourner was greeted with oat bread, whisky, cheese and butter. Depending on their inclination either immediately or at a later moment the mourners had approached the corpse, where it rested in the common room on a wooden bier, wrapped in a winding sheet, with a wooden plate on its chest containing salt and earth; salt for the spirit, earth for the flesh. Gazing upon the corpse, the mourners then reached down to stroke and touch it, so as not take their leave with any residue of ill will. They did this in silence, for no one spoke, but at every interlude when food was served Shona's cousin, her uncle's eldest son, had said grace, and during the night the mourners had formed a ring and chanted laments and danced where they stood in slow time. The first time there was dancing when Shona was present dust had risen up from the floor. People had started coughing and in the yellow light of the lamps she noticed that fleas had come up with the dust and where hopping everywhere, even onto the winding sheet covering her uncle. Fleas were not so often seen; it was more likely to be ticks, lice and midges, but at her uncle's funeral it was fleas. After that Shona's cousins had made sure every now and then the earth floor was sprinkled with water. They also chased away the hens when they got between the mourners' legs and started pecking for crumbs, and also because they did not want the hens crossing by the corpse since animals crossing by a corpse were considered omens of ill fate and needed to be killed.

After three days, at first light, they brought the corpse out of the house. At the door young Callum played a pibroch on the bagpipes. Visiting mourners came out of barns or roused themselves from the open air heath where they had slept wrapped up in their plaids. They breathed vapour and banged their hands and, if they had no shoes, stomped their bare feet as they joined the procession. The bier on which the corpse lay was carried by men who relinquished their load to others when they became tired. Several times the procession of three hundred and more folk stopped to rest on its journey. The mourners were given oats and water and grace was said until finally the procession reached the chapel and graveyard with a view of the sound where the seawater was grey as pewter.

After the sermon, women keened and Shona wept for her uncle, but an old tradition prevented her and other women from joining the men at the graveside. They watched from just beyond the stone wall of the graveyard as his corpse was lowered into the pit.

Her uncle was kin and a good man. But he was not her father. He was cautious and did not have her father's independent spirit. In the last years, and in spite of better harvests, the sept's prosperity had declined for want of her uncle's enterprise. It was he who had pressed for the handfasting with Hector. When she held her ground he had expressed anxiety for her future in a way that she knew her father, when he was alive, had not. Her father was always keen to teach her and her brother to know their minds and hold firm. But her uncle, and her aunt too, kept insisting: If after a year and a day it did not work out she could leave, they said. It did happen, she knew. Some handfasting couples did separate after the year and a day and it was not held against them, but it was the less common outcome. Most stayed together and married. Shona had not been sure about Hector, she had not been sure about herself, and she feared that at the end of the year and a day it would be no clearer to her, but that by then she would be with child and she would agree to marry Hector regardless.

If the children had lived, she thought. What would it have mattered then how she felt, how their marriage came about? The children had made her content. And Hector, too, he had cherished the children. That was when she had begun to fully appreciate another side to her husband – a side he did not often show, which he guarded against, as though afraid it would betray a weakness in him that she might employ. But the more fool he because it was that very softness that in her eyes had lifted the latch. And it was not only when he had been with the children. There had been times before that, before the children were born, when they were handfasting, and before that even, when in their encounters she had seen in him, in his smile, in his unexpected impulses, that same carefree, endearing, gentle quality.

'Over there! Look. Big ships!'

The shout came as the boat skirted the shore past the half ruined castle on the promontory of Kyleakin. Shona, who had taken control of the sail, was adjusting it to catch an easterly that would take them against the current, towards the mainland close by on the other side. For a few moments longer she attended to the sail, then she sat back, seizing the tiller again, making sure the sail was taking the wind before she let her eyes settle on the horizon. In the distance, under a broken grey and blue sky, the two ships looked small but it was immediately apparent to her that they were of a kind she did not recognize. They were big and long with many sails and two or three masts and although they appeared to be stationary she judged they were advancing at a fair speed.

'What do you make of them, John?'

The three men had stopped rowing and they were all turned towards the ships, watching in silence.

Wrinkled and toothless, but still strong, Old John turned back towards Shona and stretched out his large hands to grab both oars.

'They are men of war.' He nodded to himself. 'Frigates they would be.'

In earlier years Old John had sailed foreign seas. If he said they were frigates they were frigates.

'Might it be the Spaniards?' suggested Neil, Elsbeth's husband. He was a lean, sinewy man; fully bearded. When Shona had married Hector and moved to the mainland, Neil had elected to accompany her as a servant even though he was a third cousin of hers. 'I heard they were many in Stornoway.'

'With the Earl of Seaforth himself, now returned from France, and the other lords they are saying,' Old John agreed. 'Thee hundred of them.'

'Three hundred of whom?' asked Elsbeth.

'Spaniards.'

'I heard it was more. Three hundred and fifty,' said Neil.

Shona was silent. Everyone knew now about the Spaniards. Spain and England were at war. The precise reason why was beyond Shona's ken; and probably, from what she had heard, beyond anyone's ken. But she knew Spain was making an alliance with the exiled Scottish King James against the English Hanoverian King George and the Covenanters. In some way, she imagined, it would account for the Spanish troops disembarking on the Isle of Lewis a month or more past. Word had it that the troops were to be garrisoned at Eilean Donan castle, a day's journey from where Shona lived. Storms had driven their ships back once already, but if it was them trying to arrive again Shona was as sure as she breathed that another battle was in the making. Why otherwise would they be taking over the castle? And what would they be like, these Spaniards? All she felt certain of was that they must be of the Roman Church. Covenanters they would not be. Yet of the Roman Church or otherwise it would not halt the desolation that was sure to come. Shona recoiled at the thought of the men folk going to war once more. Sheriffmuir was a scarce four years gone. *That* battle had resolved nothing. Both Jacobites and Covenanters claimed victory, but did anyone understand the need to be fighting at all? And what victory was there for all the men who had gone away whole and never came back, or came back maimed and useless? Life was bloody and bitter enough without the added strife. It should not be like this. There must be a better way than bloodshed. But bloodshed is what it had been from the day she was born, from the day her parents were born, from the day her grandparents were born. When the bards recounted the deeds of the clans, now and in the past, it was bloodshed that dominated the recitations. Would there ever be a time when men would not kill each other? Shona wished it were so. *In the name of the Holy Mother, and of Jesus, who has died for our sins; but how can I believe that it will ever happen, that peace will settle here in my lifetime? This is hard for me. Hard to believe. Hard.*

TWO

Captain Alejandro de la Rueda stood by the forecastle. In his ears was the sound of sea sweeping past the ship and of wood creaking and the snort from the horse when he stretched out a palm with an apple on it. The horse, one of several Galician mountain ponies, had been poorly and thus transferred from the lower deck to a stall next to the cow where it could benefit from fresh air. De la Rueda was not directly responsible for the battalion's animals. That was under the quartermaster sergeant, but de la Rueda liked horses and so he had brought it an apple.

After feeding and patting the horse, de la Rueda turned to head back to the quarter deck. He was of medium height, broad of shoulder and narrow of waist; a dark complexioned man just turned thirty. Although his square face bore a thin scar from the side of his left eye down to his upper lip, he eschewed the use of make up. His nose was prominent and he sported a narrow black moustache interrupted by the scar that reached the corner of his mouth, where, as now, it ached a little in cold weather. Another tuft of dark hair grew under his lower lip. His eyes were small, close set, dark as to be almost black, and they mostly contained a watchful expression. Stepping past coiled ropes and a sailor on his hands and knees scrubbing the deck, but in no hurry, de la Rueda then paused to lean against the side of the ship and stare out at the approaching land mass. Here the land is mountainous, he thought to himself; more like at home than that place we left. To Captain de la Rueda's eye the Isle of Lewis had appeared flat, but here, as the ship sailed into the narrowing sea loch past the Isle of Skye he saw rows of mountains ahead close by on either side. Quite a few were heavy with snow. A little, it reminded him of the mountainous inlets close to the sea in Galicia where his regiment was quartered. A little of home too, perhaps, for it was also mountainous where he came from at the foothills of the Pyrenees. He was thinking of home, the green valley where his aged mother still lived, when a small vessel in the distance caught his eye.

From the pocket of his yellow embroidered coat de la Rueda brought out a wood and vellum telescope. It was of novel design and an instrument he was not accustomed to; a parting gift from Cardinal Alberoni to the three senior officers. After a little confusion de la Rueda managed to stretch it and place it to his eye. A small coastal boat with a square sail presented itself. He could just make out the crew, one of whom at the helm had to his surprise every appearance of being a woman. But the boat was far away, moving in an opposite direction, so he could not distinguish the woman too well.

And yet de la Rueda kept looking, trying to make out the woman as if it were a matter of importance. Of course, he knew it was ridiculous, this fixation he entertained that she could be somewhere in the world – a woman who did not exist, who was only a ghost in his mind; a fantasy, a face in a picture he had seen long ago. Yes, but a face seared in his soul. *And one could say the same thing about God, could one not? Who could see God actually in the flesh? And yet we know he exists. I know he exists without ever seeing him, so why might that not be her now as strange as it seems?*

De la Rueda believed in such things as miracles. As a soldier he had seen more than one miracle occur in the battlefield. Ridiculous it might be, absurd, but it did not seem to him beyond the realm of possibility that one day he could meet the very woman whose face he had seen in a picture and who in past moments of desperate need, had appeared to him in his mind like a presence, like the Madonna herself, sustaining him when all was about to fail.

Indeed, as de la Rueda peered through the telescope he now had a peculiar tingling sensation on the back of his neck. It was not for the first time. On several occasions over the years he had had this sensation on seeing a woman from a distance only to discover on closer examination that it was not her. But it was rare for him to have a presentiment. And there was something about the woman in the boat, as distant and undefined as she was, that he thought he could detect as familiar to him, as something he could recognize deep within himself and which, mysteriously, was able to transcend time and distance.

'Anything of interest, captain?'

At once de la Rueda lowered the telescope. All previous thoughts went from his head. Straightening his spine, he lifted his right hand, surrounded by a frilled lace cuff, to remove his gold-rimmed tricorne.

'At ease, man.'

De la Rueda placed the hat back on his wigged head and proffered the telescope. 'Nothing much, sir. Care to take a look?'

'I have my own, thank you. But what do you make of these things, anyway?'

'They could be useful. I would rather mine were made of tougher leather though; to be truthful, I do not think mine will last.'

'No. You are right. They do look flimsy. The people who invent these things do not know what a campaign is, they are not soldiers, that is the trouble.'

Like de la Rueda, Colonel Nicolas Bolaño, commanding officer of the Galicia Battalion, was dressed in a yellow silk coat with white piping and tails, white stockings, buckled shoes, and white waistcoat over white frilled shirt, but his gold epaulettes were bigger, his tricorne fancier, he wore an elaborate sash and there were insignias of his rank on the ornate cuffs of his jacket. In complexion he was paler than de la Rueda, a detail emphasized by the white powder on his cheeks. He was also two inches shorter, but his lack of height he made up for with a curling waxed moustachio, a peacock strut, and an air of authority.

'It should not be long now, captain. How is the gunpowder?'

'The kegs are in good order. Dry and secure, when I last checked this morning.'

Bolaño nodded. 'Well, all that awaits us now is to disembark. And let us hope there is good news from our Armada.'

'It does seem a little odd.'

'What do you find odd?'

'Well, the Armada sailed two weeks before we did, sir.'

'But from Cadiz,' Bolaño reminded him.

Cadiz was in the south of Spain and their two frigates had sailed from San Sebastian, in the north. That would help to account for the discrepancy. But de la Rueda found it odd even so. He would have expected the invasion fleet to have by now reached England or Wales. From what de la Rueda understood, the fleet was rather smaller than what the Scottish lords had requested. Only twenty eight ships with five thousand soldiers, gunpowder, cannon, and fifteen thousand arms. Not sufficient to march on London, depose the Hanoverian king, and win the war against England. But that was where de la Rueda's battalion and the Scottish Jacobite lords came in. Their little force was intended as a diversion. It was hoped the battalion would aid the Scottish lords in getting their tribes to rise and so draw English troops north, which would relieve the pressure on the invasion force.

Bolaño was about to add something when the Earl Marischal descended the steps from the poop deck and stopped by the railing to look out at the passing landscape. The earl wore a green velvet frock coat and black breeches and below these patterned yellow and black hose. Beneath his hat and wig he had a long ruddy face, lightly powdered, and lively blue-grey eyes. He was young; too young, it appeared to de la Rueda, to hold not only a general's rank in the Spanish army but also an equivalent one from the exiled Scottish king. But maybe I am being deceived, de la Rueda speculated. After all, do they not say the man served in Flanders under the famous Duke of Malborough?

Presently another noble, the Marquis of Tullibardine, emerged from the door that led to the officers accommodation. He was tall, approximately the same age as the Earl Marischal. His face was rounder, softer. He had an upturned nose and mannerisms that had a feminine quality to them.

De la Rueda had spoken to the Earl Marischal on several occasions and found him to be of an energetic and, on the surface at least, congenial disposition. But he had spoken less with the Marquis of Tullibardine, who he found polite, though with a manner that was both more reticent and petulant. The marquis wore clothes in a style similar, if quite a bit fancier, to other gentry de la Rueda had observed while on the Isle of Lewis. It was, to his eye, a pleated and belted short skirt of a patterned brownish red colour that then spread out from above the belt in a sort of blanket which was gathered and draped over his shoulder. Under this garment of fine wool he wore a doublet and a silk shirt with wide cuffs. His knees were bare, but he wore patterned hose and a large black hat with a white cockade.

The Marquis of Tullibardine and the Earl Marischal at first kept their distance, standing a few yards apart, eyes looking about everywhere but at each other. But after a moment the earl said something which made the marquis turn towards him. They then bowed their heads to each other and the earl took out a silver snuff box from his waistcoat as the marquis came to join him.

'Look, they do not appear to be at each other's throats any more,' said Bolaño softly, not to be overheard. 'It bodes ill to have all this dispute in the chain of command.'

As Bolaño was speaking the earl turned his head towards him and gave a nod.

Bolaño nodded back and pulled on his moustachio.

'I am being entreated,' he said, and went to join them.

Watching them discreetly, de la Rueda recalled that a couple of weeks past, while on the Isle of Lewis, the earl and the marquis and four or five other Scottish lords, including the Earl of Seaforth, had held a council of war, first on the frigate and presently in the upper chambers of the stone built lodge overlooking the harbour. De la Rueda did not have the seniority to be present at the meetings himself, but his colonel had been there and had relayed to de la Rueda much of what had transpired.

It appeared that there was more than one faction at work among exiled Jacobites. Their King James had his court in Rome, but his military commander, the Duke of Ormond, was based in France and Spain. It was the Duke of Ormond together with the Spanish Foreign Minister, Cardinal Alberoni, who had given command of the expedition to Scotland to the Earl Marischal. But that was not how it turned out. After the long journey when they arrived on the Isle of Lewis and disembarked the troops to give them rest, the Marquis of Tullibardine and company had arrived, having for their part sailed from France.

At first it appeared the marquis was the bearer of good tidings. He said that he had credible information that the Armada had been spotted making good progress towards the coast of England. But further questioning made it apparent that his information was at best rumour. The precise whereabouts of the invasion fleet could not in fact be ascertained. For hours the Council went around in circles, unable to agree. Finally the Earl Marischal, who seemed to be of a stubborn and at times tempestuous nature, announced after several meetings that he was now ready, regardless of the situation with the Armada, to proceed with the objective charged to him. He was duty bound, he said, to land the three hundred Spanish troops allocated to him on the Scottish mainland and thereafter raise an indigenous army with a view to diverting English troops north.

The colonel had told de la Rueda that the Marquis of Tullibardine did not dispute the Earl Marischal on this issue. These Scottish lords were both sworn to the Jacobite cause. The marquis, indeed, for all that he presented an elusive and reticent manner, had turned Jacobite against the very wishes of his father, the Duke of Atholl, and as a consequence had been disowned by him. But regardless of the depth of his sentiment, the marquis was nevertheless of the mind that if err they must they should do so on the side of caution and wait for definite intelligence as to the arrival of the Armada. The invasion had little chance of success, he argued, with a mere three hundred Spanish troops and an uprising of the clans in Scotland. The Earl Marischal conceded it would be a risk, but he countered that the longer they remained on the Isle of Lewis the greater the risk of them being discovered and encircled by the English navy. He pressed for them to trust in the safe passage of the Armada and to proceed to the mainland whence they could begin their part of the invasion by raising the clans and taking the town of Inverness which by all reports was inadequately defended.

From what de la Rueda was told by his colonel at this juncture the discussion became heated. The Earl of Seaforth, who was the overlord in this part of the world, could not make up his mind whether to side with the Earl Marischal or the Marquis of Tullibardine. Although a Catholic and no less a Jacobite, it had appeared to Bolaño that Seaforth was more concerned about the danger to his estate than his support for the cause. Seaforth was the largest landowner in the region. He was deep in debt and depended on the rents he received from his tenants, but he had told Bolaño that if the insurrection failed he stood to lose everything. He had said it to Bolaño almost as a boast, for he was a vain man. The other commanders present, chiefs of their clans, took differing sides each, until their arguing turned bitter and personal and tempers flared, eyes flashed, hands tightened on hilts. The marquis however had been concealing a trump card. He announced that the exiled King James had appointed him commander in chief of the military forces in Scotland. To demonstrate he unfurled with a flourish his commission of lieutenant general, one rank higher than the Earl Marischal. Bolaño said such was the earl's surprise and anger that he had gripped the side of his chair and all the colour had drained from his young face. Even through the powder on his cheeks one could see his skin turn bloodless. As for the marquis, he thought it best to stay quiet for a while. He got up from the table and went to stand by the window. Bolaño was of the opinion that the marquis was held in little regard by the Earl Marischal for his military abilities. Both perhaps had ranks too high for their experience, but while the earl had served with honour in foreign fields, the marquis had served only in the battle of Sheriffmuir and his command had been at best indifferent. When the earl spoke again to the marquis' back there was a tremor in his nasal voice. Very well, he declared. Since the marquis out ranked him, he would relinquish command of the ground forces, but he would retain command of the frigates, over which, being Spanish, the marquis had no jurisdiction, and which had been expressly entrusted to him by the Spanish Foreign Minister. The marquis had no answer to this, for unlike the earl he did not have a general's rank in the Spanish army as well.

By the time the meeting ended that day little had been resolved. But more discussions were held over the next days, which Bolaño attended. Tempers were held in check by a veneer of civility. At last the Earl of Seaforth reluctantly gave way to the Earl Marischal. The marquis remained intent on waiting for news of the landing in Wales or England, but the others now so strongly protested against further delay, for fear of the arrival of the Royal Navy, that the marquis finally also acquiesced.

So here now, in this uncertain way, we arrive. Tomorrow, God willing, we disembark. After that... well, who knows? As Cervantes says, Everything is life until you die... We are pawns, all of us, high and low, we are but pawns to God's obscure design. Another adventure it will be in any case, though God forgive me, how weary I am now of adventures.

Again de la Rueda found himself thinking of home, wishing he could be there even though he had not visited home more than twice in five as many years. But the last occasion had tugged strongly at his heart. It was pleasant in the valley where the de la Ruedas had their estate; sheltered and fertile and he could remember how much he had enjoyed being there even if almost he had himself killed by a bear.

Farmers from around and about had approached him because a rogue bear was coming down from the woods. As well as scaring peasants it had broken into a barn and devoured two goats. So de la Rueda and others had tied an old donkey in a field on the edge of the wood on the north bank of the valley. They chose a moonlit night, smeared themselves with horse manure, and hid among the trees. De la Rueda had his musket primed. As a precaution he had also loaded a pistol. After a few hours the bear appeared. It came ambling into the silvery moonlit field, looking about, sniffing the air. A huge brute. The donkey went into panic, trying to break loose from the rope. The bear approached the donkey with what appeared to be curiosity, but a moment later its paw came out and with a single swipe it felled the donkey. De la Rueda, from his position behind a large oak tree, took careful aim and pressed the trigger. But the musket did not fire and the bear, hearing the trigger, raised its head from the donkey and came forward to investigate. De la Rueda threw the musket down and brought out the cocked pistol. The bear covered the short distance in a flash. It came around the tree and was upon de la Rueda when he fired. The bear fell back but not before its claw had slashed his chest. It was about to attack again when the others came up. The bear then turned and ran off. A few days later it was found dead in the forest, shot through the heart. De la Rueda's wound was superficial, but his deed was much retold by the folk of the valley. At the end of his stay he had sat under the dappled shade of the pear tree in the orchard, his naked back against the trunk, and wanted never to leave again. The more so since his father had now died and responsibility for the estate had been passed to his sister and brother-in-law, neither of whom inspired de la Rueda with total confidence.

But the army had him under contract for another while. Some, like the colonel, born soldiers, embraced the vagabond life. Other officers, less dedicated, came from families with good connections. When the life became too burdensome they found ways to escape their obligation. But he was of Jewish seed. Every day de la Rueda had to show he was more of a Christian, more of a soldier, than his fellow countrymen. That his parents had converted to the Catholic faith before he was born was scarcely sufficient. Protection did not come so simply. When de la Rueda was a child, his uncle, a bookbinder in the city of Corunna, and convert though he was, had been expelled with his wife and children. Where the family was now de la Rueda could not be sure. In Greece, he believed. And his grandmother in Castille, before de la Rueda had been born, had been burnt at the stake after first being made to convert. De la Rueda's parents had been spared, for his father, a merchant of repute, had gained the patronage of the Count of Fuentenueva. But for a convert it was always tenuous. The army, the count had suggested, would be a good career for the young de la Rueda. It would put him in good standing, and if he were to distinguish himself it would reflect to the glory his family. De la Rueda's father had not disagreed. As for de la Rueda himself he was seventeen and hungry for adventure. He joined the regiment of the line as a cadet. And now, thirteen years on, he was a captain, with honour to his name, a veteran of several battlefields and seven times wounded. But he was weary. The flavour had gone. All de la Rueda wanted now was peace and rest.

And to find that woman, he dreamed in idle moments

With the Isle of Skye receding behind the two frigates, the sea loch began to narrow until hills appeared closer by on both sides of the water. Then a castle came into sight. It jutted out from the shore into the sea loch, near where a river debouched. More directly behind the castle the ground rose steeply with fields beginning to turn green and a few small scattered dwellings from the thatched roofs of which smoke billowed. The castle itself was made of grey stone and was reached from the shore by a narrow bridge onto a projecting islet of rocky ground. To de la Rueda the castle, while dramatically placed, seemed run down, almost derelict, and rather smaller than he was expecting. When he put his eye to the telescope he could see people on the battlements but not the crowds he had vaguely anticipated.

As de la Rueda gazed through the telescope orders were barked through megaphones and sailors appeared in part uniforms that were blue and white with bits of red and dark top hats or red caps and bandanna. The sailors feet thudded on the wooden deck as some made their way to the rigging and others to their stations by the cannons.

De la Rueda put away his telescope as Colonel Bolaño left the Scottish nobles and came back to him.

'What do you make of the castle, captain?'

'It appears well positioned, sir. But smaller than I foresaw.'

'Yes, well... The Scottish lords assure me they have information from the Earl of Seaforth that it has ample space for between fifty and a hundred soldiers. So that is how we shall proceed. I will disembark here. I will look the castle over and decide how many soldiers to garrison and whether it will be suitable storage for our munitions.'

'Yes sir.'

'If I decide to stay on, which is most probable if the Earl of Seaforth awaits me as arranged, you will remain under the Marquis of Tullibardine's command until the remaining troops and provisions are disembarked.'

'At that harbour where we picked up the pilot earlier, sir?'

'The same, captain. I am told it is no more than two leagues from the riverside by the castle. There is a track from the harbour, although I understand there are few in this part of the world that will accommodate carts. But that is not our concern.'

'Do you still intend to place Captain Stapleton in command of the castle garrison, sir?'

'Yes, why?'

De la Rueda hesitated.

'I know what you are thinking,' said Bolaño. 'But on that Lewis island he did not touch a drop. Not a drop. And we will need someone who can speak the language and can get on with the natives.'

Stapleton was Irish. There were several Irish among the troops. De la Rueda's second in command of his own company, Lieutenant O'Flanagan, was Irish. When the battalion was assembled out of the larger regiment the Irish contingent had been chosen for their knowledge of the Celtic world. The Irish all knew some English or Latin and while their Gaelic was different it was hoped it would be sufficient for basic communication. It had appeared to make sense back at home, in Spain, before they sailed, but after a month in Lewis de la Rueda had discovered that in fact the Scots and the Irish understood little of each other's Gaelic, while on the other hand the Scots of the 'gentleman' class were surprisingly conversant, quite apart from English and their own tongue, with French and Latin. To one degree or another many of the Spanish officers, and even some of the troops, knew French, Latin, or both. His colonel was multilingual, although he spoke no Gaelic, and de la Rueda himself, whose home was on the border of the Pyrenees, spoke French almost as well as he did Spanish. Had it been up to him he would not have considered the fact that Stapleton was Irish sufficient reason to put him in charge of the garrison at the castle. He liked Stapleton. He was a bluff, forthright man, and his record was good. But he was old now. Too old to have come on this expedition, really, de la Rueda thought, for he feared it would make Stapleton overly cautious. And he had a weakness for drink. It was true that Stapleton had not touched the liquor in Lewis, but too often de la Rueda had seen drunks stop and start again.

'Anyway, Captain Stapleton will have Mendez with him,' said Bolaño, lifting his hand to pull at his waxed moustachio.

De la Rueda, for other reasons, thought even less of Lieutenant Mendez than he did of Stapleton.

'I will have a word with Mendez myself,' Bolaño went on. 'I will give him authority to take over should Captain Stapleton become indisposed under critical circumstances. Everyone knows the captain has a problem but I am personally obliged to him.'

Bolaño did not elucidate and de la Rueda thought best not to ask. He trusted the colonel. It was not his affair.

It was midday when the frigates dropped anchor. Sailors moved about on the top deck everywhere. De la Rueda went down into the cramped, gloomy lower decks to make sure the soldiers were kept busy, not least in hauling up the barrels of gunpowder, ammunition and provisions to the top deck. When he came back up, the launch on the port side of the top gun deck had already been taken out of its cradle and was being lowered by means of ropes and tackle onto the water. De la Rueda gave orders for the officers and soldiers not on guard duty or engaged in labour to assemble. The soldiers emerged in their uniforms, which were the opposite of the officers: white, piped with yellow. They lined up tightly on the quarter deck, bearing muskets. Above them, on the poop deck, Colonel Bolaño, now with de la Rueda and the other captains gathered behind him, gave a short speech. At the end of it the soldiers responded with a cheer, then Bolaño and the ship's captain raised hats to each other, after which Bolaño stepped down from the poop deck, and followed by Captain Stapleton and Lieutenant Mendez, made his way to the ladder on the port side of the ship.

Once an escort of soldiers and the officers were aboard, de la Rueda stood by the ladder at attention, his tricorne under his arm, watching as the launch was rowed away and towards Eilean Donan Castle, less than five hundred yards distant.

Two hours later the launch returned with Lieutenant Mendez. He reported to de la Rueda that the colonel had met up with the Earl of Seaforth and would be staying on in the castle, which he judged adequate for storage, and the transfer of men and supplies was to begin immediately. This would amount to forty eight soldiers, three hundred barrels of gunpowder, one thousand muskets, fifty barrels of ammunition, plus armaments and provisions. De la Rueda put himself to work at once. He had signals sent to the second frigate and went from here to there issuing orders, making certain nothing was overlooked. All the launches, with barges tied to them, from the two frigates and other vessels from the mainland, were employed to ferry the supplies in a relay system that required all hands available.

By midnight it was too dark to unload more. De la Rueda went down to his berth in the officers' quarters. The cabin was so small it contained little more than his bunk. De la Rueda took off his coat, hat, and boots, put them away neatly, lay down on the straw mattress and pulled a wool blanket over himself. In an instant he was asleep. His servant awoke him at first light. He put his clothes back on and went out on deck, where, under a sultry sky, he spoke to other officers and gave orders. Afterwards he went inside for some food.

Again the unloading started. It was not until late evening that the transfer of cargo was completed and the last launch was hauled into its cradle. From the poop deck the ship's captain gave orders for the anchor to be raised. At once sailors gathered at the capstan in the forecastle and begun to push at the spokes. Slowly, with loud creaking sounds, as the sailors turned in circles, the anchor rose up. Now the captain called for sails to be hoisted. Sailors scrambled up the rigging in the dusky light while others on the deck took hold of ropes. Seagulls congregated overhead in the brooding, near dark sky, and the big sails flapped as they were released and deployed to take the wind.

The journey from Eilean Donan Castle to Kyle of Loch Alsh was only a matter of an hour or two. De la Rueda went down to speak to Major Santarem, who was in his cabin. Santarem was the senior quartermaster and de la Rueda's superior officer, but he was ill, so de la Rueda had taken his place as second in command. Furthermore Santarem had been ill for some weeks with little sign of improvement. De la Rueda was of the opinion that Santarem would do better to stay on board and return to Spain, when the time came, with the ships. But Santarem was refusing. Even the surgeon could not persuade him.

'I will recover when I am on land,' the skeletal Santarem insisted while perched on the edge of his bed as the ship creaked and swayed. 'It is these cursed boat journeys that make me ill.'

The surgeon, a short man with a heavy black beard, glanced at de la Rueda and shrugged.

De la Rueda did not have the authority to order Santarem to stay on board. Only the colonel could do so; but for some reason he had not.

'You must decide for yourself, Francisco,' said de la Rueda.

'I am. And if I am going to die I want to die with my soldiers on firm land. Even if it is foreign.'

De la Rueda returned outside, up onto the poop deck to join the ship's captain. A local pilot, able to communicate by gestures only, stood beside the captain as he called instructions to the helmsman. The sky had cleared of cloud and stars were faintly visible. To de la Rueda the sky here seemed much lower than at home. It seemed to him he could almost reach out and touch these stars.

THREE

For the last three or so years most mornings when Shona woke up she had entertained a conversation with her children. Rarely she got out of bed without first greeting the twins and telling them what was on her mind. She spoke to them as she would to an adult, an intimate friend, for she did not doubt that from their place in heaven, under the light of God, they were perfectly able to understand all that she felt and had to say about her daily doings on earth.

So it was this morning. As she lay under the heavy blankets conversing with her children, seeing them alive in her mind, the pain of their absence became more bearable. She was able then to confront the day and make herself rise from the covered four poster bed she shared with her husband, but who at present was away on business in Edinburgh.

Drawing the embroidered curtain aside, Shona sat on the edge of the bed in her shift. She murmured a short prayer, crossed herself, then stepped onto a stone floor covered with rugs. Beyond the end of the bed a pale light came through the small panes of the window. Shona leaned over the chest beneath the window and peering out was pleased to see that the sky was turning an egg shell blue.

She squatted over a commode, washed her hands in a basin on a stand, took off her shift and exchanged it for a fresh one.

Removing her nightcap, she stood and brushed her long, thick red hair. Afterwards she pinned it up and covered it with a white linen kertch. In the cold of winter she would put on several layers over the shift, but on a spring day such as this with its promise of warmth she limited herself to a fine woollen indigo skirt from the day before and a leather jump, without stays, which she fastened with a leather cord at the front. On her feet she put on plain, soft leather shoes and before leaving the bedroom, for there was yet an early chill in the air, she wrapped a woollen shawl around her shoulders.

Mairi was sweeping the floor when Shona entered the common room. This was Hector's house and it had not changed greatly from the time Shona knew it as a child. The hearth was fancy as ever, with a roof of its own and built against the wall. The cauldron hung from a thick chain over the fire and around it was a three legged stool and various padded chairs with short legs, and nearby a spinning wheel. To the right side of the hearth was the kitchen, which contained barrels and household utensils, most made of wood, pewter, or iron, resting on shelves or hanging from the wall. But there was also a large dresser where finer tablecloths, lace, porcelain, glass, and a few pieces of silverware were kept. On the left side of the hearth was a doorway that led into an open space big enough for a trunk and a wooden box bed, which is where Mairi slept. To the side was another larger room with its own door and window which Hector used for his study and extra storage. Beyond Mairi's box bed was a further door which led directly to a byre which also had another entrance outside. The rest of the space in the common room preceding the hearth and the kitchen contained an oak dining table, chairs with covered seats, another spinning wheel, the glass fronted bookcase and the pictures on the whitewashed walls which had caught Shona's attention as a child, a standing chest, and not least, near the table, Shona's bureau; a refined walnut object with many drawers which had once served her mother-in-law but since Margaret was now gone with the fairies Shona had appropriated for herself.

'A better day this morning, Mairi.'

'So it is. And the birds are all singing, Shona, so they are.'

Mairi, like all the servants, whether from Hector's side of the family or hers, called Shona by her name. In the past, when she first married Hector, folk had addressed her more deferentially, but Shona had put a stop to it. Although a chieftain's daughter she had not been brought up to give herself airs.

'Will you be having brose or shall I make bannocks?' asked Mairi.

'I will have bannocks, then. Is Margaret not up?'

'I have not seen her.'

Lately Margaret had been staying in her bed. She appeared to be getting stranger by the day. She must be in bed still, thought Shona, but not wanting to brood over her mother-in-law she went over to the tap on the beer keg from which she poured ale into a pewter cup. Taking it to the table she sat down and opened one of the two books that she had been perusing the evening before and had not put away. The book was in French; an elegant, tooled edition of Molière belonging to Hector. After university in St. Andrews, which Hector had attended at the age of sixteen, his father had found a position for him in Paris under the auspices of the present Seaforth's father, who was a distant cousin of The Experimenter as well as being his landlord. Two years later Hector had returned, fluent in French. Shona also knew French, but only a little and what she did know was now largely forgotten. When she was a child and her father had hired a tutor, with his usual independent spirit he had instructed the man to teach anyone in the clan who wanted to learn; boy, girl, or adult. They had few books, little paper, and a scarce pencil or two. At times the tutor was obliged to teach on the beach by drawing in the sand with a stick. But Shona was keen to learn. Of the dozen or so pupils who attended school she was perhaps the quickest, ahead even of her brother. The tutor, who was also employed as a carpenter, and occupied a small dwelling near her parents, was Irish and had been educated by Jesuits. He spoke good Latin and French. Shona liked the sound of French and the fanciful images it conjured in her mind. After she came to live with Hector she took an interest in the French books he owned and sometimes she managed to persuade him to indulge her by practising the language with her. But that was in the early years before the children came. And after the children died she lost all sense of joy. There seemed no point in anything any more, least of all in something so trivial as French. It was as much as she could manage to live from one day to the next. But in the last year a change had come about. Shona had begun to take an interest again in the more incidental, if not frivolous, aspects of life. Always she had liked to read and now the desire was starting to return to her, which is how, going through the bookcase, she had come across the Molière. However, it was only since her husband had gone away three weeks ago that she had actually got around to giving it a try. It was laborious work. Many of the words she had forgotten and others she did not understand and the sense of much that she read escaped her. The second, larger book on the table, bound in brown Morocco, was a bidirectional French/English dictionary. It was undoubtedly a help, but Shona was finding that she was having to refer to it so often that were it not for the stubbornness in her nature she was certain to have desisted. As it was, she took a sip of ale and forced herself to read what she could, consulting the dictionary as she went, while waiting for the bannocks.

Mairi, plainly dressed, an almost elderly woman now, but able and sturdy, cooked the bannock mixture of oatmeal, salt, water, and duck fat on a skillet over the peat fire. When they were ready she brought them over to the table in a wooden bowl. Shona pushed the books aside. While she was eating, it occurred to her that there was still no sight of Margaret. A flutter of alarm rose in her. She stood up from the table and went back into her bedroom. At the end of it a solid wooden partition had been erected that served for a wall, where the children had once slept. Now the small space was occupied by Margaret, who was no longer trusted to sleep in her own room and which had become Hector's study. The space contained a trunk and a wooden box bed with a curtain drawn across it. When Shona drew the curtain aside she saw that her mother-in-law was not on the mattress. From vague apprehension, Shona now felt weariness and irritation come over her. *Well, the mattress is not soiled at least. But I will not let her rule my day.*

Having swept the floor and served bannocks, Mairi was preparing to go out and milk the cow before Old John led it to pasture.

'She is not in her bed, Mairi.'

Mairi put down the milk pail and stood looking back at Shona, her face creased with soot ingrained wrinkles.

'Where could she be then?'

Shona shrugged.

It is the devil that has taken hold of the woman. But Mairi kept the thought down.

'I will look for her when I go out,' said Shona.

There were jobs Shona had of her own that wanted doing but nothing that could not wait. Servants made work less onerous for her. Shona did not object to the wealth that made such a life possible though neither could she think about it in the purely functional way her husband did. It upset her whenever she had reason to come across folk in desperate need. Her friend Eubh, whom Shona was going to help that morning, was among the better off, however. Eubh's husband, Angus Peter, was Hector's principal herder, and a drover of repute in his own right. As such he was in a semi-autonomous position which made it easier for Shona to think of Eubh as her friend. But also Eubh had no reason to envy Shona, and if in fact there were reason for envy it would be on Shona's side, for Eubh's three children were alive and she was now expecting a fourth.

After leaving the house, and beyond the steadings, Shona stopped at the burn that ran nearby. Years ago, Hector's father had planted trees and laid down stepping stones on the section closest to the house and here now Shona bent low to wash her arms and face and under her long skirt. Barefoot, she stepped on the stones across the burn, before putting her brogues on. Choosing from three directions, she followed the path that veered away from the shore towards the low hills half a mile distant, bare of trees, where stood a cluster of thatched dwellings. All the land surrounding Shona's house for several miles was owned outright by Hector. Other land, including common grazing, and which exceeded three thousand acres, was leased to him by the Earl of Seaforth. Hector then sublet this land to his tenants in one or other of various different ways. It was in the productivity and the obligations of these sublets that, since their marriage, little by little, Shona had come to differ from her husband.

Hector, she had come to realize, was made of different grain to his father, who, aside from always looking for ideas to improve the traditional agriculture, had also been intent on the welfare of the folk in his charge. The Experimenter was not a clan chieftain, such as Shona's father had been, much less a chief; his moral responsibility was in these changing times not so defined as had once been traditional in the Highlands. In days gone by, Shona knew from the tales she had heard growing up, the clans were like families; the folk worked in common and looked after one another and to the clan chief they were like his own. They paid homage to him and he in turn protected them and made as certain as he could that they were provided for, even during the years of hunger when crops failed. But in Shona's own brief lifetime everything was starting to come undone. The chiefs were breaking the bonds with their own people. Not all of them. Shona was aware that the McKinnon of Skye and others were still adhering to their obligations, but many others were not. She knew only too well how some folk were being treated worse than animals under the MacDonald of Sleat. No wonder her father had wanted to rob their factor of his brandy. Such scoundrels cared only for their own benefit. They had no regard for the families in their care. In this respect, and although not a hereditary chief, The Experimenter had nevertheless subscribed to the obligations inherent in the old ways. But Hector was avid for advancement. By bringing up the burden of debt his father had incurred, Hector was always insisting to go with the times or be undone. That was why he had gone to Edinburgh. Shona was not privy to the details, but Hector was hoping to get an exemption for the land he administered. For being Jacobite both this earl and his father had dug themselves into a pit. The Covenanters were intent on taking possession of the Seaforth land and wealth; but Hector had a scheme to avoid forfeiture of that little portion of land he administered on the earl's behalf by putting it in his own name. Shona was not deceived when Hector said he did not intend to keep this portion for himself but merely to preserve it for when it could be passed back to the Earl of Seaforth. Shona suspected that her husband would try for whatever advantage he could secure. And that in itself did not trouble her. What troubled her was when her husband had spoken of putting sheep on that land. The sums made it clear, he said. It was good commerce, plain and simple. He was eloquent when he extolled the advantages of the new breed of sheep over the old. Listening to him talk about the production of meat and wool per acre, Shona could have believed she was listening to The Experimenter himself. And it was not that he ignored the people. They could be moved, he said, and put to work on the kelp burning that The Experimenter had started and afterwards abandoned and which Hector was idly thinking of starting up again. *They could be moved.* That is what disturbed Shona. Would The Experimenter have moved them? Would her own father have moved them? They were not sheep, they were not cattle, why should they have to move?

In a small field to the side of the path, Shona found Neil and his family ploughing with two pairs of garrons. The ponies, it was clear, were not long caught and they tossed their shaggy manes as Neil drove them forward from behind the heavy wooden plough while at the same time, in order to guide it straight, his wife Elsbeth walked backwards in front of the horses and the family's young children removed stones and broke up the clods of earth behind the plough with sticks.

Shona waited and when the team halted at the edge of the field Elsbeth walked over.

'Good morning, Elsbeth.'

'Good morning, Shona'

Elsbeth was a small woman with a birdlike face. Unlike Neil she was not a member of Shona's clan. After Neil had accompanied Shona to the estate as her servant when she married Hector, he had soon met Elsbeth, got her pregnant, and married. So Elsbeth was now also Shona's servant and their house was in the settlement not far from the field. The field, like the settlement, were both Hector's, but for being personal servants, associated with Shona, the family was more secure than many.

'Have you seen Margaret by chance?'

'I have not. Has she gone wandering again?'

As Elsbeth spoke, Neil came up. He took off the dark blue bonnet he was wearing and wiped the sweat from his brow with the back of his hand. His thick brown hair and his broad beard were matted with dirt

'She has, I believe,' said Shona. 'If you do see her come for me yourself or send someone. I shall be with Eubh.'

'That I shall do, Shona.'

'Is it bere you will be sowing, Neil, or barley?

'Hector is of the opinion we should be trying both this year.'

'A mix then. When you are done with the ploughing, have the children look for Margaret if she is not returned.'

'We will do that,' said Elsbeth. 'I will look myself.'

'Only if you are not occupied.'

After the fields and the first settlement near Shona's house the ground began to slope up. It became uneven, boggy in parts, and in the further distance cows could be seen enclosed by turf walls. But other ground, though less fertile, was arable. Most of it had already been sowed with oats and early barley, yet while late in the season, a patch remained to be planted here and there. In one such sloping, close by field Shona saw five men pushing cas-chroms into the ground. It was the slow, hard labour of turning over soil too difficult for a plough. Instead each man held a long wooden shaft between his hands on the end of which was a square of iron. Above the iron a peg jutted out from the shaft and each man would stamp on the peg with his right foot, pressing the iron blade into the ground and then heaving upwards to turn the earth over. Thus the five men moved about in disjointed motion ploughing the furrows of a lazy bed clod by clod. Shona dismissed the thought of interrupting their labour to ask about her mother-in-law. God forgive her, but she had no shame in admitting to herself that she would be relieved if her mother-in-law could not be found, or if found, not alive.

Shona had to walk three miles to another settlement before reaching the cottage where Eubh lived. In this bhaile there were only five dwellings, spread apart, and Eubh's was the largest among them. It was near eighty feet long and had a foundation of stone on the top of which blocks of turf were stacked to make the walls. The roof was thatched with reeds and bracken, but some of it was starting to leak and needed repair. Near the house were a couple of tiny gnarled trees. Beyond them, a hillside where Eubh and her two oldest children were pulling up new bracken. All three were singing in harmony. Eubh was tall and angular. She had pockmarked skin but her brown eyes were quick and her features attractive, even in spite of the sooty dirt that clung to her. Under her long skirt her stomach was bulging with advanced pregnancy, which however did not deter her from bending over, seizing the bracken plants firmly in both hands, and taking care not to cut herself, pulling them up by the roots. Nearby her three year old daughter sat contentedly in the sunshine, but the two others, older by a few years, had to work like their mother and only stopped when Shona approached.

Eubh and Shona sat down near the child.

'Here.' Shona took out a block of unrefined sugar from the cotton bag she carried.

Eubh smiled. Most folk had teeth that were yellow or missing, but Eubh's were unusually white; whiter than Shona's.

'Thank you. I shall put some with the butter in the porridge. We had it like that before when Angus Peter brought some back from Perth.'

'How are you feeling?'

'I am well. From the way it kicks it is a boy, I am sure. And you? Any change?'

'Between me and Hector?'

Eubh nodded.

'Not much chance with so little happening between us any more, Eubh. Sometimes; but soon it is over and nothing comes of it.'

'But it did once. You will get pregnant again. You will see.'

Would she? Hector was the only man Shona had known in the flesh. She could not say if it was meant to be any different than the way it was. Sometimes she thought that the union of their bodies ought to give more. More closeness, more intimacy, more pleasure. Sometimes she thought it could be why she did not become pregnant. But then again, had it been so much better when she had got pregnant with the twins? She could not recall that anything very different in feeling or manner had occurred in those unions. The only explanation that occurred to her was that when she and Hector were first together she had wanted children. The twins had not come readily, but come they had and a light from heaven they had been. But after the fever took them – and not only them; many others went that year – she had not become pregnant again. Perhaps, if it had happened quickly, if she had got pregnant soon after the twins died it would have been better. But it had not happened. And now she was no longer sure. A secret part of her was relieved, glad even, so that it made her feel guilty and wonder if this was the reason why she was not getting pregnant at all? Because she was afraid. Because deep down she did not want another child only to lose it.

Eubh could not rest for long. There was much to do at this time of year. Soon both women were at work, pulling up the plants, some of which came free of the earth easier than others. They worked all morning until both women were in a sweat and had sore backs, Eubh in particular. In a few days the bracken would be stripped and the long stalks readied for repairing the thatch, but for now, their labour finished, the group went back to the house.

'Shall we sit out for a wee while?' Eubh laughed. 'I will milk the goat, then his majesty cannot say I have been idle.'

The goat was small, with grey shaggy hair and long dark horns. It had birthed recently and so had milk. Eubh untethered it from the bank of grass dotted with buttercups and bluebells and pulled it over to a flat patch of earth near some stones by the house. While Shona sat on one stone, holding the kid between her legs, Eubh sat on another and reaching under the nanny goat she squeezed and pulled on the teats. With a slight hissing sound, a small stream of milk spurted into a wooden cogg.

'There; that will do for now.'

'It does not seem a lot.'

'I have more from yesterday,' said Eubh. 'With that it will be enough for cheese.'

'How are your cows?'

'Ach, they are all off to pasture now.'

'So when are you going to the shieling?'

'Well Angus Peter will be coming down. We will fix the house and then I will go.'

'I will visit you when the baby is born. Or before if you need me.'

Shona did not finish. Her attention was caught by a man riding a pony. He was on the same path Shona had taken, far enough away that Shona could not make out distinctly the object he was carrying in front of him across the mount, but from the sight of him, and because he was not alone but followed by several men on foot, Shona knew at once what it was. And so did Eubh.

'Mother of God protect us,' whispered Eubh.

Shona stood up. 'I have to go.'

Eubh made no reply. Her face had turned pale.

Shona hurried down the hill. For a little, as she went into a dip, the rider disappeared from her view. When she emerged she could see the rider was holding up the fiery cross. The men who followed him were Neil and the others who had been working with caschroms.

The rider was not one of Shona's people but she recognized him for he was a tailor and upholsterer from the township of Loch Alsh who in the past had done work for them. He wore a brown plaid and a blue bonnet and since he was a tallish man and the pony so small his shoes all but scraped the ground. The cross he bore aloft was some four feet long and made of two rough branches bound together with rope and a rag stained dark with dry goat's blood. The extremities of the cross had been charred and also dipped in goat's blood.

'Good morning, madam,' he said when Shona came up.

'Good morning.'

The rider's beard was turning grey and his eyes were mournful.

'I am told the laird is not available, so I am sent to you.'

'My husband is travelling. I suppose you have been sent by Colonel Murchison?'

'I have.'

Old Colonel Murchison was the Earl of Seaforth's factor in Loch Alsh.

'So is the cross sent from the Earl of Seaforth?'

'I believe it is.'

The knot of anxiety in Shona's stomach turned to anger. Not with the rider, but with the symbol he bore. How she loathed and dreaded that cruel piece of wood, even at times when she knew it was merely in practice. But this time it could not be in practice, or she would have been forewarned. And now! Why must it happen now, on such a fine day, and with all the work that was waiting?

'Do you have instructions then?'

'Morvich. The place of assemblage for this territory is Morvich. In two days. All should bear such arms as they are able for the glory of King James.'

'Is this as far as you are bound?

'Yes, madam.'

Shona turned to Neil and the five other men who were gathered around.

'Do we have a runner?'

'I think John-John is about,' said one of the men. 'He will be with the sheep.'

'Who will take the cross to him?'

'I can do that,' said Neil.

'Do you need this garron?'

Neil shook his head. 'There is a fresh one by the house.'

'Tell John-John it is Morvich in two days.'

'Morvich in two days,' Neil repeated. Then he took hold of the cross and set off at a pace that for him was fast.

Of the five men remaining three were young, not far from Shona's own age.

'Murdo, are you well enough to plough for Neil?'

'Och, I can be doing it,' replied one of the two older men.

To the others Shona said, 'I am sorry'

One of the young men, strong and ruddy, responded with a laugh and fire in his eyes.

'For myself I am happy to serve.'

But the others did not appear so resolute.

'It is your turn now, but I have yet to finish paying for Sheriffmuir,' said one, shaking his head.

'The Cross has come around again too soon,' agreed another.

Shona said nothing. But as she turned to leave she knew that everywhere now, in the little time it would take for the fiery cross to pass from runner to runner, reaching every part of the territory, the folk would find themselves torn between their duty to the Earl of Seaforth and the burden of danger and hardship this would bring to their lives. It was not the same as it had been even so little as four years ago, before the battle of Sheriffmuir. Then the Earl of Seaforth had sway over his land and people. The fiery cross had gathered three thousand fighting men under his banner. But the outcome of that battle had no victor, no advantage, no progress in the Jacobite cause. The men who returned from Sheriffmuir to their families and their land found that their bitter reward was failed crops and higher rent for land that now, furthermore, had fallen into dispute. No one knew any more what land the Earl of Seaforth could, through guile, still retain as his own, and what land was being forfeited, prised from him in the name of the English Hanoverian king by the Covenanters, and what land could yet go either way. It was all in dispute, torn this way and that, but what was certain was that Hector persisted in taking the rents due. And that the rents had gone up. Hector was demanding more from men who, on account of having gone to war to the neglect of their crops and their livestock, had on their return less to give.

Shona did not approve. She did not consider it just. She could understand if men now might decide that their loyalty to the Earl of Seaforth was misplaced. If they were to become angry and reluctant to go to battle yet again she would not be one to discredit them, though others might.

When Shona arrived back at the house a wave of despondency came over her. She sat down on the bench outside the main door. Her limbs felt heavy. Life appeared to her futile. Its pleasures too few. Its tribulations too many. Were it not for her fear of everlasting Hell she thought it would not be so difficult to stand up now and walk down the bank, walk across the stones on the shore, walk into the sea.

As she sat brooding, her mother-in-law appeared from the direction of the shore, being led by two children. Margaret was not much taller than the children; all bones in these years, hunched over, and her scanty clothes – the shift from the night before – in disarray. Little remained of the person who, up until the death of her grandchildren, had preserved all her faculties intact. For several years after her husband passed away she, rather than Hector, had ruled the estate. She rose up before first light and did not stop until it was time for bed. She kept her person tidy and had the last word on everyone's affairs. Shona came to resent this. It irked her that

Hector did not challenge his mother. Margaret both spoiled him and ruled him and she was cunning in the ways she came between him and Shona. But after the twins were taken to heaven Margaret lost her zest and with it her reason. It was not sudden. In small ways she began to neglect her person, she forgot things and took less interest in the accounts of the estate. Hector now began to take over more and more. Shona could not care one way or another, for with the passing of her children grief consumed her. But over time, as Shona became more aware of the world around her, the further decline of Margaret and her constant increasing demands provoked in Shona a shortage of patience, a violent irritation which her sense of guilt alone managed to assuage.

'We were told to lead the mistress home, madam. Or a kelpie will snatch her, my father says.'

For clothes the two girls wore disparate pieces of cloth roughly sewn together and which had since merged into a single grey-brown compound of natural dyes and dirt. Their cheeks were rosy. They were strong, healthy girls. Shona felt a pang of rancour that it was them she was looking on and not her own children, but grudgingly this was replaced by sympathy as she assessed their tangled hair and unwashed skin.

Margaret simpered. Saliva dribbled from the corner of her open mouth. Her eyes, while they did not avoid Shona, did not respond to her either.

She would be better off with the kelpie. The devil surely has her.

'Wait here,' she told the children.

In her room Shona kept a jar of boiled sweets. They had been little raided since her children died, but now Shona pulled the glass lid off and took out two.

Outside again, she gave one to each child. 'Put them in your mouth.'

The girls did as they were told; hesitant, until their eyes lit up.

'Thank you, madam.'

The girls left, swift footed, heads close together. Margaret half made as if to go after them, but Shona seized her arm and called for Mairi.

Mairi came out from the house.

'Fetch a chair, Mairi.'

Mairi went into the house and came out with a chair. It was placed by the front door and they sat Margaret on it, in the sunshine. Shona then went into the store room from which she emerged with a length of slender hair rope.

It was not the first time Margaret had been tied to a chair. Nor did she appear to mind. She did not resist when Shona tied one end of the rope to a leg of the chair before passing it repeatedly over and around Margaret's body and finally making a knot at the back of the chair. The rope was not so tight. With effort Margaret could have freed herself. Shona wanted only to forestall accusations from Hector that his mother was not being watched over, or from the bite of remorse should harm come to Margaret in her wanderings. This way no one could say she had not tried to restrain her mother-in-law.

FOUR

De la Rueda had seen virtually no houses of substance since his arrival; the lodge on the Isle of Lewis, and this one now, which belonged to a baronet and was not long built. Smaller than the one on Lewis but less spartan, it stood in a garden still being planned, was lime white on the outside, and had two floors. The ante-room de la Rueda was shown into by a servant was on the upper floor. It had green walls, pictures in gilt frames, polished furniture, and a carpet with a floral pattern. Against the wall to the right of the window were several padded chairs and sitting on one of these a man who looked about de la Rueda's age.

The man had only just returned from Edinburgh, where he had acquired a dark red velvet frock coat of the latest fashion and which he now wore with assumed modesty. Under the coat he wore green and blue tartan knee breeches, a waistcoat patterned like the breeches, and a flounced white shirt. Above his narrow, sharp face, and grey blue eyes, he displayed a wig tied back with a green ribbon.

He averted his gaze when he saw de la Rueda enter but a moment later he changed his mind and stood up. He was three inches taller than de la Rueda, and slimmer. De la Rueda bowed. The other bowed in return. He correctly judged that the Spanish officer in the yellow and white uniform would be ignorant of Gaelic and probably English but might speak French or Latin.

'Ah... sir... *Latine loqui tibi?*'

De la Rueda understood. But his Latin was rudimentary.

'*Francais?*'

Hector was pleased. Opportunities to show off his command of French were few.

'*Un peu.* A little. Hector Matheson of Clachmore. '

'Alejandro de la Rueda. Captain in the Galicia battalion. At your service.'

'I have, ah, heard the situation may not be as it seems, captain.' Hector's tongue felt odd in pronouncing the rusty vocabulary. 'If this be true it is *très regrettable.*'

De la Rueda put his hat down on a chair and clasped his hands behind his back.

'What can we do? A false rumour. We are in the hands of God.'

'Indeed. But yet ours is a just cause.'

De la Rueda nodded. 'Are you a military man yourself, *Monsieur?*'

Hector smiled thinly. The question touched a part of himself which he would rather not confront.

'Here, in our country all men have the good fortune to be... ah... ah... warriors.'

Absent warriors, thought de la Rueda, for so far he had seen little evidence of their presence. Like his colonel, when he arrived he had hoped to find thousands of Highland warriors armed, ready to march, but he had seen no gatherings, no armed men.

'Yes, so it seems; your country is not like ours.'

The barb passed Hector by. 'Do you not have... ah, *bandes, clans?*'

De la Rueda grinned. He had one front incisor missing. 'In my country the *clans* are not necessary. We fight each other well enough without. '

It took Hector a moment to realize the Spaniard was speaking in jest. And even then he was not certain.

'You are fortunate, captain. You acquaint yourself with… the… the customs of other lands. For myself, I have been in Paris when I was a younger man. Do you know Paris?'

'No *Monsieur,* not Paris, but I am acquainted with other regions. My own home is close to the border with France.'

'Ah, I see. And you come from there now, from your home?'

'From another part of Spain. Not my home. And before I was in Italy. Three years.'

The double doors opened at the other end of the room. Some ten nobles were rising from a long polished table in the adjoining room. Among them were the two earls, Seaforth and Marischal, the Marquis of Tullibardine, his brother Lord George Murray, and the Brigadiers Campbell of Ormidale and Mackintosh of Borlum, this last an old soldier with a badly scarred face.

The Earl of Seaforth was among the first to come through the door. In contrast to the alert Marischal and the more reticent Tullibardine, Seaforth was a boisterous popinjay given to the overuse of make up. His eyebrows were painted black, his face whitened with lead powder, while his cheeks and lips were rouged. His wig fell in long white curls. He wore shoes with large buckles, and was dressed in black velvet under a blue coat with a red sash. In passing he bowed to de la Rueda, who bowed back, but it was to Hector he spoke in Gaelic. 'Good day, Matheson. I am sorry to keep you waiting. Come, let us take some air.'

As the two men left, Colonel Bolaño appeared in the doorway and beckoned de la Rueda into the room with the long table. De la Rueda joined his colonel and the Earl Marischal to stand by one of the windows. Behind them, standing in a huddle at the far end of table, sharing snuff and talking amongst themselves, was the Marquis of Tullibardine and others.

'The news is not good, I regret to inform you, captain,' Bolaño said in Spanish.

De la Rueda braced himself. Beyond the small, square window panes, looking down, he saw Hector, the Earl of Seaforth, and another man slowly walking together on a path to the end of the garden.

'As you may have heard, the rumour of a landing has proved false. We were wise to show prudence but now we have other information and this time it is beyond dispute.' Bolaño paused. He was grave, troubled. 'It comes from an envoy; a holy priest under disguise bearing letters sent by the Duke of Ormonde himself. A storm at Cabo Finisterre has favoured our enemies. Our Armada is destroyed. The men of war have had to scatter. I imagine they are severely damaged and are making for safe anchorage wherever they can.'

De la Rueda felt a jolt. A moment of distress and shock before he reminded himself that it was no different from olden times. He had in mind the attempted invasions of a century and more before when three times the Armadas had also been wrecked by storms. And now it was twenty eight ships, arms, provisions, five thousand troops; soldiers, sailors, horses... who could say how many were drowned? Yes, a catastrophe. The black hand of Fate, sure enough. But for himself, personally... well, no one could say he had ever doubted his duty. He had arrived ready to serve, but now imagining it would no longer be necessary de la Rueda discovered that though distressed on the one hand he was happy on the other to think that soon, God willing, he would be re-embarking for home. A glow spread through him as once more he saw himself out of uniform, sitting in the sun under the shade of a pear tree on his estate.

'*Mas no nos rendimos.* We go on. We do not surrender.' It was the Earl Marischal speaking to him in Spanish.

The words and the keen expression on the earl's young face came as a blow to de la Rueda.

'I am sending the frigates back to Spain forthwith,' continued the earl, switching to French, a language in which he was more comfortable.

'Empty?'

'That is the decision,' said Bolaño, now also in French. 'The frigates will be in danger if they remain.'

De la Rueda's disappointment was in no doubt this time. The fleet was lost but he would have to remain here now. *A country that is not my own. Cold. Wet. And where my fate has yet to play.*

'Some of us were of the opinion the call to arms would be best abandoned,' the Earl Marischal confided, and by this he meant the Marquis of Tullibardine. 'But all have now been prevailed upon to raise fighting men from the clans. Four years ago, over ten thousand were raised, captain. The battle almost went our way. If this time we can raise the same number or more, by the grace of God victory may yet favour us.'

Without our Armada? The man has faith, I must grant him.

James Keith now came to summon the Marischal. He was the earl's younger brother; scarcely twenty four years of age and looked even younger, on account of his being a little plump, with fresh skin and rosy cheeks that did not require powder. But his looks were deceptive. Bolaño had told de la Rueda that James Keith had played a creditable role in France and Spain as a go-between for the plotters.

The Earl Marischal and his brother excused themselves and went to join Tullibardine and his group.

'Let us walk out,' said Bolaño.

Outside a breeze came from the sea. It had a balmy seaweed and grass odour that was almost perfumed. The sky was blue and grey. It was not cold and at the moment, at least, not raining. A little more sunlight, thought de la Rueda, and it would be ideal.

'Our magazine is all in one place,' said Bolaño. 'It worries me.'

De la Rueda waited.

'I mentioned my concern to the Earl Seaforth and he spoke to a certain Alexander Macrae, an important man in these parts and also, as I understand, a priest in their church. We have been offered the use of an empty house. I want you to look it over. If you think it adequate move… what? Say a hundred kegs of powder, and cartridges, muskets – a few hundred at least – and provisions to the house.'

'I will see to it.'

'Someone will come for you tomorrow to show you where the house is. Please arrange the transfer as quickly as possible. I am told there are rumours abroad of manoeuvres by our enemies.'

'I have heard something of the sort myself.'

Bolaño raised his eyebrows.

'Lieutenant O'Flanagan. He stopped at the inn, the one near that place they call Loch Alsh when I sent to him for the baggage left behind. Some traveller informed him of troop movements not four days march from here.'

'With our Armada destroyed – in confidence, captain – I fear the moment of opportunity has passed. The Marquis of Tullibardine and the Earl Marischal can never agree on how to proceed. Tullibardine shows too much caution, and Marischal is now perhaps being a little intemperate... but well, we must do as we are commanded. It is our sacred duty.'

They came to de la Rueda's mount. It was a grey Galician pony, somewhat larger and not so shaggy as the garrons in this part of the world. A young, dark skinned ensign, no more than eighteen, jumped to his feet from the bracken nearby and gave an order to the six soldiers who were reclining in the long grass. They grabbed their muskets, stood up sharply in their increasingly grubby white uniforms and took off their conical hats with their right hands.

Bolaño frowned at their uniforms, then held the halter while de la Rueda climbed onto the saddle. De la Rueda lifted his tricorne. Bolaño released the halter and started back to the house, which was where he was lodging. De la Rueda, with his escort marching behind him, set off on the path that would circumvent the hills by the shore and take him to his camp four miles to the east.

After a couple of miles on the hard wooden saddle de la Rueda decided to dismount and walk. They passed by a settlement of four or five turf dwellings. Meagre patches of ground were ploughed.

Some old folk and labouring children and women stopped to watch them pass. To de la Rueda's eye the people appeared more healthy than not but in comparison to the peasants in his own country they seemed dirty, insufficiently and strangely dressed, and their dwellings blackened hovels. Beyond the settlement, unexpectedly, an armed clansman went past travelling in the opposite direction. He was barefoot; a big, loose limbed fellow wearing a plaid. Attached to his person was a sword in a leather scabbard and a targe on his back. It was the first such weapons de la Rueda had seen. Under the blue bonnet, his long hair was loose and a beard covered his face. When the man came close he skirted them by taking to the heather on the side of the path. De la Rueda he greeted with a glance from his bright blue eyes and a word in Gaelic de la Rueda did not understand. Then he was gone with swift loping strides. The soldier in de la Rueda was impressed by the man's speed and bearing.

It was evening and it had started to rain when de la Rueda's party turned away from the shore and towards the camp. This could not yet be seen for it was on a flat field in a dip between low hillocks. Further to the party's right, close to a small river, were more fields, a few scattered dwellings, and a church. After two miles or so the party passed between the two hillocks and now the rows of white tents appeared spread out in lines.

De la Rueda, who had climbed back on his pony, dismounted with his clothes soaking from the rain that had started whipping down. The pony was led away by a soldier wearing an oiled cape. De la Rueda went into his tent, which was above head height and contained all the furnishings corresponding to an officer of his seniority. His servant was waiting for him. He was a short, older soldier; a barely literate but proud man who had a habit of muttering to himself and who in spite of a limp walked always with his chest stuck out. While the servant attended to a small iron brazier, and with the rain drumming on the canvas above, and already beginning to leak through, de la Rueda opened a trunk and brought out a dry change of uniform. Before changing he removed his wig. His natural hair was chopped short and without the wig he looked younger, closer to the age he was: a year under thirty. After he had changed uniform he sent his servant for food and to request Lieutenant O'Flanagan's presence.

The servant had returned and was heating up a pot of potatoes and salted meat when O'Flanagan stumbled in.

'Sorry, sir. I was not told you were about to eat.'

'We can talk while I eat.' De la Rueda stood up from his bed.

O'Flanagan, several years older than de la Rueda, was tall and stooping, with a face that was narrow, stubbornly red and unpowdered. His small, spiteful eyes were bloodshot. De la Rueda knew at once that O'Flanagan had been drinking because that was usual for him. It was a hindrance, but this had to be weighed against O'Flanagan's usefulness in other ways. Among the four Irish officers who had been assigned to the battalion he was the one who spoke Scottish Gaelic best, his mother having been a Scots woman who had moved to Ulster.

'Have you drunk a lot today?'

'No no. Not at all, sir. A sip or two this evening playing cards, nothing more.'

De la Rueda took the bowl of hot food his servant handed him, put it down on a small table near the brazier and sat down on the only chair – foldable, made of leather and wood.

'Would that be potatoes you are having, sir?'

'So it appears.'

De la Rueda took the demijohn passed to him by the servant and poured himself wine into a wooden cup.

O'Flanagan eyed the wine but he was not offered any.

'Now there is a strange thing, sir. About potatoes. We grow them in Ireland and I have heard that they are now being grown in England, too. But here the people will not grow them. In a bad year, and here that is quite often, their crops are ruined but they will not grow potatoes.'

'Maybe they will not grow.'

'If potatoes grow in Ireland they will grow here. No, it is pure stubbornness. They are set in their ways.'

'Is that bad?'

O'Flanagan grinned. He had uneven yellow stumps for teeth. ' A man who is set in his ways puts up a good fight, sir. Both sides used them in Ireland. Of course it was much before my time but their qualities... well, they are known to us.'

De la Rueda had heard this before from various sources. In years gone by Scottish clansmen had fought as mercenaries in Ireland, and more recently clansmen had fought on the continent, too. At close quarters, in battle, it was said their first charge was especially savage.

But de la Rueda had not summoned O'Flanagan to talk about potatoes or the Highlanders' fighting skills. After a sip of wine and a few mouthfuls of stew, he said, 'The colonel wishes to move a portion of our powder and munitions as a precautionary measure to a different location. A house near here which I am to inspect tomorrow and if suitable arrange for the transfer, so make sure you and your men are available tomorrow after reveille.'

'Very well, sir.'

While finishing off his meal de la Rueda decided not to inform O'Flanagan of the loss of the fleet. They were proceeding with their own plans regardless, and O'Flanagan would discover the news on his own quick enough.

'That is all, lieutenant. And I want you sober tomorrow.'

O'Flanagan decided to keep a straight face. He bowed and put on his tricorn. Watching him leave, de la Rueda noticed that it had stopped raining and the sky beyond the open entrance of the tent was overcast but bright. *At home it would be dark already, But here it does not become properly dark at all at this time of year. A strange country. Do they expel Jews? Burn them? There is much I do not know about it.*

Tired, de la Rueda decided to go to bed. He closed the flap on the tent, took off the top layer of his uniform, but not his underwear, lay down on the thin wool mattress of the camp bed and pulled the heavy blanket over himself. Soon he was asleep but not an hour later, as happened to him now and then since his battle wounds in Italy, he woke from a recurring dream. The dream had morphed many times over from its inception. Mostly he could not remember it afterwards but two features remained constant: A sensation of dying and a woman's presence saving him. Often in these dreams the woman's face was blurred, but he knew who she was even if he had himself never met her. In fact de la Rueda could not say if there was any reality to the woman at all, as in being a person of flesh and blood, but in his mind her being burned bright. On two occasions in the past he had seen her visage so clearly it had pierced his soul. The first time was after joining the army when he came across the portrait of her in a shop in Ciudad Rodrigo. The second time was in Italy when wounded in battle he lay between this world and the next. Had she not appeared to him then, like an angel from heaven, it was de la Rueda's belief that he would have succumbed and passed to the next.

At five in the morning, one hour before drum roll, three clansmen arrived at the camp. They were made to wait while a sentry went to de la Rueda's tent. For all his years as a soldier, de la Rueda still resented leaving a warm bed. He dressed grumbling to himself but once he was outside the frosty air and soft light immediately brought him awake.

The three clansmen wore plaids and were armed with dirks and broadswords in scabbards. One of them also carried a musket, and another a pistol. The one who wore the pistol was better dressed. His greenish plaid was of a finer wool and fastened to his shirt with a fancy silver clasp. He wore other accoutrements of horn and silver as well, and knee breeches and leather shoes with holes in them. A sprig of ground pine was attached to his blue bonnet, which, de la Rueda understood, was to indicate the clan to which he belonged. His youthful face was clean, his eyes sharp, his frame limber. To de la Rueda he introduced himself as Murdo Macrae. He spoke very little French but had some Latin. With that and sign language he conveyed that he was charged with taking de la Rueda to meet the reverend Alexander Macrae, who would then show him the house were the magazine could be stored.

Orders were given. De la Rueda invited the party to join him for breakfast. The cooks were already up and preparing to feed the troops by heating a gruel of chick peas in iron pots over peat fires. This morning it would be accompanied not by campaign bread, but the leavened wheat bread that came around once every seven days. Such bread was baked in a portable metal oven, heated by a peat fire, large enough to contain dozens of loaves at a time and protected from the rain under an improvised shelter. As de la Rueda led the men between the rows of tents to the mess his nostrils dilated with the pleasing aroma of fresh bread. Only three of the six forty-eight man companies occupied de la Rueda's camp; one of the three other companies remained at the castle and the two others were billeted at separate locations. Some troops were with Colonel Bolaño. These were well taken care of. They had drier quarters in barns than de la Rueda had himself, but still he had been told that they were complaining because they had no proper bread. The natives did not much eat leavened bread and de la Rueda's camp was the only one to have an oven for the wheat flour and yeast that had arrived with the provisions. Murdo Macrae, who had tasted leavened bread on his travels, ate the breakfast with a certain relish, sitting on a crude bench at the equally crude officers' table. Murdo's companions were more hesitant. They did not favour the chick pea gruel, but they were less averse to the bread and wine.

De la Rueda left the camp in command of the next senior officer, Captain Paez. Then, having been joined by Lieutenant O'Flanagan and an escort of several soldiers, the party set off with the clansmen for the church. None were mounted since they did not have to travel more than a few miles.

Before mid-morning they arrived at the church, whose foundations were laid, legend had it, in pre medieval times by St. Dubhthach. For the area it was a substantial structure of grey stone some thirty yards long and seven or eight wide. To one side was a knoll, and around the building a cemetery with stone crosses and tombstones, some weathered, others new. One of the weathered tombstones was of a knight who lay with his hands folded over a sword on his chest. Past the heavy wooden doors the nave was illuminated by light from glass windows partly stained blue, red and green. Two rows of wooden pews faced the chancel where stood an altar overlooked by a large wooden cross. De la Rueda immediately liked the plainness of the church. In his own land the ostentatious splendour of church interiors gave him a feeling of suffocation. Even though a soldier, he found it hard to accept the pillage and bloodshed committed by his countrymen in the New World in pursuit of the very gold that adorned the Spanish churches. He judged it contrary to the teaching of Christ, as he did the Inquisition and the execution of heretics, witches, and yes, convert Jews such as himself.

Leaving his companions behind with the soldiers, Murdo led de la Rueda and O'Flanagan through a door to one side of the altar. A short passageway led to a vestry where an old man was sitting, wrapped in heavy plaid, hunched over a table writing on a sheet of paper with a quill. There was a large fireplace in the room, which de la Rueda was not expecting, smouldering with a brick of peat. The old man half stood up from his chair. Although tall, he had a humped back. When he spoke it was in good French, a language he had once taught as a schoolmaster in Fortrose.

'Good morning, gentlemen. I am the Reverend Alexander Macrae of Kintail. Please...' Placing the quill into an ink pot he indicated the few chairs around the table.

De la Rueda took one of them. Besides the table he noticed there were other pieces of furniture, including a glass fronted cabinet containing books. That was something that had not failed to impress de la Rueda. The country appeared to him barbarous. No towns, no roads, primitive hovels for houses, foul food, people wild and unwashed, and yet the gentry among them all appeared to speak Latin or French and they had books; more so even than in his own country.

For a moment the old man spoke to O'Flanagan in Gaelic, then he turned to de la Rueda. 'And how do you find our country, captain?'

'It is agreeable, sir.'

'But far from your own is it not?'

'I do my duty.'

A glow that de la Rueda could not quite describe, a sort of mixture of torment and joy came to the reverend's yellowish eyes.

'Many are the fallen on our side, captain. And now I am hearing some people mutter as I never heard when I was a ghillie. *What for*? The burden is heavy. We have seen too much of war. And they are not wrong. *I* have seen too much of war. Two sons. *Two*. And a son-in-law also I have that are fallen at the battle of Sheriffmuir. Women without husbands. Children without fathers. The townships in ruin. It lies heavy on the heart, so it does. But those that speak thus, they forget that we fight for that which is rightfully ours. Am I wrong, captain? Would you say I am *wrong*?'

When de la Rueda remained silent the reverend bunched his thick, gnarled fingers into a fist.

'We shall not sell our freedom cheap. We are men. Life without honour is no life. And no Hanoverian pig's arse will tell us how to worship. Here we are Episcopalian; it is our creed and let me say it is not so different from your Church of Rome. We have bishops and some of us will say the rosary. I and my successors will welcome a Holy Roman mission here. That is why in my sermons I cannot fail to exhort my congregation to stand firm and give up their men to the last one. I say again, to the *last* one if that is what must pass to restore our rightful king and defend our faith.'

The reverend fell silent; depleted, but de la Rueda noticed that the crumpled, translucent skin on his hollowed out countenance had gained a little colour. He wondered how it was that some people, no matter the cost, could be so steadfast in their faith? De la Rueda himself had no such inexhaustible store. It always seemed to him that at any moment his faith might fail to sustain him and that his weakness or hunger would prove to be greater than God's sustenance.

'Yours is a most noble enterprise, sir,' de la Rueda said. 'And in my capacity as an officer allow me to say that my battalion is proud to be of service.'

The trace of a haunted smile flickered on the reverend's countenance. Then he stood up and shuffled to a sideboard. He came back with a flagon and a small, two handled, wooden quaich bowl.

'French brandy, captain. *Allez-vous prendre un petit drame*? Would you care for a small dram?'

'With much pleasure, sir.'

The reverend poured a little of the amber spirit into the quaich and handed it to de la Rueda, urging him on with a gesture. De la Rueda downed the potion in a gulp and handed the quaich back. The reverend then repeated the procedure for O'Flanagan and Murdo, and finally he took a dram for himself.

The house stood with two or three humbler dwellings on the shore a distance west of the church. Murdo gave de la Rueda to understand that the tenant was another who had fallen at the battle of Sheriffmuir and the widow and her children had moved away. As store space it was possibly a little cramped, but it was accessible and the thatch roof was in good repair, which was de la Rueda's main concern. After conferring with O'Flanagan and Murdo, he decided that O'Flanagan would return to camp with instructions for Captain Paez to send transport ponies to Eilean Donan Castle, while he himself and Murdo went ahead by boat to arrange matters at that end.

Two soldiers and two clansmen accompanied de la Rueda and Murdo on a boat that was made available to them by the reverend. It rained on the journey. De la Rueda judged that the woollen clothes of the clansmen were resistant to the rain, though only to an extent. It appeared to him that the clansmen must spend much of their waking hours wet. And yet they remained unconcerned, even cheerful, which he could not say for himself, or his two countrymen, who had oiled capes for protection but had sour looks on their faces.

At Eilean Donan Castle de la Rueda was greeted by Captain Stapleton, a square set, paunchy, older man who had been attached to the Spanish army since his youth when he had jumped an Irish ship.

While waiting for the battalion's ponies to arrive, Murdo set off to look for additional native ones, and also boats. In the storerooms behind the castle's curtain walls soldiers were put to work, under the charge of Lieutenant Mendez, setting aside the munitions due for transport. Since de la Rueda and Stapleton were not presently needed they ventured indoors, out of the rain. The castle was the property of the Earl of Seaforth but before the arrival of the garrison it had stood unoccupied for a number of years. Its furnishings were few and the walls damp. Even so de la Rueda considered Stapleton's quarters, which where adjacent to the main tower, more amenable than his own at the camp. They sat at a table and Stapleton brought out a demijohn of wine and hard Spanish cheese. On the stairway past the heavy door the muffled sound of soldiers moving crates and sacks could be heard.

'So it is settled. We go inland?' said Stapleton.

'I am not privy to the detail. A call has been sent out for insurrection and we are awaiting the result.'

'And when will that be?'

De la Rueda shrugged. 'I am told soon. Once there are the numbers, we march east, where the Highlanders expect to gather more fighting men. That is all I know.'

Stapleton was silent.

'But without our fleet, what chance?' he asked. 'I know the English. They will not leave it to the Scots to settle it amongst themselves. The Hanoverian king will be after this whole country. His forces will come to the aid of their protestant Scottish brothers. With the fleet, perhaps we had a chance, but now...' Stapleton pulled a face and took a mouthful of wine.

'Our prospects do not look favourable,' de la Rueda agreed. 'But you have served longer than I. We both know how rapidly a situation can change on the field.'

'What do you make of the generals?'

'The Earl Marischal is keen. He has a sharp mind. And so does his young brother. The Marquis of Tullibardine is more cautious. I cannot speak for the others, although there are seasoned warriors among them.'

'And the Earl of Seaforth?'

'Vanity and moods, but the colonel informs me he is staunch in his beliefs. We shall see...'

'P*or cierto*. Indeed,' said Stapleton, grimly. 'When this is over, sir, if I am alive, it will be my last expedition.'

Stapleton, unusually, had risen through the ranks. De la Rueda thought him an able officer in spite of his drink problem. However, his service was due to end and he had left a young family behind in Spain; reasons, de la Rueda mused, that could serve, should circumstance require it, to make him more cautious than was strictly necessary.

'I wish you well in retirement.'

Stapleton responded by refilling their glasses.

After a crust of flatbread and more cheese, de la Rueda nodded off in his chair. When he awoke he went out to the yard, where the munitions and provisions were now piling up ready for transport. He was counting the barrels of gunpowder when Murdo and various companions arrived with nine garrons. Some looked ill fed, in poor condition, which privately annoyed de la Rueda, but Murdo assured him they were able to carry loads. As a rule, so de la Rueda had been told, the horses in these parts ran wild to be rounded up only as and when needed. Added to the Galician ponies there would be some twenty altogether. Also, according to Murdo, they would have two boats available, one towed as a barge, but de la Rueda doubted that it would be sufficient to make the complete transfer.

Stapleton could not speak Scottish Gaelic but his childhood had been spent in Donegal and if he concentrated and it was spoken slowly he could understand its essence. That, along with de la Rueda's Latin, allowed the three men to confer. As a result it was decided the transfer would be done over two days; one journey that same day by horse and, with the tide, by boat under the direction of Murdo, and more journeys as necessary the following day.

It was mid-afternoon when the Galician ponies arrived from the camp. They were given water and hay while kegs of gunpowder were loaded onto each side of their harnesses. The garrons were loaded with sacks, muskets, boxes and barrels. It was in the twilight of late evening when the convoy of twenty pack horses, de la Rueda, his escort, and the necessary Highland drivers, left the grey walls of the castle. After crossing from the islet to the shore they turned right on the rough trail of stones and mud that twisted between the shore on one side and steep slopes on the other. At intervals there were clusters of dwellings and fields on either side of the track where the ground allowed. Smoke rose from the turf or thatched roofs, and occasionally people and goats or sheep were to be seen. But there was little evidence of the Highlanders' small black cattle, for these by this time of year were all being grazed up in the hills. In between the ploughed fields and settlements the slopes were all but treeless, overgrown with heather, grass and where the ground had still not given way to bracken, swathes of bluebells. The tops of the slopes were rounded, although sometimes rocky; the higher ones flecked white with the last of the winter snow, and in between one slope and the other were gulleys with fierce burns rushing down and narrow valleys. The sky above was grey and white. Eagles glided in and out of the clouds while closer to the shore gulls reeled and screeched.

A chill wind rose up from the sea. De la Rueda felt it going through his bones, even while he walked. In front of him the ponies heaved and farted, their loads swaying from side to side as they advanced in single file. They were moving well now, which had not been the case at the start. Then whacks and curses, not much to de la Rueda's liking, were needed to drive them forward, but having made the journey once the Galician ponies could sense the extent of their return, so that the closer they came to their destination the more they speeded up.

The twilight had deepened into an inky darkness when the convoy reached the house. As de la Rueda was expecting, since they had been his orders, a full company of soldiers were waiting to unload the ponies and move the munitions indoors. The officer in charge was Captain Otero, the youngest of the captains, and there were two lieutenants and two ensigns. Tired, with little for him to do, de la Rueda left Otero to take charge, and with his escort headed for camp.

De la Rueda's eyes were closing when at last, cold and groggy, he stumbled into his tent. He slept soundly until the drum beat woke him early next morning. An hour later he sat down at the table in the officers' mess. Breakfast was the usual chickpea gruel. There was no bread, but that was compensated by two slices of Spanish sausage. De la Rueda was chewing a mouthful of sausage when he noticed that further down the table O'Flanagan's usual place was empty.

'And O'Flanagan?' he called to the lieutenants. 'Where is he?'

'Do not know, sir,' one of them spoke up.

De la Rueda needed to talk to O'Flanagan. He had orders to do with the further transfer of munitions.

De la Rueda returned to his breakfast. Presently Captain Otero appeared and sat down, yawning, his young face unshaven and sleepy.

'Did you see O'Flanagan yesterday, Juan?' de la Rueda asked him.

'Yes, I had my men unload the boats. He was there.'

'On his own?'

'Yes. I do not know why. I thought maybe you had sent him, sir, but he soon left.'

'Did he say where he was going?'

'No.'

De la Rueda frowned.

'Was the inventory in order?'

'Yes. Everything has been counted and it is now under guard.'

'So you and O'Flanagan did not come back together?

'No. He was gone by the time I finished. It was late. I have only had a few hours sleep.'

De la Rueda returned to his breakfast. He would have thought O'Flanagan would want food wherever he had been, but he still had not shown himself when the officers were dispersing.

'Still no sign of O'Flanagan,' de la Rueda mentioned to Captain Paez, his next in command and who was sitting opposite.

'No.' Paez was short, chunky, with bandy legs. 'Strange.'

'Shall we go to his tent?'

The two officers walked between the tents and past soldiers labouring or doing drill. O'Flanagan's tent had the flap down. Paez pulled it up and de la Rueda bent down to peer in. The bed, a humbler version of de la Rueda's, was made up and empty. De la Rueda stepped in and opened the trunk. O'Flanagan's spare uniform was there, neatly folded, but there was little else.

De la Rueda went back out.

'I think we had better call the officers.'

Paez frowned. 'Very strange. Do you think he is with a woman?'

'Around here? Have you seen any available in this forsaken part of the world?'

'I have not looked, but women are always available somewhere. Maybe he has a woman in one of the houses.'

'But we have no camp followers,' de la Rueda insisted, unconvinced. 'I will summon the officers.'

FIVE

'And what am I supposed to do?' Hector demanded.
'What would your father have done?'

'That is the difference. He *lost* land. He *lost* money.'

'*He* discarded no one.'

Hector, sitting at the table opposite his wife, caught the fire in her green eyes. He did not want a fight but he would not back down – not all the way.

'I can find somewhere else for them,' he allowed.

'Where?'

'I do not know yet.'

'Do you know what happens to your tenants at all, Hector?'

'What nonsense. Of course I know. Everything is written down. What they have from me and what they owe me; it is all there in my accounts.'

'But now you talk of moving them - '

'Some of them. Those that are profitable can stay where they are. I am thinking of starting up my father's enterprise with the kelp burning. It was not profitable when he was alive. Now times are different. There is more demand. The price is rising. There is land for the ones I move to build houses by the shore.'

'You speak of them to your discredit. Do you think they have no desires of their own? What will you do if your plans do not proceed as you wish? And you keep putting up the rents! Soon even the profitable ones will not be able to afford it, and then what will you do? Throw them out like other gentry are now doing? Whole families are wandering the land destitute and starving. Have you no pity?'

'It is not my concern what other landlords do.'

'But it is your concern what happens here on *your* land.'

'What is my concern is to make my estate profitable. That is all.'

Shona had heard enough. She stood up from the table and left the room. Outside it was drizzling. She lifted a wooden pail, pulled the hood of the arisaid over her head, and marched towards the shore.

Hector looked down at his bowl of brose without appetite. The disagreements with his wife unsettled him. He had been home from Edinburgh little more than a week and already they were at odds. It appeared to him that she was intent on bending him to her will, as if his own will did not suffice him unbent.

And by what right does she belittle me against my father?

In his lifetime the Experimenter had got deep into debt. Wadsets deposited in Edinburgh had not been redeemed. All that experimentation – a plough constructed by himself that never exceeded the old; potatoes from the New World no one but himself would plant; even the kelp burning... and the dykes, the drainage, as much as they gave benefit, it had not been sufficient to counter the losses.

Someone like John Mor, however – his mother's cousin – now there was someone Hector could admire.

From little, John Mor had made much. Not for him wasteful experimentation. He had driven cattle to Crieff himself, assailed as he was by treacherous chiefs and blackmailers. And he had traded for gold, only gold, and after that same gold was stolen from him by the Earl of Seaforth's father, Kenneth, John Mor had gone and taken it back. No one knew how the old chief found out where the gold was kept, but he was in straitened circumstances and perhaps he thought that as the chief of the great Mackenzie clan he was too powerful to be confronted. But John Mor had done just that. He had entered Brahan Castle in secret and put his dirk at the old earl's throat. Restitution or death. So of course the earl had chosen to return John Mor his gold. And now his children, Hector's own cousins by marriage, owned great estates. Of course Shona would counter that John Mor had dispossessed no one. Maybe not, but his children had no fear of such. Not for them the runrig ways of John Mor's time, of his father's. They were for the new: Enclosure, pasture, direct rents... What counted now was ink and paper. No one could take a lord, a chief, at his word as in olden days. This is what his wife failed to grasp. No one could say they had land to own any more unless it was on paper. So what was he supposed to do? Not make good his father's debts? Leave everything as it was? Not take out charters for land that would soon belong to another if it was not his? What nonsense! But that is not what I object to, she would say. He knew how his wife thought. She thought he had to take account of the people without consideration for his own benefit. That it was a Christian sentiment he did not doubt, but it was not practicable. Even the chiefs of old had kept an eye on their own benefit. All the contrary could lead to was ruin. They would soon be paupers if he went down that path. Could she not see it?

Hector sighed. His gut was twisted in a knot. On the one hand he wanted to defy Shona; on the other he wanted to placate her. Either way he was afraid of her effect on his emotions. But the insecurity he was feeling was not all on account of his wife's defiance: also it had to do with present events. The fiery cross had already been around once while he was away in Edinburgh. Too early it was said, so clansmen had not left for the meeting place at Morvich or had started going back to their homes, but now the fiery cross was going around for a second time with more urgency, and, unlike four years ago at Sheriffmuir, this time Hector had the anxious, heavy feeling that he could not avoid going to war.

It was foolish. Such haste did not augur well. And now after the loss of the Spanish fleet, from where would come the necessary men and arms? In Edinburgh, Gregor Campbell, who had his ear where it counted, had left him in no doubt as to the resolve and resources available to the Government. What Hector could not understand was how Seaforth so wilfully failed to heed his own good sense. There was no disputing the ardour that had come upon him. When Hector had spoken with him, a mere few days ago, he had been expecting the earl's usual prevarication but instead the man had spurned the impediments as if they were of no account. Yet Seaforth was a fugitive. He was attainted and his lands forfeited and he could not even reside in his own castle for fear of apprehension. *He has had to live in exile abroad, and now he comes back – earl, lieutenant general it may be – but self deceived if he imagines the clans will rise as they did for Sheriffmuir.*

And for me there is no way out. I am given the command of a company. The earl expects me to make up for Sheriffmuir. I will have no children to bury this time. No pretext not to risk life for a cause that does not much sway me. Seaforth believes, the Marischal and his brother believe, Tullibardine, Glendaruel... they all burn with ardour. And it is not religion so much. It is the union with England. It has a bad semblance, it oppresses our spirits, our way of life. But I see advantage in it. I see opportunity for myself where Seaforth and his kind only see surrender and diminishment. Yet I must do as I am bid. I go to war even though I cannot endure the smell and sight of blood.

Hector had first discovered his aversion to blood when he was a child of eight. On a winter morning when a snow storm raged outside he had gone with his father into the byre where old Angus Og was living behind a sturdy wicker work partition of the same kind that separated the cows from the goats and the geese. Angus Og, thin and stooped over, smelled liked the byre itself. He never washed and changed his clothes only as and when the Experimenter handed him a cast off. For meals he was given a bowl from the family pot which he would take into the byre to eat, where he had a stool to sit on, and a pallet to sleep on. Hector knew little of Angus Og's life, only that he had a way with animals. When the cow was bled that time, the old man had passed his hand down over the cow's shaggy head and muttered something Hector could not hear. At once the beast had come under a spell and become utterly still. Then Angus Og had taken the knife and made a cut in the cow's neck so expertly its tail did not so much as switch. Hector on the other hand had gone faint. As he stood by his father in the gloom watching the blood seep from the cut and into the bowl that Angus Og held under it, Hector felt nausea welling, his skin went cold, sweat broke on his brow. But he knew he must not escape. He forced himself to face the cow. When they left the byre, through the short passageway that led into the house, Hector's legs were trembling. He could not understand why he was so affected by the sight of blood and later, angry with himself, he had taken hold of a nail and deliberately scratched his hand. But that blood had no effect on him. Nor had he felt qualms when he sat down to eat the blood taken from the cow, mixed and cooked with oatmeal.

Still, the aversion to blood had not gone away. Although he had practised with mock swords, he had where possible avoided real ones. Then, when he was seventeen, not long after he had returned from university, and before he went to Paris, a traveller called Rory MacQueen stopped by the house. He was selling pots but as well he was a sword master. The Experimenter thought it a good opportunity to hire him in order to advance the skills of Hector and ghillies under his patronage.

Rory was a man of rough appearance. He had a broken nose and scars on his arms and face. Hector was afraid of him and had the certainty that Rory knew this and had soon taken the measure of him. For two days Hector and the other lads practised the guards, feints and thrusts that Rory taught them. On the third day Rory asked for a volunteer to a contest with himself. A couple of the lads were keen but they deferred to Hector. In his mind Hector understood that he would not be in mortal danger, for the sword master was his instructor, not his enemy, but steel swords would be in play and there was the risk of blood. Hector felt as if his body were made of stone. At that moment he realized clearly that he was not a warrior. He was game for battles of tongue, pen, and mind, not for battles of the body. Yet if he was in terror of fighting the instructor, he was in greater terror of the ignominy of not doing so. He had little choice. With a supreme effort he managed to make his limbs obey him and he stepped forth on the grass, barefoot, broadsword in his right hand, targe held up on edge in his left hand.

The bout was soon begun. After the initial dread, when his limbs trembled and he could not breathe and he feared he was going to fall, he was thrown into the spell of the combat. Everything became sharp, lucid, and instantly demanding. He parried, lunged, stepped aside, lunged again, aware of Rory and his weapon as a threat that had to be kept at bay, but not as the thing of terror it had been moments earlier. And then it came. Blows out of nowhere to his arm and hand that released his grip on the sword, followed by a rough shove from close up that sent him sprawling to the ground. Rory's sword had cut his upper arm. Blood was flowing. But Hector was dazed. He did not notice it. His first feeling was of elation, happy that he had gone through with the bout, but when they helped him to his feet and he saw the blood running from a deep cut he became light headed and queasy. His heart beat fast. He thought he would faint. Rory took a look at the wound and shrugged. He told Hector he would treat it and it would soon heal, which it did.

Besides the practice duel, Hector had gone on several stag hunts, and if an animal was to be slaughtered he made a point of forcing himself to witness it. But he knew that it was not him, that it was forced, and for all his years of practising swordsmanship and military manoeuvres, for all the tales of bloodshed he had heard from the bards, he remained haunted by the elemental fear that come the day on the battlefield, the sight of blood would unman him.

But unless he went looking for a proper duel, or even a cattle raid of perilous nature, it was not something he could know for certain, because there were no calls to arms. The years before Sheriffmuir had been peaceable. Even private feuds among the clans were few, and the fiery cross was sent out only in practice. No one here favoured that foreign king the English had unlawfully put on the Scottish throne. No one here favoured the forced union of the two countries. But it was bringing peace of a kind for those who would put their efforts into their cattle and their harvests rather than their swords. Only there was pride; the Highland touchiness Hector himself knew he suffered from. Pride was stuck like a barb in the throats of some chiefs and lords. As with Seaforth and the other lords now, the Earl of Mar had likewise thought he could afford to make mischief. But he was a fool. 'Bobbing John', Popping up this side and that, and now he was fled to France, attainted and forfeited the same as the Earl of Seaforth who had fought by his side at Sheriffmuir. But Sheriffmuir... what had it served? Over a thousand dead, it was said. *I myself could have been among them. I could have left my body on the battlefield had it not been for the children...* The fever had struck them all, the whole family. Hector was the first to rise from the sick bed. But the day he rose his twin children died, one after the other. Hector did not want to live. He put on his plaid and seized his weapons. Grief was tearing him in two. His only thought was to give his life in battle. He did not want to live. But it was too late. Sheriffmuir was over. The battle had been fought to a standstill and the clansmen were returning to their homes. Hector, in torment and weakened by the fever, had fallen off his pony and when found he was brought back to his dead children and ailing wife. He had wanted to die then, truly. But time had passed. The prospects now had become less dark. He saw how he might live; not whole of spirit, yet well enough to partake of the comforts he had and to put his mark on the earth. The way a dog pisses. Only fortune had come to stalk him again. He had avoided battle once but he could not see how he could avoid it again unless by subterfuge. Deceit, an excuse for not going, was an idea he could entertain but not one that gave him ease. He had to know himself as a man, not as some cowardly serpent in the heath, despised by everyone, himself included. He could not see that he had an alternative. He must obey the call but it made him clammy, sick in his soul.

Shona tried to stop herself from thinking by picking cockles. Now that the tide was out, beyond the rocks and seaweed, a stretch of pale sand was covered by clear water. Shona, with her dress tied up around her waist and the water at her shins, moved about while peering down to spot the round white shells which she would then pick from the sand and put in the pail she carried in one hand. It was soothing work and she had almost found her calm restored when there was a flurry further out to sea. Seagulls were diving on a passing shoal of mackerel but two powerful sea eagles, from further above, came diving onto the gulls to snatch the fish from their beaks as they rose from the sea. Shona watched the squawking melee with disquiet. She had no more regard for gulls than she did for eagles, but it was the way the eagles swooped down so imperiously to steal the fish the gulls were catching that set her thinking again about her husband. He, too, was swooping down; taking land from people who had not the means to lose it. Ever since the children had died, since Sheriffmuir, her husband had been going about like he could not care what others felt. The tender aspect of his nature had always seemed to Shona difficult to bring out. Now, with the children gone, it came out hardly at all. He was raising the rents without a qualm. When she protested that folk could not afford to pay, he countered that he was only doing his duty by the earl. But was he? The earl had no choice; he was attainted, his lands were being forfeit and if he did not lease them to Hector while he could, others would have them. This much was true. Only Hector was paying the earl a low rent but he was charging the tenants a high rent and keeping the difference. Hector was anxious to become rich. Shona did not hold that against him. A portion of her could admire him for it, the way she had admired her father for his freebooting. But everything her father had done had been for the clan, to keep it safe, while everything her husband was doing was for selfishness alone. On some highland lands folk were starting to leave because of the rents – or worse because they were being thrown out to make room for enclosure and sheep. Some families had gone to the New World. Others had nowhere to go – to the east coast, or to the mines in the lowlands where folk were said to die of starvation and overwork. Hector was saying he would not do that. He was now talking about kelp burning, saying he could find somewhere else closer by for those folk intent on staying; but even if he did, it would not be as good as where they already were, and he would be losing their rents, too, which made no sense unless he had other plans for the land, like enclosing it and turning it into crofts for higher rents, or putting sheep on it. The Experimenter had enclosed some land, but she did not know that he had ever evicted anyone. Shona could not believe Hector's father would have done something that meant forcing folk off tacks that were theirs to plough. And her father would never have done that. Not even the Earl of Seaforth wanted to send folk away. He was not so bad a man, some said, even if he was vain. He commanded loyalty, unlike other chiefs and lords who had stopped caring altogether, if ever they did, for their own clan. And now her husband was taking after them, going down their path, the devil take him.

Hector was at his writing table in his study, working on his ledgers, when noises came from outside. The small window above the table was not one he could open, so he went into the common room beyond which Mairi was standing at the front door talking with three men, all armed, and one of whom held the fiery cross. Hector recognised the deep voice of Lachlan 'white eyes' Murchison.

'Show him in,' said Hector.

Lachlan Murchison was Hector's largest tenant. Unlike Hector, Lachlan did not own any portion of land in his own name. All of it was leased, but this aside, in other respects Lachlan was in the same position to Hector as Hector was to the Earl of Seaforth. Though some of Lachlan's land was leased from Colonel Murchison – Seaforth's factor in Kyle and a very distant relation of Lachlan's – the larger part he leased from Hector. Lachlan's farm, which adjoined Hector's, was considerably smaller – a few hundred acres – and though he had subtenants of his own they were much fewer. Lachlan owned some cattle and collected some rent but the greater portion of his income he derived from two illicit stills which were said to produce the best whisky in the region. Secure enough to consider himself an independent farmer, Lachlan was nevertheless always looking for ways to advance himself. A little above average height, of strong build, with a thick neck and large hands, Lachlan's most salient features, beside his somewhat porcine face, were his very white skin, pale eyelashes, and near colourless eyes; hence his nickname White Eyes. Few dared call him by his nickname, however, for while Lachlan had a loud laugh and gave every impression of being jovial and welcoming, he was known to bear a grudge, and folk who had dealings with him often had reasons to discover how devious and ruthless he could be. Lachlan, who was some five years older than Hector, was unmarried and lived with his sister and family, but he was known to lust after women. Most of these women, or their husbands, were in no position to protest. With these Lachlan was quite blatant in his advances, but with others who could challenge him he was sly.

'The Sassenach navy has been sighted,' Lachlan said, as soon as he entered the room, leaving his two companions, who were his vassals, outside.

'Where?'

'Yesterday when I took orders from Colonel Murchison I was told three ships of the line were at anchor off Kyleakin.'

Hector took hold of a silver quaich from the sideboard in the kitchen and brought it over to the table with a bottle of his best whisky, which in fact was Lachlan's own product. The two men had a dram and then Lachlan reached into his plaid and pulled out a sealed letter. Hector, trying not to show his perturbation, broke the seal and read the orders sent to him from Colonel Murchison on behalf of the Earl of Seaforth. Afterwards he tore up the letter and threw the pieces on the peat fire under the cauldron.

'My Lord Seaforth wants our company armed, provisioned and ready for deployment,' said Hector.

'Is it Morvich again the meeting place?' asked Lachlan.

'It is.' Hector turned to Mairi, who was at the hearth. 'See if you can find my wife. And send me Neil.'

Neil was not far. He was walking up and down sowing the field he had ploughed some days before. He dropped everything when Mairi spoke to him and hurried to the house. Soon Mairi also located Shona on the shore.

When Shona heard Mairi call out and saw her stepping over the stones and seaweed she knew something unexpected had occurred. Her first thought was for her mother-in-law. Had she died? A flash of relief, if not joy, went through Shona. At once it made her ashamed. But when Mairi said Hector had received orders from Colonel Murchison, Shona's mood immediately became sombre, ambivalent, and if the sense of shame lingered it was now for entirely different reasons.

As she arrived at the house she caught sight of a Neil hurrying off with the fiery cross under his arm. It had been too early last time, but surely not again? She could not credit it. *Something is afoot.*

The front door of the house was open. Hector and Lachlan stood beside it while Lachlan's men had started moving things out from the store room, where besides the goods Hector sold to his tenants and cottars he kept other supplies for general and personal use. At the sight of Lachlan, Shona felt herself withering inside, but it was not the moment now to consider her feelings. Among the things emerging were targes, swords, a couple of Lochaber axes, three matchlock muskets, barrels of foodstuff such as butter, cheese and oats. Hector had a pencil and he was counting and noting down in a ledger everything that came out. Lachlan was standing with his big hands on his hips watching the others work. When he saw Shona approach he looked at her with a combination of unabashed lust and deep anger. Shona met his stare with a defiant one of her own but immediately she turned away from him, determined thereafter to ignore him. Over the years, ever since she had known Lachlan, he had made advances on her; insinuating, trying to grope her when Hector was not looking, and once, when he had arrived at the house at a time when Hector was not about, he had put his hand over her mouth and lifted her and carried her into the rear of the storeroom where it was dark. He had seized her so swiftly and quietly that Mairi, who was a little distance away in the kitchen, had not noticed. But Shona fought him off. Lachlan had not calculated on Shona managing to knock over some iron implements onto the floor just at the point he was attempting to force himself between her legs. The noise had alerted Mairi, who came to investigate. With Mairi appearing Lachlan had to desist, but he was angry, of that Shona was certain. Before he left, Lachlan hissed to her a warning not to mention anything to Hector. So she had not, because she had no desire to court trouble, and after all, the violation had not succeeded.

'Three English men of war have weighed anchor off Loch Alsh,' Hector told Shona. 'Murchison is of the opinion there will be action soon.'

'So what does he want of you?'

'I am to gather the company and march to Morvich.'

Hector glanced at his wife sideways and chewed on his bottom lip. He was a handsome man. His face was perhaps a little too narrow, but his eyes were clear, like blue-grey pebbles under running water, and long limbs and straight features. Handsome, but frowning now, chewing his lip, and tall as he was, he looked to Shona like a frightened child. Abruptly she felt sorry for him. A captain he might be but was he a soldier? Some men, she knew, were born to fight. They thought little of killing, and it might be the brave among them thought little of being killed, too. But her husband? She could not see him as that kind. Commerce and scheming was what he was about.

'Murchison says Glendaruel and even Rob Roy have answered the call. And there will be others to our banner.'

Rob Roy? It took Shona a moment to place the name. Rob Roy MacGregor the reiver; a man some said was good and others bad, but either way managed to have himself spoken about.

'Have Covenanter troops been sighted, then?'

'They are gathering at Inverness. That is all I know.'

'We are not in immediate peril?'

'Maybe not,' said Hector. 'Though it depends what the English ships do.'

'This time there shall be no quarter,' said Lachlan, who would be second in command of Hector's company. As he spoke he had somehow managed to press close to Shona. 'Is that not so, men?'

'It is,' one of them responded.

Shona's skin shuddered. She stepped away from Lachlan.

'The fields will be abandoned. And the cattle,' she told Hector, bitterly. 'And nobody knows why.'

Hector knew she was right to an extent but he could not say it, not in front of Lachlan and the others, and perhaps not even without them. The cause – which king, which religion, which country – might not matter any more to him than it did to his wife, but honour and duty could not be so lightly dispensed. They were all tangled up inside him in ways that if he could not fully comprehend, he could still less easily elude.

'I will be leaving this evening. Those who cannot come today must follow on tomorrow.'

Shona was about to reply when Margaret came out of the house. The old woman stood in the doorway, dazed and dishevelled. Shona went over. There was a wet patch at the front of her long shift and in her eyes a blank, quizzical expression.

Shona took her firmly by the arm. 'Come back inside, Margaret.'

After a moment of resistance, the old woman allowed herself to be taken inside. With Mairi's help she was led into the small, windowless room that was hers and where they put a dry shift on her. Then she was led to the hearth and placed in the low chair with a high round back of woven grass she had owned most of her life.

More sounds came from outside. Shona went to the window with little panes of thick, uneven glass and peered through. Neil, his eldest son, and two cottars, were driving several garrons to the house. The cottars were dressed in long shirts and breeches. They were barefoot. One wore a ragged plaid over his breeches but not the other. Unlike Hector's subtenants, the cottars had no land leased to them. They and their families were labourers. They were given food and a roof in return for their labour. Earlier this morning they had been repairing a dyke on one of the inland fields; young, vigorous men with wives and children. Now they were arriving to be given arms and sent away, it may be, to die.

Shona turned to Mairi. 'Put more barley in the pot. And see what salted meat there is.'

More men would be arriving during the day and even tomorrow and she would not see them leave hungry. Presently Neil's wife, Elsbeth arrived. Shona got her to help sort out the clothes Hector had in store and which would be provided, if not to all the men, to some. After a couple of hours the ponies were packed and some twenty men had gathered. A few arrived armed with their own weapons, others would be armed from Hector's stock, and others were hoping to receive muskets and other weapons from the lords and the Spaniards. Besides weapons, the men brought such personal belongings as they could. Some had their own wooden bowls, those who did not were provided out of Hector's supplies. Thus equipped they were called into the house where their sporrans were filled with meal taken from a barrel and their wood bowls with a meaty broth ladled from the cauldron. Shona knew all of the men; she had conversed with them at some time or another, and there were two or three with whom she was more familiar and were it not for her status she might well have considered as friends. But even with those she was closest to it seemed pointless now to make small talk about day to day affairs in view of the enormity of what lay ahead for them. For all that, not a few of the men were cheerful. They were talkative and their eyes glowed. These men were filled with emotion for their country, their people, their creed, and they were happy to have life made so simple that all they had to do henceforth was obey and fight.

It was late but still daylight when Hector went into the bedroom and got dressed to leave. Trying to suppress a feeling of anxious gloom, he put on linen underclothes and over these a reddish, tartan patterned one piece suit woven of fine wool and consisting of stockings, trews and shirt buttoned at the front. On top of this Hector would normally have put on a plaid, but the weather was warm, so instead from a trunk he brought out a coat which had belonged to his father, who had also had the rank of captain. Hector was a couple of inches shorter than his father, so the coat was somewhat long on him. It was dark green, made of wool lined with red satin and had a tapered waist and silver buttons. It also had two holes where the Experimenter had been wounded in battle, once with a musket ball, and once with a dirk, but the holes had been repaired to near invisibility. Finally Hector put on leather shoes with buckles and a blue bonnet with a single eagle feather and a sprig of broom, which was the symbol for the clan.

His weapons, which he had brought in from the storeroom, were waiting for him on the table in the common room. Hector glanced at his wife, who was standing by the hearth, then he took off his coat and strapped two narrow cross belts over his suit to which he attached various accoutrements, such as a snuff horn, a small dagger, and two pistols bought at his own expense in Inverness several years ago. After this he put on another belt around his waist with sporran, various pouches, and a long dirk in a scabbard. Then he put his coat back on and over this he buckled up the shoulder belt that held his broadsword in a scabbard, and finally he put on a powder horn and another shoulder belt that held an ammunition box and bags and pouches.

Shona, watching him, felt a softening in her core. She was overcome with sorrow and pity. To her it seemed he was getting dressed to die. Her heart ached as he reached over to seize the musket resting against the side of the table and turned to face her.

Neither of them spoke. Margaret, who appeared to be asleep in her chair, abruptly raised her head and stared at her son with sudden, as it was brief, comprehension.

'God protect you,' she said, clearly.

Shona wanted to let her husband know that she loved him. She did not want him to go away thinking that she held a grudge against him. He looked so forlorn and defenceless and in need of courage, but just as she was about to go to him he broke the spell, bowed stiffly, and turned to leave the house.

Shona did not move. She understood Hector would prefer it that way because there were no farewells that could reassure him or mitigate the inevitable. He was on his own. In the hands of God. And they both knew it.

SIX

Although Lieutenant O'Flanagan was unarmed and waving a none-too-clean white shirt, he was nevertheless acutely aware of several musket barrels levelled at him from the Worcester's longboat as it came to rest in the shallow water. A naval officer and four marines soon detached themselves from the fifteen or so men in the boat and waded towards him.

'I speak English,' Lieutenant O'Flanagan said at once. 'And I wish to surrender.'

Young Lieutenant Weston looked surprised. 'Who am I addressing?'

'Lieutenant Edward O'Flanagan. First Company of the Spanish Batallion Galicia.'

'Oh. So you are one of those Irish with the Spaniards we heard about. Do you come alone, sir?'

'I do. I saw your longboat from along there.' O'Flanagan indicated a vague spot along the shore behind him. He had in fact been making his way towards Glenelg, with a view to somehow finding a way south to England, when from the hillside he spotted the longboat leaving its parent man of war, at anchor in Loch Alsh, and start rowing towards the few dwellings on the shore. Immediately O'Flanagan saw an opportunity for himself. He hurried down the hill and back towards the shore near the houses, where, gasping and sweating in the muggy evening light, he removed his shirt and managed to attract the longboat's attention.

'You had best return to the ship with us, then, where you can speak to our captain,' said Weston, pleased to have found by chance precisely what he had been asked to look for – information on the rebels.

After climbing the rope ladder onto the fifty-gun two-deck Worcester, O'Flanagan was immediately escorted to the captain's quarters where he introduced himself to Commodore Boyle as an Irish officer who wished to desert and had information to impart in return for protection.

Boyle was a sick man. Under a resplendent blue, gold, and white uniform that now appeared too big for him, his body was wasting away. In the mornings he spat up blood. At night he sweated. He had a sense that his life was coming to an end. Meanwhile he kept himself going by an inflexible act of will. It had been that way all his life. He had gone to sea young and throughout his years of service had endured his fair share of hardship and privation. Boyle believed in discipline. He despised men like this Irishman who could so callously dispense with his honour. To Boyle it demonstrated a lack of inner discipline.

'Let us hear your information, sir,' said Boyle, from his chair behind a desk covered with charts, staring up at O'Flanagan with jaundiced eyes.

'The Spaniards have a company of forty eight soldiers and munitions garrisoned at the castle, but not all munitions are held there; a portion has been transferred to a different location.'

'And you know where this magazine is?'

'I do.'

'Is it within range of our guns?'

'I believe it would be. Aye.'

'What are your reasons for coming over to us, sir?'

O'Flanagan decided he could live with the commodore's contempt.

'I have debts and women difficulties in Spain. I have no desire to go back. Or to Ireland.' He was about to add: *And I am done fighting*, but thought better of it.

'Have you information on the castle? Is it well guarded? Are they in good spirits?'

'No. I would not say they are. The Spaniards will fight for honour but this is not their country. Since the destruction of their Armada their spirits have been low. Also the clans have been slow to rally. They appear to have little stomach for another battle. It is said they lost a thousand men at Sheriffmuir.

'Do they have cannon at the castle?'

'Our ships brought none from Spain. I cannot be sure if the castle has cannon of its own, but I think not.'

Boyle thought for a moment. He was not happy with the Flamborough. Earlier in the day after his three ships anchored half a mile from the castle, he had sent out a flag of truce. But the longboat had been fired on. His ships had responded with fire of their own, but they were too far out so he had ordered the ships closer in. In so doing the Flamborough had hauled out of line and this had displeased Boyle. He expected less sloppiness from a man who until recently had served under him as first officer. Consequently he confined Bignell for neglect of duty. But Boyle also liked to think of himself as a fair man. He would give Bignell the opportunity to make amends.

'Very well. I will transfer you to the Flamborough where you will be at the disposal of Lieutenant Bignell. If your information proves correct and we destroy their magazine I will pledge to keep you on board until we reach England, where you will be free to go your way.'

O'Flanagan held his tongue. A small monetary recompense for himself would have come in handy. But he judged, correctly, that now was not the time to make such a request.

The next day, under a tempestuous sky, O'Flanagan was lowered in a boat and rowed to the Flamborough. When the boat came back the three ships separated. The Flamborough set sail up Loch Duich to locate and destroy the enemy magazine while the Worcester and the Enterprise anchored closer to Eilean Donan castle.

Standing on the poop deck, wrapped up in a heavy coat, with officers on either side of him, Boyle gripped the rail with one hand and held a handkerchief over his mouth with the other. He coughed violently, spitting out phlegm and blood into the handkerchief. When he recovered there was perspiration on his brow and his face was white. Boyle turned to his first officer as a squall sharp with rain lashed the deck.

'There is too much movement, Mr. Smith. Have a stream anchor laid and prepare cannons.'

'Aye, aye, sir.'

The stream anchor took time to lay. It involved launching a boat and running a hawser through the capstan along the length of the ship to enable it to pivot by the bow and thus for the broadsides to be better angled to the line of fire.

When the anchor was set and the firing line adjusted, Boyle gave the order. A moment later his ears resounded with the cannonade of the eighteen and twelve pounders. Although a strong wind was blowing, he caught the whiff of gunpowder as he watched dust and debris fall from the castle walls and figures scurrying along the battlements to escape. Thereafter the cannonades were kept up every few minutes, not only from the Worcester but also the Enterprise. Little damage had been done when the ships had fired on the castle the day before, but now that they were closer by a quarter of a mile, so that they were just some five hundred yards from the castle, and the line of fire better adjusted for the ship's movement, Boyle could see the splintering and cracking and tumbling of the castle's west walls taking place. Still, he thought the destruction was slow and it was getting late in the day.

'Mr. Weston,' he said, turning to the officer who had brought him O'Flanagan, 'I am in a mind to force matters. Have launches loaded with several barrels of gunpowder and such men as you can accommodate. If you reach the castle unopposed demand surrender and blow up what you can.'

'Aye, aye, sir.'

While Weston prepared to leave the ship, at the castle Captain Stapleton was taking shelter in an alcove near the gates and having a fierce discussion with his second in command, Lieutenant Mendez. Both Bolaño and de la Rueda had erred in their assessments of these two men. Bolaño had thought Mendez would serve to strengthen Stapleton's resolve should he succumb to the bottle, and de la Rueda had thought Stapleton old and cautious, quite apart from his drink problem. But although Stapleton had a flagon at his side and was taking frequent swigs, the whisky, if anything, was serving to harden his resolve. The weakness was not with Stapleton so much as with the dark, good-looking, younger Mendez.

'We cannot get at their ships, sir. There is no hope for us; we must - '

Mendez was interrupted by another cannonade. A large chunk of stone from above crashed on the ground in a cloud of dust between the two officers and a few soldiers huddled by the steps going down to the lower storerooms.

'If we could get to their ships....' Stapleton coughed, peering through the swirling dust. 'What we need is a boat with gunpowder on a long fuse and a few brave volunteers...'

'Send them to their death, sir? The English guns control the shore line. We have no option but to surrender. We must surrender!'

Stapleton took a swig from the flagon. In Spain he had a young wife and children waiting for him. For over thirty years he had been a soldier. He had fought in five campaigns. This would be his last before he retired. He had nothing left to demonstrate. But still it rankled; he was reluctant to give in without a fight only because his lieutenant wanted him to.

'I will see if I can get a message to the colonel. One of the Highlanders can take it.'

Mendez opened his mouth. He was going to protest it was useless to send for reinforcements but Stapleton snapped, 'Do not say anything, lieutenant, or I will report you for dereliction of duty.'

At the castle gates, Stapleton handed a written message to one of the few Highlanders present and asked him to deliver it to Colonel Bolaño, who was at the Jacobite camp with the lords a few miles away. But very soon after the Highlander departed a soldier called Stapleton to the ramparts. Climbing the steps, he looked out to sea; there, under a rain-streaked, windy, slate grey sky, he saw boats with armed marines preparing to be lowered into the water from the two men of war. *Ah, they are coming for us now.*

Stapleton hurried back down and started issuing orders. Thinking to deny the enemy easy entrance, he had a squad of sentinels take a small keg of gunpowder to the wooden steps on the outside of the curtain wall under an un-gated entrance gap some eight feet above ground. The resulting explosion damaged the wall a little but more crucially it demolished the steps. *That is one way they cannot get in now.* Coughing from the smoke and stench of gunpowder he looked beyond the burning timber and saw that three boats had started rowing away from the ships. It would not take long before they arrived. He hurried away, giving orders, looking for Mendez.

Lieutenant Weston saw fleeting movements along the parapets when he arrived at the islet but no one was firing down at his party. Jumping out of the boat, Weston and his men scrambled through rocks and slippery seaweed up to the castle walls, where, however, with the wooden steps in ruins, entrance through the gap would be perilous. After a moment, Weston gave orders for the party to split and skirt the castle walls to find another entrance. Inside the castle, meanwhile, Mendez was disobeying orders. He had been told to fire upon the invaders from the battlements or from wherever there was a sighting of them, but Mendez was prevaricating, delaying giving any orders at all, so that the white coated soldiers scurried about in confusion getting different orders from their sergeants. Stapleton, swigging whisky after reinforcing the castle gates, now started for the forward battlements to sort out the confusion, when he was called by a soldier who said the landing party was gaining the walls on the other side by the tower. Stapleton hurried back down and with a few soldiers following he crossed the courtyard and up the steps, but he had hardly reached the landing under the battlements when he was confronted by blue and white enemy troops with swords in hand, muskets and bayonets. Stapleton put down the whisky flagon and reached for his sword, not quite sure himself which of the two actions was the more determined. But even as his hand grasped the hilt he knew that without the presence of reinforcements, and at the total mercy of the English men of war, it would not be sufficient to suffer, perhaps die, for honour alone.

Captain Stapleton decided to surrender. A not dishonourable choice under the circumstances.

But less morally clear was Stapleton's failure to prevent the store of munitions falling into enemy hands. And exactly this same dilemma, to destroy or surrender the munitions, had meanwhile also presented itself a few hours earlier to the officers guarding the magazine in the house further up the loch after they spied the Flamborough approach.

In a curious reversal of age and temperament it was now the young Captain Otero who was hesitant and his older lieutenant who was more forceful.

Lieutenant Iturralde, an experienced officer, understood at once where the power lay when he watched the Flamborough appear like a huge lumbering beast on the dark water of the loch and slowly heave broadside, its cannons on display, not four hundred yards from the shore. There was no doubt in Iturralde's mind that the house they were guarding was close enough to the shore to be within range of the cannons. Even if they put up a defence it could not prevent the enemy from blasting the house to bits, should they so choose. So Iturralde decided, unlike Stapleton's oversight later in the day, that their only realistic option would be to destroy the magazine themselves before the enemy managed to get any part of it. His superior officer, Captain Otero, a pleasant but inexperienced officer whose commission had been purchased for him by a wealthy uncle, was not convinced, however.

'Their strength is superior,' Iturralde insisted, raising his voice against the wind that whistled past the open doorway of the house. 'If they come ashore in number we must blow the house up as we retreat.'

'Without a fight?' Otero had not been in battle before. Little more than twenty years old, he was anxious to make an impression. 'That would hand them victory. It would be a dishonour.'

Iturralde, a man with a nose like an axe blade and fierce eyes, looked straight at Otero.

'If they engage us we will have to surrender and they will take our magazine. We have no artillery, and not enough men to rebuff a strong attack unless Captain de la Rueda or the colonel himself arrives with reinforcement.'

But Otero was reluctant.

'I will have a message sent to the camp.'

'Very well, sir. But if you have no objections meanwhile I will make preparations.'

Before Otero could speak, Iturralde went into the house and past the munitions and provisions to where a group of soldiers were guarding the other entrance to what had once been a byre.

'Right, We need to find some fuse chord. *Vengan*, get to it.'

The soldiers helped Iturralde go through boxes, prising them open before they found one containing a coil of fuse chord.

'Three barrels of powder should do it,' Iturralde told the men. 'If the sons of the great whore leave their ship and come for us I want to see this whole lot go up.'

At the camp, which was only a few miles from the house, de la Rueda had not long finished reading the last dispatch from Colonel Bolaño when at the door of his tent, and in the company of Murdo, the messenger from Captain Otero arrived. De la Rueda read the note, requesting orders. For some moments de la Rueda was at a loss. It was obvious there must be a spy or more at work for he could not believe it was chance alone that made the ship anchor where it did. And if they knew about the magazine they would be after it. His blood, if not his reason, said an effort should be made to defend the magazine, but that would be contrary to orders he had just received from his colonel: The castle was under attack from enemy ships and would fall, for the cannonades were severe. He was obliged to leave the garrison to their fate while awaiting orders from the Scottish lords. Meanwhile de la Rueda was to have his troops confined to quarters and ready to march at short notice.

So how much risk was the magazine worth? Taking into account his orders, not much. But on the other hand there were already thirty men stationed at the house.

Abruptly de la Rueda made up his mind. He turned to the ensign who had taken over O'Flanagan's place.

'Have my company armed and ready to leave at once. And send me Captain Paez.'

De la Rueda thought he could risk a small auxiliary force. He would go himself to ensure nothing foolhardy took place. If there were cannonades or a landing party superior to his own he would sacrifice the magazine. If not it might be that with his additional troops the magazine could be saved.

As de la Rueda was getting ready, buckling on his sword, he glanced at Murdo, who was seated on the stool – the silver hilt of a dirk sticking out of his plaid, sword and targe strapped to his back – and thought he would like to talk to him. De la Rueda did not care much for silence. But Murdo had scarce French and de la Rueda's Latin was hard work and there was no sign of O'Flanagan, who could have translated. The *cabrón* had disappeared. Vanished. Was he lying drunk somewhere? Or with a woman? Or – No. Would he? *But he is Irish. Not Spanish. Irish. And I heard he had troubles in Spain. Could that be where the information is coming from? That treacherous son of the great whore has gone over, turned spy. Is it possible?*

Within the half hour, de la Rueda and some forty soldiers, along with Murdo and two clansmen, left the camp fully armed at double pace. The wind was brisk against them and the ground boggy, which, added to the weight of their equipment, slowed them down. Once again, though, de la Rueda found himself admiring the long, relentless strides which took Murdo and his companions over grass and heather and occasionally obliged them to hold back, waiting for de la Rueda's troops with strained patience.

The troops had to ascend a rise before reaching the shore where the house was located. As they were nearing the top of the ridge there came the sudden, reverberating thunder of cannon fire. De la Rueda scrambled to reach the top of the rise. Breathless, he looked down. The house was intact but two launches, one already arrived, the other close behind, were at the edge of the tide. Quickly, de la Rueda counted some twenty men to each launch. His own troops, meanwhile, were hastily retreating up the incline behind the house. What for, he could not know, unless it was in order to retreat out of cannon range, which he calculated would be at its limit with regards to the house. Was a defence possible? He was debating with himself when there came a second cannonade. Turf flew up, one ball fell just short of the house. The enemy marines meanwhile, dressed in blue and white, were now scrambling from the boats, muskets at the ready, while behind them puffs of smoke rose up from cannon portals on the two deck man of war.

De la Rueda was tempted to give battle. Troop numbers were on his side and the ship would not fire on its own men. But the ship could deploy reinforcements quicker than he could, and he had orders to keep the regiment confined at camp. Then, as he hesitated, he saw a lean figure who appeared to be Lieutenant Iturralde emerging from the house and running up the slope behind it. Not a couple of minutes later and even before he joined his companions the entire house exploded with a blast that took the roof off and sent chunks of debris flying in black smoke and dust. The enemy, gathering on the shore, stopped in their tracks. Some threw themselves down as bits of stone crashed about them, chunks even reaching the water. As the smoke dispersed red flames rose up from within the broken stone walls, consuming what was left of the roof, and de la Rueda's soldiers stood up from the heath and with looks behind them started hurrying towards the rise.

Well, that settles it.

When de la Rueda got back to camp he sent out forward sentries, put the troops on alert, and called Otero and Iturralde into his tent. The men were sombre and their uniforms dirty. Otero, however, had a look of petulance on his young face. He was soon insisting that he had not given the order to blow up the magazine. The lieutenant, he said, had acted on his own initiative. De la Rueda sighed and asked Iturralde if this was the case. The lieutenant said it was, because he did not want the magazine to fall into enemy hands, but that he might have acted otherwise had he known that reinforcement would reach them in time. Otero opened his mouth to make a reply when a soldier appeared at the tent door with a Highlander in possession of another dispatch from the Colonel.

As de la Rueda read it, standing up by door, a frown appeared between his eyes. The enemy had captured the garrison and was transferring the soldiers along with Captain Stapleton to the ships. The castle would be be blown up and levelled. All munitions in the castle should be given as lost lost. Colonel Bolaño ended by saying that at last clansmen were starting to congregate and there was now talk of an army under the Marquis of Tullibardine preparing to march imminently. Colonel Bolaño himself expected to gather the battalion as soon as he received orders from Tullibardine and asked for a report from de la Rueda by return.

'The garrison has surrendered,' de la Rueda told the officers. 'No mention of casualties, so I cannot enlighten you on that score.'

Stepping over to the small table, he opened the box which contained his writing implements.

'Captain Otero,' he said. 'You were in charge of the company and yet it was Lieutenant Iturralde who made the decision to blow up the magazine. That is not good enough. This time I shall let it pass but henceforth I expect you to show the authority commensurate with your rank.'

Otero reddened. 'Yes sir.'

'Lieutenant Iturralde. You took the correct action. But with a small change of circumstances it could very well have been the wrong action.'

'Yes sir.'

'That is all. Captain Otero you may return within the hour when I shall inform the captains of our present situation.'

The officers left. De la Rueda sat down, wrote his report on a piece of parchment, folded it, sealed it with melted red wax, and handed it to the soldier waiting, who departed in the company of the Highlander.

It had been an unfortunate day. The loss of the munitions, intended not only for themselves but also for the clansmen, and the capture of the garrison, made de la Rueda unhappy. Since the loss of the Armada it appeared to him that the general situation was going from bad to worse, and, since the frigates had been sent back home, without means of escape for the battalion. The one bright ray was that the clansmen appeared to be gathering, finally. *Well, it will soon be known what sort of army these strange Scots can muster.*

An ache in his muscles reminded de la Rueda of the small stock off brandy he carried. He stood up and from his second trunk pulled out a straw-covered demijohn. Standing over the small brassier, which the orderly had already lit, he twisted the cork out and took a swig direct from the bottle. *Ah, that is better.* H pulled his chair closer to the brassier, sat down, and sent his servant to enquire about food since the dinner hour was past.

Captain Paez appeared. Not long after him Otero came in, having smartened himself up, but looking somewhat sullen still. De la Rueda brought them up to the moment. There was a discussion, much of it to do with O'Flanagan, but no one could give any information as to his whereabouts.

'Perhaps the colonel can find something out from the natives,' said Paez.

'*Pues sí.* Let us hope so,' agreed de la Rueda.

The servant came back with a pot of decent stew. Two Highland cows provided by the Earl of Seaforth had been slaughtered earlier that day, so there was fresh meat in the stew. There was no bread but the cook had added four olives. De la Rueda was pleased. Olives, as with other prized Spanish victuals unloaded from the frigates, were now in increasingly short supply.

Captain Paez, who had already dined with the other officers, stayed behind while de la Rueda ate. Afterwards de la Rueda invited him to share a little brandy. If de la Rueda had anyone in the battalion he could call a friend it was Paez, because they had known each other in the Italian campaign, before joining the battalion's parent regiment. In spite of his bandy legs and short stature, Paez was a skilled swordsman. Back in Spain he had fought several duels and like de la Rueda he also had a scar on his face, though his went in a different direction, across the bridge of his squat nose.

'You know what I do not like about this country, Alejandro?' Paez said, sitting on a block of wood on one side of the brassier.

'What?'

'The sun. Here it makes a poor showing.'

'Yes, but also sometimes we can get too much of it at home.'

Paez, who had taken off his hat and wig, slowly shook his bald head. 'For my part I miss it. There is too much dampness and rain here. I have a great fear of drowning. I remember when I was a small boy there was a woman who was possessed and tied stones to herself and her two children and threw herself into a deep *alberca*. I used to play with the boy and I saw them all dead in the water. Ever since then I have been afraid of drowning. For me it is the worst death.'

De la Rueda grinned. 'If it is here, Ramón, it will be by ball or sword. I will wager you on that.'

'But with the sun,' said Paez. 'I want to feel the sun before the Lord tallies my account.'

After Paez had gone and de la Rueda went to sleep he again had the dream in which a woman appeared to save him at the moment he was on the point of death. Only this time, in all likelihood due to the day's events and his conversation with Paez, not only had the context changed but most importantly for just an instant he saw her with startling clarity: He was standing on the rise and he thought that if he ran fast enough to the house he could get there in time to save the magazine before the cannonade from the man of war hit it. But when he reached the house and was trying to remove the barrels and boxes it began raining so hard that the house filled with water. With the water at his waist and rising, he tried the door but it would not open. Then he heard a knocking sound on the window and saw a face pressed against the thick, opaque panes. He could not make out her features, but he was absolutely certain the woman was someone whom he knew intimately and whom he loved. He tried to break the window but could not. The water was soon at his throat. He saw the woman take a heavy stone and start smashing it against the window. The water covered his mouth and nose. He began to drown when all at once the window broke. A hand reached in and pulled him towards the broken window. Sputtering for breath, with water in his eyes, he looked out and at the instant he saw her face with complete clarity he woke up.

In the morning de la Rueda had news that the ship had left. He eased guard and made an inspection of the camp. After that he had various disputes and disciplinary matters to attend to. A young lad of seventeen had stabbed an older soldier in the hand before he was restrained. It was not clear yet why. De la Rueda had them both and various witnesses crowded into his tent when Murdo appeared. De la Rueda stepped outside and spoke to Murdo in his meagre Latin, wishing he had O'Flanagan to help him, but he understood that a group of clansmen had arrived and would be setting up camp nearby. Their leader, Murdo made himself understood, wanted to meet him.

De la Rueda left Paez to take over. The clansmen's camp was about a mile from the battalion's on a strip of land next to a stream where a few dwarf trees clung to the bank. The sky was milky, overcast, but not raining. The clansmen were about forty in number. They had with them no shelter but had brought several ponies and three tiny, shaggy black cows and two goats. Because it was a warm morning, some of the men had removed their plaids and were lounging about on the heather in their long yellow or white shirts. A fire was still smouldering from the night before. Their weapons, including some muskets, were stacked nearby. Most of the men had beards and their hair was long. As de la Rueda moved among them, where they sat or stood in groups, he could sense their appraising, curious stares. From near the fire a man stood up, left his group, and stepped forward. He had a short reddish beard, alert pale eyes, and dark curly hair, going grey, under a blue bonnet with an eagle's feather. He was about the same height as de la Rueda; considerably older, square set, broad in the shoulders and with long powerful arms and large hands. He, too, had taken off his plaid, and wore instead tartan trews, a shirt of good linen with frilled neck and cuffs and over that a dark waistcoat embroidered along the edges with a fancy design in gold thread. Around his waist was a belt with two pistols attached and also a dirk in an ornate scabbard.

When Murdo introduced de la Rueda to him, Rob Roy, as he was known far and wide, bowed shortly and then held out his hand. De la Rueda, surprised, took it and felt a strength in it superior to his own for all that Rob Roy was a much older man.

Rob Roy spoke a few words of French, which he had learnt as a child with a tutor and later at university. However, it was barely sufficient; when he spoke the words came haltingly, with a struggle and long pauses in between. Murdo chipped in with his Latin when they reached an impasse, and as a last resort, when that failed they used gestures. In the end de la Rueda was able to gather that Rob Roy and his men had come from the other side of the mountains, a march of several days, and that he was expecting one of his sons to arrive presently with more troops. He managed to make de la Rueda understand that enemy troops were gathering at a town called Inverness and battle could be expected soon. Finally, Rob Roy pointed to himself, made gestures of being hanged and showed de la Rueda a silver coin, which he took out of a leather pouch on his belt, for Rob Roy liked to be certain he kept money close to his person ever since he had been robbed of a large sum by a man he trusted and which had nearly been the cause of his undoing. De la Rueda had difficulty understanding until Murdo said in Latin, '*Proscribo. Ipse est proscribo.*'

'Ah, *Bandido,*' de la Rueda said in Spanish, and grinned. '*Bandido.*'

Rob Roy looked momentarily disconcerted, but then he tapped his own chest and laughed with a frankness that at once made de la Rueda like him.

'*Oui, oui. Bandit,*' said Rob Roy.

SEVEN

It is the same as last time. Men fight and women are left with all the work. But the ploughing, the harrowing, the sowing at least was done, which to Shona was a relief.

The furrowed earth on the fields around her house was of dark loam. The Experimenter had made considerable effort to improve it by adding manure and silage and rotating crops, and Hector had continued the practice, so that in some of these inbye fields, the first to be sown with oats in early April, already green shoots were showing. Now all anybody could do was pray the crops would not succumb to wind or rain. Shona was thinking about this as she and Elsbeth followed the two ponies past the fields towards the heathery slopes beneath steep hills. In her mind's eye she could see how in a few months the corn might cover the ground, their green, golden heads higher than her waist and rippling in the breeze with whispering wave-like flurries. Folk would be pleased if it was a good year, knowing they had corn to see them through the winter. Of course it might not be fine for everybody, as much as she wished it, for there would always be some to suffer want. And now with war once more on their threshold there was no knowing what cruel travails were to come. Sometimes Shona wondered how anyone managed to live at all in the face of so much that was unpredictable and, because of it, full of menace. It seemed to her astonishing that humanity had not died of fright but had somehow endured generation after generation since the time of Christ. When she went to church, which was quite often even though it was a journey of several hours, and took communion and listened to the sermon, she felt quite sure that everything was according to God's plan and therefore she need not fear; but there were other times, times such as now, when the violence in God's plan seemed to her more than was just for her or any fellow mortal to bear. It was at such moments that she questioned the value of life, and her ability to endure it, and, though she knew it was a sin, she would feel a little flame of rebellion burn in her soul.

The peat had already been cut and stacked in mounds by the hand of others when the women came to the bog. Elsbeth stopped the ponies by one of several trenches from which the peat had been extracted. Shona took her shoes off and rolled up the sleeves of her shirt before helping Elsbeth fill the wicker panniers with peat blocks. The work, not arduous, was soon accomplished. Had Shona wanted she need not have accompanied Elsbeth, but the departure of Hector and the men had made her restless. She could not sit long without an urge to escape in movement. If it was outside, walking, labouring, all the better. As a child, and although the daughter of a chieftain, she had not been spared labour. Whatever any other child in the clan had to do she was made to do herself. Right up to when she came to live with Hector there had been time for study but not so much for leisure. Then it changed for her because while her parents had folk they could command they were not like the folk that served Hector and his mother. For them servants were present to do their bidding just, and since besides Mairi there were several more available as needed, it allowed for self-indulgence. But Neil and John, the servants Shona had brought with her when she married Hector, had come of their own free will. They had *asked* to accompany her. And Shona liked to think that if ever they asked to return to the sept lands, her brother would take them back. John was old now, and she liked to let him be, looking after the animals in the byre, calling for him only when she had to. As for Neil, well he did her bidding but he was no servant. Or if he was it was only in Hector's eyes, for Shona had known Neil since they were children. They had played together and were distantly related by blood. This was not unusual. In the old ways of the clan, families often rose and fell from one generation to the next so that power and privilege outwith the chief was not assured. Neil's grandmother had been a cousin of Shona's grandfather.

On the return journey the two women halted the ponies and for a little sat to rest on the heather at a spot with a view to the sea. The morning was warm, dry. In the distance the sea shimmered silvery blue and green like the wings of a dragon fly. There, far away, Shona could make out a tiny spot which made her think it was a ship, perhaps even one of the English men of war that were said to be lingering still after demolishing the castle at Eilean Donan.

'I heard all the Spaniards at the castle were taken prisoner; did you hear that too?' asked Shona.

'I did,' said Elsbeth.

'Who did you hear it from? Hamish?'

'The pedlar? Not so. I was going to tell you, my sister in Kyle sent word. Her husband, Callum, he was sent back after he hurt his arm falling off the horse he was riding.' Elsbeth paused. 'He was fou my sister says.'

'So what does he tell?'

'The castle was blown to ruins with the Spanish gunpowder the English captured. And not only the castle. A house in the Crow that was keeping more Spanish gunpowder and arms was also blown up. And the Spaniards guarding the castle are now prisoners on the English ships.'

'They will be fed at least,' said Shona. 'And their fighting will be over.'

'Rob Roy, the one with the price on his head, has arrived with forty men and is staying near the big Spanish camp, Callum says. Men are gathering in their hundreds now, ready to march on the Earl of Tullibardine's say so.'

'Are you worried for Neil?'

'I am,' said Elsbeth. 'I only wish it had been him and not Callum who had hurt his arm. Are you worried for Hector?'

For the merest fraction Shona hesitated, then nodded. 'But it is different for me, not having children now. Or thoughts that I could not make ends meet.'

Elsbeth was silent.

'I will take care of you and the children should anything happen to Neil. You have my word.'

'I pray he will come back safe,' said Elsbeth. 'And Hector... And for victory. I pray for that too.'

But if they do win and Hector returns victorious, how will that change anything here? Oh there will be celebrations aplenty. The bards will make song and poesy like in past glorious times. And it may be Scotland will have its own parliament like it had before. And its own king! She would not object. It pleased her to imagine a Scottish king on the throne. *And if Hector distinguishes himself he will be made a major, or even a colonel. And all very fine. Only how much blood is to be spilt in its cause? And even in victory how will it change anything here, from day to day? How will it stop rents going up? And will it lower taxes? Make cattle worth more? All the things we depend on, will it really change any of that? Colonel, major, or captain, my husband will carry on as before, seeking to turn every transaction to his advantage.*

Still, she must not think harshly of her husband. She must not. She knew how he had suffered when their children died; she could not blame him if it had dried up the pity in him.

Shona could remember how much freer Hector had been when the children lived. It was the best time for them because before that there was the Experimenter's death to deal with and before that the deaths of her own parents. And their courtship, too, the handfasting, it was quite often a battle between them. Hector was fastidious. It was the one thing that had always irked Shona. His clothes had to be folded just so. The broth neither too warm or too cold. Everything always in its place and accounted for. Her own father had not been remiss. He had kept a careful tally on all that came in and went out. But Hector, if he could, he would have put every least blade of grass down in his ledgers. It was by knowing exactly what he had, he often said to her, that he could ascertain what he could afford. And more than once he had suggested that if she wanted to find out the consequences of poor management she should accompany him to the gaols of Edinburgh and Glasgow which were full to bursting with lairds and gentlemen unable to pay their debts. Shona did not doubt it. High society no less than low was mortgaged to the neck. And in her part of the world, being Jacobite, the more so because the ruling power was out to crush them. It was harder for Jacobites to trade and make commerce. Shona understood all this. And she was sorry that she could not show Hector more often that she understood his preoccupation to avoid the entrapment of debt that so many others were prone to, including The Experimenter, and even the Earl of Seaforth.

But it suffocated her. Hector's narrow, fastidious ways suffocated her. And yet… it was true, always there had been those moments when he surprised her. She would think he went one way and it turned out he could go another. As a father she thought he would be like most men, that he would not express more interest in the children than was strictly beholden and would be quick to scold. But he surprised her. She could not remember that he scolded them more than a couple of times in all the six years of their immaculate lives. He said not a word against Gregor that time he was two or three and wanting to put his hands everywhere and he pulled off the table the jug that Elsbeth or Mairi had forgotten to remove. The handle broke and Margaret was furious. She grabbed Gregor and was about to thrash him when Hector came to Gregor's rescue. He picked Gregor up and would not let Margaret near him. Hector loved the twins. She could not deny it. It was as if the tumultuous force of their natures could open up a part of him he more often put away and guarded against. Because she had seen it, too, even before the children, like that other time when she had not been able to make up her mind if she wanted to handfast with him or not.

Her father and The Experimenter were already making the contract between them. But her father would not force her against her will. If she made up her mind to refuse Hector he would accept it even if he did not care to. Her father had told her so himself when she had confessed her misgivings to him. But then Hector came over on The Experimenter's behalf to buy timber from her father. It was not the most carefree of times, for her mother had been dead less than a year and they were still grieving. Hector seemed to have matured since she had last seen him at her mother's funeral. His tall body had filled out, his voice had less of a quiver, and he came over as more confident even if he was not quick to help her brother and father with work. Shona suspected it was concern for spoiling the look of his bonny attire. And his embroidered velvet jacket, tartan trews of fine wool, and shoes with buckles *were* bonny. Shona had to admit that he cut a good figure. But it irked her, his preoccupation with himself, and she was thinking that maybe she would be happier with a man who was poorer and had not the means or time to be so concerned over his deportment. Yet it so happened that on the second or third morning Donald came running to say that a cow with a calf had got stuck in a bog. The cow, although in the common herd, was one of her father's. So they all went to help pull the animals free, including Hector. Before they left Shona caught Hector looking down at himself, his clothes, with an expression of horror. She thought with disgust that he was going to refuse. But he came along after all. And when they arrived at the bog, where the cow was sunk to her belly and the calf behind her near to its neck in one of the quagmires not easily perceived because of all the reeds growing thereabouts, Hector managed to surprise her by his sudden willingness to do his part.

They all got covered in mud getting to the animals and tying ropes around them. The calf came out easy enough, but they had more trouble with the cow. Finally her father sent Donald for a horse. He came back with one an hour or so later and so they managed to pull the cow out, though not before a flurry of its hooves sent mud everywhere, some of it landing on Hector's face, which made Shona laugh.

The next day it was Beltane. Her father still adhered to the old ways in some regards and so in the evening he made certain the hearth fire was completely extinguished. By then Hector's clothes were dry and some of the mud had been shaken off but he was no longer quite the bonnie sight he had been when he arrived. If he minded, however, he did not indicate it. When in the evening they joined the folk of her clan on the hillside he was in good cheer. There, under a sky that was still bright, a bonfire was lit. Warm and illuminated by the flickering flames, the clan gathered around to drink ale and share food the women had brought and then one of them took out a fiddle and another a whistle and they made music and sang and the bard pulled on his long white beard and recounted tales of old. Hector was happy. There was laughter in his grey eyes and he made easy conversation with her folk. After the fire died down the children and then some older folk started jumping over the flames. It was said the higher they jumped the higher the corn would grow. On the spur of the moment Shona took Hector's hand, pulling him to his feet. He came along willingly when they joined the jumpers. At the end of the night, like other folk, Shona and Hector lit torches from the fire and took them with them, each ready to light the other's torch if one of them was blown out, and in this way they arrived home to light the hearth with the new flame from the bonfire, which marked the beginning of a new year.

That night changed the way Shona thought about Hector. She saw that there was more to him than encountered the eye and that it was to his favour rather than against: A seam of kindness, so it seemed to her, where the two of them could meet and agree. So when not long afterwards the handfasting was again brought up by her father, this time she found that her misgivings were far less. In fact, one day, imagining a future with Hector, she suddenly decided that she would tell her father that she would agree to the handfasting. Before that could happen, though, her father drowned and after his death she was so stricken that she could not dwell on her future with Hector. She only started thinking about it again when it was brought up by her uncle. He was insistent. It was clear that her uncle was not thinking of her happiness alone, he was also calculating the alliance between their clan and The Experimenter's fiefdom. Shona felt she was not ready. With her father alive she had felt secure to handfast. If it did not work out her father would take her back. But she did not have the same confidence with her uncle. However, her uncle kept on with the insistence until she was wanting just to get away from him and be done with it and so she agreed.

The year and a day they had lived as man and wife had not gone perfectly. They had quarrelled, but there had been good times, too. They had a room of their own in the house, the one Hector now used for a study, and they had travelled to Glasgow and Inverness. At the end of the year and a day she was pregnant. They were struck with wonder when not one boy arrived but two. And soon Hector came to dote on them. Then The Experimenter died. He was sitting in his chair after supper and just like that he died. It was so quiet and sudden no one noticed until later when Margaret wanted him to come to bed. His eyes were open but he would not respond. He was dead.

After The Experimenter died Hector began to take over the management of the estate. At times he and Margaret clashed for she desired to retain control, but it was certain the faeries had put her under a spell for her faculties were not as they had been when The Experimenter was alive. Hector took charge of the ledgers, which were poorly kept. Soon it became apparent that his father had left behind much debt; mortgages taken on the land and spent on enterprises that were then abandoned or brought small profit. Shona could see why Hector would want to put an end to such folly. As a first step he decided to write everything down. It was long the custom everywhere not to keep books on the tenants but to trust to word and memory. Hector, however, insisted that custom had to change, he was going to write everything down and eliminate by good management the wadsets his father had accumulated. Shona only started to think differently when it appeared to her that some of the demands Hector made of the tenants were becoming too burdensome.

They can afford it, he said, and she could not deny that there were a few richer tenants who were canny and not doing so badly from cattle and corn and sublets of their own, but it made her suspicious of what else Hector might do without regard for her opinion or sentiments. He did not ask her what she thought, and she did not expect him to, but she could not help wishing that he would.

When Shona and Elsbeth arrived home with the peat a woman was standing near the door, hands busy knitting. She was some years older than Shona; small, plump, and tidy. Under the white mutch over her dark hair her face was clean but creased with apprehension.

'Good morning, madam.' The woman came forward shyly, her feet bare under a long brown woollen skirt.

'Good morning.' Shona could not immediately place her.

'Fiona, madam. My husband is Donald Peter. We have a five shillings tack on the Three Rowans.'

Shona remembered now. The couple lived a fair distance away. She saw the woman rarely, but her husband Donald Peter was well known. As part of his rent payment Donald Peter gave Hector labour when it was needed. He was a short, cheerful man. Always active; poor but admired and envied for the way he had managed in the space of five years to turn the worthless, heather covered acres he rented into land yielding productive crops of oats and bear.

'Do you wish to speak to me in private?'

'Yes, madam.'

While Elsbeth began to unload the ponies, Shona led the woman into the house and into Hector's study, closing the door behind her. A hen was sitting on Hector's desk. Shona shooed it off.

'So what can I do for you?'

'It is about our tack, the one Donald Peter rents.'

'How is Donald Peter? Has he gone with the men?'

'No. He was going to, madam. He was at Sheriffmuir like everyone. Only this time both his ankles swelled up and he is lame and in fearful pain he is, too.'

'I am sorry to hear it.'

Fiona paused. Shona waited. Beyond the room came muffled sounds of the peat being stacked by the hearth.

'If you will allow me, madam, I have come to ask for your help if you can give it.'

'What is it about?'

'Our rent… Lachlan. We are being told he has offered his lordship fifteen shillings a year for our tack.'

'Which Lachlan? Lachlan White Eyes?'

'Yes, madam.'

'How much do you pay now?

'Five shillings.'

'In kind?'

'We have nothing else.'

'Do you know if my husband has accepted Lachlan's offer?'

'I am praying to God he has not. If he has we will be evicted. When my husband took that land from The Experimenter I was set against it. I told him he was away with the faeries. It was five acres of worthless bog, but my husband listened to The Experimenter. Few listened to that good man, but my husband did. He dug channels to drain the land, and he planted the kale The Experimenter gave him. Well, madam, that was near fifteen years ago, and now those five aces give better yields of corn than any land around and about us. Lachlan cannot match it. Even at fifteen shillings he will not make a loss.'

'And can you pay that much?'

Fiona wrung her hands and looked at Shona anxiously. 'We make a little more than what Lachlan is offering his lordship, but what is left over would be scarce enough for our needs. We have four children and two grandchildren depending on us. And even if we were to offer fifteen shillings his lordship could choose not to take it.'

Would he? Would Hector not see the injustice? Shona imagined he would. After all their years of toil to improve the land he was not going to take it from them only to pass it on to someone else. But then how did she *know* what arrangements Hector had made with that pig Lachlan?

'And what is the most you can pay?'

'As long as we have our cattle and the crops do not fail we can go to ten.'

'That is twice what you are paying now?'

Fiona nodded.

'Should anything come of it, I will help you in what I can,' Shona said after a moment. 'I will send you a message.'

'God bless you, madam.'

After Fiona left, Shona and Elsbeth went on a second journey for peat. On the way back they stopped at the settlement that was about half a mile from Shona's house. This settlement consisted of nine dwellings placed close by each other. Four of the thatched houses were occupied by tenants of Hector's. Each of the tenants had a share of land to plough in the rigs that were allocated to them every year on a rotation basis, so that the more productive strips of land were distributed without favour. They also had small individual parcels of their own and a share in the common grazing for their cattle. The five other houses were occupied by cottars. These men and their families did not rent land from Hector but instead worked on his fields as labourers in exchange for subsistence.

Besides this settlement, and two or three small farms with their own sub tenants, such as Lachlan's, there were several other settlements of various sizes on Hector's estate containing both tenants and cottars; but the cottars, and at times even the tenants, who lived in the settlement nearest the estate house had greater involvement as servants in their masters' daily affairs. Thus, besides being farmers and labourers, the folk in this settlement were also craftsmen; one of them was a blacksmith, another a carpenter, Elsbeth herself was a weaver, and there was another woman who knew much about dyes. Shona spoke to this woman now, the wife of one of the tenants, and though not strictly a servant, she could not refuse to do as bid, which was to come presently to the house and help Shona and Elsbeth with a particular red dye that was difficult to use. Elsbeth's and Neil's own house was straight opposite the woman's, on a patch of grassy land where a tethered goat along with several geese and chickens were grazing. Elsbeth went there to speak to her children, who were being looked after by her eldest daughter. This girl was eleven and was not Neil's child for Elsbeth had been a widow when Neil married her. The girl and the four other children soon emerged from the house to help Elsbeth unload the peat bricks from one of the ponies, since Shona was giving Elsbeth a load for herself. Shona, standing by, watched the children carrying the peat bricks into the house, all in a line and not even the youngest, a three year old, exempt. Watching him totter into the house on his short bandy legs, holding a peat brick in both arms against his chest, Shona smiled, amused, but hiding a stab of sadness.

When Shona got back to the house she had Mairi help her unload her pony and take the peat inside. That finished, they went outside and by the wall of the barn, which was at a right angle to the house and separated from it by a broad gap, they built a small fire with bits of wood and some peat. The fire was not long going when the dye woman and Elsbeth appeared. The dye woman had a creel strapped to her back, which she put down on the ground. The iron dye pot was brought from the house, so too the creels of unspun wool, already shorn from the fleece, that was to be dyed. From her own creel, the dye woman then brought out the ladies bedstraw plants that she was going to use and under her supervision the women stripped the bark off the plants and placed the roots in the water that had begun to boil in the dye pot. When the woman judged the roots were sufficiently boiled the liquid was drained from the pot into another container. Now the pot was filled with several layers of wool and a sprinkling of alum powder and the bark of the plant in between. To this was added the root liquid which had been removed and then the pot was heated up again over the fire. At the appropriate time, again judged by the woman, the wool was stirred and removed from the fire. The ladies bedstraw was a plant with yellow flowers but now when the wool came out of the pot its colour was of a soft, translucent red. The dye woman nodded to herself and declared it accomplished. Once removed from the pot the wool was hung up to dry from the rafters in the barn.

The day had gone by the time the dyeing was finished but the sky was still bright. The gentle breeze smelt of the sea, and the green of the grass and early foliage on the trees across the brook glowed and sparkled. Reluctant to go inside, Shona sat on the bench outside her front door, hands folded on her lap and thoughts of nothing in particular drifting through her mind. Then she remembered Fiona. Her thoughts became preoccupied. With a frown she stood up and went indoors, past Mairi who was making cheese in the kitchen, and Margaret who was sitting in her fiddleback chair head lolling on her chest as she snoozed, and into Hector's study off the passageway to the byre. The walls of the study where limed and whitewashed but on their uneven surface near the door there was a small loose stone. Shona removed the stone, took out a key, replaced the stone, and went over to the desk. In all the years she had been married to Hector, and although she had long known where he kept the key, she had not once looked at his ledgers. On the few occasions she had been tempted, her scruples had prevented her. She kept her own accounts for such household expenditure as was hers to manage and for her own small private capital. The ledgers Hector kept for his transactions with his tenants or his dealings with the Earl of Seaforth, however,

Shona had decided were not hers to know. As a woman she had no legal entitlement to any part of Hector' estate, a fact of which he had more than once reminded her when she had disputed his methods, so she had drawn a line at actually delving into his accounts. But now that Hector was not here, with the immediate future so unsure, and after Fiona's appeal, Shona made a decision and sitting down in Hector's chair behind the writing table that had been The Experimenter's, she inserted the key into the single drawer beneath the writing surface and pulled it open.

There were two board and leather bound ledgers. She put them on the desk, chose the more recent of the two and opened it. It took Shona a while to go through the pages of the accounts from the beginning of the year, for she kept being distracted by intriguing entries to do with stocks, services, and payments received and given, most in kind, a few in money, but finally she found the entry under the month of March. It was written in pencil, in Hector's small neat handwriting: an advance payment from Lachlan to Hector for the five shilling tack rented by Donald Peter and to be transferred to Lachlan at the end of the year after the harvest for an annual rent of fifteen shillings.

For some moments Shona could not think. She did not want to think. Without her realizing, her hand closed the cover of the ledger. But closing her mind to the unease was not so simple. She knew that Hector had been raising the rents, and more steeply in the last couple of years, but not every rent was equivalent. Much depended on the individual circumstances of the tenants and Hector's personal relationship with each. Even so she had noticed figures in some of the entries that had seemed odd to her, excessive in their demand, and now abruptly she reached to open the ledger again, intending to examine them more closely, when a sheet of paper partially slipped out from behind the back cover. Shona removed it. There was a crude diagram in pencil on one side of sixteen rigs and various other parcels of land, all numbered. Staring at the paper, Shona realized it referred to the Silverwater bhaile. She turned the paper over and there was a list of the tenants who cultivated the particular rig or land which corresponded to their number. As well as the names of the tenants, the respective acres were graded for pasture from good to indifferent, and the number of cattle and sheep the various sections might accommodate. There was no date, but Shona knew that if Hector had written it all down on paper it was not idle fancy. Her past arguments with him on the subject of moving tenants from their holdings, when not evicting them altogether, it seemed had not swayed him in the least. She had hoped he might have backed down, for it was not a subject that had come up again since when Hector had appeared to relent by making out it was only conjecture and saying he would find employment or land elsewhere for any that were evicted. But there was nothing on the sheet of paper to indicate this. No reference to being moved anywhere. And where would they be resettled? It was clear to her, turning the sheet of paper over in her hands, that their eviction was something Hector fully intended. It was beginning to happen elsewhere. She had heard of *bailtean,* settlements disappearing in one or two places. The folk all moving away, forced from their homes, going to work in the mines or the salt pans in the lowlands or wherever they could and their land turned over to sheep and cattle.

I cannot let it happen. But how? How can I stop it? God forgive me, but if Hector dies in battle I will stop it. And if he does not die, I will try to stop it even so. It must not happen. I must look for a way.

Shona closed her eyes. It made her quail to think of Fiona and others – whole families, destitute, thrown out, with nowhere to live because of her husband's greed.

EIGHT

Many of the Spanish soldiers were stripped down to their waists, for the morning was hot and muggy as they carried stones to where the breastworks were being built on the steep slope. When not dug up from nearer by, the stones first had to be collected from the scree on higher ground, loaded onto ponies and conveyed closer to where the walls were being built. The greater portion of the battalion's three hundred soldiers that remained after the capture of the castle garrison were being put to work at this task. But the Spaniards were not alone, for time was of essence and they were being aided by clansmen under the command of Sir John Mackenzie and Rob Roy MacGregor – anyone, in fact, who was handy with stonework.

'It does the men good to work. They have been idle too long.'

Colonel Bolaño, who had taken off his coat and bandoleer and passed it to the servant behind him was nevertheless resplendent in a frilled shirt under a yellow silk waistcoat.

'Was it your suggestion, sir?'

De la Rueda stood beside his colonel, unarmed but in full uniform, near the summit of the slope, watching the soldiers at work some yards further down.

Bolaño pulled at the waxed ends of his moustachio and then waved his hand at the midges which in between the flurries of mild breeze tried to land on his face.

'Well yes, and I tell you, the Marquis of Tullibardine looked at me like I was mad when I insisted on it. The men here think only of charging, that is their way of fighting. They are not regular soldiers; and as I said to the Marquis, we Spaniards have our own ways. We put up barricades, we dig in, we hold our ground.'

De la Rueda took in yet again the terrain around them. In essence they held the high ground at the end of a narrow glen. To his right a small river ran along the glen floor some few hundred feet below. Beyond the river there rose a pointed greenish brown hill, close by as the crow flies and its summit a little higher than where de la Rueda was standing. Scattered groups of men could be seen moving about below the summit. Altogether there would be some two hundred of them, de la Rueda knew, commanded by the Marquis of Tullibardine's brother, Lord George Murray. Opposite the hill, on de la Rueda's side of the glen, and to his left, was a gulley and stony slope that rose several hundred yards higher than where de la Rueda stood, and here, a few hundred yards distant, the Earl of Seaforth was taking command with another two or three hundred men, whom de la Rueda could also see moving about among exposed outcrops of rock. Meanwhile, the track that followed the river at ground level had already been roughly blockaded, which meant that when the enemy came into the glen they would be confronted with a blocked exit and their foe concentrated above them on two sides and the centre in the rough shape of a horseshoe.

'The ground here is steep,' de la Rueda remarked. 'We are well placed if they come to us from below.'

'How else?' said Bolaño. He turned and pointed to the scree high up behind them. 'If they were to try and dislodge us from above they would have to come over that ridge, which they cannot, I am told, as the difficulty would be too extreme. They can only arrive through the valley below.'

'Is there any other news on their numbers?'

'No. If there are more reports I have not been informed. We can only hope their numbers do not increase because frankly, as we both know, the numbers on this side are far less than what we were told to expect. Of course, I imagine there would have been greater enthusiasm from the natives had our Armada landed with success.'

'That would have changed the whole situation,' agreed de la Rueda. 'But from what I have seen, the native troops, though few, appear willing.'

'But not disciplined,' insisted Bolaño. 'Only some of them, I believe, have experience of battle.'

'Are you thinking of the one four years ago, sir? I have been told it was fiercely contested. Both sides claim victory.'

'Yes. A substantial engagement. Fifteen thousand men on this side, but not many of those are here now. One of the commanders of the enemy in that battle is the same man who now leads the enemy against us. A certain Major General Wightman. A professional soldier. And highly experienced by all accounts.' Bolaño paused. 'But on our side it is not the lack of experience in the native troops that worries me so much. It is the chain of command. The lords should have settled that issue with their exiled king, in France, months ago. Instead, as you know, they quarrel and agree on little, and then mostly with bad grace. Personally, between you and me, I think the Earl Marischal should have been placed in overall command. I suspect he will take a risk where a more cautious commander will not and we both know what that can mean for victory. But well, it is the Marquis of Tullibardine who has pulled rank, so want it or not we shall have to obey his orders. Should I fall, captain, you need to know that your duty is to the Marquis of Tullibardine so long as he remains in command. No one else.'

'Yes sir. I shall keep it in mind.'

'Let it never be said that our battalion served with dishonour.'

'You can trust me, sir.'

From his waistcoat pocket Bolaño removed a small round silver and mother of pearl snuff box. Since he knew that de la Rueda did not indulge, he did not offer him the box, but opened the lid, removed a pinch of powder and inserted it into his right nostril. At that moment Rob Roy came by. Rob Roy had removed his plaid and wore trews, embroidered waistcoat and shirt. Like most others, he was not at that moment fully armed.

'Good day, gentlemen,' Rob Roy said, in bad French.

De la Rueda and Bolaño replied in better French. Again de la Rueda was struck by Rob Roy's strong physique and the restless youthful vitality in his pale brown eyes for all that he was now a man of years, his curly shoulder length hair more grey than ginger.

Rob Roy looked up at the sky, which after the earlier mugginess had turned clear blue, grinned, pointed down to the floor of the glen, then raised his large hands and moved them about in front of him.

'Natare,' he said, in Latin. 'Natare.'

'*Que dice*?' Bolaño asked, before turning to offer Rob Roy a pinch of snuff. 'What does he say? Does he go to swim?'

De la Rueda smiled. '*No sé*. I do not know. I think so.'

Rob Roy accepted the snuff box, took a pinch, turned the box about in his thick fingers, and then, after handing it back with a bow, he called in Gaelic to his men working with the Spaniards on the barricades. Moments later a few dozen of them were abandoning the walls and following Rob Roy at a swift pace down the steep incline.

'That man is a famous bandit in this country, I am told,' remarked Bolaño. Then he chuckled. 'For a moment I feared he was going to pocket my snuff box.'

De la Rueda laughed along. 'Yes, he indicated to me as much -'

'What? That he was going to pinch my snuff box?'

'No sir, no. That he carries a price on his head.'

'Do you know why?'

'Not too well. A gentleman who is related to the priest back near the camp tried to explain it but we did not get far. His French and my Latin are equally insufficient.'

'In any case, the Earl Marischal informs me this Rob Roy has a reputation for daring exploits. A cattle rustler without equal.'

'I have noticed he commands the respect of his men,' said de la Rueda.

After reaching the bottom of the slope, Rob Roy's group started making their way across the glen to the river.

'Ah, you see, captain,' Bolaño nodded to himself, 'they are going for a swim.'

'It is a good day for it.'

'Indeed. But the breastworks must be finished *cuanto antes.* I am aware that the enemy is not expected for another day or two, but still, let us err on the side of prudence.'

'Yes sir.'

Bolaño nodded and moved off, with his servant behind him holding his coat, back up the slope to where the camp was located on a small plateau under the continuation of the scree and ridge higher up.

De la Rueda went down to the breastworks. They were being erected in segments, spread across the face of the slope; stone walls in rows of three, one behind the other, and intended to be a couple of feet thick and twice as high. The soldiers worked on them mostly in silence, unlike the Highlanders, de la Rueda had noticed, who often sang in unison while working, although now and then his troops would pause to take breath or exchange animated banter. As de la Rueda walked parallel to the lower wall in the main segment he heard one young soldier, who had just put a stone in place, say to another, 'And why can the Scots go and bathe? Are we not going to spill blood the same as them?' The other soldier, aware of de la Rueda's presence, did not answer. De la Rueda, however, had heard and he decided the soldier was not wrong. He had been in enough battles himself to know how prized a carefree hour was to a soldier before his moment of reckoning, so he now climbed the slope again and trudged some three hundred yards on flat ground until he came to a large, rounded stone shieling beside another stone enclosure that was used by local herders for a pen. The shieling itself was built low and with a roughly thatched roof. Outside it, since the weather was turning fine – the breeze balmy, with a mild scent of honey, when not now and then a whiff of human waste – the generals and lords were gathered. One or two of them, such as James Keith and Glendaruel, were sitting on the heathery grass, but Tullibardine was seated on a stool under a parasol, wearing trews and a fancy frilled shirt, a sheathed broadsword by his side, two silver pistols on a belt across his silk shirted chest, his snub-nosed face flushed and a little peevish as he conversed with an officer de la Rueda did not know. Colonel Bolaño was not in this group, but was outside the door of his white and blue tent, which had been erected some twenty yards away from the shieling. There were several other tents scattered about, including de la Rueda's, but all the Spanish soldiers below officer rank, as well as the hundreds of clansmen, were now sleeping in the open. Altogether there were some six hundred men on this slope, and de la Rueda could see the native clansmen scattered all around him, in small and large groups, fraternizing, drilling, or attending to their weapons; broadswords, targes, dirks, and Lochaber axes, but also such muskets as had been given to them either by the Scottish lords or out of such Spanish munitions as had been spared destruction from the men of war. In the main, however, the clansmen had little familiarity with fire arms, so groups of them were being taught by the more experienced to employ the muskets and sporadically, near and far, the stillness was interrupted by the sound of abrupt volleys which left small puffs of gunpowder floating up in the soft breeze. Bolaño had received a visit from the Earl Marischal when de la Rueda arrived. Both de la Rueda and Bolaño had more regard for the Earl Marischal than they did for Tullibardine. Besides their suspicion that he would make a better commander, he had a more pugnacious and engaging personality. He also spoke and understood Spanish, having passed time in their country. But now, ever since he had been deprived of command by Tullibardine pulling rank on him, the earl was like a fish out of water, with no troops of his own to command. Unlike Rob Roy, Glendaruel, or any of the other dozen clan chieftains, or officers, who had arrived with their own bands of men, the Earl Marischal, having sailed from Spain, had arrived empty handed. Deprived of overall command he had to make do as an adjunct in the Earl of Seaforth's camp, and it was in this capacity that he was conversing with Bolaño, both men seated on camp stools under the flap of Bolaño's tent, while nearby them, four hobbled Galician ponies grazed on the patches of grass between the heather. Further behind the horses was a large tent holding the regiment's dwindling comestibles. The magazine, with all the ammunition and muskets, was in another tent, further away. Provisions for the clan troops was held apart, some in the main shieling, but also in native tents, which were easily distinguished from the Spanish tents because they were a different shape and far rougher in colour and style.

De la Rueda lifted his tricorne to his superiors with a slight bow.

'*Bueno dias, capitán,*' the Earl Marischal greeted him, a preoccupied smile on his long, ruddy face.

De la Rueda returned the greeting, then addressed Bolaño.

'With permission, sir. I wish to allow the men working to take turns bathing in the river since they have witnessed Rob Roy taking his men to do so.'

Bolaño considered. 'Very well. Go ahead, but no more than one company at a time, if you please.'

'Yes sir.'

Before going back, de la Rueda stopped at his tent. His servant was on his knees outside scrubbing de la Rueda's spare trews on a washboard placed in a small wooden tub, as if no battle were imminent.

'Rodolfo, my spare boots, please.'

'Straight away, sir.'

Rodolfo hobbled to his feet and went into the tent. De la Rueda sat on a clump of heather and pulled off his boots. The leather sole was clearly coming apart. *This damp climate does footwear little good. It is no surprise the natives go mostly barefoot.*

Beside the boot, both his woollen socks had holes in them. When Rodolfo came back out with the spare boots, de la Rueda gave him the socks as well.

'See if you can mend it all. And if not, find someone.'

'As soon as I have done the laundry I will see to it.'

Once de la Rueda had spare boots and socks on, he took off his coat, handed it to the servant, and then went back down to the breastworks, looking for Paez. He found Captain Paez among a group of other officers near a separate row of breastworks being erected further along the slope. While the lower ranks worked the officers chatted dissolutely. When de la Rueda approached they stepped back to let him through.

'Some of the Scots have gone to the river to bathe,' de la Rueda said to Paez. 'Our troops may do the same – one company at a time, decided by lots, at half hour intervals.'

Besides his own companies, de la Rueda also had responsibility for the companies formerly commanded by Major Santarem, the senior quartermaster, who remained ill and incapacitated since first arriving on the Isle of Lewis. Major Santarem's second in command was Lieutenant Hurtado. When de la Rueda got back to the breastplates which the men of his two companies were working on, he approached Lieutenant Hurtado, a tall young man with blue eyes, who, rather than hang about, had stripped to his waist and was working alongside the men. De la Rueda sent Hurtado in his place to arrange the participation of his two companies in the drawing of the lots. Within half an hour the first company had been chosen and divided into two groups of twenty four men each, who headed separately down the slope to find somewhere along the river where they could rest and bathe. Neither of de la Rueda's companies had drawn the lucky straw, and his soldiers, watching others go down the slope before them now hurled after them loud, jocular profanities, to which the targets responded by turning around, making obscene gestures, and shouting back profanities of their own.

De la Rueda grinned.

'Patience,' he said, to the men near him. 'Your turn will come before the day is out.'

And it did, although by the time the second of de la Rueda's companies had their turn it was near evening. De la Rueda himself accompanied the last of the groups. At the bottom of the slope they turned right, to where the glen narrowed considerably and the little river tumbled between rocks into a deep pool. Although the sun had gone behind the hills, it was still warm and bright, so the men pulled their clothes off in their entirety and the very few among them who could swim jumped naked into the dark pool while the majority stepped into the shallower water between the rocks further down. Like the Highlanders themselves there were many among the Spaniards who were afraid of the deep pools and could imagine malign spirits dwelling in them. De la Rueda, a swimmer, went for the pool. For an instant he felt the chill of the water as he jumped in, but in a moment it passed. Once he was accustomed to the water he did not want to get out. He cavorted and joked with the men, for a little while all of them forgetting the distinction of rank. When finally he got out of the water, the breeze, without the sun to warm it, felt cold on his skin. Soon dry, he got dressed quickly, and called his men to head back. The men grumbled on the way up the slope. Mostly it was about food. Scarcely anything was left of the comestibles that had been unloaded from the ships over a month ago, and such oats, fish, and meat that had been available to them from local stocks was now being diverted to feed the clansmen. De la Rueda's men had not eaten a solid meal in two days. Hearing them complain now of hunger, he resolved to speak to the sergeant quartermaster at once. The troops must be fed before any battle commences, he reminded himself.

On his way to the quartermaster's, at the top of the slope, where it started to flatten out, de la Rueda was stopped by a tall clansman, dressed in a plaid, armed with pistols and a dirk, and on his head a blue bonnet with a single eagle's feather and a sprig of broom attached to it. He was flanked by two other clansmen. One of them was Lachlan; to de la Rueda's eye this man seemed so white as to look almost like an albino. The men were armed with broadswords and targes strapped to their backs.

'Ah *capitaine, un plaisir de vous revoir.* A pleasure to meet you again.'

De la Rueda could not place the grey eyes and youthful face smiling down at him.

'We met while waiting for the lords to… ah... conclude a meeting?'

'Of course. I remember now, *Monsieur*. The pleasure is mine.'

De la Rueda was still having trouble remembering. Nevertheless, he removed his hat and bowed.

Hector returned the compliment.

'I am under the instructions of my Lord Seaforth to join the troops commanded by John MacDonald,' said Hector. 'And I believe he is to be attached close to your company.'

'I heard more troops were being moved to the centre,' said de la Rueda. 'That is good, *Monsieur*, *if* the attack comes where it is expected.'

Hector frowned and laughed self-consciously. Those two contradictory gestures revealed to de la Rueda all he needed to know regards the gentleman's experience of war.

'I am informed the enemy has little choice. All roads lead to Rome, as it is said.'

Now de la Rueda laughed. 'In that case, let us hope the enemy is directed to Rome.'

But de la Rueda was not totally persuaded. He had been in too many battles not to know that they had a way of turning against expectations. In his experience a battle's success or failure was often the result of something unforeseen that only appeared as events unfolded. They were all expecting the enemy to attack the centre, for it was at the centre that the only feasible route through the glen presented itself. So long as they held the high ground in the centre, de la Rueda could not disagree that theirs was the stronger position against an enemy hemmed in on the floor of the glen. Still, although terrain and disposition of troops was greatly in their favour, de la Rueda nevertheless wondered if they were not taking too much for given. With a sense of unease, he recalled a battle in Portugal twelve years ago that his side had lost when it was assumed victorious.

'Have you been in service long, captain?' Hector asked, as they began walking towards the camp.

De la Rueda nodded. 'I was eighteen when I joined. And you, *Monsieur*?'

'No. I am made captain, but ah...' Hector fumbled for the French words. 'I... I... have... ah.. no knowledge of battle. I am an *agriculteur.*'

'You have a farm?'

'*Oui.* Most is for cattle. I have corn too, and, well... I collect – how do you say? taxes? louer? for my Lord, the Earl of Seaforth.'

'l'*fermage*?

'Oui, *l'fermage*,' agreed Hector.

'And the men you command, what is their experience of war?'

'The young men have none. But the older ones, some of them were at a big battle four years ago. Sheriffmuir.'

'*Oui oui.* I have heard it spoken of.'

'I was to go myself,' said Hector. 'But before I could my children died.'

'I am sorry to hear it.'

'Do you have a family, captain?'

'Family yes. A wife and children, no.' De la Rueda smiled. 'But I also have a farm.'

'Yes? In Spain?'

'Unfortunately, my estate suffers from my absence. I am not often there.'

'*Effectivement.* A farm requires much care to prosper. Is the soil good?'

'It is adequate. It rains less than here. Our fruit is excellent and there is much wheat.' A sudden yearning came over de la Rueda. It was always the same when he was reminded of home; only now the sense of nostalgia was unusually acute, for it came with the fear that his life could end very soon. *I may never see my home again*, and then immediately, superstitiously, he stamped the thought out: *Only the present. Think only of the present.*

Hector was intrigued by de la Rueda's mention of his farm. He liked this Spanish officer. He was civil; and upright of bearing, a man not to be trifled with, Hector judged. But now, before Hector could enquire more, they came into the camp.

'I must attend to my men, *Monsieur*.' De la Rueda stopped and touched his tricorne. 'We shall speak again.'

Hector bowed.

De la Rueda went straight to the quartermaster sergeant. The sergeant, one of the cooks, and the two soldiers tasked as guards were sprawled on the heather outside the tent when de la Rueda approached. Upon seeing him, the men at once rose to their feet. Both the cook and the quartermaster sergeant were, if not fat, on the plump side.

'Let me see exactly what you have left.'

The sergeant fumbled with his shirt and trews. 'Not much at all, sir, apart from the whisky.'

He was referring to the two barrels the Earl of Seaforth had donated to the battalion. De la Rueda thought he could already smell it on his breath.

They and the cook went into the tent. The sergeant began to indicate the few barrels left containing such edibles as chickpeas, salted meat, barley and oats. Olives, cheese, rice, and wine, the troops – if not the officers – had not tasted for two weeks now.

'Is there any rye flour left?' de la Rueda asked.

'No sir. Nothing… well, half a barrel.'

De la Rueda turned to the cook. 'If you mix it with what is left of the barley can you make sufficient bread for everyone?'

The cook pulled a face. 'There would not be much, sir. And it would have to be campaign bread; we have no yeast.'

'But you would have enough?'

'Well... just about.'

'Do it then,' said de la Rueda. 'It can be handed out tomorrow for breakfast. One bread for every soul. No exceptions. And tonight you can serve whatever there is left here. I do not want anything left over by the time we go into battle. *Nothing*. Is that clear?'

Before the cook could reply a soldier appeared at the tent entrance. The colonel required his presence at headquarters. De la Rueda gave final commands to the cook and quartermaster sergeant and made for the shieling. Outside it, in the deep glow of the evening sun, the lords and senior officers were gathering, while lower ranks came and went or stood ready. Colonel Bolaño was conversing in French with the Earl Marischal's younger brother, James Keith, and an officer of Seaforth's, Brigadier Mackintosh of Borlum, who de la Rueda had met previously on several occasions. The brigadier was a tall sturdy man of advanced age dressed in full clan regalia, with bushy eyebrows and a strong face that drew immediate attention for it was badly disfigured by scars.

'The enemy has been sighted,' Bolaño told de la Rueda in French. 'Their army is camped to the north, a few hours march from here.'

'It is too late now for them to march further,' said the brigadier, in excellent French himself. 'But we can expect them tomorrow. I venture they will be keen not to delay further, for tomorrow, it so happens, is also the birthday of James, our King.'

'I was not aware,' said de la Rueda.

'It will give added credence to whichever side is victorious.'

'Brigadier MacIntosh will be joining us,' said Bolaño. 'He will be standing by, should his advice be required.'

De la Rueda did not object. From what he had been told the old brigadier was an experienced soldier, who for a time had served as a colonel in the French army and had fought battles in Flanders as well as in this country and in England.

'Any intelligence now on their numbers?' asked de la Rueda.

'About the same as ours, it appears,' interjected James Keith, also in French. 'There are Swiss and some Dutchmen with them, and dragoons...'

Bolaño pulled on his moustachio.

'There is a rumour the enemy also arrives with a new type of small cannon,' observed Mackintosh. 'And I may venture it will cause us some inconvenience, for we have no cannon of our own.'

Bolaño switched to Spanish, 'Our soldiers need to be ready, captain. What are their rations like?'

'I am seeing to it now.'

'And munitions?'

'We have sufficient. I will inspect the magazine again.'

After de la Rueda left the lords, he went back down to the breastworks. These were now all but finished: stone walls in rows of three spread across the face of the knoll. The clansmen, too, had started making fortifications of their own, but these were only rough trenches and with the arrival of evening they were being left unfinished. Weary clansmen and Spaniards were heading back up the slope, their bodies bent and silhouetted against the low sun. After a cursory inspection of the breastworks, de la Rueda gave orders for the remaining soldiers to cease work. In the company of several officers he then returned to camp. All about on the undulating ground, more flat than steep, groups large and small of Spanish soldiers and clansmen were gathering. It was warm, even with the breeze, but here and there for the sake of it, or it may be to dispel a chill of the soul, some groups had managed to light small fires; the clansmen had gathered heather and blocks of peat from nearby shielings, and the Spaniards, not to be outdone, had dismembered empty barrels. Among the Spaniards, and besides the officers, were a few soldiers who had basic words of French, Latin, or Flemish, depending on their education or the foreign campaigns in which they had served. Likewise among the ordinary clansmen, if to a lesser extent, there were a few who knew the odd word of Latin, when not French, but predominantly the language barrier was insurmountable and so the two nationalities kept their groups apart – the Spanish closer to the breastworks, and the clansmen more northwards towards the ridge. As de la Rueda passed among his compatriots, he stopped here and there to speak to a soldier or an officer and to check on the muskets, stacked conically, with butts on the ground and muzzles joined at the top. Afterwards de la Rueda made his way to the magazine, which was further in the distance, in a tent guarded by four soldiers. He checked the kegs of gunpowder to make sure they were dry, the surplus muskets, bayonets and Toledo steel swords, and the wooden boxes containing paper cartridges and lead musket balls. Satisfied all was in order, he stepped past a few tethered Galician ponies into another large tent close to the magazine. Here a dozen or so infirm men were lying on beds of straw or heather. There were various boxes and one empty bed. Some of the men were too ill to notice him, but one lifted himself up. 'They are out back, sir.' De la Rueda stepped out and went around the tent, where he found Major Santarem and don Ignacio, the surgeon, reclining on the heather with a portable chessboard between them. Santarem looked as jaundiced as the last time de la Rueda had seen him. Black circles surrounded his sad eyes. Don Ignacio, a short, bearded man – usually corpulent but less so at present – was more cheerful; perhaps because he was winning the game of chess.

'We are expecting battle tomorrow at the latest,' de la Rueda informed them.

'Yes; the colonel sent someone to inform us,' replied Santarem. 'When battle commences I am to be given care of the flag, that is if God gives me strength.'

'Do not fret, Alonso,' said don Ignacio. 'I will have something for you to ingest. It will give you the strength you need.'

Santarem sighed heavily. 'I'm dying like a dog. What kind of death is that? I want to go out like a man, not like an animal. For the love of God.'

De la Rueda did not know how to console him.

'I will see you tomorrow.' De la Rueda lifted his tricorne and left.

A trumpet sounded. At Once a frenzied scramble started for the cook's tent. With food in such short supply, the rota was starting to break down. Soldiers pushed and jostled and argued over which company's turn it was to be served first. De la Rueda found Paez at the cook's tent and between them they resolved the confusion. Their orders passed to lieutenants and ensigns who then passed it on to the sergeants. There was grumbling and curses among the troops but gradually an orderly queue formed. Only two of the smaller cauldrons had travelled with the soldiers. These hung from a triangle of poles over peat fires, full to the brim but still without the capacity to fully feed three hundred men; so as each soldier held out his wooden bowl he was served a scarce half ladle of watery chickpea broth to which was then added separately a sliver of salted meat and a handful of raw oats. Even then it was meagre fare for men who had not tasted food for over a day. Some complained about there being no bread. The cooks roughly assured them there would be bread in the morning.

De la Rueda's own tent was nearby but inside it was bare, for transport had been restricted to horse numbers, and while Bolaño had made room for the captains' tents, much of their contents, along with other tents and a large quantity of general baggage, had been left behind. Still, de la Rueda considered himself luckier than the Scottish lords who were having to bed, when not out in the open, crammed into the shieling next to the pen. At least he could sleep undisturbed, except by his servant, and his ensign who was invited to share the space, and with shelter if it rained. From the canvas hold-all he had allowed himself to bring, de la Rueda removed his bowl and spoon and returned to the cook's tent. It was not yet his company's turn to be served but de la Rueda, like all officers, could pull rank. With his bowl of food he returned to his tent and sat in the doorway, eating. Although well past sunset there was no indication of nightfall. A soft rose coloured gloaming pervaded in which de la Rueda smelt the smoke of fires and heard the garrulous voices of men who were settling down to eat together. Finally, soldiers from his own company came back with bowls of food and gathered near his tent to eat and talk loudly, and when the eating was over, to commence on the local whisky that had been donated.

De la Rueda was tired but he could not sleep just yet. When he had disembarked he had arrived with several large flagons of brandy as well as wine in his personal baggage. Now all that remained was a few sips of brandy at the bottom of a demijohn he had brought with him. He decided to take a couple of sips now and leave the rest for breakfast in the morning. The strong spirit immediately gave him a lift. Somewhere deep within him he knew he was afraid. Everyone was afraid. The clansmen, some of whom he could hear singing in the distance, no less than his own men. And the enemy, too, would be afraid. It was in the nature of war to be afraid. *But even more than afraid I am tired. I am tired of war. Tired of being a soldier. If I die in battle this time so be it. I am alone in this world and it will be a release.*

NINE

Stupefied by whisky, with a thick cushion of heather underneath him and ten yards of fine wool to wrap around himself, Hector had nevertheless passed a harsh night in the open. He had been assailed by terrible nightmares, and while it had not rained the damp rising from the ground had passed through the heather, the wool, and into his bones.

Hector's limbs ached when he woke up. And he had a violent headache. Though abruptly, superseding both, was a maelstrom in his gut that made him want to vomit and defecate. At once it sent him stumbling in his silk shirt up into the hills behind him, where there was nobody camped since the ground was too boggy and where a number of the other clansmen, including the Marquis of Tulibardine, were already doing their business. After the digestive upheaval he cleaned himself as best he could with reeds and bog water.

Weak and queasy, Hector returned to his sleeping place and put on a pair of tartan trews. Had the day looked to be fine he might have forsaken the plaid. But as so often happened the dawn had arrived cold and overcast, so he began the process of putting on his plaid. After laying the ten yards of russet coloured fabric flat on the ground, he started reducing its length by pleating it. When this was done he passed a belt under it, lowered himself onto the pleated fabric and lay down on his back. Next, taking hold of one side, but without rising, he wrapped it around himself. Then he wrapped the other side. Sitting up, he now fastened it with the belt around his waist and rose to his feet. Before going further he paused to put on his father's embroidered indigo jacket. With the lower part of the plaid hanging down to his knees like a pleated skirt, he then seized the remainder of the cloth, which also hung from his waist, and joined the two corners at his left breast by passing one side of the plaid up the back of his jacket and over his shoulder and the other side of the cloth up his chest. Finally, he fastened the two ends together with an ornate silver clasp.

Once the plaid was on, he strapped the broad leather belt across his chest that held his pistols and broadsword in a scabbard. Then he strapped another belt around his waist holding his dirk, ammunition pouch, and sporran. To finish he put on the cord holding his powder horn, then leather boots and the blue bonnet with the eagle's feather.

The clasp, the silver closure on his powder horn and his ornate Inverness made pistols were visible signs of ostentation, but in comparison to the lords and other gentlemen among the clansmen Hector's attire was modest. He told himself that if he fell in battle he did not want the enemy to benefit from his wealth, but a truer reason, and one which he found harder to admit, was that he superstitiously, and perhaps mistakenly, hoped that by avoiding attention he was more likely to escape with his life.

Hector did not have an appetite for the handful of raw oats he carried in his sporran. Without eating he went directly to the shieling, which was a scarce fifty yards distant. There he found officers and lords starting to assemble around the Marquis of Tullibardine, who was now sitting on a large stone, half dressed, a plaid loosely covering his shoulders, shaving himself with the aid of a shaving knife and a mirror attached to the inside lid of a box perched on another stone.

Close to Tullibardine a group of five gentlemen were passing around a carved wooden quaich. One of them, seeing Hector, motioned him over.

Hector accepted the proffered vessel, which contained strong ale.

'I do not believe we are acquainted,' said the man who had motioned to him.

Hector bowed and introduced himself.

'Lord Lochiel,' said the other, returning the bow.

He was a large man, near sixty, with a straight gaze and a hard but not unpleasant face. He did not wear a wig. Under the bonnet with three eagle feathers, his still brown hair was cut in a straight line above his ears and the tail at the back was tied with a red ribbon. His coat was rather fancier than Hector's.

Hector knew the name. Lochiel was chief of the Cameron clan. He had a reputation for being an ardent Jacobite, although a few years back he and other clan Chiefs had come close to betrayal by offering the Hanoverian Duke of Argyll to change sides. When the offer was not accepted they had reverted to their former Jacobite stance.

'Do you bring men with you?' asked Lochiel.

'Nineteen,' said Hector. 'And I believe six more to be passed to me from my Lord Seaforth.'

Lochiel himself had arrived with a hundred men. 'And where are you to be placed?'

The sup of ale had mysteriously eased Hector's headache, but less so the tightness in his chest, the queasy apprehension. 'This is what I am waiting to find out, my lord.'

'I may tell you now, sir.' Brigadier Mackintosh of Borlum spoke up. 'It was agreed yesterday with my Lord Tullibardine that as you speak French your company is to stand by immediately behind the Spanish breastworks, where you may be needed to reinforce the Spanish position. I may also require you to personally relay messages to my Lord Tullibardine.'

At that moment a scout came running past them. He stopped before Tullibardine, who had just finished shaving and was now standing up. Gasping, he told Tullibardine the enemy had left their camp and had been spotted on the drove track approaching the descent into the glen.

Tullibardine sent the scout with this news to the Earl of Seaforth, and the Earl Marischall and company, who were camped higher up among the rocks across the gulley. Tullibardine's brother, Lord George Murray, who was across the river on the slope of the knoll to Tullibardine's left, would have his own scouts, so there was no need to inform him unless by flag, but Tullibardine now turned to the group Hector had joined.

'Well, gentlemen.' A sombre expression appeared on his otherwise soft face. 'It is time for us to prepare. Pray, gather your men and take up your stations. May God protect you. But before you go we will toast to our sovereign king whose birthday it is today.'

A quaich was filled with whisky this time. Holding it in both hands the Marquis said, 'I raise this quaich to our rightful sovereign, his majesty over the sea, our gracious King James the Fifth and Eighth. May God grant him long life, and to us, on this day, his birthday, victory over our enemies.'

The marquis lifted the quaich, toasted, 'The King,' and took a sip. Each lord or officer who thereafter received the quaich echoed the toast before taking a sip himself and passing the vessel on.

After the quaich had been filled several times and gone around to all the assembled officers, the group began to disperse.

'I will show you where you are to be placed,' said Brigadier Mackintosh of Borlum, stepping over to Hector.

Hector noticed that when the Brigadier spoke the scars on his face seemed to wriggle.

At the edge of the steep slope descending from the flatter terrain the brigadier stopped. It was some twenty yards above and, when facing outwards, to the left of the breastworks. On the breastworks itself already Spanish troops had started labouring again, finishing off the walls.

'You may position your men here,' said Mackintosh. 'As you can see, Glendaruel will be over there,' Mackintosh pointed further to his left where some three hundred yards away clansmen were also finishing off the rough trenches they had been digging the day before. 'Further up is Lord Lochiel and Rob Roy, and then, across the gully over there, my Lords Marischal and Seaforth.' Mackintosh turned around and pointed to the round, nearby top of the knoll behind him and to his left. 'My Lord Tullibardine and others will be somewhere up there.' Mackintosh turned back around again. 'I will be with Colonel Bolaño further along the breastworks around this edge of the slope here, and Captain de la Rueda down there on that side.' Mackintosh paused. 'You may expect orders from myself or my Lord Tullibardine. Or the Spanish commanders should the situation merit it. Your principle duty is to serve as reinforcement should at any moment we find ourselves hard pressed in this sector.'

Hector's head reeled.

'And if Lords Glendaruel or Lochiel should require my assistance?'

'I expect you will receive the order from myself or my Lord Tullibardine,' said Mackintosh. 'But if it is in the throes of battle and there is no one you must use your discretion.'

'I will assemble my men,' said Hector.

'You are due six more from my Lord Seaforth, are you not?'

'Yes, sir.'

'I will see that they get to you.' Mackintosh paused. 'Take your cue from Captain de la Rueda if there is no one else. When I served for France in Spanish Holland I became acquainted with a Spanish gentleman, Colonel Rosales, who, Captain de la Rueda has informed me, by remarkable circumstance was his commanding officer when he first joined the army.' Mackintosh smiled a little at the coincidence. 'I believe you will find the captain an able commander.'

Hector made his way back up the slope, and past the camp headquarters. Everywhere, Spaniards and the clansmen were now busy arming themselves and gathering into their respective squads and companies. The mood was not febrile. It was clear that hours must pass before any confrontation became possible. Nevertheless, as Hector walked between the men he could feel the change of humour; the tense, rising anticipation. And the muskets, the swords, the dirks, axes and targes had all of a sudden shed their discretion, when not adornment, and were now bristling like bared fangs.

The men were mostly assembled when Hector arrived at his patch.

'Are all present?' he asked Lachlan.

'They are,' said Lachlan, his colourless eyes inscrutable, but his thick lips turned down in a sardonic expression that while not openly sneering seemed to contain a hint of mockery.

Hector tried to ignore him and began counting the men himself. Two of them were attending to three garrons, making sure they were securely tethered and had pasture. Other men were seeing to their weapons, in particular those who had muskets. Most were sitting or standing about, fully armed, some barefoot, their faces unwashed, their hair long and unkempt under the blue bonnets, and their plaids most of them grubby, ragged or patched.

'I have my orders,' said Hector. 'We are to stand in reserve, close to the Spanish breastworks. Six men from my Lord Seaforth will join us.'

Lachlan turned to the men. 'Quick now. Come on, line up.'

The men did not have the discipline of regular soldiers, and the larger part of them disliked Lachlan; a few would have willingly stuck a dirk in his back, but obliged to obey him, they began to assemble in a loose marching double line. Meanwhile, Hector checked the small pile of baggage that was being left near the garrons and picked up his musket. At the head of the column, he started leading his troops the short distance to their position on the field. When they arrived, Hector saw that de la Rueda was now at his position, conversing with another officer. Hector turned to his troops, thinking to place them favourably in the uneven terrain. But almost at once Lachlan took over the initiative. Hector was discomfited. He thought he should be taking charge, but Lachlan was one of the small number of clansmen who had fought at Sheriffmuir and so had experience of battle. Because of this Hector felt he had to defer to Lachlan. Also Lachlan had brought a few men of his own. And he had a forceful personality that Hector did not entirely approve but at the same time found hard to oppose.

A part of Hector, while knowing that it was wrong, could not help admiring Lachlan. And in particular for the ruthless and cunning way he had set himself up as an independent farmer. The man had started out with nothing even if it was true, as everyone said, that he had got to where he was by cheating the husband of one of his sisters. Originally it was this man who had held the leases to the farm, which was smaller than now and leased in the main from Colonel Murchison, Seaforth's factor. But the lease holder had fallen ill and so had entrusted his brother-in-law, Lachlan, with driving the eighteen head of cattle the land supported to market in Fort William. Lachlan came back empty handed claiming he had been waylaid and robbed. Since folks' wealth, then as now, depended on cattle, the farmer had to declare himself ruined and was forced to move away with his family. No one now knew where. It was believed he had gone to the New World. But after he departed Lachlan mysteriously appeared to gain wealth. He entered into a contract with Colonel Murchison to take over his relative's farm. Soon after, he took leases out for land from The Experimenter, and afterwards from Hector himself. Shona objected. She told Hector she could not abide a man she believed had swindled and dispossessed his own family. Hector could not argue with her on that score. What Lachlan had done was by common consent abominable. However, secretly Hector could not deny a certain admiration for Lachlan's gumption in the face of economic necessity. This was something his wife could not understand. Women were not given the virtue of sober reflection. They were too much at the mercy of their humours. How could his wife ever fully comprehend his own position with regard to his tenants? He had to pay back the wadsets his father had taken out or lose the land. One or the other. His father was a gentleman, but mistaken in his methods. Through his negligence of the indispensable his father had allowed himself to endanger his estate, leaving Hector with no option but to secure it. In his eyes financial profit was the only way, so over his wife's protestations, and dislike of Lachlan, he had not turned the man away when he had asked to lease land. It was now several hundred acres that Lachlan sublet from him, aside from grazings, paid more in kind than in coin, but every little amount that went down in the plus side of Hector's ledgers reduced the same in the minus side.

Hector's six men from Seaforth arrived. They were all from the area. Their leader was a robust man with dark eyes and a round, bearded face that was more vexed than jovial. He was a blacksmith by trade, who had his own forge and also a hostelry of a kind on the drove track just past the glen. A keen hunter of deer, he knew the area well. Hector had employed his services twice in the past, when his own blacksmith had failed him, so the blacksmith knew him enough to voice his anxiety.

'It was different at Sheriffmuir, your lordship, where I was also,' he said, rolling his eyes, the frown lines on his face etched as black as his bushy beard from unwashed years of soot and peat smoke. 'The battle was at many leagues from here, it was. But this is at my very door.'

'How does that make a difference?'

'I do not say it does; I do not except if by misfortune fate does not favour us.'

Hector noticed that below him Captain de la Rueda, who had finished conferring, now, in turning, looked up the slope. The two men caught each others' eye.

'Do you not anticipate a good result?'

'Och, I do, indeed I do.' The blacksmith's frown remained, however; he did not look persuaded.

'The terrain here is greatly to our advantage.' Hector wanted to banish the thought of any upset. 'The enemy will be boxed in while we command height, with a clear view of their disposition. I cannot see the enemy ascending the ground here with ease.'

The blacksmith nodded lugubriously. 'There is that. We have the advantage there, so we do.' But his mind was telling him different. While the steep terrain would make ascent of it hazardous for being slow it would likewise make descent of it hazardous for being too fast and uncontrolled. The blacksmith could not visualize an easy charge down the slope, which was the usual way his people went into battle. This labour of holding ground, of building walls and digging trenches was something new in his experience. He had certainly not seen it at Sheriffmuir. They should have won that battle beyond dispute had they just known to press their advantage. The men were willing at Sheriffmuir. They had rallied from far and wide for King James and the glory of God. But not this time. Men, the blacksmith knew, who should be here now, on the king's birthday, were not. They had prevaricated, they were looking for reasons to stay home, and when they heard the Spanish Armada was not to be landing after all, that it was destroyed at sea, they were given all the reason they needed. The blacksmith had almost not come himself. He had no vocation for clan feuds or war. Sheriffmuir had given him his fill. But when the fiery cross had come around he could find nowhere to hide. The devotion to his church, his country, his king, and his kin, was more compelling in him than his desire to elude the consequence. Even his wife had known that he must show up, even if he was the only man to do so. But it was with sorrow and apprehension that he took out from their hiding place the double sided broadsword and musket that he now carried. And when the blacksmith had joined the others who answered the call and he saw how they were few and how uncertain their resolve, he feared that the enterprise was off to no auspicious start and far too close to home. If the battle was lost, his house would be among the first the enemy would come across in their victorious rampage, and which was the way of war. Once they ascertained that he had fought against them, they must raze his house and put it to fire. Everything he owned, everything he had toiled for, would be lost whether he was alive or dead. Of course, once dead he would not be inconvenienced by the loss.

Upon his wife, however, it was certain to visit destitution and great hardship. The blacksmith could seek consolation in the notion that at least he had no male children to share the calamity, and his two daughters were married and their families out of harm's way, but the fear of his life coming to an end in total and sudden ruination gave him little respite for all that death itself, the actual idea of dying, did not cause him undue alarm.

Without warning the enemy appeared. At the far end of the glen, in between the treeless slopes that narrowed to a vanishing point, was a space where for a brief moment men on horseback showed themselves. They were so far in the distance they appeared no bigger than ants and no sooner were they seen than they were gone. But seen they were and it brought with it a hush that fell on Spaniards and clansmen alike. They stopped their labouring and talking and stood motionless on the hill side under a flossy grey sky, waiting. Again horses and riders showed themselves, only now they came persistently, a few at the fore, banners aloft, and then a long compact body of them moving over the ground like a whitish-grey caterpillar with a red streak at the top. These were the dragoons, mounted infantry, and while it imparted little to the Spaniards, the clansmen were all aware of them by repute when not actuality. The blacksmith, in particular, knew them at close quarters and his stomach churned.

After the cavalry had disappeared from sight there was a time lapse, and then the infantry appeared, a long phalanx moving more rigidly than the horsemen and too far away yet to distinguish the individual components of their uniforms.

De la Rueda had brought out his telescope and was pressing it against his right eye, absorbed in trying to assess their armaments and numbers, when a soldier came up to him. Colonel Bolaño was requesting his presence. De la Rueda went around the breastworks and up the hill where the Colonel was standing, his own telescope in hand, with three captains at his side, including Paez.

'Well, what do you think?' Bolaño asked him.

'Fifty to a hundred cavalry from what I can make out. The estimation we have received of their troop numbers look to be correct, although I do not know if they have all appeared, sir.'

'Did you sight any mortar in your telescope?'

'No sir.'

Bolaño pulled on his moustache. 'I understand it is something new in this country, this mortar of theirs. But I have heard of it before. A Dutch invention. Very small. Easily transported in carts.'

'Is it certain, sir?' asked Paez.

'That they have such?' Bolaño nodded vigorously. 'The intelligence is reliable I am assured. What is not certain is how effective the mortar will be. No one here is able to testify to having witnessed their use.'

'If their range is short they will have to be brought up close,' said de la Rueda.

'But in any case it will be out of range of our muskets.'

De la Rueda was silent.

'We have no fall back position. Though with God's help it will not be needed - so long as we stand firm. Their mortar must not make us retreat.' Bolaño was thinking that he himself, had he been in overall command, would have wanted a second redoubt further back, possibly above and behind the shieling; somewhere to reassemble should the enemy break through. But Tullibardine, while present, never appeared to be fully engaged in the planning. Was it that he doubted overall victory was feasible, without reinforcements, after the loss of the Armada? The Marischal and Seaforth showed themselves more bellicose. He did not think the lords would give up without a fight, but quarrel as they did with Tullibardine they were not in ultimate command. Tullbardine was putting all his cards on this one position. So here it would be decided, right or wrong.

'Even if they have mortars,' said Paez. 'It is better here than down there.'

De la Rueda saw a horse and rider appear, still some distance away, but no longer so ant-like, the two main components just about distinguishable to the naked eye. The horseman emerged fast from around the profile of a slope before stopping abruptly on the drove track in the narrow bank to the right of the river. De la Rueda brought out his telescope and when he trained it on the horseman he saw that the man had a telescope of his own through which he was scanning the terrain in de la Rueda's direction. The soldier wore a red coat faced with blue and grey trews. His horse was white. Once stopped he appeared in no hurry to move on. He was making a thorough scrutiny of the terrain.

'Their scouts,' said Bolaño. 'It will not be long now. I must see to the flag. I will be with Santarem, if you need me. Or Tullibardine.'

Bolaño left.

'What do you make of it, Alejandro?' Paez asked de la Rueda.

'The ground is in our favour. I cannot speak for their mortar.'

'Will their cavalry be of use?'

'Only if we go down to meet it. Their horses will flounder on these slopes.'

Paez hesitated. He opened his mouth but closed it again.

De la Rueda lifted his chin 'What is it?'

'I know what it is,' said young Captain Otero, who was standing close by. 'Ramón feels the men from here lack resolve.'

'There ought to be more,' said Paez. 'Two or three thousand, anyway. And what are they? A thousand?'

'The enemy are not more. We know that.'

Paez wanted to say: *But they are professionals. They are not farmers. On our side they are farmers.* However, he remained silent.

De la Rueda observed that the men had started going back to work on the walls. Their white uniforms were all filthy and they seemed tired. They had had bread this morning, but flat and little of it and now there was nothing else to sustain them. If there was battle today it was best to have them rested.

'I think the barricades are now high enough, do you not, Ramon?'

'Yes. I agree,' said Paez.

'We will give the men a rest. They can concentrate on their weapons.'

Paez nodded. De la Rueda went back around to his sector, taking Captain Otero with him. After giving orders to cease work on the battlements, he made a point of going about exchanging civil words and a little banter with the troops. Of the three hundred Spaniards there were four or five de la Rueda knew either from previous campaigns or regiments. Bolaño, on the other hand, knew a larger proportion, for all the officers and not a few of the lower ranks had been personally selected by the colonel when he came to assemble the battalion. In a previous posting Bolaño had been a major in a private regiment, for until a few years ago most of his country's regiments were privately owned. But now it had become policy for the government to establish an official army. Bolaño had been promoted to lieutenant-colonel and transferred to a government regiment. Not a few of the troops he had selected for the battalion were known to him from previous service. Some of the lower ranks had come out of press gangs and were inexperienced. But many were experienced soldiers. De la Rueda, who himself had transferred from a private regiment, was less familiar with the men on a personal level. But since he was in command and he depended on them as much as they depended on him, he now went about trying to put them in good spirits.

TEN

An escort of dragoons surrounded Major General Wightman. The dragoons wore red coats and were mounted on grey horses. Wightman himself sat astride a black horse with a docked tail and was attired in white trews, a black hat with a large cockade, and an elaborate blue and gold coat. A slender man with a florid face, Wightman presented to the world a studied, unrevealing mien that yet, according to circumstances, could break out in expressions of warmth or anger, or more often querulous dissatisfaction.

At that moment, as the party rode towards a promontory, Wightman's expression was of the latter variety, for it had taken longer than he desired for the baggage to be moved up from Loch Cluanie. Ever since his army had left Inverness, some five days ago, constant difficulties had arisen with transport and provisions. His superior, Lieutenant General Carpenter, had been bedevilling him from the beginning. He had withheld finance and complained to the undersecretary when Wightman wrote out credit notes in Carpenter's name. But did Carpenter expect the army to live on air? And how was Wightman to pay for horses and the civilian handlers needed for them without funds? As it was, in the trackless country after Glenmoriston, a number of the handlers had deserted, taking the horses with them, so that today Wightman had had to arrange several return trips to the camp in order to bring all the baggage forward. His force was now in place at last, or as best as Wightman could manage even if not entirely to his satisfaction, but meanwhile the larger part of the day had gone. It was approaching mid-afternoon, which left only a few hours of adequate light to initiate and conclude an engagement. Under other circumstances Wightman might have delayed until the following day, but he felt it had to be this day. Not tomorrow. Today was the tenth of June. It was the birthday of the Jacobite king, the pretender, and so the best of possible days to defeat his vassals. Wightman, indeed, could not help an almost superstitious belief that his victory depended on the battle being fought on this day. But Wightman was diligent. Marlborough himself had commended Wightman for his conscientious planning. He had a cautious side to him as well as one that could be bold. Hence his present exasperation, the feeling he had of being caught between the need to thoroughly prepare for battle and the impatience to initiate it.

The promontory where Wightman and his escort came to a stop was less than half a mile from the enemy. Here Wightman was beyond musket range, yet close enough to catch glimpses of distant moving figures and of white uniforms massed behind the fortifications on the slope of the bluff more or less opposite him.

Already Wightman had decided that with so few hours of daylight remaining any action by his troops had to be used with maximum force for there to be a quick and successful resolution. But as he surveyed the enemy lines he began to fear that vigour alone would not suffice, for quite clearly he could see that the enemy had every advantage in terms of terrain. They were spread out in the rough shape of a horseshoe on the high ground across the narrow glen. On Wightman's far left, and across the river, they occupied a small hill and the slopes of higher hills behind it. On his far right they occupied the rock outcrops and scree in between a sparse pine wood and a gulley. And on the steep bluff in the centre, some few hundred feet up, were the shallow trenches and stone fortifications manned by clansmen and the Spaniards. That they were Spaniards, Wightman knew from spies and the white uniform. As for their fighting capabilities, Wightman suspected that they would show themselves resolute. Ten years before he had served in Spain at the battle of Almansa under the Earl of Galway. Then he had been able to assess the Spanish character and witness at first hand their fighting spirit. He knew that the Spaniards were often slow to coalesce but when they did they would be stubborn. They had much regard for honour, which they would hold dear on a foreign expedition. Most importantly it appeared to Wightman that by concentrating the Spaniards in the centre ground along with fortifications and heavy support from the clansmen it was there that the Jacobites were expecting to be attacked. And this especially as there was no other way through the glen except along the side of the river past the bottleneck of the centre ground. In effect the enemy's dispositions had all the markings of an ambush. But what if instead of deploying with an attack to the centre as they expected him to, Wightman reasoned in his fastidious way, he began with an attack at the extremities, where they were weakest? Even at these points the ground was much to their advantage, but they were less prepared, and he had one weapon available it was certain they did not. Pondering, Wightman began to feel confident that with the coehorn mortars, the element of surprise, and disciplined unrelenting musket fire, he could succeed in dislodging the extremities. If the centre then weakened by diverting reinforcements, it could open a space for him to concentrate a frontal attack on the fortifications, again with the support of mortar.

For a little longer Wightman turned the plan over in his mind. Doubts persisted, risks and counter offences that he wanted to consider in more depth, but time was running away and suddenly his mind was made up. After exchanging a few words with his adjutant and another grandly dressed officer, Wightman turned his mount around and headed back to his troops, who were massed out of sight behind a slope line.

Wightman had roughly one and a half thousand troops at his disposal, including some Dutch and Swiss infantry and several hundred dragoons. In numbers he had expected the enemy to present itself with considerably more and he had worried that his own small force would be insufficient for the task, but spies, along with his own present reconnaissance, now confirmed to him that unless the enemy had troops in the background he did not know about their numbers were similar to his own. With this in mind Wightman spoke to his second in command, Colonel Clayton, who was an old friend and a soldier for whom Wightman had high esteem. Clayton, a physically strong individual with bandy legs and a bald head, who in times of battle eschewed wearing a wig and even a hat, nodded in agreement as Wightman outlined his intentions. Once the two had worked out a plan, Clayton set off, surrounded by his retinue, to instruct the regiment of foot that he commanded and which bore his name.

On the cone shaped hill at the one extreme of Jacobite forces, and across the river from the Spanish breastworks, the Marquis of Tullibardine's younger brother, James Murray, was disconcerted by the appearance of enemy troops deploying across the river and over the lumpy ground towards the hill which he controlled. It was not what he was expecting.

'What are they doing?' he asked MacAngus Peter of Dunollie. 'Do they intend to attack?'

MacAngus Peter was as puzzled as Murray.

'Their horses will never get up here.'

The two men stood side by side in the grass half way up the hill watching Wightman's left wing advance. Formations of red coated infantry scurried like strange insects to gain ground around the far side of the hill. But Murray's square, large-jawed face with small darting eyes was more fixed on the forty or so dragoons, wearing conical hats, who advanced on their horses in a line broken only by a scattering of hillocks in their path. Behind the dragoons were platoons of infantry and a few pack horses.

'It is too much effort for a feint.'

'A little closer and we can pick them off,' said Murray. 'Have our sharpshooters placed within range. I will send for the men on the high ground.'

Murray went over to a group of clansmen gathered nearby while MacAngus Peter, who was fresh faced and little older than twenty, hurried off to place sharpshooters behind the scattered rocks and trees at the foot of the hill. After dispatching a messenger to the contingent of clansmen hanging back on the high ground behind the hill to venture down and reinforce his own troops, Murray set about dispersing his men on the slope off the hill, some low down, others concealed in the hollows or behind scattered trees higher up. But even as Murray was doing this, Wightman's bombardiers, behind the screen of dragoons, were lifting down four coehorn mortars from the pack horses. The coehorn was a small object; it had a muzzle less than two feet long which projected from a boxed wooden platform. Once the boxes had been placed on the ground the two bombardiers to each cannon soon had them armed with powder filled shells. Bombardiers in long coats, each holding a botefeux a foot or two long, lit the fuse and a moment later there were loud bangs, the cannon jumped and recoiled, puffs of acrid gunpowder rose up, and four balls could be seen rising under the blue sky in a slow arc. Colonel Clayton, from a little way back, watched keenly as the first bombs exploded in landing on the ground. Immediately the mortars were loaded and fired again. Clayton, deciding the time was now, gave orders for two of his platoons to advance on the hill that started to rise in front of him just out of musket range.

Clayton's platoons, four soldiers deep, were in danger of breaking up because of the rough ground but one way or another they managed to maintain a steady barrage of musket fire as they advanced, one line firing as the line behind loaded. The clansmen, meanwhile, had placed their sharpshooters forward ready to fire as soon as the enemy came within range. The government troops fired more or less blindly, for they had no sharpshooters of their own and the clansmen were well concealed behind rocks, trees, or flat out in the long grass. But what the clansmen were not expecting were the bombs that exploded all about them with fearful smoking bangs that sent shrapnel flying and lifted earth and stone from the ground. Few if any of them had seen the like before. The resolute among them held their positions and started picking out targets among the red coated troops now only a few hundred yards away. Soldiers began to fall. The sharpshooters' fire slowed but failed to altogether halt the advance, and some clansmen were becoming unnerved by the unrelenting bombardment. In ones and twos they began retreating, slipping back up the hill behind them. Murray, crouching in the grass further up, among more of his troops – out of musket range though not of mortar – called out to the men to hold their ground. Though nervous, and dismayed by the unfamiliar bombardment, he told himself he held the stronger position and he was anticipating the arrival of the contingent of clansmen hanging back on the high slope behind his hill.

'Did you make sure they were called?' he asked John Anderson, a short dark man who was his adjutant.

'I did.'

'So what is keeping them?'

Anderson did not say what he thought: that perhaps the men had no stomach for the battle, that they were waiting to see who fortune favoured before they committed. Instead he was about to reiterate that they had been sent for three times already when a bomb exploded as it fell to the ground not much distance away. Almost at the same time as Murray was deafened by the detonation he felt a sharp thud against his thigh. Murray saw the surprised expression on Anderson's face and a little behind him a clansman keeling over into the grass. Then he looked down to where he had felt the thud on the side of his thigh and saw blood seeping through a ragged tear in his patterned red and green trews.

'You are hit,' said Anderson.

'He over there is worse.'

Anderson turned around, saw the clansman lying on the ground, and called out until other clansmen came over to assist.

Among them was one who carried a leather back pack and knew sufficient to pass for a field medic. He had a quick look at Munro's thigh, then went over to the other casualty and came back moments later declaring that he was dead. Soon clansmen gathered to carry the corpse up the hill. The field medic cut open Munro's trews, looked at the wound more closely and declared that it was not deep. From his bag the field medic took out some loose spun wool and linen strips. He was placing the wool over the wound before wrapping it when in the near distance, close to the bottom of the slope, flames and smoke began to rise from the ground. For some days it had not rained and the exploding bombs were setting the dry heather alight. The remaining sharpshooters, many of them in the heather themselves and seeing the flames advance towards them, were obliged to retreat regardless of their desire to do so.

Murray looked about him. The bombardment had ceased but below him chance favoured his enemies for the summer breeze was fanning the heath fire in his direction. And behind the flames and the smoke the red coated enemy advanced, firing at Murray's men as they scattered and retreated. Murray wanted to rally; it was on his mind to draw a line on the higher ground behind him. The Jacobite cause for him was all. Like his brother, by joining the rebels he had disobeyed his father, the Duke of Atholl, and sacrificed his inheritance. He believed his country could never be free so long as it was ruled by a foreign king and he was distressed at the thought of letting down his older brother, the Marquis of Tullibardine, whom he admired and whose approval he was always seeking. But the reinforcements had still not arrived and if the few men he had with him were intent on retreating he could not see how to make them do what they would not.

Wistfully, Murray glanced across the glen to the bluff, where he knew his brother would be watching now, hoping to catch sight of a victory. But how? Reinforcements were nowhere to be seen. And all that had been in Murray's favour was collapsing. He could not see how he could put it all together again, how he could stop the heath fire, stop the cannonade, stop his troops fleeing.

'We will retreat,' said Murray, grimly, to his adjutant and the other leaders gathered around him.

MacAngus Peter and MacKenzie of Avoch wanted to fight on. They were young and proud and their blood was up. But after the short exchange they too had to agree. Murray was helped to his feet. Two strong clansmen put his arms over their shoulders and reluctantly the party started moving up the hill, away from the battle.

Wightman knew better than to indulge in thoughts of victory. It was his superstitious experience that such rash prognostications were more often a harbinger for defeat. As his left wing advanced on the hill, he was quick to note, however, that the enemy appeared reluctant to put up a strong resistance. Wightman had expected the reinforcements on the slopes behind the hill to come down. For this reason he had kept back part of his troops on the left, fearing that if the reinforcements arrived they could come around from behind to try to encircle his army. But the hundreds of clansmen on the high slopes were holding back and those on the hill were retreating as his own troops advanced. Yet he was sustaining casualties. Wightman had ordered the field hospital to be brought as forward as possible. The two tents and the surgeons were located not far behind him, and sitting on his black horse, surrounded by his retinue, he was receiving reports of sharpshooters among the enemy that were taking a toll on his soldiers. Wightman could not help a sudden anger when a dispatch rider came up to inform him that Lieutenant Hurst, a protegé of his, and the son of a distant cousin, had been killed. But he was quick to suppress the feeling. He told himself his attention must focus only on outmanoeuvring the enemy. Accordingly, Wightman waited, receiving reports, now and then leaning over to pat his horse's neck or lifting a thin telescope to observe the battle across the river. When it became evident that the enemy had been dislodged from the hill and were retreating to the higher slopes behind, he felt secure enough to conclude that no attempt would be made to encircle his army from that side of the river. He could now deploy to his right, and so he addressed the officers about him, giving orders for the assault to begin on the Jacobite left.

The assault was initiated by a contingent of Sutherland militiamen under Lieutenant Mackay and two grenadier companies from Montague's regiment. The militiamen, while fighting for Wightman's side, were themselves Highlanders. Due to the day's heat they had removed their plaids and were mostly clad in shirts and trews. As irregular troops they were less constrained by army drill, so were able to advance more swiftly towards the steep slope that rose from the glen floor in between a scattering of trees on the far side and a gulley that separated it from the central bluff on the near side. But the Dutch and English grenadiers, who were closer in and lagging behind, marched in narrow formation and at a slow pace so as not to become out of breath when they closed with the enemy.

At the far left extremity of the Jacobite horseshoe, watching their advance from behind scattered outcrops of rock on the ridge-line some four hundred feet above the floor of the glen, were the Earl Marischal and the Earl of Seaforth with a battalion of two hundred and fifty men. For a while it was not altogether clear which way the government troops would veer. They could at any moment turn and attack the centre as predicted. But Wightman had surprised them with the unexpected attack on their right, across the river, and the Earl Marischal had a strong, uneasy feeling that Wightman would again do the unexpected. It was becoming ever clearer to Marischal that the enemy's intention was to weaken their flanks, and although he could not perceive its ultimate aim, he anticipated the assault would be not on the centre bluff held by the Spaniards, but here on themselves. The Earl Marischal was younger than Wightman; he did not have his military experience, but he was a general, he had served under Marlborough for several years and fought at Sheriffmuir, and beneath his loquacious manner, he had a pugnacious mind. To counter Wightman's anticipated move, Marischal thought they must prepare at once to outflank the government troops as they ascended the slope, but the

Earl of Seaforth, another general in rank, would not agree, and Marischal had not the means to persuade him. The difficulty was that Marischal had no troops of his own to deploy, whereas Seaforth, who was in his own land, had brought more clansmen to the battle than anyone else among the Jacobites. The clansmen on the ridge with Marischal would obey him only on Seaforth's orders and Seaforth was of the mind that an outflanking manoeuvre would be premature.

'We must wait to see where they go,' he told Marischal.

The Earl Marischal had better relations with Seaforth than he did with Tullibardine but he did not think much of either man's soldiering. Both, he thought, lacked rigour and boldness, and though he had little reason for it, since he was a bit of a dandy himself, he ascribed Seaforth's hesitancy to his soft French upbringing and weakness for finery.

'We delay at our peril. We must attack now while we can make it count.'

But Seaforth remained indecisive. He bit his lip and frowned; opened his mouth and closed it again. Finally, after further words, Seaforth decided that Marischal was right after all. But it was too late, for now both men watching from behind the rocks saw the ascending militiamen veer away from the gulley and make a sharp turn to their right with the clear intention of closing in on them by coming around the end of the ridge.

Immediately Seaforth gave the order to fire. A first volley of musket fire erupted from behind the scattered rocks and hollows on the ridge. Puffs of gunpowder rose under the early evening sky which was now for the first time in a few days beginning to cloud over. The militiamen halted, sought cover where they could, and began to return fire. The platoons of grenadiers behind them steadily closed the gap. Once the reinforcement was complete the government troops began to advance again in spite of the increasingly steep and uneven terrain. They kept up continuous musket fire. Seaforth's men returned fire with urgency. Again government troops began to take casualties more than the

Jacobites, who were less exposed and commanded the higher ground. But while some of Wightman's soldiers keeled over and slumped onto the grass, most others came on determinedly, all the while gaining height. Seaforth, seeing them closer with each passing moment, became nervous; there was little possibility now of attacking by an outflanking manoeuvre, and for a frontal charge it had become obvious that the terrain would not serve. The Highland clansmen were feared for their fast and ferocious charges. They had won many a battle this way, sword in hand. But such a tactic depended on the ground being suitable and here it was certain that were they to charge they would fall over, stumble, or overshoot.

'If they draw level they will surround us and have the advantage in numbers,' Marsichal warned.

'I will send for Coul.'

Sir John Mackenzie of Coul was next in line on the Jacobite horseshoe. He had two hundred men with him but was at a distance, on the other side of the gulley. Seaforth sent a messenger over, hoping Coul would not delay. Meanwhile the government troops, now almost level, began to extend and thicken their line of fire around the end of the ridge on the broken terrain above a scattered line of trees. Urged by their officers, the three hundred or so soldiers kept up volleys of musket fire that, if not accurate, was relentless. The clansmen were soon dismayed by the onslaught. Not a few were beginning to leave their positions and slip back when the reinforcements from Coul appeared. But while Coul himself was keen, not all his men were eager to respond. Some lagged and came slowly, others appeared dispirited. Even so, for a while, the presence of Coul's men strengthened Seaforth's position. They returned fire. Yet it was not sufficient. The government lines continued receiving reinforcements from below until they were threatening once more to advance. After a short exchange with Marischal and Coul, Seaforth decided to send for more reinforcements from the centre. However, an hour later it was only Campbell of Ormidale who showed up with a few men and orders from Tullibardine to sort out the confusion. Ormidale was a dour man of imposing physique who was able to give an appearance of ability which he lacked. He was known to be brave and, like the other leaders, had commanded troops in battle, but he did not allow much room for the unexpected. Although the Earl Marischal was insisting that they needed to repel the enemy advance at this point, Ormidale remained convinced that the main thrust of the assault would be on the centre and would require every man to repel it. Seaforth sided with Marischal. He asked for Rob Roy and his eighty men to be summoned, as they were next after Coul on the horseshoe, but Ormidale was reluctant.

At the same time as Ormidale was resisting, Wightman had decided to send yet more troops. The battle was not turning out quite as he had foreseen, for he had hoped to draw rebel troops away from their centre to their left extremity. If they sent no reinforcements it made an assault on the centre more hazardous for him. On the other hand quite clearly he could see through his telescope how the rebel clansmen were slipping away individually or in small groups from the fire fight. They did not bolt altogether, but they moved to higher ground, out of musket range, and there waited to see which way to go. *Their heart is not in it.*

Wightman was not the only one to have this thought. Rob Roy cursed when he saw the trickle of desertion starting across the gulley between him and Seaforth. If anything made Rob Roy contemptuous it was lack of courage. He did not care so much for causes. He himself had decided to join the battle out of an inclination for adventure and calculated reasons of self-interest. As for the cause itself, he like so many others inclined to the Jacobites but without ardour. But regard for personal loyalty and a word given on the day meant a lot to Rob Roy. It felt to him unmanly and undignified to see the clansmen retreating without a proper fight. If they would not give the example he must do so himself.

At the moment Rob Roy began to urge his men forth, Seaforth took a musket ball in his arm. In the flurry of shock that followed, while Marischal and others jostled him to safety behind a larger rock, Seaforth lost his hat and wig. Suddenly he looked less imposing, more vulnerable and frightened as he stared out of a face streaked with white powder and sweat. But Seaforth had arrived with a surgeon among his retinue, who was at the hospital tents, behind Tullibardine's headquarters, and he said he must go there to have his wound attended. A party hurriedly assembled and braving enemy fire led Seaforth away from the ridge. His retreat was taken as a sign by many of the vacillating clansmen and soon they began to leave the field as well. Rob Roy and his men now on their way across the gulley to reinforce Seaforth encountered this growing exodus. Rob Roy shouted at them to turn around and go with him back to the ridge. But the clansmen paid him no heed, or to Glendaruel either who had also decided to come with some of his men to Seaforth's assistance. Then, as the advance and the firing from the government forces continued, it became apparent to Rob Roy that the ridge was being lost and there was little they could do to prevent it. For the sake of his honour, Rob Roy advanced with his men to exchange a few volleys of fire with the enemy, but when he saw that it was having no effect he ordered his men to retreat with the others.

Very soon the Dutch grenadiers with their Scottish and English counterparts began to overrun the ridge-line. The Earl Marischal spoke hurriedly to Ormidale. Their concern was now the obvious danger that with the ridge-line taken the enemy would succeed in making an encircling manoeuvre from above on their centre in order to cut off any strategic retreat.

As they crossed the gulley they met up with Glendaruel and Lochiel who had a number of men with them. They decided to consolidate what troops they could and form a firing line among the low rocks on the stony, sandy ground that continued up to a long high summit. This sudden example of valour struck a chord among a small number of the fleeing clansmen and they turned back and came to join the line.

ELEVEN

'Look at them. They are not holding ground,' said Bolaño. 'Even Rob Roy is retreating now. For God's sake, *why*?'

De la Rueda, from behind the breastwork, could see the clansmen abandoning their posts, retreating up to the scree on the mountainside, where they gathered in loose groups. Meanwhile, down below him, on the floor of the glen a few hundred yards from the foot of the bluff, a line of dragoons mounted on grey horses advanced slowly. Behind the dragoons came packhorses and a small number of troops. The uniforms of the troops and the loads on the packhorses alerted de la Rueda. He lifted his telescope. The mortars had been dismantled but de la Rueda recognized the components. He himself had been at the end of the little devils in Italy. *An attack will start soon and it is not looking good. Their commander knows what he is doing.*

De la Rueda lowered his telescope. 'They are bringing mortar up. I think they are coehorns. I know them from Italy.'

Bolaño took a look through his own telescope, then brought it down.

'Well that would explain the bombardment across the river. And now they must have moved them over. I am going to speak to Tullibardine. As soon as any of them are in range, open fire if I am not back.'

Bolaño went up the slope to where it flattened out on the edge of the plateau and where Tullibardine was standing with a group of his men, including Borlum.

A sudden fierce volley of gunfire reverberated from the near distance to de la Rueda's left, but the sloping and uneven terrain to his side prevented him from seeing the action. The clansmen some forty yards further up and to the left side of de la Rueda's breastwork were leaving their hastily dug trenches and moving out of sight. De la Rueda spoke to his ensign.

'Go and see what is happening and report straight back.'

Below, the dragoons were less than three hundred yards from the foot of the bluff.

'Make ready.'

As de la Rueda's soldiers raised their muskets, from behind the dragoons a platoon of infantry came forward as if to overtake them but instead of heading for the bluff they moved to the side of it, towards the fortified barricade, which de la Rueda could not see but which he knew was by the river blocking the narrow entrance of the glen.

The ensign returned and reported that a rear-guard line of fire had been formed on the edge of the gulley and was being strengthened. While the ensign spoke de la Rueda observed the dragoons below moving their horses to one side, away from the centre, as mortars were positioned on the ground with their attendant bombardiers in their long blue coats and tricorn hats. They were a little too far back to make an accurate target, but behind them de la Rueda observed a figure on a black horse come forward at a fast trot and turn to head for the dragoons. The figure on the horse was resplendently attired; the gold on his coat and elaborate hat shimmered even though the sky was now overcast. He appeared to be a general, one of their commanders, if not the commander himself, and de la Rueda calculated that the dragoons were almost within range.

At that moment a feeling of déjà vu came over de la Rueda. All the battles he had fought were different in their circumstances, yet they had all had moments like this when he experienced this abrupt shift in perception, as though his life was no longer his own to control, that it had been taken out of time itself and given over completely to his guardian angel. His fate had been decided for him before, and it was again. He did not want to die here in this land that was not his own. He was afraid. But what would be would be. Quickly de la Rueda crossed himself, then he gave orders.

The order passed along the line of troops massed behind the stone fortifications and within minutes a platoon of twenty or so men were detaching themselves from their companions and gathering by de la Rueda. Once they were assembled, de la Rueda left his position, leading the men away from the breastworks to a hollow he had spotted further down the slope to the left. The men were the best shooters in the two companies under his immediate command, and now, that much closer to the dragoons, he gave the order to stop.

Just then the eighty or so dragoons dismounted and gathered before the general as he dismounted. Then the mortars opened fire. De la Rueda turned to watch the bombs rising in the sky in their curving trajectory before they started to descend.

'Prime and ready! Prime and ready!' he shouted as the mortars exploded.

In seconds the soldiers had loaded the muskets with gunpowder and pushed the balls down the barrels with ramrods.

'Shoulder your firelocks... Fire!'

De la Rueda could not be sure if the dragoons that went down were wounded or taking cover but he saw a couple of horses take hits. One horse ran off before it collapsed and rolled over, legs up. The other horses stamped and bucked, threatening to bolt, too, but dragoons took charge of them and started leading them away. The main body almost at once lined up in defiance of the bullets that came down on them. A number of them detached themselves, ran forward, and taking position, began to fire back at de la Rueda's men. The remaining majority started marching fast towards the foot of the bluff. The general ran back to his horse, mounted, and took off back to where he had come from – a little knoll out of musket range where his retinue and several hundred troops awaited him. De la Rueda's attention was on his exchange of fire with the dragoons, who, it was apparent, were at a disadvantage and poorly placed to inflict harm on his men. But the main body of dragoons had now turned to face the bluff, right under the breastworks, and spread out in long lines were starting to make for the slope itself.

Holy Virgin. They are coming up for us.

At once de la Rueda gave an order for his men to return to the breastworks. As they started back, a platoon of infantry that was coming in behind the dragoons turned towards them and began firing. The men threw themselves on the ground, then it was a rush to reload and return fire before the soldiers could advance upon them. But while they managed to detain the soldiers without sustaining casualties themselves, they were at the same time being prevented from reaching the breastworks.

Looking in that direction de la Rueda could see what was becoming a mass exodus; clansmen hurrying away, abandoning their posts. From his position it was difficult to see more than the end of the breastworks, but from what he could make out it was apparent that his troops were firing down upon the forward dragoons in good order. But this did not stop their advance up the steep slope; moreover they were spread out and at moments concealed by the uneven surface of the slope which made them difficult targets. Meanwhile the remainder of the enemy troops, which had until then stood back, were swiftly advancing towards the bluff. And so too the enemy platoons that had besieged the ridge-line were starting to come across the gulley towards the centre.

The battle was being lost. It had reached that critical moment when fate makes up its mind. De la Rueda recognized the signs. He had seen it all before. Win or lose, however, his duty was to fight until ordered not to do so. Only a matter of yards separated him from the breastworks, but his men would be dangerously exposed. Their safer approach was to reach the breastworks by retreating in a backwards circle and coming in from above.

De la Rueda quickly sent half his men ahead under the protection of a firing line. Moments later he sent the other half, himself being the last to leave.

Hector was about to leave himself when he saw the first ten Spaniards emerge from the side of the slope to his left and scramble up fast from below him before circling to join their companions at the fortifications. One reason he had not left already was that Borlum and Tullibardine were lingering above him even while clansmen were deserting all around. This included Hector's own company. Of Lachlan, his second in command, there was no sign. He was gone with the others, who were breaking up without him being able to prevent it. Men were simply leaving, making for higher ground, where, as if to give them a hand and make their escape still easier, it was becoming misty. But several of Hector's men, including Neil, remained with him, and this was another reason he would not leave just yet. Whether from the likes of his social peers and superiors or his servants, Hector could not bring himself to let others see him as a coward or even a faint-heart. He had felt afraid all the while, cringing at the thought of seeing blood, and nothing so far had occurred to give him an opportunity to demonstrate that he was not the coward he feared himself to be. The sound of musket fire, the bombs exploding – a few quite close to his post – and the sight of the enemy ever closer, all terrified him. He felt his legs tremble and his arms go rigid. His body was paralysed yet his mind raced with wild thoughts. Then the other ten men appeared. De la Rueda came up close behind. Suddenly the Spaniard immediately in front of de la Rueda fell. Hector saw the man fall to the ground on his side. De la Rueda stopped. Hector watched de la Rueda crouching on the grass, talking to the man, helping him to stand. Another Spaniard went back and between them they were starting to bring the Spaniard up the slope when fifteen or so yards below them a soldier appeared. The soldier raised his musket to his shoulder and fired. At that distance he should not have missed but for some reason he did. De la Rueda, turning, saw the soldier and dropping his injured companion drew his pistol while the soldier was reloading his musket. At the same moment another soldier appeared, and still another, spread out. De la Rueda fired. The first soldier fell backwards, but the other soldier came up fast drawing his sabre. Without thinking or willing it Hector found his body suddenly free of the fear that immobilized it. He could have been a bird, he could have had wings, for he scarcely felt the ground as he left his post, pistol in hand, rushing down to de la Rueda's assistance. The other Spaniard with his wounded companion turned to face the third soldier advancing to Hector's right; de la Rueda himself, though, was suddenly in difficulty, for the soldier below him had in an instant drawn his sabre before de la Rueda had time to discard his pistol and draw his own sword. As the glinting blade of the sabre swooshed across towards him, de la Rueda had time to take in the blue eyes and gasping breath and the moustached grimace on the face of a soldier who was larger than himself, but he did not have time to draw his own sabre. For the merest instant he was certain he was going to die. A sense of resignation was coming upon him when there was an explosion of pistol fire close behind him and he saw the soldier reel back. But the ball merely carried the soldier's conical hat; he was not injured and he kept hold of his sabre as he recovered his balance.

Hector was upon him before de la Rueda. It was all his body now. Hector had no thoughts in his mind beyond the immediacy of action. He had dropped the steel pistol and drawn his silver handled dirk, but it was a moment too late to prevent the soldier from taking a swing. The sabre caught his arm with a first blow and then came down cleaving through his hat and onto his skull. From that moment on Hector ceased to be aware of himself except in brief flashes. He had yet to feel pain even. Darkness came over him as the soldier, himself wounded by the thrust of Hector's dirk to his side, stumbled back. De la Rueda had managed to draw his own sabre and he struck the soldier on his neck. The soldier spun backwards, falling down the slope. Other Spaniards arrived, for they had turned back and hurried to help once they had seen the difficulty their captain and their wounded companion were in. They made a line of fire. Neil and two other clansmen arrived. Between them and the Spaniards they lifted Hector and carried him up to the safety of higher ground. From beginning to end the fight had taken a scarce three minutes. And the assault by the dragoons on the slope of the bluff would not exceed half an hour before Tullibardine, seeing how clansmen were retreating all about him without a proper fight, decided to abandon the field and take flight while he still could.

Some among the lords objected. Others were undecided if to flee. Borlum cursed and said they must fight on. Bolaño, too, declared his troops would make a stand if so commanded. It would soon be nightfall, he indicated, which would give them the opportunity to rally for the next day. Tullibardine looked this way and that. There was a look of wistfulness and distress on his snub nosed face, but his small mouth was puckered stubbornly.

'And where is the bread to come from? Will your men fight without bread, colonel?'

Bolaño had to admit the marquis had a point. He could not see his troops wanting to fight on without shelter and rations. But as he was about to agree, the Earl Marischal, who had arrived moments before, said there was no time to discuss anything now. They could do so once they were safe but must leave for higher ground at once. Even as he spoke, Tullibardine was starting to walk away. Marischal turned to Bolaño.

'Will you help me hold our enemies back, colonel? That will give our men time to retreat.'

Bolaño pulled on his moustachio. 'How shall we do it ?

'Bring your men back here,' said Marischal. 'I will gather as many as I can, and we will hold a firing line, moving back as they advance.'

'Very well.'

Bolaño hurried back down to the breastworks. He arrived just as de la Rueda was arriving himself.

'We are moving back now. We will keep them at bay as long as we can. The Earl Marischal will show us where to stop.'

'Yes sir.'

De la Rueda gave orders. In good formation the troops hurriedly began abandoning the breastworks and retreated towards the plateau not far above. Hector, carried by Neil and others of his company, came with them. When they got to the plateau, Tullibardine and his people could be seen leaving for the high ground below the ridge, which had become enveloped in mist. Only Marischal, his younger brother Keith, Ormond, Borlum, and some hundred clansmen remained to join the Spaniards.

'Someone must go to the hospital tent,' Bolaño told de la Rueda. 'They will have to surrender here. The rest of us will provide the rearguard and follow Tullibardine for now.'

'Are we to surrender?'

'We must. We have no provisions.'

In that case I am no longer needed. De la Rueda motioned towards Hector, who lay on the ground nearby. 'That gentleman just saved my life, sir. With your permission, I will take him to our surgeon now. Perhaps he can do something for the gentleman. I will give them the order to surrender myself.'

'And you will then catch up with us?'

'I do not think the gentleman can surrender, sir.'

'Spit it out, man. There is no time to waste.'

'I would like to make sure he escapes safely.'

'You say he saved your life, Alejandro?'

'Yes sir.'

'Very well. You have my permission. God protect you.'

De la Rueda turned and walked over to Marischal. In French he asked the earl to explain matters to Hector's men. Marischal and de la Rueda went over to where the men were gathered around Hector.

'Who is in charge?' Marischal asked in Gaelic.

Neil was thinking Lachlan would be in charge now that Hector could not be. But Lachlan and the others in Hector's company had taken flight. The blacksmith was another who was in charge, but he was Seaforth's man, and he was keeping quiet.

'I must be, your lordship,' Neil replied reluctantly, looking sideways at the blacksmith.

After Marischal explained, Neil and two clansmen spread out Hector's plaid in such a manner as to hold him while the three men and de la Rueda each grabbed a corner and thus were able to lift him and carry him, if with difficulty.

Marischal hurried off to catch up with the Spanish troops and his own men as they marched towards the scree on the mountainside above them. De la Rueda and his group went towards the hospital tent a little distance behind the stone enclosure and shieling that had served as the Jacobite headquarters. Meanwhile the mist that had been gathering around the ridge above the high ground was being blown downwards by a chill breeze. As far as the Jacobites were concerned this was to their advantage since it made pursuit difficult. Already the edge of the mist was approaching like a white wall under the darkening sky when the men reached the hospital tent.

In the small tent the surgeon was attending the casualties who had arrived before de la Rueda. Three Spanish soldiers were injured, including those that had come to his aid, and a lone clansmen had somehow found his way there in spite of the Scottish lords having their own surgeons. Besides these wounded were the Spaniards who had been ill before the battle and Major Santarem, who had been tasked with keeping the flag but had been too ill that day to manage even this. The surgeon, though occupied, soon went to Rueda when he appeared at the tent entrance and helped bring Hector in and lay him down on a pile of heather.

'He saved my life,' said de la Rueda. 'See what you can do. The battle is lost. When the enemy arrives here you will need to surrender.'

'Where is the colonel?' asked Major Santarem, staring out of his drawn face.

'With Tullibardine. I believe the lords will make their escape and then our troops will surrender.'

'Have you the enemy close behind, Alejandro?'

'They are not far. This mist that has come down should help us though. And it is getting darker now. I do not know when they will be here. Soon, when the mist clears, but I have been ordered to tell you to surrender.'

Hector was unconscious. His hair was matted and his face blotched with streaks and patches of fresh and drying blood. There was blood also on the slashed clothes around the wound on his arm. Don Ignacio worked quickly. He spread a piece of lint smeared with an ointment over the wound on his head and then wrapped it with a bandage. For the wound on Hector's arm he cut the clothes away with scissors. Then he held Hector up and sticking his fingers in his mouth to force open his lips he gave him a potion to drink from a small metal cup.

'His head wound is bad. I cannot say if he will live,' the surgeon told de la Rueda. 'What are your intentions for him?'

'These men will try to get him home. I will accompany them.'

'You will not be able to carry him all that way; I cannot see how.'

'No. We will tie him to a horse.'

'Keep him well wrapped up. Make sure he drinks water. And I will give you a potion for him to take in a few hours time.' The surgeon paused. 'If he is still alive.'

'God willing he will be.'

As a child Neil had attended school lessons with Shona. But not many, for he was not inclined to book learning. He knew the rudiments of reading and writing in Gaelic and he had scarce words of Latin. Thus, by making signs to each other and interjecting with the odd word of Latin, he and de la Rueda managed to communicate at an essential level. Outside, nearby, they found the hobbled Galician ponies. There were ropes and wood saddles, too, among the provisions in the hospital tent.

A pony was saddled. Hector was taken outside and lifted onto it. While they were tying him, for a brief moment Hector appeared to awaken. He sat up straight, opened his eyes, mumbled, but then slumped down again onto the pony's neck. Once Hector's legs had been secured, his waist was tied to the pommel and his arms on either side of the pony's neck were tied by passing a rope under it. De la Rueda did not want to take more than one horse, lest it be needed by his sick compatriots, but at the last moment he unshackled another pony.

The mist was dense and the light inky dark when the party left.

TWELVE

The route by which the main Jacobite army had arrived at the battlefield was now inaccessible to the retreating clansmen. The easier ground on the floor of the glen was passing to Wightman's control, which meant that the only safe escape was by the back routes on higher ground across the mountains. Neil was not familiar with these mountains, so the party's guide was the blacksmith. When not hammering metal he herded cattle and hunted in the locality and thus knew the lie of the land. Even so the combination of mist and semi-darkness made progress slow and considerably more hazardous than it already was. The blacksmith went first along the trackless ground. Behind him came Neil. Next the pony carrying Hector. Then de la Rueda, and last the spare pony and four other clansmen. De la Rueda could see Neil's back appearing and disappearing in the mist, but he could scarcely see the blacksmith or, should he turn his head, the four clansmen at the rear. As the little plateau came to an end the ground began to break up into all manner of hills and gulleys. De la Rueda stayed close to the flanks of the pony, so that it would guide his steps but also to keep an eye on Hector, whose long and bony bulk lurched from side to side, sometimes sliding so far that in spite of the ropes de la Rueda became afraid he was going to slide off the saddle. Then, when he could, he would move to the side of the pony and put his arm out to hold Hector firm. But where the ground was difficult this was not always possible. 'Prohibere!' he would call out instead. No one, even Neil, understood this word, but the sound of de la Rueda's voice made them halt. Hector would be pushed up into the saddle again; the ropes would be adjusted and retied and once again the party would move on.

Underfoot much of the ground was heath and not too steep for the horses. But at other times the terrain became far rougher; rocky, narrow passes with dangerous drops, and also watery bog or loose stony shingle. How the blacksmith knew to navigate in such conditions, when barely able to see more than a few feet around, de la Rueda could not say, but the blacksmith gave no indication of being in doubt, except for once when he led them into a gulley and then stopped. De la Rueda watched him and Neil conferring. The other clansmen came up and they conferred for another while. De la Rueda could not inquire as to the subject of their lilting talk, but he had a feeling they were at a loss which way to go. Finally the blacksmith turned about and they started marching back the way they had ventured, de la Rueda believed, although the scarce visibility was confusing his senses.

After the gulley the breeze freshened and the mist started to lift. It became possible to get glimpses of the hills rising all around: dark, of different sizes, and some peculiar shaped, flat at the top, or long, or knobbly.

The journey became quicker as the mist dispersed. But they were far still from their destination. At a tiny lochan they stopped. Hector was slumped forward over the horse. The bandages they had put on him were congealed with blood. One of the clansmen gave de la Rueda a bowl, which he filled with water, took over to Hector, and lifting his head managed to get a little of it down his throat. At one moment Hector opened his eyes and appeared to force himself against the rope, trying to sit up. Very soon he became unconscious again, but the small signs of life gave de la Rueda hope. In his time he had seen soldiers recover from wounds so grievous he would not have thought it possible. He himself had recovered from serious wounds. De la Rueda judged Hector stood a chance, so long as he did not come off the horse and the journey was not prolonged to excess. *And a surgeon. May God grant him an able surgeon.*

After the lochan the descent in places became treacherous. The drops were sheer. Few plants grew on the sandy, rocky soil. In one stretch the only way down between the outcrops of rocks was by a narrow funnel of loose scree. De la Rueda became so concerned for both Hector and the pony that he decided to lead the pony by its halter, murmuring to it softly in Spanish. But if a mishap was avoided there, circumstances were less fortunate an hour later when, even though on firmer ground, one of the clansmen at the rear inadvertently stepped on a loose stone which came away and rolled from above down onto the spare pony. The stone was large enough to momentarily scare the pony, making it jump forward, which in turn made de la Rueda throw himself out of the way as the pony collided with the one carrying Hector. That pony then slipped and stumbled on the large, uneven rocks that were about. When de la Rueda had recovered and the party was moving on again it became apparent that the pony carrying Hector had gone lame. So they stopped, untied Hector, lifted him off the saddle and lay him on the ground, where now and then he made a gurgling sound. De la Rueda gave him more water. They saddled the spare pony, put Hector on it and tied him down.

It was now over six hours since they had left the battlefield. The mist had dispersed and the sky above the hills, while dark and sprinkled with a faint dusting of stars, gave enough summer light for them to find their way among the shadows.

As they were setting off a party of a dozen clansmen caught up with them. They stopped briefly to confer with de la Rueda's party. Hearing them speak, de la Rueda wished to know what they were saying but there were none among them who knew French or Latin. Presently the clansmen moved on ahead at a swift pace.

Finally, towards dawn, after hours of travel they descended from a corrie to a narrow glen where a river ran and the banks were flat enough to allow for good progress. The lame pony which until then had managed to keep up was lagging behind. De la Rueda did not know what to do about it. Should he shoot it or leave it be? He decided to leave it be, for he liked horses too much to think of killing one while it stood any chance.

More parties of clansmen caught up with them. Fields began to appear by the sides of the river. They passed a settlement and at last emerged from the glen towards the shore of loch Duich. De la Rueda was hungry and his legs ached when they reached the ford, which was at a crossroads, where they encountered numerous clansmen who had arrived before them. As yet they had no wood or peat and no fires going. All bore their weapons still, and they stood or sat resting, talking, the few lucky among them sharing snuff or what they had left of their oat rations. The very poorest cottars among them did not have plaids, but most did, even if they were of poor quality, and many of them had re-arranged the top part of this garment in such a way that the cloth fell over their heads and shoulders like a hood, keeping them warm.

Beyond the groupings, other clansmen were already wading the shallow water of the ford, crossing to the opposite bank. When de la Rueda's party arrived, and the pony stopped, he went to look at Hector. The bandages were seeping blood and his eyes were closed, but his hands held fast to the horse's thick mane and from in between his arms, where his head rested, came sounds of breathing.

Neither Neil nor the blacksmith had so far made any significant overtures towards de la Rueda. Unable to communicate except by signs they had behaved mostly as if he did not exist, but now Neil came up to him and reaching into his sporran he took out a meagre handful of raw oats to offer them. De la Rueda did not refuse. He put the oats in his mouth, then stepped over to the water's edge and kneeling, he sipped the cold water with cupped hands to wash the nourishment down.

Unexpectedly a figure appeared at de la Rueda's side. In the dark de la Rueda did not recognize the man until he lowered the hood covering his head. It was Murdo.

'*Estne bonus, Monsieur*? Are you all right, sir?' As on previous encounters Murdo included the odd word of French with his Latin.

De la Rueda nodded. '*Oui. Merci.*'

'You are alone?'

De Reuda felt too tried to struggle with Latin, but he obliged.

'I... *Monsieur* here, he... he saved my life.' De la Rueda shrugged.

Murdo spoke to Neil and the blacksmith in Gaelic. The blacksmith gestured a farewell to de la Rueda and left.

'*Ego auxillium vobis.* I will help you,' said Murdo.

The horse was led across the ford, which was only a few feet deep. De la Rueda took off his boots before crossing, thinking to salvage what remained of them. Once on the other side they were in territory familiar to de la Rueda, for the regiment's camp had been no more than three miles distant, and still closer the church Murdo took them to, where not many days before de la Rueda had met the Reverend Macrae.

After Murdo knocked on the heavy door it was opened at once. Several men came out. One of them, who appeared to be in charge, gave Hector a quick look and then, giving instructions in Gaelic, watched as three other men lowered Hector from the pony and carried him inside. Murdo and de la Rueda followed. The church was not as it had been the first time de la Rueda had visited. The pews were pushed and stacked to one side and the stone floor was taken up by improvised beds of heather and straw. The beds – some not yet properly divided – were empty except for two in which lay the shadowy shapes of injured clansmen; one of them groaning loudly, the other silent.

Hector was lowered onto a table, where, in the light of several cruise lamps, the bearded man who was in charge immediately began to peel away Hector's bandages. Observing the man's skill, as well as his attire of trews and jacket, de la Rueda surmised he would be a surgeon or a physician if not both. The injured clansmen were only a few yards away from de la Rueda and in spite of the cool breeze passing through the hall he caught a whiff of gore and raw flesh.

Murdo had absented himself, but now he reappeared with the tall, stooped figure of the Reverend Macrae.

'Ah, *Monsieur capitain*, we meet once more,' the minister greeted him in his good French.

De la Rueda, who had lost his tricorne in the battle, bowed his shorn, wig-less head.

'The pleasure is mine.'

'Come. If we are needed the surgeon will know where we are.'

De la Rueda followed the minister down the passageway into the vestry. In the large fireplace a small cauldron simmered on a peat fire which glowed in the penumbra and was watched over by a stout woman, wearing heavy clothes. The remainder of the vestry looked empty. The cabinet de la Rueda had noticed on his previous visit was gone. So too the table, which was now in service to the surgeon. Three chairs and a plain wooden cross on a wall remained, and there were four beds of straw and blankets.

The minister spoke to the woman in Gaelic, whereupon she picked up a wooden bowl by the fireplace, and rising from the compressed hay she had been sitting on, filled it from the cauldron with a ladle.

'Please, be seated; have some food,' said the minister.

The gruel was no more than a little dulse and salted fish cooked in water. But it was warm and de la Rueda was famished. He sat down and supped from the bowl. When he had finished, the woman took the same bowl and filled it for Murdo.

'Our cause is lost, I fear.'

The minister, sitting on the chair beside de la Rueda, sighed and interlocked his hands tightly in front of him, as if in prayer.

De la Rueda grimaced. 'The way of war.'

'I am told the skirmish was short. I would rather a long battle with victory than a short one without. But if lose we must we can be thankful it was short. As you can see, *Monsieur*, we have only one surgeon of our own here at present. We are not sufficient to cope with many wounded unless other physicians avail themselves. But those will scatter with all the rest.'

'There will not be many in need of care,' de la Rueda agreed, thinking of how the clansmen had disappeared into the mist rather than fight. He did not question their mettle. No, he had been a soldier long enough, and had fought in foreign battles often enough to know that how fighting men accounted for themselves on a particular day depended not so much on courage as on the circumstances that were able to unleash it. What had been lacking, de la Rueda thought, was not courage but the example of leadership.

'I do believe the Earl of Seaforth may have been wounded,' de la Rueda said, remembering that of the natives in his sector the fight had come largely from Seaforth and Marischal.

'Murdo here has already told me,' said the minister. 'The Earl has his own surgeon with him. If he has not arrived already he is being taken to a house not far from here where he will be better concealed.'

'Is it not safe here?' asked de la Rueda.

'I pray it will be. We may know in the days ahead when the enemy's immediate intentions become more apparent.'

'What is it you fear?'

'Not for myself.' The minister unclasped his hands and twisted towards de la Rueda with dark fire in his eyes. 'They may do with me as they wish but I will not, *I will not* give that foreign swine who calls himself a king an oath of allegiance. What they may do to this church and the wounded here I cannot account for. Burning and hangings, that is what usually occurs after a battle, is it not? In my judgement you will be better gone from here before they arrive.'

De la Rueda, exhausted as he was, straightened his back. 'I feel I have a duty to make sure the gentleman arrives home safe.'

The minister shook his head. 'As you wish. The laird is a gentleman of means. He may have a place to hide once he is on his own land, but before he can be moved we must hear what the surgeon has to say.'

'Of course.'

'In any event the enemy have first to clear the barricade that is blocking the glen. Any movement towards us will be noticed. We have men that will harry their advance, so in my estimation I would say we are safe –'

Howls interrupted the minister. They were coming from the passage into the church. The minister went off to investigate. De la Rueda followed. In the nave several men were holding another man down on the table. He had a piece of rope tied between his teeth while the surgeon sawed through his forearm. It was only a matter of moments before the man passed out and the howls ceased. Turning his head, de la Rueda saw that Hector was lying on a bed near a window. His eyes were closed but he did not have the appearance of a man who was dead. De la Rueda, who had seen many corpses, knew this at once. The bandage on his head had been replaced. Although stained with fresh blood it was wrapped neatly over his skull. He was not sure about the bandages on his arm.

De la Rueda sank into an empty stack of straw nearby. In spite of the noises, the smell, and the presence of more wounded arriving, he fell asleep. It was however a sleep he fought against; a sleep that stunned him only briefly before the minister's voice awoke him.

'If you please, *Monsieur*. You will be more comfortable in the vestry.'

De la Rueda stood up, shaking the drowsiness from himself, and looked towards Hector.

'The surgeon thinks he will mend. He is not finished with him yet. We will know more later in the day.'

There were now twelve wounded men on straw beds in the nave, including the man whose hand had been amputated. The surgeon and his three assistants had not stopped all night. A thirteenth man was on the table being bandaged when de la Rueda walked past. The surgeon's clothes had become splattered with blood.

In the vestry, the minister showed de la Rueda one of the straw beds where he could lie down. Before he could pull the blanket over himself he was asleep. When he opened his eyes again it was daylight. He stood up, for a moment disorientated. The surgeon was close by on an adjoining pile of straw, face down, snoring. Yet another pile was occupied by Murdo. De la Rueda went out along the short passageway into the nave, which was illuminated by light coming through the large green and blue stained glass windows along the walls. The wounded lay on their beds, some making sounds, most silent, while the old woman from the night before moved among them, serving them broth of some kind by dipping a wooden bowl into a pail which an assistant was carrying for her. De la Rueda stopped by Hector's bed. He was asleep. His bandages were encrusted with blood. His face was gaunt, the skin covered with perspiration. When de la Rueda leaned close he heard his breathing was rapid and shallow. *He has fever. That may not be bad. In Spanish Holland I too had fever after I was wounded.*

The church doors were ajar. Outside it was warm but raining softly. A green field sloped away towards the nearby river that joined Loch Duich. Black cattle were grazing on the pasture and in this light the water in the river and the loch was more dark blue than grey. Suddenly de la Rueda grinned, happy to be alive. Even the rain he liked. Walking out into it he thought he had not been in another country where the weather changed so quickly. Two fully armed clansmen watched him from a distance as he circumvented the cattle. Past the cattle it was not far to the estuary at the banks of the loch. Looking across to the other side he could see a number of armed clansmen camped there with fires going. By now de la Rueda had learnt that their woollen plaids would keep them warm even when wet and that the rain, unless very heavy, would not disturb them much. What de la Rueda wanted to know, however, was what the troops were doing there, armed as they were. For an answer he had to wait until he had defecated and washed himself at the edge of the water and returned to the church. There he found the minister standing in the doorway, stooped over, holding a bible in his hand, talking to a tearful, barefoot woman dressed in little more than rags and with three young children gathered around her. Breaking off his conversation with the woman, the minister explained that her husband was one of the wounded brought in and he had died overnight. The deceased was a local man, a cottar, and they were waiting for the woman's neighbours to arrive so the body could be taken and buried. The minister said something to the woman in Gaelic before switching back to French.

'I have information for you this morning. Your compatriots have all gathered at a place only a few miles from here and are today surrendering to Wightman.'

De la Rueda was not surprised, but abruptly a thought occurred.

'I hope you do not think, *Monsieur*, that I am putting myself before my duty.'

The minister appeared perplexed.

'I was told by my commanding officer that our troops would be surrendering. I had his permission to accompany the gentleman, which I do as a deed returned.'

It took the minister another moment to understand. 'Of course, *Monsieur*. I beg your forgiveness. It was never a thought of mine to hold your honour in doubt.'

They went into the church, silent, in mutual embarrassment. The minister excused himself, asking de la Rueda to wait. De la Rueda lingered near Hector. Other people entered the church. A young woman looked about her in confusion before she gave a cry and hurried over to the side of one of the wounded. The children, but not their mother, of the man who had died, came in through the open doors and went over to their father's corpse. The older of the children, a little girl, was holding what appeared to be a small bunch of wild flowers. Like her brothers, she was skinny and filthy, the rags that covered her mere scraps of soiled cloth sewn together. De la Rueda watched her with momentary keenness as she went up to her father and tried to get the flowers under his hands, which were folded on his breast. She did not immediately succeed, for she could barely reach, but there was such devotion in the attempt that it tugged at de la Rueda's heart. He was reminded of another time in Spanish Holland when, just as a battle was to start, a woman had come running up and handed one of de la Rueda's fellow soldiers, a sergeant, a basket containing a swaddled baby. The woman was a camp whore whom the sergeant had impregnated and she wanted to be rid of the baby, battle or no battle. No one in de la Rueda's company hesitated; the baby went into battle, passed in its basket from soldier to soldier as the situation demanded, and their enemy never touched it. The infant escaped mortar, grenades, and sword in hand combat as if the Mother of Jesus Herself had looked over the infant, the one being that was innocent and unblemished in the midst of the carnage.

Just as the girl was turning with her two smaller brothers to leave the church, a man with a wild look in his eyes, and his shirt, for he wore no plaid, soaked in blood, stumbled through the doors. When he reached the passageway into the vestry he started calling out in words de la Rueda could not understand. Very soon the minister appeared with the dishevelled surgeon and one of his helpers following behind. While the surgeon and his helper attended to the wounded man, the minister shuffled over to de la Rueda.

'I have spoken to the surgeon. He can do no more. He is of the opinion it would be best for *Monsieur* Matheson to be given over to the care of his wife. One or more of *Monsieur* Matheson's men are camped with the troops across the bay. I am sending Murdo now to fetch them so it can be arranged to have *Monsieur* Matheson transported home.'

'Is it far to his house?'

'Not by water. If the weather holds.' The minister added, 'and we do not run into the English men of war.'

'Are they still here?'

'They sit out at sea, I am told... Now, I believe you have not yet supped. Please, let us go to the vestry.'

De la Rueda followed the minister past the table where the surgeon was preparing his instruments while his assistant was holding down the patient. De la Rueda noticed that the man had a deep gash across his exposed stomach, the result of a sword thrust. In the vestry the cauldron was simmering, unattended. The minister ignored it and went over to a nearby barrel de la Rueda noticed for the first time. Taking a wooden bowl from the top of it, he stooped down with difficulty to place it under the tap. De la Rueda saw amber liquid flow into the bowl.

The minister struggled upright, proffering the bowl with a thin smile. 'Ale. It arrived in the night while you were sleeping.'

De la Rueda imbibed the strong bitter liquid gladly.

'There is no bread, but I will get you some oats.'

From a depleted sack near the barrel, the minister took out a handful of raw oats. He passed the oats into de la Rueda's spare hand.

'I must now attend to the burial. The boat will not be leaving until dusk, when it will be safer from the men of war unless we are attacked here before then.'

'What shall you do if you are attacked?'

The minister's hunched, bony shoulders gave a lopsided shrug. 'There is not much we can do. We shall disperse, taking with us such wounded as we are able. Now if you will excuse me.' The minister turned to leave. De la Rueda stood still for a moment, then on impulse he reached into the leather pouch under his jacket, attached to the cross belt holding his pistols. Inside the pouch was a concealed slit containing another pocket and inside this pocket were four gold coins plus several lesser ones of silver. They were all Spanish coins but de la Rueda was aware that foreign coins had value in Scotland, since its own currency had been banned and English currency was in short supply. The coin of least value de la Rueda had was *dos reales*. He was not exactly sure how far it would go, what it could buy, but something anyway. Hurrying out, he caught up with the minister as he was proceeding across the nave.

'Pardon *Monsieur*, but I observed the little girl place flowers on her father's breast. The man who died...'

The minister's white eyebrows lifted.

'It appears to me the family must now be in severe distress. I would like to give the little girl something for her mother, if you will help me do it, please?'

'And what is it you wish to give?'

De la Rueda passed him the small coin. 'In my country it could buy a chicken certainly, maybe a lamb. I do not know what it could be worth here.'

The minister peered at it and nodded.

'I know not what it is worth myself, but I can find out. I will speak to the widow when she receives it to make her understand. Your generosity will not go unnoticed.'

The minister handed back the coin and they went out of the church. The widow and her children, now joined by her brother, and two others who carried wooden spades, were gathered in the graveyard. The minister beckoned the woman to come close. He spoke to her in Gaelic. De la Rueda saw her face express confusion bordering on consternation, followed by something like baffled acceptance. With a quick look in de la Rueda's direction, the woman said something to her daughter and pushed her towards him. De la Rueda bent low. Bringing out a smile he handed the girl the coin. The little girl's dark eyes blazed at him, then, hearing the minister speak to her, she handed the coin to her mother, who at once and without a glance closed her hand around it tightly.

The minister spoke to the woman again and it was only now that she appeared to credit the unexpected gift. Her eyes brimmed as she glanced at de la Rueda once again and spoke to the minister.

'She asks me on her behalf to express her profoundest gratitude, *Monsieur*. She prays that Our Lord may bless you.'

De la Rueda responded with a short bow. The group then turned away and started walking in between the lichen speckled tombstones and Celtic crosses towards the far end of the graveyard, which had no headstones and was reserved for common folk. As they did so the little girl turned and looked back at de la Rueda. He raised his hand to her, then turned himself and was proceeding back towards the church when he noticed a long stone tomb with the effigy of a knight carved on it. The effigy was worn by time and the elements but the main details were distinguishable. The knight lay on his back in a suit of armour with his hands folded on his chest over a sword. De la Rueda was no expert in history, but he was curious and he had read a dozen books. The knights of old, he knew, were soldiers at the service of Christ and their lords. Where this particular knight had come from he did not know; but here he was buried, here he had died, and for reasons perhaps, de la Rueda reflected, that were now lost to memory. The knight had fallen in battle, perhaps; one more battle among the hundreds, nay the thousands of battles in the world that history no longer recalled. And yet each of those fallen warriors had been a man replete with hope, fear, passion.

A man had a duty to live by his honour. In de la Rueda's estimation honour was greater than life itself. *Only I have seen so much of battle now. So much of waste and destruction that sometimes it becomes hard to keep honour true, knowing which part is God's work and which the Devil's own.*

Looking up from the grave, de la Rueda noticed a boat being pushed onto the shore by four men. Although it was a few hundred yards away, he had no trouble recognizing the limber figure of Murdo among them. De la Rueda moved away from the grave towards the shore. Once the boat was secure, Murdo, with the others following, came up the slope.

With his usual mixture of gestures, French and Latin, Murdo made de la Rueda understand they would be departing presently and asked if he knew where to find his uncle. De la Rueda responded with few gestures of his own. Murdo went off in the direction indicated. Among the men who stayed behind, de la Rueda recognized Neil and two of the three other clansmen who had accompanied Hector. Soon Murdo returned with the minister.

'Are you able to row?' the minister asked.

'I am. Yes.'

'Then we require only one more. There will be two other wounded men in your boat.'

They went into the church. The surgeon had gone back into the vestry where he was stretched out, snoring as he slept. A glass bottle was on the stone floor beside the hay. The minister and Murdo conferred, then Murdo shook the surgeon. He awoke brusquely, frowning and muttering. While the minister spoke, the surgeon picked up the glass bottle and shook it to ascertain if anything remained. Morosely he stood up, his trews, shirt, and jacket still grubby with dry blood and gore. In the church the surgeon stopped to make a brief examination of Hector, who was half awake and bathed in sweat, and then spoke to the minister.

'*Monsieur* Arnott will give *Monsieur* Matheson a potion to drink,' the minister informed de la Rueda. 'And he says you can bathe his brow with sea water when he is in the boat. The rest is up to God.'

The surgeon moved on to examine the two other wounded who were going in the boat. De la Rueda went to stand under the wooden cross on the wall above the chancel. He joined his hands together under his chin and looked up at the cross. Overcome by a sense of frailty, he began to pray, giving thanks to God for his life and asking for his sins to be forgiven and for Hector's life to be spared.

Hector was carried the short distance to the shore in his own plaid by four men, each grabbing a corner of the cloth. The other two wounded men were able to walk; one, who had a shoulder wound, without assistance, the other, who had a thigh wound from musket shot, hopping and with support. Once on the shore the invalids waited for the boat to be turned around and pushed into the advancing tide. Hector was carried out and placed behind the mast, on a couple of planks that came from the minister's barn and were placed across two of the boat's benches. In this way Hector was able to lie with the upper part of his body prone while avoiding the water in the bottom of the boat. The other two invalids accommodated themselves sitting up as best they could. The able bodied men squeezed aboard and took an oar each. The last to leave the shore was de la Rueda.

'*Bien Monsieur,*' said the minister. 'Let us hope we meet again in more favourable circumstances. God willing, our people shall be free of the unholy German swine.'

'God willing. I am much obliged.'

'*Dieu vous accompagne, Monsieur.* God go with you.'

De la Rueda, with his boots under his arm, bowed, turned and stepped across the pebbles into the water. Murdo, who was in the water by the boat, steadied it while de la Rueda climbed aboard and took hold of an oar. Soon, under Murdo's command, the boat was being turned and rowed westward beneath a cloudy sky that continued to shed a fine penetrating rain. In no time de la Rueda's clothes were soaked but the effort of rowing kept him tolerably warm. Further out, a square sail was raised but the men did not stop rowing. In a while they passed before the jagged ruins of Eilean Donan castle. The men became silent and gloomy in the presence of the charred, demolished walls protruding from heaps of rubble. As if to rid themselves of the reminder of their defeat, once past the sight, the men, following Murdo's lead, broke out in a Gaelic version of a defiant Jacobite song:

What, shall a German cuckold and his Fool,
An Ox and Ape o'er generous Britons rule,
Whilst under them like Dogs We sneak and howl?
Not whilst our Royal, James is to the dore,
A Prince Whom Europe's Princes All adore...

During the moments of rest, de la Rueda, his arms and back aching from the effort of rowing, would turn his attention to Hector, giving him water to drink and trying to ease his discomfort by adjusting his plaid and body where he lay. The plaid was soaking wet but de la Rueda thought that might not be a bad thing considering his fever, and, indeed, when he felt Hector's brow it seemed to him that it was no longer so hot. Sometimes Hector's eyes opened and he stared out with a look that de la Rueda thought was of someone who was not in full possession of himself. There were flickers of awareness, and once he appeared to recognize de la Rueda, but immediately he drifted off again. Sometimes, too, Hector's mouth would move and he would make sounds which, however, were inarticulate, difficult to hear amid the sounds of sea and wind and the creaking of the boat. But several times he cried out so loudly that all in the boat could hear. Each time this happened de la Rueda feared Hector was about to die – for not all died silently, many a time had de la Rueda heard soldiers cry out in their last moments – yet Hector's cries, so it would seem, were not those of a man torn away so much as of one refusing to give in, fully engaged in the struggle to fend off the claw.

After a few hours the boat rounded the sound of Kyle, where, close to the mountainous shore of the Isle of Skye, they could make out an English man of war. To their good fortune its sails were furled and it was too distant to cause more than fleeting concern. As the man of war dwindled from sight, Neil took over the helm from Murdo and began to guide the boat towards the shore. In the west, out to sea, the lowering sun had broken through dark clouds in a long a streak of yellow and to the sides of it the rain could be seen as it fell in moving bands across the surface of the green sea. Screeching seagulls careered above the boat as its sail was lowered and Neil turned the prow inwards, aiming for the breakwater The Experimenter had built at some expense. The tide had not yet turned sufficiently for the boat to mount the shore itself but the little bay protected by the breakwater was shallow and sandy. Once the boat dropped anchor two of the able men jumped into the water, which came up to their thighs, and waited for Hector to be lifted by the others, with Murdo and de la Rueda helping.

Neil said he would go to inform the house and fetch help. Once Hector was out of the boat he was carried by a man on each side of him the few yards to the shore. There he was laid on the grass bank beyond the pebbles and seaweed. Murdo managed to make de la Rueda understand that he could not tarry as he had the two other invalids to deliver at a place some leagues distant. While they stood speaking and gesturing in the dark light de la Rueda noticed a pale house peeking among trees behind him in the near distance.

'*Vale, Monsieur. Mar sin leat,*' said Murdo, using both Latin and Gaelic.

'*Adieu, et merci pour tout.* Goodbye and thank you for everything,' responded de la Rueda with a short bow.

As Murdo and his companions were retreating into the water, figures emerged hurrying down from the house: Neil and two women arrived first. Behind them a third woman approached with a fast but contained motion. She was small of stature and wore a long dress. Her head was bowed against the wind and rain, and covered by what appeared to de la Rueda as a long shawl which was held close to her face and which fell over her shoulders. Observing her, and without yet being able to see her distinctly, de la Rueda nevertheless felt inexplicably alert. It was an awareness not dissimilar to the one that came to him in the taut moments before battle. At that instant, for no reason that he could fathom, he had a sense of being on the edge of something momentous.

The woman was only a few yards from him now but the arisaid was pulled up over the lower part of her face and her gaze did not acknowledge him, intent as she was on the recumbent figure of Hector. But she did not rush forward. It was the other two women who at once knelt on the wet grass beside him. As they did so they turned to look up at the other woman, who stepped past de la Rueda and stood staring down at Hector while speaking in Gaelic.

A moment later she turned. As she did so the arisaid dropped away from her face. De la Rueda felt a violent shudder go through him. A hollow opened in his very soul. His heart thumped. The woman's eyes rested on him for the merest instant then moved beyond him to gaze back towards the house.

It is her face. They are the same. She is the woman in the picture.

De la Rueda was filled with holy fear.

FOURTEEN

When Shona saw Hector lying on the grass she was thrown into confusion. Ever since she had examined his ledgers she had been telling herself that it would please her if he never came back. She could imagine a situation where she was a widow, free to run the estate as her heart and her conscience dictated. In idle moments she had permitted herself to imagine it as a place where food and shelter would not be denied to the deserving and where true Christian compassion would triumph over cruel self-interest. But her fantasy was not free of guilt. Though she told herself her husband was unworthy, yet to wish him dead was a step too far. Any such notion disturbed her deeply. She drew back in alarm from the animus, from the cold anger that she felt. She told herself that all she wanted, in reality, was for Hector to show a little more charity, a little more concern for the folk that came under his scrutiny. Shona's resentment was not constant. It waxed and waned. Along with her thoughts that it would be better if Hector did not exist were her guilty, fervent prayers that he should return to her from battle safe and entire. So now, with Hector on the ground, wet, wounded, and unaware of her, Shona stood wrestling with her emotions, waiting to know which one prevailed.

In the end it was pity. She felt pity for her husband.

Now Old John approached, waddling on rheumatic legs and panting as he dragged a farm sledge behind him. As always, he was ingrained with dirt. His long grey hair and beard were matted and the plaid he wore day in day out never washed. But de la Rueda gave him no glance. His mind was stunned. He saw nothing and nobody but the woman.

It was only when Shona spoke and moved to help the others lift Hector onto the wooden sledge that de la Rueda broke out of the trance and in silence joined in. The sledge was too small to accommodate Hector's full length. With his legs dragging on the grass and both Neil and de la Rueda pulling on the rope, and the women helping as they could, Hector was transported up to the door of the house. There they lifted him by his plaid and carried him inside. Margaret was sitting in her chair near the hearth. Her brow creased and her eyes flickered as the group struggled by at the other end of the common room, but these small gestures of Margaret's were of bewilderment rather than comprehension. Although she caught a glimpse of Hector, and it awoke vague stirrings in her, she could not remember who he was.

Hector was laid on the bed. Then Shona turned to Neil, becoming aware of de la Rueda's intense gaze on her but too preoccupied to give it thought.

'Neil, when you arrived did I hear you say it was French the gentleman spoke?'

'I only know what Murdo, who is the nephew of the Reverend Macrae of Kintail told me.'

'And what did he tell you?'

'Some words of Latin he has. And that other language he speaks well... French, aye, I think it will be.'

'Not English?'

'No. I believe Murdo said French.'

Shona looked down at Hector. His eyes flicked open and for a moment she thought he became conscious of her, but she was not sure. It was dark in the room, for a lamp had still to be lit and little of the late evening light penetrated the small and opaque panes of the single window.

'Does the foreign gentleman know medicine, Neil?'

'That I cannot say, but I believe not.'

'What have we to do, Mairi? You know better than I.'

'Hector is wet through. Change him, Shona, give him broth, and send for MacQueen of the plants.'

Alisdair MacQueen was a physician. Opinion of his merits was divided, but he lived not far away and was a distant relation of Hector's.

'Light a lamp, Elsbeth.'

While Elsbeth went out to light a lamp from the hearth, Shona opened a trunk from which she removed one of Hector's many spare shirts. As she did so she was trying to assemble sentences in French, a language she was confident of reading but which she had not spoken, and then mostly with her tutor, since she was a child.

Returning to the bed, Shona still avoided looking directly at de la Rueda, but she heard herself say, '*Mon mari, Monsieur... merci...* My husband, *Monsieur*... thank you...' She could not think of anything else in the language. Turning away she at once began undressing Hector with Mairi and Neil joining in.

De la Rueda stood rigid. But while outwardly little showed, inwardly he was startled to hear the woman speak words in French, even though badly. *You are Captain Alejandro de la Rueda. An officer. An experienced man. You are not a callow youth. Remember who you are.*

Elsbeth came back with a lit cruisie lamp.

De la Rueda stepped up beside Shona, '*Si vous me le permettez, Madame.* If you will allow me, madam.'

He placed his arms under Hector's side and began to help lift his limp body in order to change his clothes. Shona scarcely noticed. She was overwhelmed by her husband's condition. It was more than pity, it was distress. It pained her, frightened her to see the pale flesh so limp and with the brown, stained bandages wrapped around his arm and head. Her husband breathed fitfully, grunted, but he was unable to awaken. Would he ever? *Please God be gentle with him. He is not a cruel man. He can change. I can save him.*

Once Hector's clothes were changed, Shona sent Mairi to prepare a bowl of broth. At the same time her thoughts finally turned to the Spaniard. Neil had told her he believed Hector had saved his life in the battle but he did not know much else, other than that the battle was lost.

'Elsbeth, see what spare bedding we have. The gentleman can stay in the barn.'

Elsbeth went to the bedding trunk. Shona turned to face de la Rueda.

'If you please, *Monsieur*,' she managed to say, raising her hand with the palm towards her.

De la Rueda understood. With a bow of his head he silently followed her out of the room. Shona went over to the cauldron, which Mairi had lowered on its chain and was now stirring with a big wooden ladle. A red glow came from the peat fire.

'Is there sufficient for the gentleman?' Shona asked.

'I have added more water,' said Mairi.

Shona took a wooden bowl from a shelf and under the vacant stare of her mother-in-law went to the cauldron and filled it with a thin broth of barley and salted meat. At the table she gestured to de la Rueda, who was suddenly hugely hungry. Shona did not stay with him but went back into the bedroom where she helped Elsbeth gather bedding and carry it out. De la Rueda, sitting at the table, supping the broth, watched Shona pass through the common room. He was exhausted, too tired to think, but deep down he had strange, tumultuous, clashing feelings of joy and doom.

Out in the barn the women filled a linen bag from the small amount of straw that remained from the previous year. Among the boxes and barrels and farm implements there was also a quantity of heather used for thatching. After separating some of the heather the women filled a mattress cover with straw and placed it on the heather and then added two rough, thick woollen blankets, sheets, and a feather pillow. *It will have to do.*

After Shona had prepared the bed she returned to the house and approached de la Rueda, who sat at the table with his head against his chest. His head jerked up, his dark eyes opened wide and she thought she detected fear in them. *But why should he be afraid of me?*

'If you please, *Monsieur...*' Shona pointed to Elsbeth and switched to Gaelic. 'Show the gentleman his bed, Elsbeth, please.'

De la Rueda stood up and bowed.

'*Merci, Madame. Bonne nuit.* Thank you, madam. Good night.'

Shona turned to Mairi. 'Will you take charge of Margaret? '

Mairi took hold of Margaret's arm, to help her rise and lead her to the little box room adjoining the bedroom. Shona followed with a bowl of broth. While Margaret was being put to bed, Shona sat on the edge of her own bed, and lifting Hector's head carefully, so as to avoid disturbing the bandage, she tried to feed him with a horn spoon. Hector did not respond immediately, but once she managed to get a little of the broth beyond his lips he started swallowing it and his eyes opened. Although the glow of the lamp gave only a dim yellow light she saw the initial vagueness in his eyes give way to a single brief flicker of recognition. One of his hands touched her, then fell away again, and his eyes closed. But when she continued to feed him, he continued to take it down.

Mairi came out of the box room and stood at the end of Shona's bed.

'He is eating,' Shona said.

Mairi crossed herself. 'Blessed be Mairi Mother of God.'

'Tomorrow early I will send for the physician. If I need you I will wake you.'

'Good night then, Shona '

'Good night.'

After Mairi left, Shona lay down beside her husband but she could not sleep. She wondered about the Spaniard. Why had he come with Hector? What was he doing here, away from his own kind? And it seemed to her every time she had ventured a glance she had encountered his dark eyes staring at her with disconcerting intensity, as though he were burning inside. It was unsettling. She must speak to Neil again in the morning in case there was anything he had not mentioned. The foreigner was a handsome man. And civil. His attire did not seem to her that of an ordinary soldier. Perhaps more a gentleman's. An officer? But he was tense. In shock... frightened? Or was it all in her mind? Most likely it was in her mind, for what did she know, really, about men and the affairs of the larger world? The only other foreigners she had met were a few English and an Irish husband and wife when she had gone to Edinburgh and Glasgow with Hector. And, of course, that portrait painter. What was his bis name? De Medina. Did she not recall that he originated from Spain, too? A strange man. Impossible to forget. And far too forward with her.

Hector stirred and mumbled. Shona leaned over and felt his face with the back of her hand. He was perspiring but did not feel hot. She did not think he needed, just now, to be cooled with water. But lying back again, her thoughts would not be subdued; they, and the pain she felt in her body for her husband, continued to keep her awake. Finally she got up and went to the common room where she put a lump of peat on the fire and then sat by the hearth and pulled over the spinning wheel.

De la Rueda did fall asleep. After Elsbeth left, taking the lamp with her, he removed his belts holding sword and pistols and lay down in his clothes on the rough mattress. He pulled the blankets over his shoulders and was instantly asleep. But two hours later he woke up. Shona's face was impressed in his mind. Her face was the face of the woman in the portrait and in his sleep the portrait had come alive and started speaking to him. After he awoke he was unable to fall back asleep. He lay in the dark. An owl hooted close by and there was a rustling sound from a small animal. *It has finally happened. But not as I anticipated. I do not know what I anticipated. I thought if it ever came to pass it would be sent from heaven. I thought my faith if not my virtue would be rewarded. But can something from heaven be sent that is not pure? She is a married woman. She is the wife of the man who saved my life. How then can it be sent from heaven? But it is her, nevertheless. It is her. She is the woman in the picture.*

It was a couple of years after joining the army that de la Rueda had seen the picture for the one and only time. He had stopped with his regiment in Ciudad Rodrigo. The Portuguese king had changed sides. He had broken the uneasy truce between Spain and Portugal by coming out in support of the English and the Dutch against the French. De la Rueda's part of Spain, Bourbon Spain, was allied to the French. Battles were being fought on the border lands between Spain and Portugal. De la Rueda was a twenty two year old ensign attached to a private regiment. The regiment was due to march the next day towards Portugal where de la Rueda anticipated being in battle for the first time in his life. Meanwhile he, two other ensigns, and a lieutenant, were off duty. Others who were off duty stayed behind to whore and gamble with the camp followers, but de la Rueda and his companions preferred to acquaint themselves with Ciudad Rodrigo, a medieval city within sight of the regiment's camp by a river on a dusty yellow plain beneath hills. A high stone wall surrounded the city, in whose centre was a cathedral, squares, arcades, and narrow streets. After the two hour walk to the city under a hot sun the group were thirsty and when they came across a tavern they decided to enter. But in front of the tavern, on the other side of the street, de la Rueda noticed a shop front. He had no particular reason to notice the shop, other than it was a shop that sold furnishings – trunks, chairs, tables and the like – but for some reason, while his companions went into the tavern, he stepped over to glance inside the open door.

A portly man with a bald head and a wrinkled face was sitting in the blue shadow of the interior. He had small bright eyes that at once fixed themselves on de la Rueda.

'Come in, young man. Come in.'

De la Rueda stepped inside.

'You are not here to buy,' the shopkeeper went on, conversationally. 'A book maybe?'

De la Rueda laughed. 'I have nowhere to keep one. And it will be more than I can afford.'

The shopkeeper nodded. 'I bought the contents of a whole house last month. No one in the family was left so it all went to auction. These chairs, books, those two trunks and that picture over there, it is all from the house...'

The picture was resting against a wall on top of an oak chest of drawers. It was in a carved gilt frame shaped as though with layers of leaves. The strong sunlight, coming through the doorway, caught the edge of the painting but not sufficiently for de la Rueda to see it clearly. Mildly curious, he stepped around a table piled with books, marquetry boxes, a standing mirror, and other items, and stopping close to the painting, staring at it, he saw his fate.

How could he ever know why? He was in an uncommon mood that day. The notion that he would soon be going into battle for the first time no doubt had an influence. He was afraid of what was coming but at the same time he was eager, strangely joyous. And while he knew his duty was to violence and blood, yet he felt his soul light within him; not murky, weighed down in his flesh, but clean, chaste, submissive to a power higher than himself. So perhaps, in that receptive condition, he was able to see beyond mere pigment, beyond even what the painter of the portrait had intended. For the portrait was not of special magnificence. Even de la Rueda, who had little knowledge of art, could tell that the outline was perhaps too soft, and the tones perhaps too even. Also he could make out brushstrokes in the black background. But the longer he stared at the portrait of the head and shoulders of a young woman, which is what the entire painting consisted of, the less the imprecision of its execution appeared to matter. Before his eyes it was as if some kind of divine witchery were taking place, giving the portrait a life beyond anything the painter had attempted or wished for. He did not judge the woman either beautiful or angelic but she was striking. A foreign woman, possibly, for her hair – piled up in ringlets, and it appeared to be her hair, not a wig – was red. A dullish auburn in the actuality of the painting but in his mind already a vivid gingery red such as he had seen rarely, and then only in French women. The plumpness of her pale, powdered cheeks, and the prominent bump in the bridge of her nose, marred her feminine delicacy with a coarseness that, however, for de la Rueda was an instant source of fascination. But above all it was her eyes. They were large and pale green and de la Rueda had the uncanny certainty that they were not a fiction, that the artist could have painted them better or worse, angry or sad, a hundred different ways, and it would make no difference. The intangible essence that he perceived was not in the pigment. It was somewhere in the space of his own mind. He had the sense that through the woman's painted image he was looking back at himself. She was not here in the flesh. She was not present. Yet he *knew* her. He did not doubt that somewhere she existed. He felt her in his soul, suddenly, like a shard of glass.

That had transpired eleven years ago. He had not asked the shopkeeper anything about the painting. To speak of it at all felt like sacrilege. Nor had he contemplated trying to purchase it. Besides having little money and nowhere to store it he knew that he would not need to look at it again. He would carry the woman's image, as she appeared in his mind, wherever he went.

And so he had. The mysterious essence of her look had never deserted him. The battle that he experienced two days later was severe. Some of it was reduced to sword in hand. He killed two men and received several cuts himself. After such a strong experience he could have expected his encounter with the painting to show false and pass like a fleeting whimsy. But it had not. Neither had it passed after he had lost his virginity to a whore, for he had been a virgin when he came across the painting. The battle, however, changed him. Everyone is changed by their first encounter with death and carnage. Afterwards he felt a thirst for life. The fornicating and drinking, the duelling and gambling, the wild excesses that he saw soldiers indulge in no longer appeared to him so unappealing. 'Less church and more brothel, de la Rueda,' his lieutenant used to advise. The lieutenant, of course, was not taking into account that he was a Jew – a convert but nevertheless a Jew. Caution, the fear of discovery, was never far away, for while the Inquisition was dormant it had not been abolished. Now and then one heard of some poor *marrano* being punished or expelled from the land. Convert Jews such as himself were advised to become more pious and better Christians than the Christians themselves. But after the battle self-restraint did not bring de la Rueda comfort and he did not feel innocent any more. Something of the wholeness of life was shattered for him. His mind sought oblivion, but his senses indulgence. Off duty he began to drink and gamble. The camp whores he managed to avoid because they were diseased and because there was not one of them that attracted him. But after his regiment moved to the north, one time his platoon was sent to the garrison at Salamanca for supplies. The troops had one night of freedom in the city. De la Rueda went drinking with companions in a seedy tavern. A dark haired woman with skin like ivory became bold and sat on his lap. He could feel her haunches pressing down on his cock and her hair brushing his face. He was somewhat drunk by then but cognizant of events. Abruptly she appeared to become nervous. She said she had seen her husband just come through the door and she must leave right away. She wanted him to go with her. He did. Leaving his companions behind he followed the woman out through the back of the tavern. There in the alley way she pressed herself against him, she put her hand on his cock. He became erect. He would have taken her there, in the open, but the woman wanted a room. She said she was afraid her husband would find them. There was another tavern down the alley that had rooms. De la Rueda had decided it was time. He was not concerned as to the degree of the woman's sincerity. What mattered to him was that she had succeeded in arousing him and he wanted to lose his virginity. De la Rueda paid for a room above the tavern. They fell onto the bed at once. The woman was eager. The feel of her body, firm yet soft, rounded and fluid, came to him as a surprise. He had a good idea of what he needed to do from seeing animals, and on several occasions people, doing it, but he was clumsy and he fumbled to find his way in between her legs. She was helping him when at that very moment the door burst open and a man came in and around the side of the bed brandishing a sword. Before de la Rueda could disengage himself the man had adroitly seized de la Rueda's own weapons, which were on a chair by the bed, and now he was shouting at the woman, 'Whore, whore. I am going to kill you!' De la Rueda got off the woman, confused and alarmed that the man had taken hold of his weapons. He feared he would have to defend the woman barehanded. The woman made a show of weeping. But the man would not be appeased. Square set, with a moustachio and glaring eyes, he declared the woman his wife and began to demand from de la Rueda compensation. De la Rueda, getting dressed but without his weapons, began to realize he had been set up. It was all a show. She was a whore and he was being robbed, but without his weapons he had no defence. He was forced to hand over every coin he had. Wisely the robbers did not take his weapons, for that would have caused more provocation than it was worth. Even so, de la Rueda was furious and ashamed. Once armed again he went in pursuit but by then the robbers had vanished.

Over the years there had been other women. Some had been whores. In Spanish Holland he had had an affair of several months with a Dutch widow. She was a good woman and he was sad to part from her when, after the campaign, his regiment embarked to Spain. And a few times he had met women that under another star could have led to intimacy, even love. But fate was against it. Life carried them in different currents. Perhaps if the allure had been sufficient he would have risked all – military career, reputation, all to cross over, but he had held back, hesitated, and before he knew it the object of his desire was gone, out of reach. *She is not the one. When I meet the one I shall be seized like I was with the woman in the painting.* And sometimes, in his fantasies, he dared to imagine that it was her, not the painted image of her, but her in the flesh that he would meet. Of course it was absurd. He could see clearly that the notion of coming upon the incarnation of a painted image had no grounding in reality. It had been a mental aberration, a folly of his youth. Yet for all that he could not quite let go of the belief in its possibility. Greater miracles had happened in life. Had not our Lord Jesus raised Lazarus from the dead? Had not Moses parted the very sea and the Mother of God answered all manner of prayers? If God when planning the destiny of mankind had arranged, in His almighty wisdom, for him one day to meet the woman of his dreams, the woman in the painting, why then should he be one to disbelieve? So while his realist self had put her out of mind, relegating her to idle moments of fantasy, his more credulous self, the one that believed in the world that could not be seen, had felt her presence all the while in his soul, like a shard of glass. And waited, quietly waited.

But this? A married woman? The wife of the man who had saved his life? No, it could not be. Lying in the dark he concentrated hard to locate differences in the face of the woman and the face in the painting. And certainly, when he thought about it, it seemed to him that they did not match so closely after all. The woman had a face that was narrower, not so fresh; definitely older, sharper, a more experienced expression, and their mouths were not the same. The woman in the painting had a mouth that was small and perfectly formed – heart shaped – but the other had thin lips. He had not seen but for a small part the woman's hair, for she kept it covered, so he could not be sure even if they had the same colour hair. Was it not possible he was making too much over too little; fabricating similarities? Or mistaking minor similarities for true likeness? That is how the very Devil employed his guile. He tricked your mind. He put temptation in your path by confounding you with false images until you could no longer say the difference between honour and dishonour, virtue and sin, good and evil. For it was sinful, of that he had no doubt, to be lying here entertaining thoughts of the woman as anything other than the wife of the man who had saved his life. *I will leave tomorrow. Or the day after at the latest. I shall make my way back by one means or another to the church and I will put myself at the mercy of the priest. If I must thenceforth surrender to the enemy as I suppose my colonel and the regiment have done, so be it. And if I am to be imprisoned or executed, so be it. What*

I cannot do is open myself to the Devil's guile. I will not sacrifice my honour. I will not be damned. I will not!

Alarmed by a sense of profound moral danger, as if already he could detect the first whiff of sulphur, de la Rueda threw the blankets off, stood up, and with his hands interlocked at his chest he began pacing in the dark by the side of the bed. He prayed to God for protection – against his own weakness, against false images, against the loss of his honour.

While de la Rueda prayed, Shona at last fell asleep. One minute she was hunched over, her foot pushing on the pedal that turned the spinning wheel and the next she had fallen back in her chair and was asleep. When she woke up she went into the bedroom. Hector was asleep as before. Once more she lay down on the bed, but thoughts crowded her mind. Abruptly, reaching a decision, she stood up, wrapped her arisaid about her, and left the house. Outside it had stopped raining. The owl had stopped hooting but now a cuckoo sounded in a tree nearby. The sky was clear, a pale purple scattered with tiny stars. It was yet an hour or two before dawn but there was light to see by. Walking quickly, Shona followed the path across the burn and by a field furrowed and planted with growing bear. On the other side of the field was a cluster of houses. Shona stopped before one of them and knocked hard on the door. After a moment Elsbeth's voice came from the other side. Shona replied and Elsbeth opened the door.

'I am sorry to disturb your sleep, Elsbeth.'

'Is it Hector?'

'No. He is sleeping. Can I speak to Neil?'

Elsbeth stepped aside.

'I will wait here,' said Shona.

Neil came out, adjusting his plaid. His shorn hair stuck up in tufts, his eyes were inflamed and wild. Immediately Shona regretted having disturbed him.

'I am sorry, Neil. You can have all this day to rest if you wish. I am sure you must need it.'

Neil was silent but his expression eased.

'I need to ask you about the foreigner. Do you know if he is an officer?'

'He is. There was only one or two above him.'

'Is he hiding for his life, Neil. Or is there another reason he is here?'

Neil pulled on the end of his long beard, frowning.

'I cannot say why the Spaniard is not with his kind, Shona. But after I came down from the battlefield with Hector and the Spaniard, I was speaking to some men. They told me they had witnessed Hector go to the assistance of the Spaniard.'

'When? During the battle?'

'They were with Hector.'

'Were you not?'

'I was. But Hector, seeing that Rob Roy was getting into difficulty further up the hill, sent me and others to help out against the enemy and what happened with the Spaniard was later. But John the Cobbler and the others who were with Hector will know what happened – it may be, if they saw it.'

'Why would they not?'

Neil gave a shrug of his strong shoulders. 'When you are fighting strong yourself you see little that is not before your eyes..'

'Were you told what assistance the Spaniard received from Hector?'

'The Spaniard was outnumbered by the enemy, and I believe Hector arrived in time to help dispatch the assailants. John the Cobbler said Hector saved the Spaniard's life. I know not else, Shona, but those that were there may tell you more.'

Shona fell silent. It could be a day or several before the others returned. But she had found out sufficient to think on. It could explain what the Spaniard was doing here, though it was confusing to her emotions where her husband was concerned. Once again it appeared that she was receiving impressions of him that conflicted with her intensely. How was she to judge when there was so much at odds in him?

'Thank you, Neil. I will not trouble you again today.'

'Och, you have never troubled me, Shona. It was of my own free will that I followed you here.'

Shona was moved. Unexpectedly she remembered her father, for Neil's father, also called Neil, had served her father. He had been one of those who crewed her father's boat and tended his cattle. Shona had spent many hours with Neil and his sister when she was a child. She could remember small childhood secrets with Neil known only to the two of them.

Shona sighed. 'It is not the same, Neil. Everything is changing. Look at that Donald of the War, how they say he neglected his kin. I fear the trust is going. That is what I see. And it is starting to happen everywhere. Even my husband… ach, for some folk who forget the old ways it is all about making a profit.'

'I heard more folk were being thrown out on the White Sands bhaile. The one belonging to Mackinnon. They will be having nowhere to go now.'

'Will they be headed this way?'

'For the Lowlands it may be, more likely. There is work to be had in the mines I am told.'

'God help them. The mines are no good place from what I hear… Well, I am happy to have you back, Neil. And I am glad you are safe.'

Neil was silent. Women had their own anguish, he knew, but the violent anguish of battle was not one of them.

As Shona returned to the house the crow of the cockerel joined the call of the cuckoo. To the east the sky was turning a pale pinkish lavender. Shona's skin felt warm. *It is going to be hot today.*

Mairi was already up when Shona entered the house.

'Do you know who there is to fetch MacQueen?'

Mairi stood adjusting her clothes and kertch. 'That will be Roddy. The boy is fleet of foot, like his father.'

'Is he not in the shielings?'

'His mother will have stayed. He has come back to finish some jobs by the house. He was asking after his father but I could not tell him.'

Roddy's father was one of their runners. He was also one of those who had gone to battle with Hector and, though due back at any time, had not yet showed up.

'Can you go to the boy now. Will he know the way?'

'I expect so.'

'He is to say to the physician that my husband has been wounded in battle and to come at once. That is all.'

Mairi went out.

Although the day promised to be hot the peat fire was never left to go out. When needed, however, it had to be cleared of ashes. Shona, noticing now, picked up a wooden pail nearby and with a straw brush and a small wooden shovel began to pile in the surplus ash. Once the bucket was full she carried it out of the house and to the far end of the stables were she scattered it on a gentle slope that was gradually being levelled and over which a thin, mossy grass was growing. On her way back the Spanish gentleman appeared to her. He was stepping out of the barn but he saw her at the same instant and they both stopped. For de la Rueda it was as if he had not seen her before, as if it were for the first time. All the thoughts that had troubled him through the night were momentarily displaced. Her presence there, standing by the house, was like that of a divine apparition. He did not think of good or bad, of right or wrong. *It is her, the woman in the painting.* And it was a thought reinforced by a first sight of her hair; for she wore no hood or cloth over it and while not piled up in ringlets, as in the painting, it was nevertheless red – long, thick and red.

His clothes are filthy. I must see that his clothes are washed. As she turned to enter the house she saw his head bow to her and felt his eyes on her back. The peculiarity of it was that she did not object. She did not feel herself threatened. Rather, she wondered what it was that made him stare at her so? At the door, when she was about to close it behind her, she glanced up and saw him standing as he had been. His scarred, unshaven face was rigid, but the intensity of his stare also contained softness, a child-like wonder. A little flustered, leaving a door ajar, for it did not seem proper to close it entirely, she passed through the store room, put the empty pail down, and went into the bedroom.

Hector was lying on his back. Through the window the first shaft of dawn light illuminated the upper part of his torso. As Shona went to the beside his head turned slightly and his eyelids flickered open.

'Oh, you are awake!'

Recognition came into his grey eyes.

'I believed I was dreaming.'

'No. You are at home.'

Shona touched his brow at the edge of the bandage. Her fingers came away damp.

'My head is sore.'

'You are wounded, Hector. I have sent for Alisdair MacQueen. With his help and God's you will mend.'

'My mouth is dry. I need tò piss.'

Shona went to the commode and removed the chamber pot, which after using hours before she had emptied and washed, and took it to the bed. Lifting the bottom part of his shirt, she placed the ceramic chamber pot between his legs and lifted his penis to the edge of it. Hector grunted and winced. Finally a trickle issued into the pot. Shona wondered how they were going to manage if Hector needed to shit. Margaret they could sit on the commode mornings and evenings, but she doubted Hector would be well enough to sit for a while. They would have to hold him in place, she supposed.

'Are you hungry?' Shona asked, when Hector was done.

He shook his head. 'Water.'

Shona went to the common room, poured water from a flagon into a pewter cup and went back to the bedroom. She sat on the edge of the bed, gently lifted the back of Hector's head, and placed the cup to his lips.

'A foreign gentleman,' said Shona, standing over him after he had drank, 'a Spanish officer I believe, accompanied you here.'

Hector was silent, his eyelids closed, but just as Shona thought he was going to fall asleep again, he opened his eyes.

'I remember. I went to his aid.'

'Well, he has accompanied you home.'

'Is he here?'

'I have accommodated him in the barn.'

Again Hector closed his eyes.

'I may see him now.'

Shona put her hand on his shoulder.

'Later. I will bring him to you later.'

'I have an axe in my head,' Hector said.

Shona went into the common room. The cauldron was dry. She lowered the chain and poured water into it. When the water warmed she and Mairi could bring it down and give it a good clean. For breakfast she could make porridge. Or bannock. Bannock and ale, she decided. Moving to the barrels and the sideboard that was against the front wall of the room, under the window opposite the table, she placed flour into a bowl and mixed it with water and a pinch of salt. Afterwards she flattened it with her hand and put it on a metal skillet which she rested on a tripod over the fire. While the bannock was cooking she went back and poured herself a draught of ale from the beer keg.

It felt too warm by the fire, so Shona took her breakfast over to the table. She ate quickly, breaking up the bannock with her fingers and washing it down with gulps of beer. Disparate thoughts crowded her mind, some unexpected and disturbing. Pushing them away, she turned her mind to household chores, but soon she was distracted by the notion of her need to communicate, presently, with the Spanish gentleman. Going to the book cabinet she removed the English-French dictionary, bound in brown Morocco, and brought it over to the table. Sitting down again, she went through the coarse pages, looking for words that would fit the sentences she started constructing in her mind.

When Mairi returned an hour later, Shona was still at the table with the dictionary open in front of her.

'It is done. The boy went off fast as a hare.'

'Hector was awake earlier. May it please God to help him… Did you see our guest outside?'

'I did not.'

'He was by the barn door when I went out. His uniform is black when we are told it is yellow. Shall we see what he can wear while we wash his attire? And he has not yet eaten.'

'Nor have I.'

'I will see to Margaret, then, while you eat,' said Shona. 'Afterwards we can attend to the guest.'

Hector was sleeping when Shona went past the bed. In the box room Margaret was awake but utterly silent. Lately Shona was doubtful that Margaret recognized her. Margaret lived in her own world, far away from everything and everyone. Folk said that when people went strange like that it was because of the fairies. Shona did not doubt that fairies existed. She had seen their glow often. Everyone had. But if it was fairies it would not be the Seelie Court. Only the Unseelie Court, who were the Devil's own, would be so cruel as to enslave Margaret's mind.

Margaret was obedient when Shona got her to rise and sit on the commode. More impatient than usual, Shona gave Margaret perfunctory attendance before leading her out to her chair in the common room. By then Mairi had finished eating. The two women went back into the bedroom and opened Hector's clothes trunk. There were several spare shirts of Hector's, and folded at the bottom of the trunk was also an old plaid that had belonged to The Experimenter and which Hector never wore.

'The shirt will be too big for the Spanish gentleman,' said Mairi.

'It will have to do,' said Shona.

The women left the house together, Mairi carrying the clothes. When they could not spot de la Rueda, Shona, overcoming her reluctance, banged on the barn door. De la Rueda was returning from the burn where he had drunk water and tried to clean himself up when he heard the noise. Coming around the side of the barn he was overcome again the moment he saw Shona.

'Bonjour, Monseuir.'

De la Rueda pulled himself together, bowing from the waist. *Do not be an imbecile.*

'Give them to him.'

Mairi proffered the clothes.

Shona tried to smile as she pointed to his uniform.

'Ah, *merci Madame.*' De la Rueda took hold of the clothes.

How do I say it? I have forgotten. Shona frowned, resorting to gesticulations. 'If you please, for… for eat,' she managed.

'Ah *Oui. Merci.* Thank you. I will change.' De la Rueda bowed again, avoiding her eyes, and went into the barn.

'I think he understood,' said Shona.

Mairi shook her head. 'I have not heard you speak a foreign tongue until now.'

'I did not know I could remember to speak it myself.'

In the barn de la Rueda did not know what to do with the plaid. He had discussed the garment with the Irish officers and had an idea how it was assembled, but was not inclined to attempt it now. In the event the shirt, when he put it on, came down to his knees, and under these he could retain the long woollen underpants he had put on just some days ago on the eve of the battle. Though not ideal, he judged the combination passably decent.

When he came out, Mairi held her arms up to take his dirty uniform. For a second Shona had an impulse to giggle, but at once she was mortified by her levity. Hiding a blush, she lowered her head, turned, and went back into the house. De la Rueda followed.

In the common room Shona asked Mairi to serve the gentleman ale and bannock and showed de la Rueda to a chair by the table. All the while she avoided looking at him, and she did not speak to him more than to say, *'Excusez moi.* Excuse me,' before proceeding to the bedroom. Hector had his eyes closed. Shona went into the box room and stripped Margaret's bed and then began to gather various garments that needed washing along with the sheets and the gentleman's uniform.

De la Rueda sat at the table, waiting while Mairi made his breakfast. He assumed she would be a servant, but he was less certain about the diminutive old woman who sat in a chair by the hearth staring out with a look so blank it did not appear to register his presence. Was she a relation? The room itself, he thought, was lived in, comfortable without being overtly luxurious. Two hens were pecking on the floor near the old woman. The floor itself, he noticed, was of stone. And there were two silver candlesticks and odd pieces of worthy furniture, including the bookcase, and a small gold framed painting of a bird. The hearth, which was under its own roof attached to the gable end, was not so different from ones in his own country. Here they burned peat as opposed to wood but as peasants and farmers did at home they sat close to the fire, under the hearth itself. The difference, it seemed to him, was that here such a home was for the gentry. Not the nobility maybe, but certainly it would seem for the gentry, whereas at home the houses of the gentry were better appointed. His own house, indeed, compared to this, was palatial.

De la Rueda was thinking of home, picturing the house he had not seen for five years, when Mairi came up to the table and served him bannock and a jar of ale. From where he sat, breakfasting, he was not able to see Shona leave the house with an armful of washing. Outside she dumped the washing on the long grass and went back into the house for a wooden washtub which she managed to lift by its handles and carry outside. But when she went back to the bedroom for more washing she found Hector awake.

'Does your head still hurt?' she asked him.

'I have an axe in it. And now my arm hurts, too.'

'Alisdair MacQueen may bring a remedy. We are waiting for him. And the Spanish gentleman is here breakfasting. Would you care to see him now?'

Hector nodded.

Shona went to the common room. De la Rueda, who had finished eating, put down the jar of ale. In spite of himself he was wishing she would look at him. He wanted her eyes to meet his. He wanted to see just how green they were and if they matched the eyes in his memory, if there was the same expression hidden somewhere within them. *If she looks at me I may tell.* But as his eyes fell on her she averted her face, looking away and down as she spoke.

'Hector... my husband... if you please...'

De la Rueda understood. He stood up and followed her to the bedroom.

'Ah *Monsieur*, you are awake now. Excellent. Excellent.'

Hector recognized the man stepping up to his bedside. But just. Unshaven, without uniform or wig, de la Rueda could have been a stranger were it not for the familiar narrow scar down the side of his face and the near black close-set eyes. As for events, Hector's memory of them was disjointed, jumbled, and his headache would not let him think. When he tried to answer de la Rueda in French he could not think of the words.

'*Merci*,' was all he managed to say, finally.

De la Rueda waited. When no more came, he nodded and laid his hand on Hector's arm.

'On the contrary, it is I who am obligated. You did more than your duty.'

Hector was not at all certain what de la Rueda was talking about, but something in the words soothed him.

'*Merci*,' he said again. And then in Gaelic. 'Water. Is there water?'

Shona poured water into a bowl and moved past de la Rueda to the head of the bed. De la Rueda stepped back to make room. He tried not to stare, but even with the man who had saved his life lying before him, de la Rueda could not prevent his gaze from straying towards her, noticing the strong curve of her hip under the long brown dress as she leaned over to help her husband drink.

When Shona had finished, she left the room without a word. De la Rueda waited, not sure what to expect. Hector lay with eyes closed. Sounds came from beyond the bedroom, but eventually when Shona did not return, de la Rueda left the room. Now that he had seen Hector, his thoughts turned once more to his departure. He must leave at the earliest possible opportunity. He was a soldier. A gentleman. He could not deny the fierce turbulence of his emotions but he trusted himself to behave with honour. *I must not let myself fall. I must not be a fool.*

Outside, de la Rueda saw Shona and Mairi carrying between them the washtub full of clothes towards the burn. He halted by the barn door and, since the sun was reaching it, he sat down on the wooden doorstop and leaned his back against the door. A smell of manure wafted towards him. A cow appeared from behind the byre at the far end of the main house. Behind the cow came Old John, so filthy he looked as though he had climbed out of the earth. De la Rueda recognized him as one of the men who had helped ferry Hector from the seashore. The shaggy black cow was left to feed on the grass and the old man disappeared again behind the stables only to appear shortly afterwards behind three shaggy goats with their hind legs hobbled. The goats, too, were left to browse on the grass. Meanwhile, nearer to the burn and closer to de la Rueda, Shona and Mairi had filled the washtub with pails of water and were now bent over the tub soaping the clothes. They were some thirty yards distant and the branches of trees and clusters of bracken and blackberry interfered with de la Rueda's view of them, but not entirely, for he saw the servant woman place some washing in the water of the burn itself while the mistress – for it was her and not the servant – he saw hoist her dress up above her knees, exposing the whiteness of her bare thighs, before stepping into the tub itself and stomping her legs in a steady, sinuous manner.

De la Rueda felt a thud in his heart. He began to stand up, caught himself in the act, and sat down again. Deliberately he turned his face away, looking towards the animals. *I must ask her. She speaks French little and poorly but I will find a way. I cannot go away without asking her. I must know.*

FIFTEEN

Alasdair MacQueen arrived on horseback in the early afternoon. He was a hunchback, but were the hunch discounted, the rest of him, even now in middle age, was remarkably handsome. He had fine bones, clear blue eyes, and thick wavy grey hair. After dismounting from the pony, Alasdair removed two wooden boxes from the small panniers behind the saddle and with one box under each arm he limped into the house.

Hector was ten years younger than Alasdair but the men knew each other because they were distant cousins on their mothers' side. Both Alasdair's parents were dead and they had not left much of an inheritance, but Alasdair had done well as a physician and herbalist. Though his skill was disputed he was much in demand for those who could afford him. Thus, when Hector opened his eyes, after a moment of confusion he experienced a glimmer of hope when he recognized Alasdair by his side.

'I am here now, Hector,' said Alasdair, in a low, soothing voice. 'Are you in pain?'

'My head most.'

'I have something for your pain.'

Alasdair opened one of the wooden boxes. Inside it was divided into sundry compartments holding glass vials and little jars. One of the vials contained a potent tincture of henbane and other herbs, a few drops of which he administered to Hector by means of a miniature horn spoon. Minutes later Hector was senseless.

Shona stood by while Alasdair attended to Hector. It anguished her to see the extent of Hector's wounds when bandages were removed or partially removed with the aid of cold water.

'I believe the surgeon was Arnott of Inverinate. He has done a good job with Hector's head. He has been trepanned – see? Here – and the wound is clean.' Alasdair sniggered. 'No doubt Arnott will stop by for his fee when Hector recovers.'

Shona put her hand to her breast. 'God be praised.'

'The cut here on his arm I do not think is of great concern… Now, let us see what there is.'

Alasdair opened the second box, which contained compartments of powders and unguents. After he had finished mixing potions and transferring them to paper sachets he gave Shona instructions. Unlike some, Alasdair did not believe wounds of the flesh should be left unattended. His teacher, who had studied under the last Beaton of Skye, had taught him to treat wounds with clean water infused with hypericum and other herbs and to change bandages with the waxing of the moon. This knowledge he now imparted to Shona. Before he left he also passed her a vial containing an unguent. And last but not least, a good sized ceramic bottle of laudanum. He told Shona Hector must take the laudanum only when he was in severe pain. Should his fever return with persistence or his wounds swell and suppurate, Shona was to send for him again. Otherwise he would stop by in two weeks, by which time he expected to see Hector making a good recovery. No mention was made of a fee. Alasdair fully intended to charge a high price, for all that Hector was a cousin, but it could wait.

Shona went out with Alasdair to his mount and stood watching as he rode off. She felt relief now that she had an idea of how to look after Hector and had reason to believe he would improve. But at the same time she was aware that the fierce resentment had not gone away, that it was there still, buried tight inside her like a clenched fist. *I cannot face it now. When he can fend for himself I will confront him.*

When Shona went back into the house Mairi had collected several eggs from the hens. But one of the older hens had stopped laying. Shona found it outside, near the stables pecking on the ground with the others. She clucked it to her, showing it a handful of barley, grabbed it, trapped it between her knees, and with both hands twisted the hen's neck sharply until it broke. Back in the house she gave the hen to Mairi to pluck, then found an old receipt that was no longer of use and sitting at the table, with the French dictionary to help her, she wrote on the back of the receipt in pencil an invitation in French for the gentleman to dine at his convenience after sunset. Duty and good manners required it, she told herself. However, she was nervous, and she did not think it proper to approach the gentleman herself, so she sent Mairi, along with a pencil and an enamelled carriage clock.

De la Rueda was lying on his straw mattress dozing when he heard the knock on the barn door. Hardened as he was, the events of the last few weeks had begun to wear on his strength. And the delirious but portentous encounter with the woman was leaving him further exhausted.

Rising, he went over to open the door. In silence Mairi presented him with the note. De la Rueda read it, took the pencil and wrote a brief reply in French. He shook his head at the clock. With a polite smile be reached into the pocket of his silk waistcoat and pulled out a watch, showing it to her.

De la Rueda arrived at the house unshaven but bathed and wearing the clean uniform, which had dried quickly in the sun. Shona had gone to the trouble to put on a striped wool skirt over her petticoat and her best flounced, pink silk shirt, a garment she had not worn more than twice in the last few years. She also wore a silver pendant. She knew that in society women wore their hair exposed and elaborately arranged, but besides not having the time or means, a sense of modesty prevailed on her to keep her hair out of view, coiled under a finely embroidered kertch. For the same reason she did not powder her cheeks or dress up in the one society frock she owned or her double heeled red shoes. *My husband is grave, this is not a time for frivolity.* Even so, when Mairi showed de la Rueda into the common room she rose from her chair by the table and as he stopped before her she did something she had not done until that moment: she showed her face to him in full and lifted her eyes to meet his.

De la Rueda felt himself sway. Her eyes were the green of Bishop Torres' emerald ring. They were pools into which he could feel himself yearning to dive, for like pools they rippled with shadow and light and tantalizing depths. With a wrench, and a hollow feeling in his gut, he pulled his own eyes away from hers and bowed deep from the waist.

'*Bonsoir, Madame.*'

Shona made herself smile. '*Bonsoir.*' She indicated a chair across the table that was usually Hector's.

'Mairi, fetch the claret and come and sit down yourself to accompany me.'

Mairi preferred where she was. Nevertheless she came over with the three engraved short-stemmed glasses Shona had removed earlier from storage, and a bottle of French wine, one of several that Hector had procured two years before on a journey to Inverness.

De la Rueda watched Shona's hands; the competent motion of them as she employed a knife to peel the wax from the cork. When she filled the glasses the wine glowed a deep red in the soft evening light coming from the window behind the table.

De la Rueda waited until Shona raised her glass.

'*Slante mhaith,*' she toasted in Gaelic

'*Salud,*' de la Rueda responded.

Shona, who had learnt about wine from her father, judged it drinkable. De la Rueda, who had tasted much better, did not care. Mairi did not like 'foreign drink'. She liked a tipple, however, so she drank it.

De la Rueda noticed the book, bound in expensive Morocco, on the table.

'*Dictionnaire,*'

'Ah, *dictionnaire.*' de la Rueda nodded. 'May I?'

He opened the book. The English words meant nothing to him.

'How did you learn French?'

Shona looked at him blankly.

De la Rueda went to the French-English section and found the word learn. He turned the book around and pointed.

Of course. Apprendre. But it is the way he pronounces it.

'I… when… *petite*,' she said. 'Little.'

'Teacher?' asked de la Rueda. 'You had a teacher?'

Shona understood. She was pleased. '*Oui*.'

'I will see to the dinner.' Mairi put down her glass and stood up.

'*Madame*...' de la Rueda paused. His heart was beating fast. '*Madame*, I have question...' He paused again, trying to think of simple words. 'When you are young. Someone paint you?'

Shona did not wholly understand. *He is asking me a question. Something about when I was young. And why does he look at me so fierce?*

De la Rueda seized the dictionary.

He turned the dictionary and pointed to *dessiner*, the entry for draw, then raised two pinched fingers and made drawing gestures in the air.

Shona remained confused. *Is he asking me if I can draw?*

De la Rueda seized the dictionary again. This time he found the entry for portrait. He showed it to her. 'When you are young. When you are young,' he repeated.

Mairi came over with the blue and white porcelain bowls taken out for the occasion and started laying the table. She sensed a strange sort of tension. The foreign gentleman was staring at Shona with unabashed directness. Shona had a look of astonishment, and as if in a spell.

The portrait! How could he know? Impossible… Hector. Of course. Hector knew.

'My… my...' Husband. *Mari.* Is it *mari? 'Mon mari* – he speak with you, *Monsieur*?'

De la Rueda frowned. 'About your portrait?'

Shona understood his question, for the French word portrait sounded very much like the English word, which Shona recognized.

'Yes.'

'No, *Madame*. Not about that. Not portrait. He did not speak to me about that. But it is true?'

Shona understood but she did not reply immediately. Who if it was not her husband? Who? The artist himself was dead. Unless it was before he died that the gentleman had seen it? She could not think of another explanation. It seemed incredible, impossible that he could have seen the portrait that painter had done of her. Fairy mischief. Was it fairy mischief?

'You... my...' What was the word? '... um... Portrait, *Monsieur*? You...' Shona raised a finger and tapped under her eye.

De la Rueda slumped back in his chair. He could feel the strength, and along with it the tension, draining from his body.

'I saw it, *Madame*.' He counted on his fingers. 'Nine years ago. I saw the portrait in my country.'

Shona eyebrows drew close.

De la Rueda leaned forward, resorting to the dictionary. 'Spain,' he said, pointing to the entry for country and then to himself. 'Spain. My country.' He began to gesticulate. 'I saw your portrait. Do you understand? *Your* portrait.'

Mairi arrived with the broiled chicken on a plate. Shona moved the dictionary aside, stood up, and with her hands and a knife began carving the chicken. She did not know the word for 'serve' so sitting down again she just indicated the chicken and said, 'If you please.'

De la Rueda was not hungry, chicken though it be. His stomach was in a knot, but he served himself nonetheless. Shona was glad of the distraction. It gave her time to compose herself. She concentrated on the chicken, holding a bone in her hand and chewing on it. De la Rueda, doing the same, though more gingerly, noticed that Shona had good teeth. Mairi, who had few teeth, pulled the meat off the bone before putting it in her mouth.

When Shona had finished she licked her fingers, dried them on her skirt under the table, and opened the dictionary. She looked up a couple of words.

'*Pardon Monsieur*,' she said, finally. 'You acquaint... with *Monsieur* de Medina?'

De la Rueda shook his head. 'No, *Madame*. I am not acquainted with the gentleman. Who is he?'

'He...' It was now Shona who made a painting gesture.

'He painted your portrait?'

'Yes.'

De Medina. A name like mine... Another Jew! How was so much coincidence possible?

'He is Spanish? From my country?'

Shona resorted to the dictionary.

'He is dead.'

'But from Spain? From my country?'

Shona lifted her hands and shrugged. He had lived in Edinburgh. Sir John Baptiste de Medina. A famous painter, knighted by Queen Anne. The last man knighted before the cursed Union, it was said. He spoke no Gaelic, but they had spoken in English. Had he told her he came from the continent? Perhaps he *had* said something about Spain. But it was long ago, she could not quite recall. He kept wanting to touch her. She could only think of fending him off.

'Monsieur de Medina… he live… Edinburgh...'

Expelled Jews, thought de la Rueda. Had not the merchant in the shop told him the portrait came from the house of someone who had lived in foreign lands?

'So *Monsieur* de Medina is dead, *Madame*?'

'*Oui. Mort*. Yes. Dead.'

'*Quand?*'

When? Did he mean when? Shona tried to remember. She did not know what year the artist had died but Hector had found out when he went on business again to Edinburgh. It was while the children were still alive. On his return he had told her the rascal was dead and several husbands were not displeased, including himself.

'Many years.' she said. 'He dead.'

'In Edinburgh? He paint your portrait in Edinburgh?'

'Yes.'

De la Rueda was silent. He looked down at the table, then, raising his eyes, watching her all the while, he began speaking, again in the present tense, and with the aid of constant gestures, repetitions, and the dictionary.

'I see the portrait in a shop… I am in a place with many people…. Ciudad Rodrigo. It has name: Ciudad Rodrigo…. I fight in battle but I never forget… Do you understand? Your face is with me always. I am wounded in battle many times. Do you understand?... Many battles... I wounded… Battle... I am dead. But I see your face and I live. I live again. Do you understand? I am not dead. Not dead. I live again!'

Abruptly de la Rueda felt himself becoming undone. He had said too much. Revealed too much. It was for him a strange and rare feeling. It was not the way he behaved. He could see himself falling at her feet now, sobbing like a child, but these were things that would besmirch his honour, which he could not allow. With an effort he straightened his back, turned his eyes from her, and stood up.

'Excuse me, M*adame*, if you please.'

He bowed deeply from the waist, turned, and walked to the door.

'Well,' said Mairi. 'The gentleman has gone soon.'

Shona did not respond.

Mairi stood up and began collecting the plates.

Shona came to herself and began helping clear the table. Afterwards the two women took bowls of chicken broth into the bedroom. While Mairi went to the box bed to feed Margaret, Shona sat on the edge of the bed, woke Hector up, and fed him.

'Is this chicken I taste?' asked Hector.

'It is.'

'It is good.'

'Do you feel better?'

'I think I do.'

'Are you still in pain?'

'Some. It is more tolerable now.'

After Hector had been fed, Shona did not want to lie down and neither did she want to stay in the common room with Mairi, so she went out of the house and sat on the bench. The air was balmy, redolent of the sea, and there were no biting midges for it was still too early in the season.

How uncanny it was that the gentleman had seen her portrait, and in such a faraway country. Of course, de Medina, though a Scot, was born foreign. Part Spanish. And the father of children older than her, so perhaps it was one of his children who had taken the portrait to Spain? When she had met him he had been with his wife. It was only the second time Shona had ventured further than Inverness. To Inverness she had travelled more often but only twice to Glasgow and Edinburgh. It was the year before the children were born. The Experimenter was dead; Hector needed to be in Edinburgh to untangle the complicated money matters his father had left behind. He was to be gone for the summer months. Rather than leave her behind he had proposed she go with him. Of course she had agreed. De Medina was at that grand party they attended at Lord Thomson's home. Before they left he had asked to paint her portrait. For the sake of it, he insisted. He said he had never seen a face with so many adverse yet captivating proportions. Shona was confused. Did he mean the bump on the bridge of her nose? The eyes that she thought too big for her face? The hairline too high on her forehead? She had never thought of herself as other than fair, though men would look at her and de Medina seemed fascinated – sufficiently to want to paint her portrait, because there was no money changing hands. Hector was not entirely pleased. He appeared not to object to de Medina wanting to paint her portrait, but it got under his skin that de Medina would do so without a fee. There, in Edinburgh, Shona saw uncovered a side of Hector that she had not been aware of hitherto. She had thought the tendency he had to give himself graces was superficial; for show more than consequence. But with de Medina she realized that it truly mattered to him. Hector did not want to be taken for a pauper. Another man might have compared himself favourably with all the nobles and gentlemen who languished in the city's debtors prison. But Hector was always too concerned with how others viewed him to concern himself with how he viewed others. Hector's self-esteem demanded he pay de Medina for painting the portrait. He told Shona it was a matter of pride. Shona, annoyed, retorted that he only wished to pay so that he could show off. But whether for airs or honour, the fact was that they had not the means. Hector knew this. If they could not pay, he said she must decline the offer. But Shona was flattered to be asked to sit for a man of de Medina's illustrious repute, who besides painting Scotland's highest nobles had gained fame for illustrating Milton's *Paradise Lost*. She stood her ground. They argued. If Hector had revealed how much importance he gave to his position in society, she in return revealed how stubborn she could be. Over Hector's protestations she agreed to sit for de Medina at his house. Very soon though, she regretted it. On the first sittings de Medina was intent on his work. When his deep, melancholy eyes rested on her it was no more than to capture her image. Sometimes they were accompanied by an apprentice boy who ground and mixed the pigments. She sat close to where stood the easel with the canvas on which de Medina worked quickly and intensely. He was a slight man with a long curly wig, slightly hooded eyes, and a bulbous nose, yet he was strangely vigorous, and it fascinated her to watch him work in a way she had not seen before, and at something that was mysterious and new to her. But it changed when the apprentice boy was dismissed and de Medina began to turn the lock in the door. He claimed to be dissatisfied with the progress of the painting. At one sitting he kept putting his hands on her head and body to move her around on the chair more to his satisfaction. At a subsequent sitting he went further. He pressed himself against her and ran his hands down over her hips. When she pushed him away, he laughed and went back to work. But now, when he looked at her, it was with bold, lustful intimacy. A part of her that wanted to be admired was not altogether averse to de Medina's attentions. And sometimes he had things to speak of that were fascinating to her, such as the visit he had once made to Rome, or the nude sculptures of Aphrodite which he would describe to her in vivid detail and with the gleam in his eye of a rutting goat. Yet she had no strong desire for de Medina. On the contrary, the more he put his hands on her the less she wanted them put there. If she continued to attend the sittings it was because she did not wish to give Hector any excuse to gloat, but also because when she looked at the portrait it appeared to her as something marvellous, magical, which her vanity would not leave unfinished. But in the end de Medina went too far. He lunged himself on her, declaring that he was losing his senses for want of her. At the same time as he began to grope under her petticoats he tried to cover her face and neck with kisses. In trying to repel him they fell to the floor but this did not deter him. Fortunately, she discovered that although a man, he was not so strong. She was able to roll him over and get to her feet while he looked up at her on all fours, gasping. It crossed her mind to kick him. She thought he deserved it, but actually she could not be cross with him. Her outrage was tempered by her admiration for his art. As she walked to the door, he called after her, begging her to return for a last sitting, but she never did. Two weeks later she and Hector left Edinburgh for Glasgow and she never saw de Medina again. Occasionally she had wondered what had become of de Medina and the portrait, though not for long, and after she heard from Hector that de Medina had died she had scarcely recalled him at all until now.

She could not deny that it was strange and disturbing, the way the past had resurfaced. So sudden and in a manner so mysterious and unexplained. Shona feared it was sinful. She feared the mischief did not come from God but more likely it was the work of the Unseelie Court or of Satan himself. She was a married woman. She had a husband who was gravely injured. Now was not the occasion to indulge in fanciful thoughts, past or present. It was improper. She must not. And yet the Spanish gentleman was making her think of him. His story was compelling. He was no ghillie; a mature man, a professional soldier. Likely he had seen much battle, but she thought she could sense something vulnerable in him. His eyes were young when he looked at her, like a hungry child's. They gazed at her with a sort of tormented wonder. It gave her a not unpleasing sense of power. It made her want to put her hand out, touch the scar that ran down his face -

Shona cut the thought off. She tried to think of Hector. She wanted to think of him with tenderness. She took into consideration the lifetime they had known each other, the years they had been married, the tragedy they had endured together when their children were taken... but somehow it could not assuage the resentment she harboured, it could not make her want to be with him, it could not stop her finding fault with his disregard for the lives of the folk who depended on him. It did not matter to her that others had started doing no different or worse. That was always his last excuse. When he could not persuade her that his actions were essential for the preservation of their comfort, he would indicate how in comparison to his actions, the MacDonald of Sleat had started selling their tenants for transport as slaves, or how other lairds had quadrupled the rents in a single year. But Shona did not see that one ill deed justified another. She thought she could forgive Hector almost anything, but not the coldness that broke with tradition and the teachings of Christ. There had to be compassion in this world. She could not live, seeing every last stirring of joy and warmth withering inside her on account of Hector's indifference. It was mystifying to her how Hector, and so many others of his ilk, could go off to war in the name of an absent king, for a cause that not all understood, and be prepared to die, while at the same time they would refuse a helping hand to their real and immediate dependents. Shona decided she must enquire from the Spanish gentleman how Hector had aided him in the battle, precisely, to merit the solicitude he was now being given in exchange. Could she hope that it would put Hector in a different light? Less harsh? One that it would manage to draw her to him again before it was too late?

SIXTEEN

Again, de la Rueda had stayed awake much of the night. When lying in bed became impossible once again he got up to pace the barn. Going to war was easier. It was something he understood. But this torment was new to him. He had the sense that he was losing control of himself, like the moment when a soldier, overwhelmed, abandons his ground. Such decisions are made in an instant, but their consequences decide battles and reach far. What most alarmed him was the idea of losing the battle with himself. All it would take was a single wrong decision. It would not require her participation. She was the reason of his travail but she was not the resolution. The resolution was all of his own making. It would make little difference if she said yes to him or no, once his honour was besmirched. Was happiness possible without honour? Could he live with himself, regardless of her own actions, however virtuous they might be, knowing he had sullied his honour? Surely from that moment on he would become a defeated man, not himself; one of those craven, ruined, unhappy servants of the Devil. No. Never. He must not step on that path, because that is all it would take, one step. One bite of the apple. Such is temptation. No. When he arose in the morning he would go to her and request directions. No more talk of the painting. No more talk of fate. He had lived well enough, so far, without her, and he could live likewise the years that remained to him. Perhaps he could find a woman to love him who spoke his own language, back in his own country? Tomorrow he would request directions to the church. He would inquire from the minister the whereabouts of his compatriots. Perhaps the minister could help arrange his escape to Spain? Or failing that, if necessary, his surrender?

But de la Rueda, resolved though he thought himself, did not have a prompt opportunity to address Shona regarding his departure. When he emerged from the barn in the early light he found Shona standing outside the house deep in conversation with a woman, while Neil and a youth stood by. Neil was fully armed. De la Rueda sat on the bench to wait. Shona was not aware of him; it was only when she had finished talking that, in turning, she saw him.

For an instant she stiffened, as if flustered. Then she came towards him with a determined, pigeon footed gait.

De la Rueda stood up, bowed. '*Bonjour, Madame.*'

'*Bonjour.*'

Shona's thin lips were puckered and when her eyes met his they were combative.

'I... Pistol...' Shona made a gesture of firing a gun, then waved her arm as though holding a sword. 'You... I... We go.'

De la Rueda was puzzled.

'I put on my arms?'

Shona nodded. 'More men.' She pointed to his uniform but before de la Rueda could speak she turned and went into the house.

There is mischief about. De la Rueda went into the barn for his arms.

In the bedroom Shona went to Hector, who lay asleep on his side. She was on the point of waking him when she changed her mind. She doubted he would be in a condition to think clearly. Later, in a few days, when he improved, she could put him to the test. But right now she had to stop Lachlan White Eyes. He was a heartless man; more of a fox than her own husband.

From Hector's chest she brought out a plaid, a shirt, and a blue bonnet. She could not have the gentleman going about in his Spanish uniform. Of course he would attract attention, but when dressed in local attire, no more than necessary. The other option was to keep him here, out of sight, but then it was difficult to raise men immediately, even her own tenants. And he could be useful if it got out of hand.

Back outside, Shona handed the clothes to Neil.

'Please take these to the gentleman. And show him how it is done if he does not know already.'

De la Rueda was sitting on the edge of the fire pit checking his pistol when Neil appeared in the barn doorway. Neil had no clue how to explain the plaid to the gentleman, but in the event there was no need. With Neil watching, de la Rueda went through the process of laying the cloth on the ground, folding it, and putting it on.

'*Math.* Good.' Neil grinned through his beard, showing yellow, broken teeth.

De la Rueda was surprised at how light the plaid felt. On the natives the plaids had seemed to him heavy and cumbersome. But the fabric of this one was finely woven. Under the skirt the air circulated freely around his balls. And it was not cloying. De la Rueda had his own belts so he did not need Hector's. There was no pin to fasten the plaid on his chest over the shirt, but Neil came forward and with his calloused hands shyly tied the two ends in a knot.

It was in the nature of the plaid to adapt to the shape and size of the person who wore it. As a result de la Rueda did not look demonstrably ill-dressed when he emerged from the barn, fully armed. An odd note was the Spanish boots, which were still just about serviceable, but Shona, seeing him approach alongside Neil, thought the impression was good enough.

'I cannot promise you it will change anything,' Shona said to the short, plump woman beside her. 'We can only try.'

Abruptly Fiona seized Shona's hand in both of hers and kissed it.

'No. Please. Go home and wait. I will let you know what comes of it.'

'God bless you, madam,' said Fiona.

Shona turned to Neil. 'Are we ready? Shall we start out?'

Without a word Neil and the tall, thin youth – barefoot, dressed in a patched and dirty attire – set off ahead at a fast pace.

'We go, *Monsieur.*'

'*Oui, certainement.*'

De la Rueda started walking behind Shona, who wore brogues, her skirt tied up at her waist above a single white petty coat, for the day looked to be warm again. De la Rueda had no idea as to what mission they were embarking on, other than the requirement to bear arms. He wanted to ask her but there was a sense of urgency and he suspected that it would be difficult for her to explain. Whatever it was he would go along with it, so long as he was not asked to go against his scruples. As for Shona, she was not in fact expecting to have to make use of the gentleman's fighting skill. Lachlan would not have more than a few men with the cattle, for there was no reason for him to suspect her.

At the giant's stone they stopped to wait. They had no words to say to each other that could make small talk and for Shona it was complicated to explain herself in French. Thus the wait felt long for them both, charged with unspoken emotion that found no release. All they could do was to sit at a distance from each other, which made it easier, and stare about them in silence. Finally Neil appeared with three more armed men. Two with broadswords. Another also carried a musket. De la Rueda recognized one of the men from the battle. He had been with Hector's company and stood out for his large, strong bulk and wild ginger beard and long hair.

'Thank you for coming,' Shona said.

'If it helps Donald there is no need for thanks,' said the ginger-haired man.

'Are there others to come?' Shona asked.

'Eachann has gone to find Angus Peter,' said Neil. 'We will meet on the way.'

Soon after the Giant's Stone the little fields with ripening barley began to fall away. The ground thereafter rose steadily into small hills covered with grass and heather where cultivation was all but impossible. On soggier ground were peat bogs however, and here and there scattered black sheep could be seen foraging under the eye of a small shepherd boy not much taller than the sheep. Goats were more troublesome to manage, and, when not hobbled, they, like the cattle, were at this time of year gathered together under the care of herders.

After walking fast for two hours, uphill and with only short breaks, along a meandering path, the party came to a fork at the entrance of a corrie where two low hawthorn trees with twisted trunks stood side by side, and whose branches had interlocked to form a large circular canopy. These were the only two trees in sight amid a range of hills increasingly sparse of vegetation as it gained height. Under the trees a man sat with his back against one of the trunks, and next to him the youth who had earlier been with Neil, and a black and white dog. The dog appeared to sense at once that de la Rueda was a stranger among them, for it singled him out with a curl of its lips and rising hackle. Its master spoke a single word as he stood up and the dog was calm again.

Shona was glad to see Angus Peter. He was a good and able man, and the husband of her friend, Eubh.

'Hello, Angus Peter.'

'Shona.'

'Are there more to come?'

'We will be enough as we are,' Angus Peter answered. Loose-limbed, with a long nose, a prominent Adam's apple, and narrow blue eyes, he gave de la Rueda a squinting, appraising glance.

Shona understood. If more did not avail themselves it was because they would not feel safe obeying a call for arms that did not emanate from Hector. He had too much power over their fate for them to risk his displeasure. With Neil it was different, for he was Shona's man. And Angus Peter, though Hector's tenant, had strength in his position, for besides being Hector's main stockman and herder he worked independently as a drover and had his own income. As for the others, they had their own private reasons to take the risk.

'How many of them are there, do you think, Angus Peter?'

'I heard Lachlan has put another two on.'

'So he has four or five?

'Thereabouts. Reivers are on the prowl now with the battle over. By Loch Carron way, I have been told, sixty head and more of cattle have been lifted.'

'How is Eubh doing?' asked Shona, remembering that her friend was soon due.

Angus Peter nodded. 'Well enough. It will not be long now.'

'Tell her I will visit soon.'

Angus Peter reached for a long staff leaning against the trunk of the tree. He bore no sword but in his hands the staff was more than adequate. He also carried a dirk and a pistol. With Angus Peter leading they took the path to the left of the trees into the corrie that soon, passing between two tawny slopes of rock and shingle, came to the edge of an abrupt descent at the bottom of which was a long narrow loch shimmering black and silver under the blue sky.

'They will be past the loch, there,' said Angus Peter, stopping. 'We will go around the back here. I do not expect the men will give us trouble. They will know us. How many head are you wanting?'

'Enough to bring him around,' said Shona.

'Five.'

'Ten,' said Shona.

For an hour they followed the line of the left slope, keeping out of sight just under the rim. The ground was hard and stony. De la Rueda, Angus Peter, Neil, and the big man all had footwear but the two others were barefoot. Once past the slope they descended onto ground that was softer, overgrown with grass and heather. They were above the far end of the loch now and there on a knoll two hundred yards or so in front of them sat a man looking down into the terrain beyond the loch.

'That is Callum,' said Angus Peter. 'He will give us no trouble. Wait here.'

Angus Peter commanded the dog to stay, then with swift strides, staff in hand, he covered the two hundred yards and came upon the sitting man just as he appeared to sense a presence and was turning. Both Shona and de la Rueda caught the look of surprise on the man's face as he rose to his feet. Not long afterwards Angus Peter raised his arm and beckoned them.

Callum, a short, barrel-chested man of middle age, was deferential towards Shona. Although he was a dependent of Lachlan's, it could even be said that he was an indirect tenant of Shona's, for his tenancy happened to be on a part of land that Lachlan leased from Hector.

'We are taking ten head of Lachlan's cattle,' she told him. 'We will not want any that are yours or of others. If you make a mistake the cow will be returned.'

Shona, while addressing Callum, saw that already they had been observed from below. One of the men watching over the herd grazing on the soft slopes beyond the loch had started hurrying towards another man.

'We will wait for you here,' said Angus Peter. 'Is Robert in charge?'

'He is.'

'Well, he can choose the cattle himself. When you are ready, give us a signal; we will come down.'

Callum went off. The herd did not consist only of Lachlan's cattle. Mixed among them were Callum's' own few cows and those of other tenants. But the lady wanted only Lachlan's cattle. And they could say they had not put up a fight because it was Shona herself, not outlaws, who had come to take his cattle.

De la Rueda had little idea of what was taking place. Something local. A dispute over animals or land like the people had at home. It was no concern of his. He should have been off by now, gone on his way, but sitting there on the heather beside Shona he knew that he did not want to leave her, could not, until something occurred now to end the strange sense of fate that drew him and imprisoned him like a moth at a flame. *I am not myself. I am adrift. I need God's guidance. I need to find my soul again.*

'If this does not change Lachlan's mind, I fear nothing will,' said Angus Peter, sitting on the other side of Shona.

'I could not let it go by.'

'Maybe so. But it could cost you… All of us.'

Callum had reached the herd. They watched him speaking with the other two herders. All three looked up towards the knoll. Moments later they separated and began to go about among the scattered black cattle, gathering ones that belonged to Lachlan.

Angus Peter stood up. Then Shona and the others.

'I will tell you something, Shona,' said Angus Peter. 'When I was at the winter tryst in Argyll last year I heard talk about the mines - '

'The coal mines?'

'One of them anyway.' Angus Peter paused. 'Some women protested. They could not carry the coal on the rations they were given. The four ringleaders were tied to the gin wheel and made to do the work of the horse. Three fell dead from exhaustion.'

Shona was silent.

'There is cruelty everywhere now.' She remembered Hector's notes. 'Here it will be sheep that cause it.'

'They are clearing the land in some places.'

'On Skye some folk are being sold for slaves.'

Angus Peter nodded. 'He was never good, that MacDonald.'

'My father cared but now the chiefs think only of themselves. So tell me, Angus Peter, what difference will it make in the end if it is our side or the Hanoverians that has victory?'

'One cannot be sure but I think you may be right. That is one reason I did not go to war this time.' Angus Peter glanced at de la Rueda and back to Shona. 'Does the Spanish captain understand one word of our language?'

'Only one or two it may be... But we speak in French a little - '

Callum raised both arms and waved.

Angus Peter motioned to his dog and strode forward. The others followed. When they arrived at the spot where the ten cows were gathered they were left to it. Lachlan's men stood at a distance, watching in silence. Only Angus Peter's dog and the one belonging to the herders appeared to show a momentary interest in one another. Angus Peter called his dog back and started to wave the cows on. They moved slowly, mooing and defecating, up into the hills. Concealment was not required now on the return journey so they took a different route, easier for the cattle. At one point, still some way above the giant's stone, Angus Peter took his leave in order to return to the herd he was in charge of, some miles distant.

'Keep a good eye on them. You will not want to lose a cow that is not yours,' warned Angus Peter.

'I will try not to. And I will call on Eubh any day now. As soon as I am able.'

'She will be expecting you. I will tell her.'

In a moment, without further word, Angus Peter was gone. The rest of the party continued their descent, slowly, the men spread out as they drove the cattle before them over the undulating hillsides. Finally they arrived at the pens. These were the more secure permanent pens as opposed to the movable turf ones that served to enrich the soil with fresh manure. The permanent pens were two enclosures of drystone walls with a dwelling nearby. After the cattle were herded into one of the enclosures a rough wooden gate was closed behind them. From the pens it was possible for de la Rueda to see the trees behind Shona's house in the near distance and around the house, to right and left, the fields cultivated with growing barley, tall enough now to be knee-high and shimmer as the breeze passed through. Further in the distance, to the front of the house, was the stony coastline. All along the coastline, behind the flat, fertile, cultivated land that belonged to Hector, was other land cultivated on the slopes by Hector's tenants. Many of those tenants had moved to the shielings where they could tend the goats and sheep and cows in the hills away from the crops, though always some people would remain behind to attend to other labours or because they were old or infirm.

Standing by the pens, de la Rueda looked about. *It is pleasant here when the weather is warm and it is not raining.*

'If you please, M*onsieur.* We go.'

'Very well.' De la Rueda smiled. 'You will learn French yet, M*adame.*'

Shona found herself smiling back without meaning to, and though not sure she had understood him.

It was late afternoon when they reached the house.

'We eat,' said Shona, making a gesture.

They went indoors. There was no one about, not even Margaret, but there was broth in the pot. Shona got the wooden bowls out and handed one each to Neil and the youth.

'I will see how my husband is for a moment.' Shona turned to de la Rueda. '*Monsieur*?'

They went into the bedroom. Hector was awake. He was lying on his back in his shirt, the blankets thrown off, staring at the ceiling. After the air of the hills the room smelt fusty.

'Ah, here you are.' Hector's eyes flickered to Shona, and then de la Rueda. '*Bonsoir, capitain.*'

De la Rueda inclined his head. '*Monsieur.* Are you feeling improved?'

'A little. Thank you.' Hector felt the need to be polite to de la Rueda, but his tone became more querulous when he addressed Shona. 'Have you been out all day?'

Shona answered without hesitation. 'I took ten head of cattle from Lachlan's herd.'

Hector went silent. His eyes closed. After a long moment they opened again.

'Why did you do that?'

'Donald and his wife Fiona from the five shilling tack on the Three Rowans. Do you recall? You signed a lease, Hector. You have passed his land to Lachlan for ten shillings more a year.'

'What has this to do with the cattle?'

'When Lachlan brings me the lease you signed I will tear it up and you can sign the land back to Donald. Then Lachlan can have his cattle and his money returned.'

Hector began to open his mouth but closed it again. His blue-grey eyes bulged. His neck strained and his shoulders rose up from the bed. Then he went limp, turning his eyes away, but the tension remained around his mouth, which he closed with a stubborn downward curl.

When Shona saw that Hector was refusing to look at her or speak, she said to de la Rueda, 'Come, M*onsieur.* We eat.'

De la Rueda followed Shona to the common room. It was obvious that there had been a confrontation. He wondered if it had anything to do with the day's events. And had she included him in such out of politeness, to be hospitable, or because he was serving a function he was unaware of?

Neil and the youth were sitting at the table with their bowls empty. They had finished eating. Shona filled bowls for de la Rueda and herself and took them to the table. There were four chairs, enough for them all, but the youth stood up.

'I will go now, madam. If you do not need me.'

'Come by tomorrow early. I may need you for an errand. You have done well today. Thank you.'

After the youth had gone, Shona turned to Neil. 'I do not know how this is going to go. Hector was not pleased when I told him.'

'Your father's blood is strong in you, Shona. Think no more of it. It may end well.'

'Or it may not.'

Neil remained silent.

Shona sighed. Just then Mairi appeared with Margaret. There was dirt on her clothes and saliva dribbled from the corner of her flaccid mouth. Her eyes were blank, though in their depths sometimes a merest hint of recognition would show.

'She snuck out on me,' said Mairi. 'I found her near the shore.'

'I am too tired,' said Shona. 'You will have to put her to bed. Has Hector been fed?'

'He asked earlier.'

Neil stood up.

'I will be going, then.'

'God bless you.'

After Shona had finished eating she took down the French dictionary from the bookcase and with a glance at de la Rueda, she turned to leave the room. De la Rueda assumed she meant him to follow her. Outside, she sat on one end of the bench and placed the dictionary by her side. De la Rueda sat down on the other side of the dictionary. Hens pecked about in the grass, but the goats were not about for they were by the byre, on the other side of the house, being milked by Elsbeth.

'Your country,' Shona asked de la Rueda. 'Is... here... like here?'

De la Rueda pointed to the sky. 'More sun,' he replied, gesturing.

Shona understood. After only a few days both were finding that often gestures sufficed.

'And more fruit. Oranges. Lemons. Apples.'

Shona got him to repeat the words and between them they consulted the dictionary.

Apples Shona had tasted. And on rare occasions a lemon. But not oranges, although she had seen them in pictures and once a real orange in Glasgow at the house of a lord.

Again she consulted the dictionary, lifting it from the bench and resting it on her lap.

'Is much fruit?'

De la Rueda smiled and made an expansive gesture, stretching his arm out and moving it from left to right. As he did so, not for the first time Shona observed that he used his hands in a manner that was expressive and elegant. 'Whole fields, with many trees and much fruit.'

Shona thought she understood. In her mind she could see trees in profusion with oranges hanging from the branches, like the apple orchards she had seen south of Edinburgh.

'And… like here.. Mountains?'

De la Rueda nodded. 'Mountains, too. You would like my country.'

Shona appeared quizzical.

What am I thinking? De la Rueda all but smacked his own brow. *It is a sin to see her over there with me. Virgin Mary, save me…*

'Have you *champs*, in...country of you?'

'*Terrains*? Yes. I have house and land.'

'Like here?'

'Yes… My sister. She looks after my land. For me.'

De la Rueda pointed to himself and made gestures. Shona gazed at him, her green eyes amused, happy with the knowledge that she was managing to understand him. De la Rueda felt himself almost swooning again. One look into her eyes and fire went through his veins. Shona, suddenly conscious not just of his presence, but of the physicality of it, felt a sort of quiver pass deep under her skin. Immediately the air became dense between them. Whereas moments previously the space between them, occupied on the bench by the dictionary, had been manageable, now all at once it was only the air that seemed to be preventing this space from breaking down and disappearing altogether. De la Rueda knew how to wait. In battle this ability was of supreme importance. But for Shona such physical excitement was less usual. Her curiosity about men other than her husband had always been idle speculation. But here was something from within - unexpected in its intensity and thus alarming to her.

She stood up.

'I... go...'

De la Rueda jumped to his feet, lifting the dictionary for her as she bent down to reach it. It was on his tongue to mention his departure, but once again he could not bring himself to.

'*Madame.*'

Shona was turning away when a thought stopped her. She could not leave without knowing.

'*Monsieur*... My husband, how he....' What was the word. *Sauve*? Yes, *sauve*. 'How he save... life of you?'

'I...' de la Rueda pointed to himself and then to his pistol. 'I killed one man. With my pistol. But more men attacked me.' De la Rueda paused and gesticulated as he spoke. 'I had no time to draw my sword. Then your husband came to my rescue. They had a struggle. Your husband was wounded... badly wounded. But he saved me. Without him I would be dead.'

Shona understood few of the words he spoke, but the gestures that accompanied them were expressive. She understood enough to know that Hector had acted bravely in coming to his assistance. It softened the anger towards her husband.

'*Merci. Bonne nuit, Monsieur*. Thank you. Good night.'

Shona left to go indoors. De la Rueda sighed and went to the barn. He had been sleeping little since arriving. Now he lay his head down on the bed and was at once asleep.

Shona was also tired and yet, in spite of what de la Rueda had just told her, she could not bring herself to lie down on the same bed as her husband. With her emotions in confusion, she sat down on her chair by the hearth. *All manner of men can be brave in battle. Does that make a man good because he is brave in battle? It is the worthiness of a person's soul that must be judged. I would not willingly withhold Christian compassion from a soul that was worthy. But I look at Hector and in spite of everything I find in his favour I cannot bring myself to trust in the worthiness of his soul. I find always a part of it that he keeps hidden away - like his accounts and ledgers. He expects that it will not be molested, that we can get by without my having to know. But I must know. Can his soul be made good? Or is it twisted in the core?*

SEVENTEEN

Lachlan appeared the following day. He came to the house mid-morning, riding on a garron with a servant walking in front. The servant wore plaid but Lachlan was dressed the lowland way, in leather breeches, waistcoat and coat. He also wore a white peruke of poor quality, an accessory he resorted to only on occasions he thought required added authority. When the horse stopped, Lachlan could not get off it without a wide swing of his leg, for his legs were as short as his torso was long. But though stocky, he was not fat. Even his red, porcine face was muscular.

It was no small matter to have ten head of cattle taken without explanation. On the other hand Lachlan was fully cognizant of his position in the pecking order, so although furious he was determined to keep an outward appearance of civility, at least until he had managed to appraise the situation. As for Shona, she knew it must be him when the knock came on the door, but she was in no hurry to put down the wooden spoon which she was using to pile curds into a cloth for making cheese. Mairi, who was sweeping the flagstones, started for the door, but Shona stopped her. Only when the knock persisted and Shona had pulled down her green tartan skirt over her petticoats and gone to sit at the table, did she allow Mairi to answer it.

'Good morning, madam.' Lachlan bowed.

'I have been expecting you. Will you take a seat?'

Lachlan, holding a leather satchel under one arm, took a handkerchief out from under his frilled lace cuff and mopped the perspiration on his forehead as he came to sit on the other side of the table.

'How is the laird now? Does he find himself improved?' For all the politeness Lachlan could not prevent the hint of a sneer creeping into his loud voice.

'I will take you to him shortly, sir. But first you must know that he had no hand in the confiscation of your cattle. It was all my doing.'

Lachlan flushed. To conceal his rage he reached into his waistcoat and brought out a horn snuff box.

'And the reason being?'

'I want you to tear up the lease you signed with my husband for Three Rowans land. You will get your money returned and your cattle.'

Lachlan took a pinch of snuff. The distraction was momentary.

'The lease was agreed, madam. I made an offer which was accepted by your husband.'

Shona remained silent.

'It is blackmail.'

'I think of it as justice.'

Lachlan made to rise and sat down again. He wanted to rape the whore. That would be justice.

'May I speak to the laird?'

Shona led him to the bedroom. Hector was awake under the canopy. His bandaged head was propped against the oak bed rest. His unshaven cheeks were gaunt and in his eyes a gaze not entirely present. The violent headaches gave him little respite and his thoughts, driven by the laudanum he was resorting to, were full of gaps, dream-like and drifting, so that it was only at interludes that he became fully lucid.

'Good morning, sir.'

Hector recognized Lachlan, though what business he could have with him he had abruptly forgotten.

'I am glad to see your health is improving.'

'I am poorly,' said Hector, trying to concentrate.

'But improving. That is the main part. I saw it all,' Lachlan lied, for in fact, at the moment referred to, he had already been deserting his post. 'It was a brave deed you did in saving the Spaniard. A most brave deed.'

Hector looked at Shona, then back at Lachlan, who now opened the satchel and started leafing through various documents. Once he found what he was looking for he pulled out a rough sheet of paper.

'This is your handwriting.' Lachlan showed Hector the document without letting go of it. 'The lease clearly states that on the last day of September, after the summer harvest has been brought in, I am taking possession of the five acre tack on the Three Rowans in exchange for a rent of fifteen shillings yearly and for a period of ten years. We have both signed the lease.'

Lachlan put the document back in his wallet.

'And this,' he pullied out a smaller piece of paper, 'is a receipt. It is for the five shillings I gave you as an advance on the first year's rent.'

Hector now remembered the adverse discussion he had had with Shona. But he struggled to recall the details or even if it had actually occurred or was merely a dream.

'I trust the documents are in order?'

'They are. There is no wrong with the documents. But madam now wishes me to destroy the documents and have the money I advanced returned to me.'

Hector was remembering more. He turned his gaze to Shona. Her face was impassive but her eyes were watching him, waiting with a tense glimmer of appeal.

'Madam has confiscated ten of my cows. It is unlawful blackmail.'

Hector looked away. *I am at her mercy. I cannot even do my needs without her help. But it is my land, my money. She does not understand. Lachlan is not a man to be so blithely trifled with. The deal was done. It cannot be undone now if he has no mind to agree.*

'Your cattle will be returned to you. You have my word.'

'In that case there is no more to be said.' Lachlan glanced at Shona and back at Hector. 'I expect them to be returned in the same fine condition as when they were taken. And before the week is out.'

'You will be recompensed if the case requires it.'

Lachlan buckled the satchel and bowed.

'Good day to you, sir. And may you recover with all speed.' A cold glee came to his colourless eyes when he bowed to Shona. 'Madam.'

Shona kept silent. All she felt for Lachlan was loathing. He was not behaving in any way she did not expect. But for Hector her feelings were deeply unsettled, so deeply that she could not yet acknowledge them. A strange calm came over her as she followed Lachlan to the door. There, she heard Lachlan say, 'Do not think that I am not able to make mischief should I have a mind to, madam. I will remind you that the battle was lost and the earl's lands remain forfeit. I have it on good authority General Wightman is to hang such worthy rebels as he finds and put the land to fire. Your husband will be lucky to keep possession of what he has, considering where he has placed his allegiance.'

'And did you not place your allegiance there as well?' Shona snapped.

Lachlan gave a mocking laugh. 'Do you think I make the better example, then? A humble tenant farmer?'

Shona shut the door on him. Her chest felt tight as she went to the common room and sat down at the table. She did not doubt that Lachlan could make trouble. He was sly. And, though he had gone to battle with Hector, he sold illicit whisky to the Hanoverian Highland Militia. He was one of those who had no trouble flattering both sides. If Lachlan saw opportunity he would take it. And he was spiteful. But that was not what mattered. What mattered was that a family was being cheated out of what was rightfully theirs. She could not help all Hector's cottars and tenants. If Hector wanted to put sheep on the land she could not stop him. But when the Three Rowans woman came appealing to her she had not seen how to stand by. Those five acres had produced not a single head of corn when Donald took it over. She could remember the gossip she heard, how folk had said Donald had spent too much time listening to The Experimenter, how he was away with the fairies. No one believed Donald could make anything out of five acres of bog unless it was to dig up peat. But Donald had not desisted. After all the day's labours to feed themselves and their young ones, and while other folk slept, the couple went out to work on the five acres. To drain the water they dug trenches, they did what The Experimenter had done for some of his own fields, and they dug the stones out and ploughed it by hand, without a garron to aid them. They planted kale and when the kale grew they mulched it. How could she not admire their fortitude and their faith? It was nothing, those five acres when they took it over; and one day after years of toil, corn started to grow. Nobody was saying they were away with the fairies then. So by what right are the rewards of all that toil and hardship taken away from them and passed to another who has not spent a moment on that land to plant even a single grain? Her own father had been no saint. In his years of buccaneering he was sure to have offended some and disadvantaged others. But that was very different to uncaring cruelty. She had heard the same said of Rob Roy; that if bandit he be, he was most discerning and would not harm the poor. Her father had always looked after the clan. He would die before disowning one of his own for no Christian purpose. He thought only of keeping them safe. That is what the Book commanded; treat others as thou would be treated. Why could Hector not understand? If he was brave enough to go to the Spanish gentleman's assistance why was he not brave enough to do justice to Donald and his family? Was it because they were poor? But were they not mortals with souls? All this wealth he wanted for himself, to whom was he to leave it? Their children were dead. And she did not know why others had not come. If they had more children Hector might insist to her in justice that the striving was for them. But it was not. They had no children. Did he wish all the children to starve and see families suffer because his own children were taken? *God have mercy on his soul but I cannot. I will not.*

A banging sound came from the bedroom and then Hector's voice calling for Mairi. Shona stood up and went into the bedroom. Hector had managed to rise. He was sitting on the edge of the bed in his shirt.

'What is it you need?'

'Where is Mairi?'

'She has gone out.'

'Will you fetch her, please?'

Shona was silent.

'Hector, I shall ask you to consider my feelings; will you not change your mind?'

'Lachlan's cattle must be returned.'

'And The Three Rowans family ruined? Where are they to go?'

Hector looked at Shona standing at the end of the bed. Her face was angry and distraught. *She has crossed me, and now it is she who is angry when it should be me. But I am unwell. I have not the strength.*

'I will find somewhere for them if it pleases you.'

'If it pleases *me*? Do you not think of *them*? And what will you find them? Another five acres of bog they must improve or starve and then you will take away from them? Is that what you will do, Hector?'

'Lachlan is a dangerous man. He has friends among the Hanoverians, he sells them whisky. I cannot take the risk of offending him.'

The words gave Shona pause.

'Is that why?'

'Is what why?'

'Is that why you passed the land to him?'

Hector looked away. 'It is how matters are. If we do not look to our own advantage, no one else will. Seaforth and the others come over for war but they will go back to cosy exile in France and Rome. Seaforth is fortunate that myself and others choose to send him the rents even though his lands are forfeit. But you and I have no pleasant exile to go to and no one to send us rents. We are not important enough. If we are cut adrift there will be no rescue. And Lachlan will be one of those doing the cutting if he can. Unless we have him on our side. I would be a fool to make more enemies than I need on my doorstep.'

'But how are you different? Not all the chiefs and lairds are alike. My father was never one to disavow his own, and others there are like him – your own father… Oh, there are many who do not only think of sheep and cattle and rents and put profit above all else. And what is it for? It will gain you no credit with God. We have no children to leave it to - '

'We do not know that.'

'Well, there are no children that I see here… All I see is your ambition. All I see is your vainglory and folk like on the Three Rowans and the cottars and tenants you want to move only to put sheep on the land. That is what I see!'

Hector was becoming too tired to argue longer. He wanted to lie down, but the shock of what Shona had just said kept him sitting up.

'How do you know about that?'

Shona looked at him. All at once it seemed to her as if she were contemplating a stranger; someone who had the same grey eyes as her husband, the same long nose, the same tall body, but was not actually anyone she *knew*. Is he a kelpie then, an *each-uisage*? *But he has human feet, though it is said the wiliest each-uisge can even disguise its hooves. What I could do is shoot him with a silver bullet. He would turn to hair and jelly. I would like to see him turn to hair and jelly.*

Shona gave a single bitter laugh. There was cold hatred at the core of her. It alarmed her to feel it so forcefully. She had the impression that some last flicker of hope had just died.

'Have you looked at my ledgers?'

Shona did not reply. She turned and left the room and the house. The shore was not far. A grey heron flapped its long wings and took to the air as she approached. Smaller curlews also took flight. But the black and white oyster-catchers with orange beaks had nests among the rocks to defend. They screeched overhead and made mock dives. Shona moved away from them and sat down on a flat rock. Clouds gathered and dispersed against the blue sky. The sun came in and out. The breeze from the sea was warm. The brown and green seaweed among the rocks in front of her gave off a pungent smell. Beyond the seaweed was a narrow strip of sand the incoming tide had not yet reached, and beyond that the indigo sea itself stretching to a far horizon.

I should go home. There is nothing here for me. Of course, her brother might not be so welcoming and Neil and Elsbeth would ask to go with her. Not Mairi, for she was Hector's servant. But Old John, too, would ask to go. Neil and Elsbeth might be useful to her brother, but old John would be a burden now. Her brother did not have her father's skills: Too fond of the *uisge-beatha* and not enough a seafarer. The clan lands were small. By good fortune they had some timber – trees her father and grandfather had planted – and her brother was good with cattle, but to provide for more folk was not something her brother would wish for without a return or a reason. And what reason did she have that was good enough? He would want to know if Hector was beating her, or treating her in a manner that did her much ill. But she could not tell him so. Hector had not once lifted his hand to her. And if she brought up Hector's disregard for his tenants, her brother would have the names of many more to throw at her who treated their tenants with even greater indifference. It was being said everywhere nowadays that the future was not in agriculture but in the wool and meat market. Her brother himself had talked of putting the new breed of sheep on the clan land when she had gone for their uncle's funeral. He had claimed it could benefit all. But for how long? The more sheep brought in, the more land it would take. She wondered if her brother had it in him to become like Hector? But even if not she doubted he would think her scruples enough reason for her to abandon her husband. All she could say to her brother was that she did not love Hector, that she had stopped loving him, that this morning they had argued and she had suddenly watched how the last flicker of tenderness for him died in her. There was nothing. No *feeling* for Hector. That is all she could tell her brother. But marriages were made by God, he would say. She should have taken better stock of the situation when she went through the handfasting. She could not now take apart what God had put together. He would say such things, probably, and it would not be his desire to have her there, probably; but he would not turn her away. She was certain of that. *I should leave this place. Go back home. I should go back home…*

As de la Rueda left the barn to go to the house, he had come to the decision that he must finally make arrangements to leave. He had accomplished what he had set out to do and he had been here time enough. That the woman he had been predestined to meet should turn out to be the wife of the man who had saved him was a cruel jest played on him by fate. But everything happened for a reason. It said in the Holy Bible that even the hairs on a man's head were counted. God had put this test on his path to heaven. That was why man was given free will. He could quell the fire that consumed him now and be dammed, or he could save his soul. *I can live with anything. I can take the pains of a shattered heart, of destiny thwarted, but not dishonour, a soul damned, that I could not live with.* So he would ask for directions, and tomorrow early, with or without a guide, he would leave.

But it was not Shona de la Rueda met at the house; it was Hector. After he had knocked on the door, he heard a voice respond accompanied by thudding sounds. Presently it opened and both men were surprised to encounter each other.

'Ah, *Monsieur...*' said Hector.

Hector was supporting himself by means of an upturned broom under his good arm. His shirt was tied between his long, spindly legs and a small stain of wet bloody matter was sticking to the bandage around his arm. The brown stubble on his chin was turning to beard, and tufts of hair had started to grow at the edges of the bandage that wrapped most of his head. De la Rueda thought he looked improved, or at least up and conscious, but somewhat out of sorts.

'Where is the maid? Should you not be in bed, *Monsieur*?'

'I am looking for her myself... Come in... come in.'

They went into the house.

'I will rest on my bed now that you are here,' said Hector.

In the bedroom de la Rueda went to Hector's assistance and helped him recline with his back against the bed rest. Hector insisted de la Rueda pull up one of the two upholstered chairs.

'You are passing a pleasant interlude here with us, *Monsieur*?'

'Yes. But I wish not to overstay my welcome. I must try to make for Spain or surrender.'

'For Spain -'

Hector did not finish for now they heard sounds coming from outside the bedroom.

'I will trouble you to see who it is. If it is the maid I must speak to her.'

De la Rueda went into the common room. It was Mairi who had just come in, carrying a pile of loose wool. She gave a start when she saw de la Rueda, but understood his gestures and followed him back to the bedroom.

'The cattle must be returned, Mairi. Where is Farquar?'

'I believe he is home. Him and some of the others.'

'Is he wounded?'

'I believe he is not. No.'

'Then have him come over. And if you do not find him send for Angus Peter himself. See to it now, please, Mairi.'

After Mairi had gone, Hector let out a long sigh and said to de la Rueda, 'Have you a wife, *Monsieur*?'

But she is yours.

'A wife does not accord with my profession.'

'Mine does not understand me and I not her.' Hector's voice rose unexpectedly. 'I must manage my affairs as I see proper. I cannot do as she wishes. I cannot. It would be ruin!'

De la Rueda's first impulse was to say something soothing, for it was apparent that Hector was becoming agitated. 'Is something amiss? The cows perhaps?'

'So you know about the cows? What do you know?'

'Your gracious wife invited me to accompany the party when the cows were brought in. But I do not know what it is about. Regrettably your wife's French is not like your own.'

Hector's eyes became restless; when he looked at de la Rueda they had a feverish intensity.

'Good deeds for all and sundry will not bring me profit. And without profit I shall squander all I own. My wife and I will become paupers. We will be destitute. Yet she goes against me. She refuses to understand.'

'*Pardon, Monsieur*. Do you say your wife wished to do a good deed?'

'So do I. I wish to do good deeds. Why not? Everyone can wish to do good deeds; the question is does one have the means? I am sorely constrained. My father left only debts which I have struggled to repay. My wife knows this full well and yet she wishes me to turn away opportunity and renounce profit.'

'And this you will not do?'

'How will it end? There are many things I must do that give me no pleasure. If some labourers lose by my actions then be it so. The ones that stay will gain if I can make my estate prosper, but speaking to my wife of such matters is speaking to a wall. She refuses to give me credit. It has been this way between us for a long time now. For her I am the devil incarnate. By why so? She is my wife. She must do her duty. A ship cannot have two captains. This is my estate. I am the master here!'

After this outburst Hector slumped. His shoulders went limp and the focus appeared to go from his eyes.

'Is something the matter?'

'Ah… my head… There is a bottle, over there by the window, if you could fetch it for me...'

De la Rueda saw several containers on the chest top. He went over to them.

'The bigger one.'

De la Rueda picked it up.

'Yes. That one. And the spoon, if you would be so kind.'

De la Rueda brought them over.

Hector pulled the cork out, filled the small spoon, and swallowed.

'It is all that helps.'

'I have encountered many soldiers with head wounds, and with good attention they heal.'

'I feel I have an axe in my head.'

De la Rueda nodded. 'It will pass.'

Hector closed his eyes. 'I shall rest.'

As de la Rueda passed by the common room he saw that only Hector's mother was there, sitting in her chair by the hearth. Once outside, he did not wish to return to the barn. It was agreeable in the open air; warm and dry. On impulse he started walking towards the shore. When he arrived he stood for a moment staring out at the sea. Thoughts of home came to him once more. Then he caught sight of a figure walking towards him. It was Shona. De la Rueda stiffened, as if against an unexpected squall.

When Shona saw de la Rueda she was not surprised. It seemed as if he was destined to be there. She had a sense – inchoate but strong – that her life was taking an unexpected turn. And although it alarmed her, it also aroused in her a curiosity that was compelling.

'*Madame*,' de la Rueda bowed.

'Good day, *Monsieur.*'

'It is agreeable again today.'

Shona wanted to reply that it was warm but could not think of the word.

They started walking towards the other end of the breakwater, where on the shore lay two upturned boats belonging to Hector.

'I come from seeing your husband.'

Shona frowned.

'I speak to him.'

'Oh… ah… what speak?'

De la Rueda pulled the corner of his mouth down. 'Little… some things.'

'The cows?'

'No... But, well, he said you are...' How could he say this? Finally he lifted his hands and made a gesture of the two parting. 'Like this.'

Shona stopped. Looking up at de la Rueda she made two fists and knocked them together.

De la Rueda had to look away. He could not meet her eyes for long.

Shona started walking again. De la Rueda's mention of Hector made her feel constricted. An impulse of defiance rose in her yet again and not knowing how to express it, deliberately, before she had pause to consider, she reached up and pulled the kertch from her head. Then, pulling the wooden pins out of the coils and shaking her hair loose, she stepped off the grass and towards an outcrop of rocks. De la Rueda saw her hair shimmering like dark red gold over head and shoulders. He was overcome with wonder and déjà vu, for in the past he had often imagined the girl in the painting with her hair let down.

De la Rueda hesitated. But there was no escape. As Shona sat on the flat edge of a rock, de la Rueda stepped over to join her, half perching himself on another rock close by.

Shona pointed towards the sea and then at herself and then back at the sea.

'Your home?'

Shona nodded.

'Your parents? Father, mother; they live there?'

'*Morts.*' Shona knew the word for dead. 'My...' she searched her mind and found the word for brother. 'He. My brother...' She pointed again toward the sea.

'Your brother?' De la Rueda was confused.

Shona nodded. She did not know the word for chieftain. '*Ceann-cinnidh*,' she said in Gaelic. And when de la Rueda looked blank. '*Ceannard*?'

Surprisingly, de la Rueda understood then, for titles and ranks were among the elementary things he, as a commanding officer, had been obliged to learn in both Gaelic and Latin, if not English.

'*Chef*?'

'*Oui*,' said Shona, for it sounded like the English. She pinched a thumb and forefinger and laughed. 'Little *chef*.'

De la Rueda took a deep breath, making gestures again as he spoke. 'I cannot stay here, M*adame*. I must go.'

'Where go you?'

'My companions. Spanish soldiers. I go to them. I surrender. Or I go home. If I can I want to go home. To my country. What do you think? Is it possible?'

More gestures, repetitions.

'Go. You?' Shona made the gesture of a house.

'Yes.'

Shona wished she had the dictionary with her. She did not desire him to leave, if that is what he intended. She would have to help him of course, should Hector not be able. To surrender would be easier. But to escape far more difficult. Such would take time, patience, money. Did he carry money?

'We talk. Not now. With dictionary. I... '

'*Merci*. I am obliged.'

De la Rueda thought he saw palpitations under the white of her blouse. Her lips were slightly parted. Light appeared to shimmer around her thick hair, and her body – taut, voluptuous, straining against the fabric that covered it.

I want to devour her.

Shona stood up. 'We eat, M*onsieur.*'

As they started walking back towards the house Shona lifted her hair. She pinned it loosely and put the kertch back on.

Both now, as they approached the house, made an effort to become more composed.

EIGHTEEN

Mairi was in the house when Shona got back with de la Rueda. 'I was sent to fetch Farquar,' she informed Shona. 'Hector has told him to take the cows back to Lachlan.'

Shona was silent. Anger and disappointment scalded her. She felt herself sinking. *What am I to tell those folk now? They will lose their land after I promised to help them. I hate him. God forgive me I wish him dead.*

'I am sorry, Shona,' said Mairi, for while she was Hector's servant, she felt closer to Shona.

'It is not your fault. But they will lose their land now.'

'These be hard times for some.'

'Will you please feed our guest? I must speak to Neil.'

Shona left de la Rueda sitting at the table and went out of the house. She crossed the burn and passed the few trees and the field on the other side. Soon she was at Neil's house. Neil was not there but just past the open door, Elsbeth was sitting at a small loom weaving tartan cloth.

'I need to speak to Neil.'

Elsbeth stood up. 'He is with the goats. I will fetch him.'

Shona sat on the rough plank which served as a bench outside the house while Elsbeth went off. She was not gone long before Neil appeared on his own, having left his wife with the goats lest they be tempted by the crops.

'Sit down a moment.'

Neil sat on the bench next to Shona.

'Our guest wishes to go back to his own country. Either that or he will surrender. But I think our clan could arrange for him to be smuggled. I know my brother does not take after my father but one of the others may still know people who are in the trade.'

'It is possible,' Neil agreed.

'Could you get a message to my brother?'

'Will the post not do?'

'I do not trust it. Not as things are.'

'Well... Diarmad, the one they call "the stick", is crossing over all the time.'

'Is he trustworthy?'

'He does a bit of smuggling himself when he is not fishing. His sister is married to one of ours. But money will make it firm. It is going to take money to get the gentleman out of the country.'

'It is late today. But can you go tomorrow early. Where does he live?'

'By Kyle.'

'Find out if Diarmad can do it, and how much he wants.'

'I will see to it.'

'I will go back and write a letter to my brother and bring it to you shortly.'

When Shona got back de la Rueda had eaten and gone to the barn. He had decided their conversation could wait, for he was in too much turmoil to be with her. Shona now ate. Afterwards, while Mairi attended to Margaret, she sat at the table with a pencil and paper. She spent a long time composing the letter which was two pages long and which she placed in an envelope and sealed with red wax. By the time she finished, Mairi had retired to her box bed.

Shona went out with the envelope. The sky was bright although it was late. In a few days it would be the summer solstice. There would be bonfires and drink. In some houses there would *ceildihs*, full of music and stories. In some houses there would be joy, but not in others. The folk on the Three Rowans would have only sorrow and bitterness. How could they celebrate, knowing that in a few months they were going to lose all? *I have failed them. And I know not what to do about it.*

Neil and Elsbeth were sitting on the bench outside the house when Shona arrived. And Old John was there, too. They were sharing a quaich of whisky. Elsbeth brought out a low chair for Shona. She handed Neil the letter and he went into the house to put it away. Elsbeth passed Shona the wooden bowl and she took a sip. The whisky went down her throat like liquid fire.

After Neil sat down again, Shona said. 'When Diarmad asks for payment, tell him he may have it once he delivers my brother's reply.'

'That I will do.'

The quaich went round again.

'I am sorry to hear the cattle raid was of no help,' said Old John.

'I cannot make Hector come around to my way. I cannot.'

When the others were silent, Shona added. 'He is not like my father. Or even his own father.'

'Everyone is different,' said Elsbeth, timidly.

'He has not been bad to us,' said Neil, more forcefully.

'No, you are here with me; you and others are safe,' said Shona, not certain it was a conversation she should be having. 'But you can see how it is going everywhere. And now is just the beginning. It will get worse. Hector wants the land at Silverwater turned over to sheep.'

There was a heavy silence.

'I have seen his plans,' said Shona with sudden recklessness.

The quaich went around.

'All of it?' asked Old John.

'All of it.'

'Some of the arable is good growing land,' said Neil.

Elsbeth sighed. 'Folk will be hard done by unless somewhere else can be found for them.'

'How many sheep is Hector planning?' asked Old John.

'Many hundreds.'

They were silent again.

'He will do it,' said Shona. 'When I do not know. Meanwhile we keep it to ourselves. There is no need to worry folk now.'

Old John passed the quaich but this time Shona declined. Already the drink was going to her head.

'I will be going,' she said, rising to her feet.

Shona had occasionally spoken out against her husband in years past. Brief remarks of anger made on the spur of the moment. She had not ever spoken against him so deliberately, however, even if Neil and Old John were virtually kin. She had been held back by duty and respect. Even now some part of her was bothered by her disloyalty, but her discovery of the ledgers and Hector's refusal to spare the Three Rowans was provoking an antipathy that was stronger, such that his injuries even were unable to mitigate.

When she arrived at the burn a notion came to her to bathe. This was not unknown for her in the heat of summer months; though wary of discovery, she always took precautions to keep some of her clothes on. The few occasions when she had bathed naked had been for a moment only and with Mairi, Elsbeth, or another standing by as lookout. And once, years ago, when she was handfasting with Hector, they had bathed together naked in a pool. But she was not thinking of Hector now as she walked a little way up the burn, or rather if he was in her thoughts it was with the rebellious desire to be free of him. Between rocks, at the far end of the pool, a small waterfall bubbled white and made rushing gurgling sounds. The water beneath it shone in the penumbra like black glass. It was deep there. Too deep for Shona, who could not swim. The end closer to her was shallow, and here, hot and a little woozy, and with sudden, bold defiance, she began stripping off her clothes. She took off her kertch, removed her stays, short sleeved shift and skirt, and stepped out of her petticoat. Her skin was white, her breasts small and rounded, her thighs broad and strong. Without hesitation she entered the water. It was cold but bearable. She bent her knees and lowered herself until the water came up to her neck. *No one will see me at this time of night. But if they do I do not care. Let them burn me for a witch. I do not care.*

When she emerged onto the bank the wooziness was gone. Her hands and the soles of her feet were cold but the rest of her was warm. With the petticoat she patted herself dry, then began to dress. She felt refreshed and free. Why had she not done this more often, bathed in the night, naked? But she knew the answer. After the children died, grief had not allowed her to escape into momentary pleasures, and although the grief finally receded, it had not disappeared. Life for her and Hector was never the same. The guilt of being alive when their children were dead was always present. She could console herself with the thought that their souls were in paradise for all eternity; nevertheless the guilt was a chain that confined her. It had put delight and exuberance out of reach.

Back at the house she had no desire to go to bed. An unfamiliar agitation lingered within her. Unexpected images of de la Rueda troubled her mind. Too quell them, she sat down at the table with the French dictionary, a cruise lamp, and pencil and paper. For an hour or so she attempted to memorise words and compose sentences she thought would be useful. Then finally she stood up and went into the bedroom. Margaret was in the box room and Hector was in bed, snoring.

Shona had removed her stay, but she still had her other clothes on when she lay down on the bed. She closed her eyes but the images of de la Rueda kept intruding. They were boldly intimate and had an intensity that she could feel consuming her. She imagined de la Rueda's hands on her hips, his lips kissing her neck. Abruptly the presence of her husband's body beside her became abhorrent. *I will find somewhere else to lie.* She stood up and left the bedroom. But there was nowhere else for her to lie without all the trouble of improvising a bed of some kind, so she went out of the house, which she found confining, and sat on the bench.

Some clouds had appeared in the sky, darkening it, but it was still warm and there was a breeze to keep the midges at bay. She wondered if God was watching her now, or if without her knowing, fairies had cast a spell on her with the purpose of appropriating her mind, for there was sin in her thoughts, of that she was certain, she could not deny it. But if sin it was, it was a sin she could bear, for the world was rotten with excess of sin far graver than this passion awakened in her. How could God not understand that if Hector had not sinned in the flesh, he had sinned deep in his soul? Not against her, that was of little account, but against the very demand of Christ that he show charity and love. Was she then to walk on the same vile path? Be a party to his unchristian ways? Was she to make a pact with the Devil only because Hector was her husband? It seemed to her, sitting on the bench, that this would be the far greater sin. The true corrupting sin that must damn her soul for eternity.

Shona was still sitting on the bench, waiting to become so exhausted that she must re-enter the house in order to go to bed, when de la Rueda woke up. There was a pail in the barn that he might have used and which subsequently could have been added to the barrel in the byre, for urine was collected and used in dying wool. However, de la Rueda had not been informed of this custom and so he stepped out of the barn, drowsy with sleep, and around to the gable wall. A moment later, on his way back, he saw her sitting on the bench.

Instantly he stopped. His heart thumped. He felt the ground disappearing under his bare feet. *I am lost.* And there was no doubt. He had an absolute certainty of fate. It was not a fate he wanted, but want made no difference. He had seen it many times before. He had seen it in the eyes of men he was about to kill, he had seen in it the eyes of animals about to be slaughtered; it was a look of acceptance, of resignation to unavoidable fate. And that is how de la Rueda saw himself at that moment. Hector came to his mind, honour and betrayal came to his mind, but without strength. They made no impression against the overwhelming, unavoidable force of her presence. De la Rueda was not even surprised to see her sitting there. He knew she must be waiting for him. He knew she knew that just as she was destined to sit there waiting for him, he was destined to wake up in need of a piss and go out of the barn to find her there. Every step of the way was inevitable. Perhaps so from the very first moment he had set eyes on the painting those years ago it had been waiting to happen.

Both de la Rueda and Shona moved almost at the same moment. He turned to go back into the barn and she stood up from the bench. For an instant she hesitated. It was not too late. She could turn around and go into the house and hold fast to the life that was hers, the life that she knew, or she could let go of that life, now, and venture into the unknown.

Her heart beat fast and her legs threatened to buckle but she swiftly crossed the short distance to the barn. She closed the door behind her. The room became immediately dark, yet not entirely thus, for over time the rough planks on the door had warped, allowing narrow shafts of silvery light to penetrate the gaps. The outlines of their bodies were just visible to one another as they stood there, face to face. Both felt a violent force pulling them to each other. De la Rueda's mind, even more than Shona's, resisted. It was full of foreboding, but the yearning in his body, in his soul, was ungovernable. The tension could not last. It snapped, the way a storm will snap the mast on a ship. He lifted his arms. She felt his strength, the roughness of him as he took hold of her, and he felt her voluptuousness, the solid yet supple yielding of her. To both of them the same thought occurred, that it was betrayal, that it was sin, but almost as the thought appeared it was vanquished by their awareness that they were truly alone with each other now. Not out of reach of the world, but for these moments beyond caring, alone to give themselves over to the fire that was consuming them.

After it was done, they lay back, breathing hard. Abruptly they were apart and separate again. Both were dazed, unable to believe what had happened. It was not before some moments had passed that they began to acknowledge to themselves the act that had taken place. And it was an act that could not be changed. From this moment on, their lives would never be the same.

Of the two, it was de la Rueda who was soonest mortified. Here he was, lying with a woman who was not his. Another man's wife. A man who had saved his life. How was it possible? How had he allowed such to come to pass? It was treachery of the worst kind. A dishonour beyond words. Yet how could he have prevented it? And her, lying here now beside him in silence, undone, her skin touching his, had she also been compelled? Or was she more calculating? Perhaps it was not the first time she had been with a man who was not her husband? How could he know? They could scarcely communicate. And she was a woman. He could not gauge women. But compelled or willing, she had come to him. Why had she been sitting out there? Why had she not gone back into the house? Had she not the same duty to honour he did? If she were Spanish or French, even Italian or Portuguese, he could talk to her. He wanted to know what she was thinking, what made her betray her husband. Perhaps tomorrow, with sign language, in the light of the day it would be easier to communicate. It was too late now to undo the sin, but if he could just understand it… For fate was not all. It said in the holy book that God gave man free will. The painting was fate. She was fate. And he could say what happened just now between them was inevitable. It was fate. But fate could not reveal itself until it had already occurred. They could have chosen differently. Had they chosen differently they would not be here now, lying side by side. Had they chosen differently their honour would be intact. But they had not chosen differently. They had been overwhelmed by temptation, and although at this moment he was satiated, deep in his being de la Rueda had a sense of calamity. He feared that he could not prevent events from unravelling. He knew that his self-respect, which was everything, was shattered.

Shona did not have the same immediate remorse as de la Rueda. She regretted nothing. Rarely had she known physical ecstasy. On scarcely two or three occasions she had pleasured herself, and on others Hector had been able to accomplish it. In that respect he was not without skill. But life and long marriage had made their bodies dull. Novelty was already scarce before their children died. Thenceforth their physical relations became perfunctory. Now and then, when something came about to break the monotony, there had been a brief resurgence of the attraction they had experienced at the beginning. Such small moments of physical intimacy, of pleasure, had been sufficient to persuade Shona that she was content with what she had. Other men were of little interest; they were too young or too old or married or unattractive or violent or dull. But in de la Rueda she had perceived something unexpected, different, perhaps on the beach, even, when she had first noticed him while her husband lay wounded by her feet. In his eyes their encounter was foretold. Extraordinary providence made it so. Could she deny it? Could she say the painting was mere circumstance? There was a force pulling them to each other whether they willed so or not. With Hector their coming together might have been destined too, but never such fire as she felt with de la Rueda. *Never.* Lying there beside him, it made her wonder if she would not have gone with de la Rueda even had she not fallen out with Hector? Sin it might be, but God would forgive her. Was it so wrong to choose pleasure over pain, love over hate?

But it was dangerous. She could not predict how Hector would respond were he to find out. It must be kept secret.

Abruptly she sat up, adjusting her shift, brushing down her skirt.

'I go, *Monsieur* -'

'Alejandro. My name is Alejandro.'

Shona smiled. 'Alejandro...'

'Yes. That is my name.'

'I help you,' she said, trying to remember the sentences she had composed. 'Spain. You go Spain. I help you.'

'How can you help me?'

'My... brother,' she said. 'We help you.'

De la Rueda sighed.

Shona leaned over. With the tips of her fingers she touched de la Rueda's cheek, then softly she placed her index finger over his lips.

De la Rueda did not move when she walked to the door. Although he felt himself to be falling into an abyss, he was confused by surreptitious feelings that desired to be joyful. His physical body seemed to want to fight his mind. Though his zest was depleted he could nevertheless feel a humming in his sinews, a lightness that made him float in air. Already his body was starting to want her again. It was his reason that said it could not be. It was his reason denying his body. He could want her, crave her, but he must not have her again. This, he was beginning to understand, was the one small chance he might yet have to avoid total ruin. What had occurred was done now. He could not undo it. It did not appear to him at this moment that he could ever regain all that he was losing. He had known soldiers who had blown their brains out over far less. They had been accused of cheating at cards or failing to carry out an order, things it seemed to de la Rueda that were of no great significance, and yet they had deemed it such a stain on their honour as to put a pistol to their heads. He should do likewise, he supposed, but he would not. Not yet at least. It would demonstrate only that he had set too much store on his own worthlessness. Penance was another matter. A man could redeem himself through penance. There were ways of making penance that might yet save his soul. But first he must leave. She had said she would help him escape to his own country; how long must he wait? If the escape was not soon he must surrender, for he could not stay here now. The dangers were too many. *Dear Lord Jesus do not cast me adrift. I have sinned but I beseech you Lord spare my soul. Give me strength.*

Shona lay on the bed next to her husband. He was the same man she had lain beside not much earlier. He was the same but she was not. The change was exhilarating and frightening. She could still feel on her flesh the embers of Alejandro's caresses. If she died tomorrow she could tell herself that for one small moment in her life she had meant something to somebody. For she did not know what she meant to Hector, if she meant anything to him at all. His property, the way his house was his property, the land, the animals, his servants. But she did not want to live just for his whims. Women had no other choice. It was their station in life to do the bidding of the menfolk. Her own mother had always been obedient to her father, but it was possible her mother *wanted* to be obedient. It was not the same with her and Hector. They were more like the Duke and Duchess of Argyll, each raising troops to battle for opposing causes on opposing sides. The Duchess had not always obeyed her husband. And in Inverness-shire once Shona had also met a woman who had total command over her husband's estate and his commercial affairs. Were Hector less obtuse, Shona could see how they might reach an accommodation. It was possible that all her good feelings for him were not beyond repair. She did not know. Time would say. But this fornication that had happened between her and Alejandro – Alejandro. How strange the name felt on her lips -there was beauty in it. She would not despise it. What Alejandro felt now, she could not be sure. He appeared to respect Hector. And she had not the French to put her own feelings about Hector across, lest Alejandro be inclined to judge her harshly. Could Alejandro be feeling guilty and blaming her? Perhaps in his eyes, having given herself to him, she was now a whore, a witch? Perhaps her value to him had been only as a picture of purity in his mind? Well, if that were the case it would distress her. She must seek to put his heart at ease. But no matter what happened now, she would not regret it.

Abruptly Hector's good arm began thrashing. His body jolted. He muttered out loud and woke up. He turned his head towards Shona but whether because of the penumbra or otherwise he did not appear to notice that she was dressed.

'Are you awake?'

'I am.'

'I have been dreaming. My head was chopped off. I was running about like a headless chicken. Someone was running off with my head.'

Shona was not sure if it was from spite or humour but his words almost made her laugh.

Hector struggled to sit up, grunting. Shona did not move to help him. After an effort, Hector managed to get to his feet. He seized hold of the broom, and using it for a crutch, he hobbled over to the commode. He lifted his shirt and pissed. Then he drank some water from the jug on the dresser. Shona watched him with curious detachment.

'Were you able to get your head back?' she asked him, with an effort to appear herself, when he lay down again.

'I woke up. But I do believe my headache is less. Only my thoughts, they are mixed up… I cannot explain. They run away from me...'

'When you heal they may settle down.'

'I must get back to my affairs. What week is it now? Has the solstice passed?'

'It has not been.'

'When is it?'

'On Friday. In two days.'

'It will be time for the trysts soon.'

'Is that all that concerns you, Hector?'

'It is what came to my mind. Cattle tryst. If something else came to my mind I should mention it… Is our guest still here? I know I have spoken to him, but I am confused; was it today or yesterday?'

'I cannot say, but he is still here.' Shona paused. 'I have written to my brother. I am trying to arrange for our guest to escape to his own country.'

'Oh, you are? What more news is there of General Wightman?'

'I have not heard.'

'Farquar has told me Wightman's soldiers are on the move. They are harried, but intent on burning and hanging.'

This was news to Shona.

'Are they coming this way?'

'No one knows which way they will go. They cannot arrive here unannounced. We have the advantage there. But our guest cannot stay here long. If his escape cannot be arranged soon, he must go into hiding or surrender. I may have to go into hiding myself, come to that... How did you send the letter to your brother? Was it post?'

'No. Through a fisherman from Kyle, someone they call The Stick. He is married to one of mine. Neil has arranged it.'

'How much is he asking?'

'I do not know yet, not until he brings my brother's reply.'

Hector closed his eyes. Shona waited for him to speak. But unexpectedly he had fallen asleep again.

NINETEEN

The next day de la Rueda and Shona avoided each other. Both had compelling need of respite from the turbulence that assailed them. The fear of discovery was foremost in their minds. All else could be pushed back, suppressed, until on the surface at least they had regained a semblance of control. But Shona would not have de la Rueda go hungry, so she sent Mairi to fetch him and feed him while she herself went to call on her friend Eubh.

Eubh was no more at home, but on their shieling, where she was staying for the summer months in order to graze the cattle on hill pasture away from the crops, a two hour walk beyond the Giant's Stone. It was cloudy when Shona set off and the air so still that if she were to rest for any length of time infinite quantities of midges would soon rise from the ground to attack her with the thirst for blood that at this time of year started to awake in them. However, as long as she kept walking the midges could not keep pace with her. She walked without stopping into the hills until she came to the two twisted trees. There she paused to gather breath, and since there was a boggy patch of ground nearby, to scoop up handfuls of dark oily peat and smear it thickly on her face, neck, hands and legs. The peat would not prevent the midges from surrounding her but they would not be able to bite her through the layer of mud. Afterwards she took the path to her right and an hour later came to a corrie where on flatter ground above a stream stood a stone-walled pen and a few tiny thatched dwellings. While smoke came out of them there were no people to be seen. Shona was not surprised, for there was no breeze to keep the midges at bay. It was one of those resented summer days when the midges drove people indoors. Eubh's stone dwelling stood a few yards higher on the ground than the others and it was longer. Hens and hobbled goats roamed about on the dirt and grass. Shona banged on the low rough door, which was soon opened by Aileana, one of Eubh's daughters, whose bare skin, like Shona's, was smeared with peat. And so, too, was Eubh's and even the newly born baby in the willow crib by the open hearth on the stamped earth floor, for the midges, not to be deterred, managed to get in through the gaps in the two doors or the single small window.

But close up to the hearth the smoke kept their numbers down. And since there was no breeze this smoke gathered under the roof, all along its length, like a grey blanket before being sucked up through the hole in the thatch. Under the smoke, though, the air was breathable.

Shona took out the presents she had brought from the folds of her skirt, which was hitched up above her petticoat around her waist, and handed them to Eubh. These included baby clothes she had cut and sewn herself and a rattle. Eubh thanked her effusively, then pulled aside the blanket draped over the crib. Shona never saw an infant without a pang of sorrow if not envy, but she kept these feelings to herself as she cooed admiringly. Finally they sat down, Shona on a rough-hewn, low three-legged chair, Eubh on a stool. Meanwhile Eubh's two daughters, little though they were, were made to fetch freshly made cheese and oatcakes from the living end of the room. The other end, beyond the hearth and behind a rough box bed, was an open byre without a partition to separate it from the living quarters and from which came a strong stench of goat and piss mixed with manure.

'How is Hector?' asked Eubh, picking up a spindle. 'Is he improved?'

'His head hurts, but I think it may be less. And the wound on his arm has stopped seeping. Alasdair MacQueen will be coming to see him again next week.'

Eubh darted Shona a shrewd look.

'Are you worried?'

'That he will die?' Shona paused. 'God forgive me, Eubh, but when I think of what is to happen to the Three Rowan folk sometimes I…well…' Shona did not finish. But she did not have to. Eubh could guess what she must be thinking.

'I worry for Angus Peter—'

'For helping me take Lachlan's cattle?'

'He says I should not because he will be never short of droving work but I still worry that Hector might take against him now.'

Eubh began teasing wool onto the spindle.

'It would not be to Hector's advantage. And he is always thinking of his advantage. Without Angus Peter who will take care of the herds? I would not have asked for Angus Peter's help if I thought there was such risk to him.'

'So what is going to happen to the Three Rowan folk now?'

'They will have to leave, I suppose, if Hector still refuses to side with me and Lachlan gets his way. And I promised. They have children. Where will they go if they are driven off?'

'You did what you could.'

'But it was not sufficient.' Shona had a mind to tell Eubh what she had discovered of Hector's plans to put sheep on the Silverwater lands but she held her tongue. Now was not the time. They were only plans. There was as yet too much uncertainty. She did not wish to alarm the tenants who stood to be evicted.

'A band of reivers came by yesterday. Men from the battle, all armed.'

'Where they many?

'No. Only four. Two mounted. I believe one of the mounts was a Spanish pony. They were heading home Loch Carron way but when they heard it was Angus Peter who was herding the cattle up here they gave no trouble. Their spokesman said he knew Angus

Peter from the trysts, but they were only four anyway and we have more than twice as many, so I imagine they will be looking for easier pickings on their way home.'

'Did they mention General Wightman?'

'I was going to tell you. The church at Morvich was torched two days ago, which was when the reivers set off. By the grace of God the minister was able to get all but three away before the troops arrived. One of the prisoners was hanged. No harm came to the other two, who were badly wounded. But the church was burnt to the ground, Shona. General Wightman himself is now heading for Inverness with the main troops, but he is sending out parties to make mischief on the way. Angus Peter thinks General Wightman is after the Earl of Seaforth and all the lords, for according to the reivers some are hiding in the hills beyond Loch Carron and other places, but they will not be caught, Angus Peter does not think, unless they are betrayed.'

'Angus Peter may be right,' said Shona. 'But we are not so very far ourselves from the general's path. Do you think they would venture this far?'

Eubh took a moment.

'There are other places nearer by. And they would have to put hands on Hector.'

Unless they burn and hang without evidence, just for spite. But if word gets out that we are sheltering a Spanish officer they will go out of their way.

'Are you thinking as I am, Eubh?'

'What are you thinking?'

'I must move our guest.'

'It would be safer. What is to happen to him?'

'He wishes to return to his own country.'

'And you can arrange it?'

'I will know soon. Meanwhile can you ask Angus Peter to find somewhere for our guest?' When Eubh appeared to hesitate, Shona added, 'Hector wishes it, too. I have spoken to him and he thinks it for the best if our guest is hidden.'

'Then I will ask him,' said Eubh.

The following morning, before midday, two of Angus Peter's herders arrived at the house while Shona and Mairi were tending to Margaret. They said they had come to take the Spaniard to a hiding place. Shona invited them into the house and bid Mairi serve them ale and oatcakes. Meanwhile Shona sat at the table and with the aid of the dictionary, paper and pencil, composed a note for de la Rueda. Afterwards she gave the note to Mairi and asked her to take it over to de la Rueda and bring it back once read.

After being fed and taking a walk earlier in the morning, de la Rueda was reclining on his bed listening to the blustery change of weather when there came a knock on the door. He stood up quickly and went to open. There was a tightness in his chest until he saw that it was only Mairi. She handed him the folded note and waited. The note was brief.

Sir, you are move. We arrange. If you please now. Thank you.

De la Rueda went into the barn and began to put on his weapons. He wondered where he was being taken and if he would see Shona before leaving. Perhaps he would not see her ever again? The thought brought him blackness. The taste in his mouth turned bitter. He felt himself sinking. But then he remembered the man he had betrayed. If the thought of not seeing Shona again was death, the thought of having to speak now to Hector, knowing what he had done, was a hell worse than death. The shame of it made him cry out and lifting both hands he beat himself hard on the head. When he lowered his hands there were tears in his small dark eyes. He was on the verge of breaking but a voice told him that what he was feeling was mere pity for himself when what he needed to show was penance. He was not a man. He was nothing. He deserved no pity. He was full of filth, a vessel without honour; vermin, a worm, only penance could save him. When and if he finally reached home he would shut himself up in a monastery. He would become a monk. Penance, not self-pity. Only penance could earn the succour of God.

Once de la Rueda was ready he went to wait by the open barn door. Shona, meanwhile, spoke to Hector, who was awake and sitting up, his face gaunt and bearded, his eyes aware but also containing suspicion and bewilderment, as if baffled by the circumstances in which he now found himself.

'Angus Peter knows of somewhere we can hide our guest. Reivers have passed by our high ground. No cattle were taken, for we outnumber them and they know Angus Peter, but they told him the church at Morvich has been burnt to the ground and one person hanged.'

'On whose orders?'

'General Wightman's.'

'Are his troops about?'

'I am told they are. So I am arranging for our guest to be hidden.'

'If we are in danger he must be gone at once. We are not safe. I should have arranged it myself.' Hector sounded peevish and alarmed. Glancing at Shona standing by the bed, for the first time since he had returned he noticed her womanly contours.

'You have been indisposed.'

'But why do you inform me just now? You cannot just go behind my back without consulting me as you did with the cows.'

Defiance flared in Shona's breast: *If only you knew what I can do without consulting you.*

'Do you wish to address our guest before he leaves?'

'And have Mairi send for Lachlan. I am going to put him in charge.'

'In charge of what?'

Hector hesitated, for it was a belittlement that he was intending. Exactly why he had this urge to hurt his wife, especially when she was taking such care of him, he could not divine except to know that it was not new. Throughout their years of marriage he had often felt there was something in Shona that wanted to slip away. When the children were alive they had called for her attention and he had not minded; but before and after the children he had resented this elusive quality in her that was not obedient, that resisted him, that would not defer.

'In charge of my affairs,' he said.

Shona's green eyes turned bright, like a cat's. But her anger, which in other circumstances would have persisted, was at once replaced by indifference.

'Why does it not surprise me, Hector?'

'I do not know. Why does it not surprise you?'

'Because I will be myself? Because I will seek God's mercy before I seek yours? Do as you wish. I cannot prevent you. Only know that White Eyes will rob you blind.'

'He has a mind for commerce but I have no reason to distrust him.'

If it was his hand wanting under your plaid you might say differently.

'I will have our guest sent in.'

Shona left the bedroom. In the common room she told Mairi to fetch the gentleman and take him to Hector.

A terrible dread assailed de la Rueda as he followed Mairi to the house. He could not say who he feared meeting more, Shona or Hector. But when he crossed over to the house it was like a man bound for the gallows.

Mairi showed him straight to the bedroom. In passing the common room he kept his gaze averted for fear of encountering Shona, but she, on hearing de la Rueda enter, had moved to a part of the room where she would not be seen.

'Ah, come in, *Monsieur*,' Hector greeted him.

De la Rueda, in forcing a smile managed only a tormented grimace which he attempted to conceal with a bow.

'My wife tells me you are leaving us?'

'I understand I am to be hidden elsewhere.'

'*Certainement*. The enemy is about now. It would be dangerous for you to remain here.'

'Have you news of the enemy's movements?'

'A church has been put to fire. One man hanged. Wightman's soldiers now march in pursuit of our leaders. But any of our kind, high or low, will suit their purpose if they are caught.'

'Then I should be obliged not to burden your gracious self further.'

'My wife is trying to arrange your escape from our country. If it cannot be done, I would suggest you make arrangements to surrender.'

'I will do as you suggest.'

An awkward silence ensued. It was now the moment for de la Rueda to express his profound gratitude to Hector for saving his life, but he felt such deep shame that he could not bring the words up.

He is embarrassed. Hector misread de la Rueda's stricken look.

'Well, good luck, *Monsieur*. It has been a pleasure to make your acquaintance.'

'I would not be alive without your brave actions in the battle,' de la Rueda said at last. 'I am obliged to you. And may God reward you.'

Hector held up his hand. He was about to speak when de la Rueda, unable to endure being there a moment longer, bowed deep from the waist, turned, and fled the room. But as he was crossing past the common room to the main door, Shona came up after him.

De la Rueda could not look at her directly but her presence was a force he could not avoid. He took the note that she passed him. Her small hand shook, as did his own.

Sir, I arrange. We speak more.

De la Rueda handed the note back. For the barest instant he met her eyes. When he stepped through the door and towards the barn it could have been the very Devil on his heels.

A little later three of Angus Peter's men presented themselves at the barn door and with gestures made de la Rueda understand he was to follow them.

The three men set off on foot in the rain with a pack horse. Under his weapons de la Rueda wore the clothes he had borrowed from Hector. The ascent into the hills was muddy with the rain, and his spare boots had finally come apart, so he removed them and carried what remained of them under his arm. Walking barefoot was not so bad as he presumed for the water and mud served to soften much of the ground. Still, his feet were not accustomed and it slowed his progress when the ground became difficult. The men soon became aware of the foreigner's predicament, so wherever they could he was taken over soft ground and they waited for him to catch up when necessary. After three hours of walking they arrived at a stream which descended sharply to a loch. Clusters of ash, birch and other small trees grew along the stream. The men took the loaded creels off the horse and tied one each to their backs. With the pony left behind, de la Rueda was guided up the side of the stream, in places so steep they had to scramble over rocks and use their hands for purchase. But at the top the ground flattened. In between two low humps of sandy grass and shale stood a tiny oblong stone dwelling. It had a makeshift roof of heather and a door constructed from rough-hewn wood. Inside there was no room to stand upright and the earth floorspace allowed for little other than a heather bed, a hearth, an iron pot, a few utensils, and a block of wood to sit on. During his short inspection de la Rueda saw evidence of goat droppings and hair, which led him to conclude that the shelter was used by goat herders.

Since the guides could not communicate except by sign language, there was little interchange with de la Rueda before their departure. Going through the provisions left for him, de la Rueda noted that Shona had thought to include two bottles of claret, as well as salted meat and fish, cheese, and oats. Water he could get from the stream. If he was careful he calculated that he had sufficient to last him a couple of weeks. The hearth was out, but he was in no hurry to light it with the tinder box they had provided. Instead, he went out to reconnoitre his surroundings. A short distance to his right and a little further up was the spring from which the stream began to descend. The far bank of the stream became increasingly steep and wooded. He thought it would be difficult for men to cross over without being spotted if he were on the lookout. As for the land in front of him and to the left of the dwelling, it fell away in a broken terrain that was yet clearly visible as it descended to a rocky coastline with the sea beyond. Only the ground behind him, he decided, after climbing a hump to survey it, offered any small element of surprise. But even then it would be difficult if he ascended daily to where he was now standing and took a little time to study the expanse of hilly ground below for any sign of human movement. The hours when he was most exposed to capture would be in the night when he was asleep, but he wondered if he really cared so much any more what became of him. *I will stay alive in order to do penance; but if I am caught it will be God's will and no less than I deserve.*

Four days after de la Rueda was moved, Neil arrived at the house in the evening with a letter for Shona. When Shona saw the letter in Neil's large hand faintness came over her. She could say not if it was more on account of happiness or sorrow. Since de la Rueda had gone her body had felt deprived, as if a gaping hole had appeared under her skin. There was hunger in her womb, a yearning to have him close. At night she lay in bed, unable to sleep, imagining, in spite of the fear that it could be sin after all, that it was the Spaniard and not Hector who lay beside her. But she knew it was not possible. Even if Hector were to die it would not be possible. The only event that could have the least opportunity of making it possible was for the whole situation in the land to be turned around. The Jacobite cause for James would have to have been won and the Spaniards no longer enemies for her lover to have the least chance of remaining in the country. Without such all was hopeless. It had never been otherwise. A moment's sinful foolishness that she must forever keep to herself.

Shona took the letter from Neil's hand, sat down at the table, and after examining the seal broke it open.

Dear Sister,

I hope this finds you in good health and cheer. I have several men, and in particular one, who I will here not name, who with the grace of God may accomplish your request. I leave the manner of transport to myself in your hands. Once this is procured we can seek the means to complete the endeavour.

Meanwhile I entreat you to take utmost care. With fondest regards, Your brother.

The letter was not signed, but Shona had gone to school with her brother and she noted that he was still using the odd clumsy flourish on certain letters.

'We have to transport our guest there ourselves, Neil.'

'It will be for the best. We can choose the place and the time.'

'How much should I give The Stick for his trouble?'

'Are there more letters to deliver?'

'Not now.'

'Not too little, in any case. A groat maybe.'

'I thought you said he could be trusted?'

'He is a good man, but he holds a grievance easily, Shona.'

'So he cannot be trusted?'

'I believe he is trustworthy; but… well...' Neil shrugged.

'But what?

'Where money is concerned it is hard to be sure with anyone...'

Shona sighed. She had money of her own though not a lot. And she did not know how much the Spaniard had, if any, though now she must endeavour to find out. But it meant that until she knew how much money would be available and how much the whole endeavour was likely to cost, she had to be circumspect.

'So we are paying for his silence?'

Shona went into the bedroom, opened her chest, and took out the money box. Hector watched her from the bed.

'Are you taking money?'

'I have to pay the letter bearer.'

'Who is that?'

'A fisherman they call The Stick, from Kyle.'

Hector had to think hard before he remembered anything.

'The Stick? I cannot place him... Have you received a letter, did you say?'

'I have.'

'Who from?'

'My brother.'

Again Hector had to concentrate, but it was coming back to him now.

'So he will help with our guest?'

'He will.'

'And how?'

'My brother will not say openly. When our guest arrives there I will know more.' Shona hardly hesitated before she spoke again. 'I will take our guest to my brother myself.'

Hector had nearly forgotten the dispute he had had with Shona days before. He was not pleased to be told she would not be there to look after him. His forgetfulness and intermittent confusion, so it appeared, was being exacerbated by the laudanum MacQueen had left behind for him, while doing little to relieve his violent headaches.

'We have the men. There is no need for you to go.'

Shona looked at him coldly. 'He is my brother. It is best if I go.'

Hector felt his headache flaring. He and Shona had never been apart other than by mutual accord. All his married life he had assumed his wife would be at his side when there was need. That in part she resented him for managing the estate in the manner he did, and that her affections for him were not as they had once been, was a predicament he had come to accept as the natural consequence of a marriage that was not all they wished it to be. But what held true for himself he also expected for his wife. It appeared to him that Shona was breaking the boundaries implied in their marriage. She was disregarding her obligation to nurse him for the mere vanity of satisfying a desire to accommodate a guest who, in his view, had already been sufficiently accommodated. Indeed, whose life, he himself had just recently saved.

'Then you go at my displeasure.'

'I am not surprised. Whenever I venture a will of my own it is at your displeasure.'

'You are my wife.'

'Mairi will take care of you.'

'Mairi is not my wife!'

'The physician is due tomorrow.'

Hector's eyes narrowed. 'What has that to do with it?'

'I will hear what he has to say. And then I will decide.'

Hector was not satisfied. He was anxious and angry to think that Shona would not at once acquiesce. He wanted to assert himself, impose himself, but he had not the strength to rise from his bed, much less to go after her when she turned and left the room.

MacQueen arrived as he had the first time, mounted on a horse and smelling of whisky. After getting his bags and boxes from the panniers he went into the house, where he was greeted by Shona, and shown into the bedroom.

'Ah, I see you are much improved, Hector.'

'Am I? I am still not well.'

'It takes time. Yours is a grievous head wound. You cannot expect to recover in days.'

Pulling up a chair, MacQueen turned to Shona and asked for warm water. When Shona returned with the pot of water MacQueen used it to soften the bandages on Hector's head.

'Are your headaches better?'

'They come and go. I wish them gone altogether but what troubles me to excess is my mind. I cannot seem to get a grip on it. My thoughts will not settle.'

'Your humours are out of balance. It is common for men when they receive a head wound.' MacQueen pulled away the last of the bandage. Without the bandage Hector's patchy hair looked like the plumage of a fledgling bird. 'I see the skin is already healing. Excellent. I will apply a potion now to help it on its way. Then we must look at your arm.' Using his fingers MacQueen applied a salve made of herbal extracts. Then around Hector's head he wrapped a fresh bandage. This done, again with the help of warm water, he unwrapped the bandage on Hector's arm. 'You are fortunate the sword did not take your hand off. See here? The scar is dry. It is starting to heal. These war wounds are a strange business. Some folk pass away with one, and others may receive five or ten and recover to live.'

'Will I live?'

'It is in the hands of God, Hector. But I have every reason to believe so.'

'You see that bottle you gave me, Alasdair?'

'The laudanum?'

'Well, it is near empty. I want more.'

MacQueen hesitated. The value of laudanum for head wounds was disputed among physicians. It also had a reputation for being addictive. On the other hand MacQueen stood to make a profit on the sale and it would serve to pacify his patient.

'Very well,' he said. 'But avail yourself of it in moderation or it may cause you harm. Does it help your headaches?'

Hector sighed. 'It gives me dreams. Sometimes I know not if I am awake or asleep. But it makes the day go by.'

TWENTY

De la Rueda had run out of everything except oats. It was all that remained and only a few handfuls at that. No one had visited him. Strokes of charcoal on a stone by the door post marked the days he had been in the shieling. Ten so far; all but two of them without foul wind and rain. On one of those two days when he had been outside he had seen a hare. From his childhood he could remember how the peasants on his estate had sometimes dug a deep hole which was rigged with a snare and then lightly covered. When the rabbit or hare came for the bait it would fall into the hole and get trapped by the snare. De la Rueda, sitting on the earth floor, his back against the wall, for a moment imagined himself constructing such a trap, catching a hare, cooking it. The juices in his mouth flowed at the notion. But instead of hare, he was reduced to standing up, reaching for the bag hanging from a beam and extracting a meagre handful of oats. These he mixed with cold water in a bowl and sat down to eat by scooping a little at a time into his mouth and chewing it over and over. By such means he could attempt to persuade himself that the quantity was greater than it was. In two, three days, he would start to starve, unless he was so lucky as to construct a trap that could catch a hare or someone arrived with provisions.

But maybe it was what he deserved after all? If he starved here like a dog it would be a just punishment. What had happened had to be the devil's work. It had been planned all those years ago when the painting had been put in his path. Like God Himself, Lucifer could command infinite destinies within the blink of an eyelid. De la Rueda was just one more among the multitude of doomed souls trapped daily in the Devil's net. How else could such dishonour be explained? Was there anything more foul, more full of sin than to betray the man who had saved his life? He must pay – if not here now, then when he returned home. Like Saint John of the Cross, a Jew such as himself, he would take vows and cloister himself in a monastery to pray for his soul, and yes, beat down his foul flesh, starve it, squeeze it so hard Satan himself would find it too mean.

An indistinct sound came from outside as de la Rueda munched on the oats, brooding. At once he put down his bowl quietly and reached for the sword which at all times he kept nearby. But as he stood up and started to remove the sword from its scabbard he heard the whistle that the men had made him understand would announce their presence.

When de la Rueda opened the door one of the men and Neil were standing outside. Nods and silent acknowledgement were exchanged, then Neil made gestures. De la Rueda understood. He gathered his arms and scant possessions and moments later he was following the men down the way they had arrived.

The night was clear, bright with a full moon. De la Rueda's guides travelled fast and he struggled to keep up in the boots he had himself badly repaired. When they came to the bottom of the burn they passed by the side of a roundish loch, shimmering silver, and then between hills where at one moment a pair of startled grouse flew up from under their legs. Finally they arrived at the Giant's Stone, but after they had passed it, instead of turning left towards the infields and the house, they turned right. Small cultivations of early bear, now waist-high and swaying in the breeze, appeared on the hillsides, then more heath as they arrived at the edge of the coastline which they had to follow for a while before passing through a narrow rock gulley and out onto a sandy cove. There, anchored in the shallow water at the tide edge was a boat. When de la Rueda saw it he thought it was on its own but as they approached two figures rose from among the nearby rocks. De la Rueda's heart stopped. For an instant everything stopped. Waves and wind stopped. Sound stopped. Time stopped. Everything everywhere stopped for there was no room in de la Rueda's mind for other than her presence as she stood there, boldly, her eyes steady on him, her face round and pale under the hood of an arisaid drawn over her shoulders as it fell to the long skirt beneath.

As for Shona, when she saw him jolt, and caught, even in the penumbra and from a distance, the stricken look in his eyes, and his gaunt, dishevelled appearance, she too felt as though time had stopped. A sudden feverish warmth suffused her body. But it was no more than a moment before time caught up with them and broke the spell.

Stepping closer, de la Rueda bowed.

'*Madame.*'

Shona inclined her head in return. She turned to the others. 'Let us go'.

Old John, wild and filthy, lifted Shona's leather-bound trunk by its handles and, hobbling, carried it to the boat. The trunk had arrived with them on the boat, but Shona had thought it safer brought ashore while they waited. Once the trunk was placed back onboard, Old John steadied the boat while de la Rueda clambered in. But Old John could not so easily get in himself on his arthritic legs, so Neil gave him a lift. After Shona got in, hitching up her skirt and petticoats, Neil and the other man lifted anchor, pushed the boat around to face the sea, and climbed in themselves. The four men, with Shona at the tiller, rowed out to sea, the boat bucking against the waves. As they did so, Old John, who had a good voice, began to sing and the others, except for de la Rueda, joined in. After the sail was hoisted the men continued to row, but de la Rueda, Shona noticed, appeared to be flagging, rowing out of step with the others.

'Neil,' she said, leaning forward, 'do you know if there was any food left when you arrived for our guest?'

'I do not think there was much. It was all gone.'

'Pass the ale then. Our guest must be weak with hunger.'

In one of the two bags that Shona had besides her trunk she carried a matured goat cheese, oats, and dried, salted meat. The men stopped rowing when she brought these out.

For all the mortified condition of de la Rueda's mind, hunger made him seize the food and the flagon of ale when they were proffered. In his weakened condition the ale soon went to his head. He became dazed but also it gave him energy. Shona took only a small amount of food herself. She did not feel hungry but the other men joined in heartily.

Gradually, with the hours, the looming, mountainous mass of the Isle of Skye drew closer. Shona remembered that it was not so long ago she had been home for her uncle's funeral. There had been a reason beyond reproach for going then. She could not say the same this time. Tongues were sure to wag. All she knew was that it was something she was compelled to do. Hector was not the man to prevent her. She had considered it. Sitting at the table, on her own, when all was quiet, she had gone over every reason for staying. Hector needed her. It was her duty. She was his wife. She had to manage the estate while he could not. What she was wanting was against the law of God. It was mortal sin. More than once she doubted her sanity, unable to comprehend how such recklessness had come upon her. But always he was there, as he was now bent over an oar in front of her, always when she should have been worrying, fretting over Hector, ministering to his needs, this foreigner whose name she could with difficulty pronounce was in her mind taking up every corner of it. The longing she felt for him was like nothing she had known. Only death – the death of her parents, the death of her children, her beautiful children – had unbalanced her more. For Hector she had not ever felt a lust that made her womb burn. It was that, and it was knowing his lack of charity. *If he would see how I despise him for it. If he would change his ways so that I can hold my head up. But he will not. And I will not rot in this grave. I will not. I want the light. I want the air.*

Shona had no plans that were definite. She did not know what would be the final outcome of her recklessness. She had asked her brother only to help the Spaniard escape. How long she stayed with her brother, what his response would be, when she would return to Hector, or if she would return at all, where all questions to which she had no answer. Much would depend on the Spaniard. It had yet to declare itself what would happen; but even without him Shona had the intuition, both frightening and exhilarating, that her life had reached a turning point. From now on she must choose her own way and seek forgiveness only from God. Men could not decide for her. Not her husband, not her brother, not the Spaniard. If she must fashion her future on her own, so be it. And it was with this thought in mind that, after she had packed the travelling trunk and the two bags, she had made a decision that had caused her heart to flutter and her bowels to churn. From the chest of drawers in the bedroom she had removed the box containing her finest jewellery and from the large trunk with a lock on it she had removed the pouch containing the gold sovereigns, none of which she had ever spent, that had come down from her mother and which her father had divided between her and her sister when they had married and left home. The jewellery and the coins were Shona's entire wealth. It was kept now close to her body in an embroidered bag she had fastened at her waist with an ornate leather belt.

Since she was going to her brother's with Hector's knowledge, however resentful, there had been no need for the other preparations to be kept from him. All had been done in the open. Precautions of secrecy were for the safety of the Spaniard. If Hector had no reason to suspect that Shona intended going any further than to her brother's, neither did Mairi or the others except for Neil. To him she had hinted her tumultuous thoughts when, in expectation of a salmon run after the recent rain, he had come for a net.

As he was leaving, Shona had taken him around the side of the house where they could speak without being overheard.

'When I go to my brother I do not know what I will do after.'

'Why do you say that Shona? Are you not wanting to come back?'

'I do not know. I may come back when you do but I may not. I just do not know now.'

Neil had fingered the net in his thick fingers; silent, a frown on his brow.

'We are kin, Neil. My brother will not abandon you That is what I want to tell you. I will make certain.'

It had taken Neil a moment to understand. He nodded slowly. The clan ways were not what they once were. The old bonds of kinship meant little. Men's lives were to be done with as the chiefs pleased. But Shona was loyal. He had to trust her brother showed the same. He would have to take her word that the Glas sept would have him and all his family back should Hector turn against him.

A few days later when Shona was leaving Mairi had become upset. Tears welled as she had watched Old John place the trunk and bags on the sledge that was attached to the pony.

'Will you be gone long?' Mairi had asked.

'Only a little while, to make sure our guest gets away to his country,' Shona had dissembled.

She had felt guilty for not sharing her truer thoughts with Mairi, or her friend Eubh, as she had with Neil. Mairi was a good woman. Over the years Shona had bonded with her. She would never forget how good Mairi had been to her during the difficult time when the children died, but Mairi belonged to Hector's estate, there was no connection to Shona's clan like there was with Old John and Neil.

As the boat drew close to the shore of Skye it sailed past the broken walls of the medieval castle by Kylakin and then into the sound of Sleat. Here the hills of Skye on their right, and the hills of the mainland on their left, rose to face each other, their brooding, shadowy outlines close by on either side of the narrow, fast flowing channel. When after a while they approached the end of the channel, before it began to open into the sea again, Shona released the halyard to bring the sail down, then turned the tiller to point the boat landward. As she did so the men began to row hard lest the current carry the boat past the cove before it could be steered ashore. But this was familiar water for Shona. She guided the boat deftly in between the treacherous rocks upon which the waves foamed and crashed. With a last effort the boat was rowed onto the shore, whereupon they all jumped out, and standing in shallow water, pushed it as far up as they could onto dry land before dropping the anchor. Nearby two other boats, one of them considerably larger than theirs, were upturned on a strip of grass beyond the tide reach. There was also a pile of sawn logs and a new built timber hoist.

Neil and the other man took a handle each and carried Shona's trunk up the path; steep for a short while before it flattened out under the forest on the hillsides higher up. When Shona's father was alive a lookout most likely would have seen them arrive, for the booty in the cave had to be guarded, but now that the cave was little used the first to detect their presence were two dogs that broke out barking as they arrived at the first dwellings. One door opened and then another. As shadowy figures emerged, Neil spoke up. The first two figures came forward, and then more joined them. It was difficult to see in the deep twilight but they were recognized and Shona was greeted warmly. After a little talk the party carried on. They passed shadowy oat and barley fields, climbed further, and came to the main settlement, which could not be perceived except as vague structures scattered about. Again a dog barked. But now the party did not stop until it reached a house a little higher on a level strip of its own.

Shona pulled on the door. As it opened a dog growled and then yelped. Immediately it came crawling forward, tail wagging. Shona leaned over to pat its head, speaking to it. Stirrings came from further in the house and a voice said: 'Who is it?'

'It is I. You sister.'

'Shona! Is that you, truly?'

'It is.'

'I will light a lamp.'

Shortly the whole household was up and awake. Such included Douglas' wife, Kirstine, and their four children. Along with de la Rueda, Shona, and the three others it was a tight fit around the hearth. This was in the centre of the room and did not have the benefit of a chimney. Smoke gathered like a blanket under the beams before being sucked up the opening in the thatched roof.

'This is the Spanish gentleman I wrote to you about,' said Shona to her brother.

Douglas had never been much good at schoolwork. Unlike many first sons of chieftains he had not progressed to university. He could read and write Gaelic adequately, and could speak some English, but except for the odd word had forgotten such French and Latin as he had learnt. As a consequence his ruddy, affable face could only smile and nod at de la Rueda, who bowed deeply in return. Meanwhile Kirstine, a small, round woman with a pleasant manner, set about producing rough oatcakes. Then Douglas poured whisky from a keg into the intricately carved silver and wood quaich that had been his father's and grandfather's.

'To your health.' He took a sip before passing the quaich on. None missed out except the infant; even the family's next child, a four years old boy, was allowed to wet his lips. He did not like the taste and pulled a face, which made the parents laugh.

Neil and Old John had relatives they could stay with. And they offered to take the other man with them. The three went away in due course after they had been fed and given handfuls each of oats to put in their sporrans. Kirstine and her eldest daughter went off to make a bed for de la Rueda in one of the barns by the house.

'If you please, *Monsieur.*'

As Shona spoke she spread the palm of her hand. De la Rueda understood. He sat down by the hearth when Shona and her brother did, but he did not look at her. Now that the glow of the lamp allowed him to see her, he felt the stirrings of two contrary urges. The one to devour her with his eyes and the other to claw his eyes out. For the moment, however, such violent conflicting impulses were enfeebled by exhaustion. What he most wanted was to sleep.

'I have news,' said Douglas. 'It comes from our sister.'

'A letter?'

'No such. Sleepy Macphail.'

'That old man; is he still smuggling then?'

'Only a little I believe. At the moment he is buying our timber. We are fortunate. We have him on our side and he is often down Mallaig way. Aila gave him a message. She has discovered that arrangements are being made in the Rough Bounds to receive the Marques of Tullibardine and other lords. It is intended they will hide there until they can be transported to Spain.'

'It is certain?'

'What is certain nowadays? Machpail is due back in three weeks. He may bring more news then. You can speak to him yourself if you are not returned to your husband. How is he keeping by the way?'

'He is mending. But I do not know how well. Is it your idea our guest can escape with the lords – when they do?'

'That would be the plan, so it would. But first they must arrive, and then we must get our guest there. I cannot say how long it will all take.'

'But it is a start.'

Kirstine came back in. The guest's bed was ready. Douglas stood up and refilled the quaich. For just an instant Shona and de la Rueda exchanged a glance. Then, when Shona stood up, de la Rueda did so as well. Once more the quaich was passed around.

'Can sleep now, if you please,' Shona said.

'Ah, *Merci.* Thank you,' responded de la Rueda. He bowed to the family and waited.

De la Rueda followed Shona out to the barn. At the door Shona stood aside.

'Good night, *Monsieur.*' Without waiting for his reply she turned and went back into the house.

Shona slept in a box bed with her two nieces. The box bed was by the byre, which was divided from the human quarters by a partition of thick planks. Although they were tightly fitting, the odour from the two milking cows, several goats, and various fowl was pervasive. Along with the odour came heat. A little too much of it now, at this time of year, perhaps, but welcome in winter. For Shona the animal smells and warmth so close by was reassuring. Douglas and Kirstine slept in a box bed on the other side of the hearth, which they shared with their young son and infant. This box bed had belonged to Shona's parents. It was quite large, with a double door instead of a curtain and was ornately carved, as befitted a chieftain. The box bed Shona shared with her nieces was smaller. It was the same one Shona had used as a child, although now it had a different mattress and new curtains. The space inside was cramped for the three of them but Shona was too tired to notice.

Although she fell asleep at once it was only two or three hours before she woke up again. It was dark and her nieces, squashed up beside her, were sleeping soundly, but from across the long room Shona could hear the infant crying. For a moment it brought back a memory of nights she had spent awake with her own children, then she found herself thinking of the Spaniard and wondering why it was he had withdrawn into himself so. His eyes avoided her and not once had he made an attempt to converse with her. Could it be that he was beginning to disdain her already? It was a distressing thought; a stone weighing her down, sinful as their union might be, but there was another possibility as well which might explain his behaviour. It seemed to her she was perceiving in him not so much disdain of her as anguish, and why would that be unless he believed that he had gravely sinned? Yet what sin was it if the man they had betrayed was not himself worthy of commanding fidelity? Was it then betrayal at all? Was it? She could not speak for what had occurred on the battlefield. It was not for her to judge. But she could speak for what she knew. Somehow she must find the manner to explain to the Spaniard that the Hector he had been acquainted with in battle was a Hector very different to the one she called her husband. *I will not let him leave without making him understand. He must be told why I have no love for Hector, why he is no more a man I can respect. Let the Spaniard then judge me as he judges me now, if that must be, but not before he knows everything. Everything!*

Shona had brought the French dictionary with her. The book, along with sign language and the little French she could speak, would enable her to communicate with the Spaniard at the simplest level. But for him to understand more she must learn more words and structures quickly. With this in mind she resolved that in the morning early she would spend a while writing French words out, memorizing them, and practising sentences in her mind.

By dawn she had arisen. She went outside to do her toilet and wash herself in the burn nearby, for most settlements had such streams. Afterwards she stood staring about her, at the dwellings and barns scattered some yards apart, on the grass a little below and which was dissected by a continuation of the stream that ran past her brother's house. Smoke, smelling of peat, drifted up from the roofs into a sky that contained a pale violet haze – an indication that it would be a dry warm day. There were no people about, but any moment now they would start to appear and once they saw her they would be wanting to come forth and greet her. Remembering her resolution, as well as being pestered by midges, she quickly went back indoors. However, the family were themselves starting to rise and she could not easily ignore them. So she spoke to the children, in particular her eldest niece who was nearly eleven, and set about helping her sister-in-law tend the hearth and set food on the table while the animals were being taken out of the byre.

'Our guest must come in to eat,' said Douglas, sitting down at the low oak table with a pewter mug of ale.

'Do you know if he has arisen?' asked Shona.

'I did not see him,' said the Shona's youngest niece who had just come in from outside.

'Let me look at the dictionary first. There are some words I must know.'

Douglas watched Shona go over to the trunk, placed on the roughly laid flagstones that passed for a floor, and take out the dictionary.

'Do you have pencil and paper?'

Douglas stood up and went to the bureau under the window opposite the table. The bureau, like the box bed and most of the other furniture, had belonged to Shona's parents. All the furniture was of good quality, but it was scantier and, except for one or two pieces, less refined than the furnishings Hector owned. After rummaging about Douglas came back with a scrap of paper, already partly written on, and a pencil. But now the children and her brother himself came to crowd around her, waiting to see what she was going to do with the pencil and paper.

Shona sighed. She pushed the paper aside.

'Is it the French you are wanting to better?'

'It is all we can speak together.'

Douglas sat down in his chair again. 'Well, in that case I have a better idea.'

Shona waited.

'Our old schoolmaster.'

'What about him?'

'He is living in Camus Cross now.'

'Oh? So near? I thought he was in Portree.'

'He was. But he has a daughter in Camus Cross. It is my understanding he is living with her since his wife died. I could send for him. I cannot see that he will refuse if he is able to travel and we pay him. Besides, I must speak to him in any case about setting up a school for the children.'

'Do you not have that other teacher still?'

'Maclean, do you mean? We do not. He left. But the young fellow was not much good at French. It is a bit late now for the older children to be learning French; but better late than not at all.'

Shona thought for a moment.

'It would make it easier, true.'

'He could speak for you, too.'

'I am not sure of that.' Shona looked straight at her brother. 'What I have to discuss with our guest may be private.'

Douglas took a sip from the tankard and wiped his lips with the back of his hand. His eyes were inquiring but he kept silent.

'But if I could learn from teacher it would help me remember all the French I have forgotten.'

'You could speak it a lot better than I could. You were always better at school.'

'If I had been a boy I might have gone to university.'

'Well, I cannot do anything about that! But I will send someone with a message for the schoolmaster this morning.'

'I could go myself. It is not far. Can you make a pair of ponies ready? The schoolmaster may need to ride one.'

'Well… I suppose… As I said I must speak to him in any case. Very well, we will see to it after eating.'

Kirstine began filling bowls with porridge from the cauldron. The family sat down on unstable stools and chairs to begin eating at the table.

'Will someone go again for our guest?' asked Kirstine.

They all looked at Shona. Left with no choice she went out and tapped on the barn door. Below her, people and animals were starting to emerge from the dwellings. Sounds came from inside the barn. Shona stepped back as the door opened.

'*Bonjour,* Good morning *Monsieur.*'

The dark close-set eyes buried in the bearded face gave Shona a single tormented look before skittering away.

'*Madame.*'

De la Rueda bowed.

'*Manger, si'l vous plait.* Eat, if you please.'

'*Je viendrai dans un instant.*'

Shona understood. He would come in a moment.

'Good. Thank you.'

As Shona turned to leave a man outside one of the nearby houses raised a hand to her in greeting but she was too agitated to notice. Her heart was beating fast when she went back to the house.

'He will come in a moment,' she said, sitting down at the table.

The family started eating.

'How is the trade?' Shona asked her brother for something to say.

'In timber? Well, we are getting by. And we have more calves this year. Ten more. But it is not like in father's day.'

'Or even your uncle's,' Kirstine interjected. 'The timber does not make up for the brandy. And at the rate we are having to fell it, it will all be gone one day.'

'It is so, but what can we do? There are more government troops than ever in these parts now with the barracks they are wanting to build in Glenelg. I could not risk it.'

It was true. Freebooting had become an increasingly dangerous occupation. But there was another reason her brother did not take up after her father and uncle, Shona knew. And that was because he had little liking for boats. Somewhat to her father's disappointment it had always been her who had wanted to sail with him.

'The crops at least are looking to be good, so long as the weather holds. God willing we will all get by this year, but who can say what is to come?' Kirstine shook her head. 'Some folk talk of leaving for the New World. It is only the reports coming back that stops them.'

'What reports are those?'

'Folk die on the ships, it is said. The Macdonald sells his own kin for slaves, and if they do not die on the ships they die over there. Hunger, savages, illness – I know not what else.'

'The Macdonald of Sleat have long been cruel to their kin,' said Douglas. 'That is why father was happy to take their brandy.'

'Father had charity.' The words came out before Shona could stop them. 'My husband is no different from those Macdonald. He will be throwing folk off the land to put sheep in their place. The sheep will make him more money. That is what he says but I cannot abide it. I cannot!'

Both of Shona's small hands were clenched on the table top. Her green eyes flared defiance.

Various thoughts crossed Douglas' mind. He himself had never cared so much for Hector, who had always seemed to him stiff and self-regarding. But he was wounded now, in need of care, and he wondered if his sister's animosity – the intensity of it – was due entirely to the treatment of his tenants, or was it something else that was making her leave her home to be here?

Just at that moment the door creaked and de la Rueda appeared.

At once Douglas stood up, his round, ruddy face smiling, but speechless.

Kirstine told the girls to take their bowls to the hearth where they had a bench to sit on. After bowing, de la Rueda sat down on a vacated chair. As if by mutual consent he and Shona avoided looking at each other. Douglas stepped over to the ale barrel and poured a jar for the guest while Kirstine fetched a spare bowl and filled it with porridge. In spite of his inner turmoil, de la Rueda found that he was hungry.

'Can you explain anything to the gentleman?' Douglas asked his sister while de la Rueda ate.

'What do you wish explained?'

'He should know we are waiting to receive a message but it will not be for three weeks.'

'I will write it out.'

Shona brought the dictionary to the table again. With its help she managed to scribble on the paper: *We wait message. Three weeks come.* She handed the paper to her brother. He frowned, glanced at her in puzzlement, and pushed the note across the table. De la Rueda read it and looked up at Douglas, nodding.

'Merci, Monsieur.'

'He thanks me?'

'He does.'

'Ask him if he will accompany me this morning. I am going to look at some trees. Maybe he can help fell one?'

'I will just ask him to accompany you.'

Shona wrote again. To her surprise the only word she had to look up was 'ask'. The finished note passed once more to her brother.

'*Mon plaisir*. My pleasure,' said de la Rueda, after reading the note.

Douglas clapped his hands. 'A dram, and then we shall go.'

'But he has no shoes. His boots are broken.'

'Oh?... Well, he can have a pair of mine. And I will send for the ponies. Will you be taking someone with you?'

Shona thought of her friend Morag, but she would be busy now. There would be plenty of time in the next days for them to catch up.

'Neil can come with me, if he is free.'

'Very well. But you should not leave it too late.'

Kirstine went to fetch a pair of her husband's shoes. He had several pairs; some for working in and made of one piece. After she same back with the shoes she put them down on the table.

'For you, *Monsieur*,' Shona said.

'*Merci. Merci beaucoup*.' De la Rueda looked at Douglas as he spoke.

'He thanks you,' said Shona.

Douglas nodded and went for the quaich and the whisky. Shona declined the whisky. The two men imbibed, then communicated with gestures as Douglas allowed de la Rueda to step in front of him towards the door.

After they had gone Shona felt a sense of relief. It was many years since she had travelled to Camus Cross itself and she could look forward to a day out in the land of her childhood without the burden of having to think about the Spaniard, or her husband, but in particular the Spaniard. It looked to be a bonnie day. For the next hours she would try to appreciate it.

TWENTY ONE

The schoolmaster's hair had been ginger and frizzy when Shona learnt from him as a child. Now, fanning out from his skull, it was still frizzy but white. The face framed by it was pink, round, and remarkably unwrinkled. His eyes were blue and clear and they retained the twinkle that Shona remembered. But his hands were deformed, his joints swollen, and he could walk only a few steps with the help of a staff.

'As much as I would like to, dear child, I could not manage it to your brother's. I could not.'

They were sitting side by side on the long plank that served as a bench against the front outside wall. Hens pecked the ground about them. Not far beyond, after a small field with a couple of trees, a white sandy beach stretched to a tranquil blue sea. Oyster catchers with yellow beaks flew about on the beach by the seaweed and seals popped their heads above the water out by some rocks.

'My brother was hoping you might start a school again.'

The schoolmaster smiled at Shona and shook his head. 'Your brother will have to find a younger man. His best opportunity would be to write to Fort Augustus. There may be a ghillie there fresh out of school looking for a post. But if it is only for you a matter of French... well, I do not see why you could not travel here. How long did it take you today?

'Three hours, about.'

'Well, the weather is fair now. If you can travel here I can teach you. I remember you were good at languages.'

'Can we start now?'

'I do not see why not. Help me up and we will go inside to look for my books.'

Shona helped the schoolmaster inside. The house he shared with his daughter and her family was a humbler version of the one owned by Shona's brother, but not so impoverished as to be deprived altogether of a little passable furniture: A table, chairs, a bookcase...

The next couple of hours were spent sitting at the table where with the aid of a pencil, paper, and two books, the schoolmaster taught Shona the French she had forgotten. To her surprise she found that under the schoolmaster's guidance the language started coming back to her in a manner rather easier than when she attempted to converse with de la Rueda.

In the afternoon they were joined by the family, and later by Neil, who had gone to call on some folk he knew. When Shona departed with Neil, mounted on ponies in the early evening, she had already made arrangements to return the following morning.

For two weeks or so Shona saw little of de la Rueda. When she was not travelling to Camus Cross, now mostly on her own to the schoolmaster's, she was spending time with her friend Morag and other folk of her sept with whom she was close. The occasions when she mostly encountered de la Rueda were in the evenings, for then they would all gather to eat at the table. Often in the mornings she was already gone by the break of day, and during the day itself everyone was busy, including de la Rueda himself, who had taken to assisting Douglas in the myriad tasks that needed doing, not least in felling and sawing timber and transporting it with the aid of garrons down to the shore. The work was hard but it was just the kind de la Rueda was needing. He took it on with manic desperation. He told himself that he would not care if he worked himself to the grave. Anything was preferable to being left alone with the guilt that tormented him or with the force of a temptation so irresistible that even while he felt the earth being dug from under his feet he was wanting to take another bite of the apple.

Douglas was impressed by de la Rueda's appetite for work. After a few days, even though they could communicate only by sign language, the two men were getting along in an agreeable manner.

'The Spanish gentleman is a hard worker,' Douglas remarked to Shona one night when they were sitting around the hearth, before going to bed. 'I had him felling the trees in the slope above the Adders Rest today and he was going at it hard. I thought to myself, he is not working so for pleasure. A grievance, it may be, that is urging him on?'

Douglas kept his eyes on his sister as he spoke, but she did not raise her head from the wool she was carding on her lap with two hand-held brushes.

'Did you warn him there are vipers about where he is felling?'

'The vipers are further below in the gulley. Unless you count Brendan.'

Now Shona did look up.

'Has more happened there?'

'It has not so far.'

'But he makes a claim on the land?'

'He goes around saying he has been robbed. That is what we have heard,' said Kirstine, who was teasing onto a spindle some of the wool Shona had carded.

Douglas' usually affable countenance puckered in an expression of angry contempt.

'It is our land. They are our trees. It was never his father's.'

Shona was silent. She had no wish to involve herself in a dispute that was not hers. All she knew was that Brendan was a cousin, her uncle's son, and that he and her brother had been friends since they were little but had now fallen out over the woods by the Adders Rest. Brendan claimed it had all belonged to his father but her brother maintained that not so the portion above the gulley. From what Shona recalled of the many times the family's holdings had been discussed by her parents she thought her brother was correct, although there were no written charters to show it. Brendan however was adamant that those woods were his. So the two men had fallen out. Shona was sorry, because Brendan had moved across the sound to work on the army barracks that they were starting to build by Glenelg, but his wife and children were still here, spurned and ignored by folk who feared offending their chieftain.

Why is there so much strife and discord in the world? The Lord Jesus teaches us gentleness. He commands us to love our kin. Yet never do we stop fighting each other. And I am guilty, no less. Why am I not at home, as the Lord would have me be, taking care of my husband? Why do I remain here, hoping only for a sign of favour from the man with whom I have lain in sin and who now despises me? It is pride that obliges me; not love. Pride is the ruin of human kind and it will be my ruin, too.

But pride or otherwise, Shona remained determined not to let the Spaniard leave without attempting to put his heart, and her own, at ease. To this end all her attention was focused on improving her French. Besides the lessons she took from the schoolmaster she was continually referring to the dictionary, memorizing words, and rehearsing basic conversations in her mind. Deeply she wished de la Rueda would allow her to engage him in conversation, but whenever she tried, he, by one means or another, managed to avoid responding directly. Then one evening there was a ceilidh. Folk young and old gathered in a house not a hundred yards from Douglas' own. It was a mild evening, and dry, so most folk gathered outside the house itself. Douglas, in a fit of generosity and thinking to impress his Spanish guest, had a ewe slaughtered and provided ale and whisky. Shona's childhood friend, Morag, came with her children – but not her husband who was in the hills with the cattle – and for a long time they talked. All around them meanwhile people gathered and mingled. Some, old as well as young, listened to the bard, who on this occasion happened to be a woman. They gathered about her with rapt, guileless expressions, certain she must be speaking the truth when in a slow, measured way she recounted tales of water horses and other creatures that were known to inhabit certain localities and whose existence was not in doubt. While the bard regaled, the ewe roasted on a spit over a fire. Folk were too polite to interrupt and make noise. If they wanted to talk of other things they did so quietly and at a distance. When the meat was ready the story-telling broke up, ghillies cut off chunks from the carcass and began to hand them around, along with containers of whisky and ale.

De la Rueda, unable to speak the language, sat on a log beside Douglas close to the fire in silence. The festivity made him recall the *fiestas* in his own country. These, after mass and the usual procession, became lively affairs with much drinking of wine, dancing, food and games. He thought of how he might be there now, on his estate, partaking of such festivities and of the life due to him as the local squire, until the notion turned bitter. He groaned aloud, which caused Douglas to glance at him inquiringly, and had an urge to fall on his knees and pray to the Virgin Mary for the forgiveness of his sin. But politeness kept him seated. He forced himself to nod and smile and appear appreciative of the food and drink. Presently someone produced a fiddle and someone else a whistle. Folk gathered around as a lively reel sounded. Almost immediately folk started dancing on the flat ground by the fire. Married couples were less quick to venture forth, but young men, children and unmarried women with bright faces and head bands tied around their plaited hair were soon lifting their feet, many of them bare, and whirling about and linking arms. Eventually Douglas was pulled to his feet by Kirstine and they went to dance.

'*Monsieur*, we must talk.'

Wrapped in an arasaid, her outline dark against the orange glow of the fire, Shona stood before de la Rueda and for an instant he mistook her words, imagining that she was asking him to dance.

'Please, now. We must talk.'

Shona gestured. There was insistence in her voice and somehow it seemed to him that she spoke more fluidly. A feeling of panic, more than if she had asked him to dance, came to him. But panic was an emotion he had come across many times in his life, in particular on the battlefield, and not once had he allowed it to best him.

With a deep breath he pushed himself up from the log.

Shona turned and de la Rueda followed. As she walked she looked about her. Most folk were intent on the dancing or the drinking so they did not notice her leaving. But some did, following with their eyes as she led the Spaniard away. *Let them all know. Even my brother. I do not care. They can gossip all they want.*

The days were becoming shorter now that it was past the summer solstice. But till in the beginning of July there was always some glimmer of light coming from the sky. It was bright enough for Shona to see the path in front of her; a good and broad path used for hauling the logs. Aware that de la Rueda was close behind, for she could hear the shuffle of his steps, she nevertheless did not stop or turn to look at him.

Shortly, they were down on the shore. The sea wind was chilly here and the sound of the waves hummed as they left the grass and stepped between the rocks to a narrow, vertical slit on the face of the low cliff that the tide did not reach. De la Rueda watched Shona walk into the opening some three yards wide and disappear. Curious, he followed her. Shona removed a tinderbox from the pocket folds of her skirt. After placing the open box on a stone ledge, she put a piece of curved iron over her fingers and struck it sharply against a flint stone. The tinder in the box was dry, so it soon caught light from the sparks. She blew on it softly and then from another compartment in the box she took a sulphur match and lit it from the tinder. Once the match was alight she brought out a bundle of rushlights, again from her skirt. The pith of the rush soaked in tallow flared as she lit one. For an instant de la Rueda found himself staring down at her: The gracious curves of her small body, her soft flushed face, and the fire in the orbs of her green eyes made him spin. Recovering, he followed her between the rough rock wall of the entrance and into the cavern that opened up behind.

The cave was no longer used as it had once been. The barrels were all but gone except for five on the rock slab. Drips and trickles of water fell from the high ceiling, but the slab, which was extensive, was always dry. Of the five barrels, three were empty and two contained rum. The rum belonged not to Douglas but to another man. Douglas wanted nothing to do with the sea, which he feared, but his uncle's younger son, Brodie, kept the family tradition alive on a much reduced scale, and Douglas consented for a cut. So the cave was still used for a little smuggling. Because of this there were a couple of cruise lamps, one of which Shona lit from the rushlight.

'I learn more French.' Shona sat on a hump in the slab, drawing her knees up. 'Schoolmaster… from before… When I am little...'

The spluttering light from the lamp flickered across her face.

De la Rueda was surprised, interested. He could not help it. Everything about her interested him. But to be drawn in by her he could not allow. It must not happen. The salvation of his soul was hanging in the balance. *Polite but no more. Show no interest. Resist her.*

'*Monsieur*, my husband… He not… He does what... I not like.'

De la Rueda kept silent; eyes averted, lips pinched tight, but he was listening.

'My husband… People. You understand?'

When de la Rueda remained silent, Shona stood up and grabbed the sleeve of his shirt under the plaid, jerking it so that his gaze was forced upon her.

'People! He..' She searched for the word. Not finding it, she raised both hands and made a brusque shooing gesture away from herself. 'People. Family, children… He, my husband… away, away! Have no food, no house. Many people, many one day they go. Have nothing, *Monsieur*, nothing for them he give my husband. I cannot like. Never. He does bad to people. Not I! Not I!'

The words were reinforced by emphatic, agitated gestures. After a moment de la Rueda thought he understood. Her husband was sending people away. His workers, it must be. For what reason he did not know. What she was saying was not difficult to follow but it came as a shock. He realised now that he had not given particular thought to Hector's life beyond how it appeared to him. Events had occurred so fast as to leave little room in his mind for enquiry. He had not considered how the moment of madness, the intemperance and betrayal could be playing in the lives of Shona and Hector. All along he had been thinking only of what it meant to him and how it was affecting him. *The sin is there. I cannot undo it. That is for God. But I should listen to her. She wants me to know.*

'Your husband did not have to come to my assistance, M*adame*. But he did. He saved my life. It is not you I accuse. It is myself. Me. I…' de la Rueda jabbed his finger at his own chest. 'I am nothing without honour. Like fly, ppfff...' He turned his lips down and made an anguished, scornful motion with one hand.

Shona did not understand the reference to a fly, but most of the rest she did.

'My husband is no honour for me.' Her voice became strained. 'He does bad for people. They must go. Food not have. Land not have. For you he does good… He for you does good. For me he does bad. I no can…' Tears gathered in her eyes. She placed the palm of her hand under her breast. 'I for him cannot... Nothing is *here*.'

'It was a sin!' De la Rueda pointed to himself and her. 'Sin.' And when Shona seemed confused. '*Peccatum*,' he said in Latin. 'Do you understand me?'

She did. She knew some words of Latin; in particular the religious words.

'My husband does *peccatum. Peccatum mortiferum.* I cannot love my husband.'

De la Rueda said nothing.

Shona struggled with the language, with the words. Sometimes when she spoke it was as if from within a fog, but at others the words would come out by themselves.

'I cannot... live.... Live, *oui,* with a man I cannot love, *Monsieur.*'

De la Rueda was stunned. The audacity of her words struck his core. It was not what he expected from the lips of a human soul, man or woman. Was not such a demand against the teachings of God? Had she a right to choose? She was giving herself a freedom that until this moment de la Rueda would not have thought was possible to give oneself. Women were burnt at the stake for less.

'And your *devoir?'* de la Rueda asked.

Shona frowned.

'*Devoir. Obligation,'* de la Rueda tried. 'Have you no *obligation,* M*adame*?'

Shona understood, for the French *obligation* was the same as the English term.

'My husband have obligation. He this obligation do.' Shona lifted her hands and made a snapping gesture. 'I cannot... like. I stop to love. Love is go...'

De la Rueda turned his face away. The blaze of entreaty and defiance in her eyes dismayed him. Did she not regret her actions? Did she think it was no sin to go behind her husband's back and rut as they had done? But she must not regard her husband in the same manner that he did. That was clear to him now. The man he saw as his saviour she saw as debased. Did her husband merit such contempt? He would want to know more to decide if it was merited. But everything seemed to him less clear. He felt himself arriving at a territory of the mind he had not anticipated, where the path was not clear, where sin began to take a different hue, where God's judgement was suspended.

Shona waited. But she would not beg. She had said what she had to say. If he did not turn back to her she would leave, and she was on the point of it, just starting to turn when she heard him say, '*Madame*, I must think on your words. There is much I do not understand. Your husband, I think, is one man for you and another for me.'

'I write,' Shona replied. 'Understand more...'

De la Rueda nodded. He met her eyes and they were a pool he wanted to dive in. His arms ached to encircle her and draw her to him. He wanted her body, her soul, he wanted to possess her, to lose himself within her, but while he quivered with desire he was in terror of being lost, forever lost if he took her for a second time.

'I await your letter.'

De la Rueda bowed.

Well, it is a start. It will be easier to explain more in writing. I will ease his heart yet, before he leaves.

TWENTY TWO

Not a day passed when Lachlan did not wake up scheming. It was the way he had been born. As a child, one among numerous siblings, he had known extreme poverty and hunger. The relentless effort it took to outsmart his siblings for the least scrap of food, warmth, and clothing had shaped Lachlan's outlook as did the elements those gnarled dwarf trees that here and there clung to a rock in a forsaken bog. Lachlan was a survivor. Ostentation, for its own sake, held little allure for him. He was not interested in the disposition of his house or the flamboyance of his attire. These were unremarkable, for the way he saw it, money squandered was power diminished. Everything in his life revolved around the struggle to accumulate power. When he was a child he had discovered that a rope of horse hair was a valuable item. It was useful but as well it was supple and could be sold for money. So wherever he could he had collected horse hair. The ways he had done it had been various, some of them sly, and on more than one occasion he had been kicked or bitten by a horse while clandestinely cutting its tail. His siblings, except for his older sister Forbia, had mocked him, for they could think of easier ways to make rope out of grass. But he was persuaded he knew something they did not. With Forbia's collusion he stuck to it stubbornly. Then one day he had enough hair for a narrow rope, which he made himself. That rope he sold to Colonel Murchison for a coin.

Suddenly Lachlan had money, something extraordinary, something even his father and mother had scarcely owned before. It was a mere coin, but for Lachlan it was the discovery of power.

In Lachlan's universe men like Hector existed to be exploited. While on the surface Lachlan was unctuous with gentlemen, deep down he despised them for any display of weakness. Gentlemen who were born titled could not comprehend the value of what they owned. The likes of the Earl of Seaforth, the chiefs, Hector's own father, they lived as though their wealth would be there always like water. Even when their lands were forfeit people like the earl expected it never to persist; a change in the wind, a shift in government and they would get it all back. Hector, Lachlan would admit, had more sense than his father. He knew enough to want to hold on to what he had and not give in to that mad witch of a wife. He had a mind for profit, but everything was going wrong for him now after the battle, and Lachlan had no intention of letting the opportunity pass.

'What is it you are saying? Are you sure of this?'

'As sure as I am of sitting here.'

In the small windowless room, illuminated by a flickering lamp, only Lachlan and the innkeeper sat at the rough-hewn table. Voices came from the parlour beyond the closed door, for in recent times the inn had become a popular place on account all the building work for the new army barracks. Officials, government soldiers and militia were arriving like summer flies in these parts. This was one reason Lachlan was keeping out of sight, lest they unmask him as a Jacobite. But the other reason they were alone was that he and the innkeeper did not wish to be disturbed.

'I did not know she had gone with him for *that* reason.'

'The rumour is there is something between them.'

The innkeeper was a thin, nimble man, no longer young, with the pointed face of a pine martin. Like Lachlan, he was forever scheming, looking for ways to accumulate wealth. One of these was by reselling Lachlan's duty-free whisky, a distinctive product, and at the price it was sold few were tempted to enquire as to its provenance, not even the government soldiers tasked with seizing it.

'Between them how?'

'They are copulating.'

'*Copulating*?'

The innkeeper nodded. He wondered if the woman was large. He liked large women himself. His own wife was large.

'So I am told. But if it be true I cannot say. My informant is for leaving the sept. He has had a dispute with the woman's brother, though I know not what it is. He says he has been robbed, that is all. He is angry now, he sees blood; were it not for that I would be told nothing. They are like clams over there, those Glas.'

Although Lachlan owned two illicit stills he was not himself a heavy drinker. That evening he had imbibed little, and it had been his own best quality whisky, but even so the liquor now turned sour and rose burning in his chest when he pictured the green eyed whore opening her legs for the Spaniard.

'This man, your informant, does he have a trade?'

The innkeeper lifted the flagon from the table, but Lachlan burped and put a hand over his glass.

'It has matured well,' remarked the innkeeper, refilling his own glass. 'I should have no trouble selling it on. How many barrels can you bring?'

'Three.'

'I will take more if you can bring them.'

'It is all I can sell you.'

'When can I expect them?'

'By the end of the month.'

'The usual place?'

'It will be.'

The usual place was a secluded cove several miles distant. Once ashore the innkeeper's men would transport the barrels by pony. It would be at twilight and the men would be armed. The innkeeper would also provide them with makeshift militia uniforms. The locals would know they were impostors, but it would be less clear to the excise men.

'So, does your informant have a trade?' Lachlan repeated.

As the innkeeper raised his glass the flickering yellow light from the cruise lamp on the wall caught its edge, making it glitter.

'He knows boats. They all do, those Glas.'

'A smuggler?'

'I have heard that a little goes on still over there. But it is not like in the days of Red Douglas or his brother William. The present chieftain has no taste for the sea I am told, and you can see for yourself how it is around here now. Military people everywhere. I am having to take more and more precautions myself.'

'But you sell to them.'

'So I do. But you know all it takes is one Judas.'

Lachlan dropped into silence, ruminating. As he did so his white eyelashes flickered and his wide nostrils seemed to sniff the air. He had an intuition that he might be onto something, a dark feeling of being able to dominate, but his indigestion was not allowing him to think clearly. It was that whore of a woman. Why was it that she would open her legs for the Spaniard and not him? He had to acknowledge that every time he had come in contact with her a violent urge had come upon him to take her there and then. Other women did not have such a strong effect on him. Those whores as would lie with him he scorned. And women who were his social equal, or superior, he met infrequently, and when he did, they were scornful of him, or he found they were married or there was some other impediment. As a result Lachlan was unmarried, a situation he intended at some point to remedy. First, of course, he would have to get past Forbia. His older sister was the only woman Lachlan had ever feared. He had not feared his mother or his other three sisters, but Forbia was implacable. Everyone feared Forbia; her husband, her children, and other people who had dealings with her, for it was she who organized the commerce. Early on he had conceded that Forbia's ambition and guile matched and in some respects surpassed his own. She was a woman, however; she could not go about in the same way that he could. So it was Lachlan who made the deals and did the travelling. This suited him, for he could not be around Forbia long before she started getting under his skin. On his own he could do as he wanted. He did not have to think about what Forbia would think if he took a fancy to a whore. His illicit whisky dealings had taken him far and wide in the west of the country, on occasion as far as Glasgow. So although Lachlan was not wed he knew what a woman's flesh was. He had paid for it. Or two of them he had taken. One against her will but with the consent of her husband, forced by him to give herself. And another, a widow living near Ullapool who had invited him into her house, he had violated when she would not succumb. He had taken pleasure in having the woman at his mercy, lying there on the floor with her fine clothes undone, her skirts and petticoats raised above her white thighs. He had not even had to strike her. All he had done was show her a *sgian-dubh*. The look of terror on her face had thrilled him more than the act of penetration itself. It was power. He liked to watch a woman break to his will. That it had happened in this way only once was more for a lack of opportunity than another reason. Lachlan had long imagined violating Shona. The contempt and hostility he felt emanating from her served as a spur, so maddening him that once he had tried to snatch her from under Hector's very nose. Had it been the widow, he doubted she would have made a sound, but that whore of Hector's knocked things over, made noise, and he had to let her go. After that he had not been able to come near her.

'Did you know the witch tried to take my cattle?'

'I did not.'

'Well, she did. A ransom, so I would withdraw from a contract I made with Hector.' A sneering grunt came from Lachlan's throat. 'I had my cattle returned in no time. Hector understands who is paying the piper here.'

'I heard he came off badly in the battle.'

Lachlan nodded emphatically. 'Now, you see, why do you think so many held back?'

'It is the growing season. And we heard the Spanish Armada was wrecked.'

'There was small chance of victory with no more help coming to us. Everyone was feeling that. So on the day all those that could were hanging back – '

'Including yourself?'

'I could not. I was with Hector. We were placed beside the Spanish barricades. But there was no fire in our stomachs; everyone was looking over his shoulder waiting to see who would abandon the field first... But now when the fighting starts and the Spaniards get in difficulty, Hector charges down to their aid. He alone charges down. Was that sensible, when everyone else is looking to go in the opposite direction?'

'Brave?'

'Foolish. Look what he has now for his trouble: A wound in his head that is sending him mad and a whore for a wife running off with the man he rescued.'

'My informant thinks there is a plan in the making – for the Spaniard to leave the country. I did not press him for details, which I do not believe he knows. He talks only of having been robbed by Douglas Glas and coming away from the sept lands.'

'But he is still there?'

'Sometimes. He has a wife and bairns over there. Mostly he works here, repairing boats and carts for the military. He has also moved whisky for me.'

Lachlan was still not sure what he was after. That in some way he wanted to possess Shona, be it only in order to destroy her, was an impulse he could understand and felt strongly in his mind. But there was something else also; a feeling that such would not be sufficient, that if it were mere spite that was motivating him it would not be worth the effort and he would let it pass. The whore could go to the devil. What did he care? *Unless... unless...*

'Do you find your man reliable?'

The innkeeper sniggered. 'How do you judge? He likes a drink but I would say no more than many. And he has a temper. Why do you ask?'

'I am not sure. But he would need to know when to keep his mouth shut.'

The innkeeper became more alert.

'Are you wanting to use him?'

'For information. It could be. I know not what else just yet.'

The innkeeper lifted the flagon again. This time Lachlan allowed the innkeeper to pour three fingers of near transparent whisky into his glass.

'What shall I say to him?'

'Tell him I am interested in knowing everything he can discover about the whore and her Spaniard. What they do, where they go, everything. I will pay good money but only if the information is for me alone. No one else. Can he write?'

The innkeeper pulled his lips down, nodding. 'He knows sums. So maybe.'

'Well, if it be urgent you can send for me.'

'And what might be urgent?'

Lachlan looked into his glass without drinking.

'Well,' he said, finally, raising his colourless eyes. 'If he can know in advance when they plan to leave the island or such.'

Lachlan left Glenelg the next day. He travelled with his nephew, a raw-boned lad of seventeen, and an older man, a servant. The men wore plaids and, although against the law, were armed; his nephew with sword as well as dirk. Lachlan also wore a pistol. And while the other two walked, he rode a pony. Behind came another pony, a packhorse carrying the basket work creels which contained the flagons of whisky they were hawking, as well as samples to encourage larger orders from Lachlan's clientele.

There was not much in between Glenelg and Rattagan. But for an estate or two, which were not on Lachlan's list, the trail took them over a long rise of uninhabited tawny green bogland. Eagles circled in the grey sky and a small herd of deer grazed down near a river, but they came across no people, which as far as Lachaln was concerned was for the best. Sitting on the pony, he had plenty of time to ponder. He knew what he wanted. He had not been sure when he had spoken to the innkeeper; his mind had backed off, for it was a notion of extreme boldness. Yet he wondered now what power there was on earth to prevent him? Of course he would have to talk it over with his sister. If she balked he could not see how he could accomplish it. But if they had Hector's infields, the best land, they might grow all the barley they needed without buying in. If their business became big enough they might even go legal. It could be worth their while to pay the government so that they could operate in the open. Large stills in the Lowlands were starting to do this, he had heard. Not here yet. Here it was all small stills and all concealed. But he could be the first. The largest producer of whisky west of the Great Glen. Why not?

The party camped that night in the open. They built a fire, gathered clumps of heather for a mattress and slept wrapped up in their plaids in spite of midges and a soft drizzle. In the morning they descended sharply down a rocky twisting trail towards the head of Loch Duich. There they encountered soldiers building a road; close to a hundred all counted and they had been detached from General Wightman's army. Some men were digging, others using ponies to haul flat stones, yet others laying the stones into the muddy ground. The soldiers were overseen by sergeants, and at the head of them, sitting on a horse, was a captain, and a drummer wearing a uniform almost as extravagant as the officer's. In years to come it was intended for the road to extend all the way to the barracks at Glenelg. Rather than go past the soldiers, Lachlan and his men made a wide detour, not without difficulty, before reaching Rattagan, where Lachlan had a laird and one lesser gentleman as customers. Their business in Rattagan took a large part of the day. So again they spent the night on the road, this time more comfortably in a barn. The next day they crossed over by Glenshiel and passed by the Church at Morvich, where Hector had passed the night, but now, after being torched by Wightman's troops, was reduced to a roofless, charred ruin. Upon seeing it, Lachlan was mildly offended by the destruction. It seemed to him a wasteful act on a structure of stone that had been impressive to behold. However, he was indifferent to the building's religious or political association. He was not prone to superstition and did not believe in either God or the Devil, not because he had reasoned it so, but because his mind would not encompass matters that were not purely physical. As for politics, it had always been for him a flag of convenience. He was a Jacobite because it suited him in a locality where almost everyone was so inclined.

A few more times the party stopped for Lachlan to conduct business with clients who had a predilection for whisky matured over several years and with that particular smoky character he gave it by drying the barley over a peat fire. A few of his clients were well-to-do; they were landowners, lived in well-appointed houses, and would be good for a barrel delivered at a later date. Most were not so well off; they were tenant farmers, crofters, who while they could lay their hands on distillations of inferior quality, were willing to make a deal for a flagon or two of Lachlan's elixir. Thus, when the party arrived home late at night on the third day after leaving Glenelg, Lachlan had, besides the bigger future sales, brought with him four chickens in the creels of his pack horse, a bag of nails, three hides, a small amount of coinage, two sheep, and one promissory note.

The house where Lachlan lived with his sister, her husband, and their five surviving children was poor in comparison to Hector's. Its furniture was rudimentary. In size and layout it was only a little less than Douglas' house on Skye. The one difference was that the gable end that was not the byre had been partitioned off by a wall of planks. Behind the planks, which had gaps in them, Lachlan had his own small quarters, which consisted of a box bed, trunk, writing desk, a chair and a small table. All were roughly made. The floor was paved with uneven flat stones. Here Lachlan slept, plotted, and did his basic, self-taught accounts. The room had no window but had a door to the outside. If anyone wanted to enter the room they had to use that door, but no one ever did enter, even his sister, for he had made it plain that this was for him only. All the rest of the house was given over to Forbia and her family and the animals in the byre. Here Forbia reigned unopposed. It was only in his room that Lachlan felt himself independent to a degree. Once he was on the other side of the dividing planks, within his sister's sphere, he felt dominated by her presence, the same way her husband did, which is why Lachlan had appropriated a space for himself within the house.

After the baggage and the animals had been seen to, Lachlan was far too tired to want to talk. He went straight to his box bed, pulled the curtain, lay down in his clothes, and did not wake up until the next morning. Before eating he went out to do his business in the bog some yards behind his house. Afterwards he went to the stream nearby and splashed some water on his hands and face. Later he would shave, but for the moment he stood gazing beyond the three other smaller stone and turf dwellings that housed his cottars, towards the gently rolling fields of barley beyond. He did not take notice of the fowl, hobbled animals, and two or three people about. Already his mind was returning to the thoughts he had entertained over the last days. With them came feelings of power, and trepidation; but he could not do it alone, he would have to talk it over with Forbia.

As with Hector's estate, Lachlan's farm was situated close to the sea. The best agricultural land was around his house on the narrow, relatively flat ground before it began to climb steeply in rocky outcrops and hills. At one end of this strip, about half a mile distant, were two other cottar dwellings and behind them a barn as long as Lachlan's house and a few feet wider. The barn had wattle walls above a foundation of stone to allow ventilation. Inside, one third of the floor space was taken up with a round, sunken pit which contained a flue made of stone leading to a firebox above which was suspended a wattle floor. It was still too early for harvest time so there was no barley to be smoked and dried on the suspended floor. Likewise the stone threshing floor by the pit, which occupied another third of the barn, was also bare of barley. The last third of the barn, which was walled with stone, kept the two dozen or so barrels of maturing whisky, flagons, tools, a stack of peat against the wall all the way to the roof beams, and two gleaming copper stills. These were over four feet tall and almost as wide: Round, with long spouts projecting from the neck, and each stood on an iron tripod inside a stone firebox with a small flue.

Forbia was nearby, piling up staves in preparation to sitting down and proceeding to make a tun for storing the mash when the time came. She was a big, square woman, strong as a man, less pale than Lachlan, with thick lips and hard narrow eyes.

'So there you are. I was wondering when you would show up.'

Forbia put down the staves and picked up a two-handled hollowing knife.

'We came back late. We now have two more sheep and four hens. And a bag of nails. Very handy they will be, too.'

'Money?'

'Some. Our order book is now full. Robertson in Glenelg wants three barrels. He would have more if we could give it.' Lachlan paused. 'I have something I want to talk to you about, Forbia. But we must be alone.'

'Fergus will be here any moment. We had better go outside.'

They left the barn and climbed by the side of the burn up a small hillock. From here they could see all around. No one could hear them.

'So what is it?'

'Robertson has it on good authority that Shona and the Spaniard are hiding out at her brother's on Skye.'

'With Douglas Glas, the chieftain?'

'So it is. She and the Spaniard are fornicating.'

Forbia did not look surprised. 'What has that to do with us?'

'Robertson also thinks they are planning the Spaniard's escape. There is a rumour about that some of the lords are heading to the Rough Bounds and from there to the continent. The Spaniard will join them, it may be. Shona's sister is married to one of the

Macdonald in those lands. He will be taken there, it may be, but I cannot see Shona staying behind with her brother. Anyway, Robertson has a spy in the Glas clan. I hope to be kept abreast of Shona's movements.'

'Why does it matter to you?'

Lachlan ran his tongue over his thick lips. 'I want to get hold of Hector's land.'

Forbia took her hard eyes off her brother and slowly looked all around her. Of course they were alone, but she needed to absorb her brother's statement.

'And how do you propose to do that?'

A sardonic smile puckered Lachlan's mouth. 'We turn Hector against his wife and get rid of her – one way or another. And I become a better friend to him than I am already. I take charge of his land. It gets passed to my name. We grow barley and we open a distillery such as are now just appearing in the Lowlands. We pay duty but we sell far and wide. We become rich.'

It sounded too simple to Forbia.

'Hector is not strong in the head,' said Lachlan. 'The blow he received makes him strange. We can turn him against Shona. And if she should die, all the better. We could… well, I am thinking we could put Aileen to work for us... Only if she were agreeable,' he added quickly, under the full force of his sister's scrutiny.

Forbia was silent. Aileen was young and she had her father's looks. Any man would want her now, even the laird. Why not, if his wife was away whoring? But they would have to be careful. The Glas clan could make a bad enemy…

'Aileen will do as I tell her. I will think on it,' said Forbia, finally.

TWENTY THREE

Hector woke up sweating. It was the same nightmare often. Mortars exploded all about him. He tried to run but the mortars forced him back to the same spot. Then he saw the Spaniard hailing him. He ran to join the Spaniard thinking he would be safe there but as he arrived the Spaniard began sinking into the ground. With an effort he managed to pull the Spaniard out but just at that moment he fell into the pit himself and began sinking while the Spaniard stood on the edge looking down at him. He cried out for the Spaniard to help him but the man for some reason refused and a moment later Hector was tumbling into a black pit, down and down.

When he awoke he was always full of anxiety. His head ached, he felt himself utterly alone, and his instinct was to take comfort from the knowledge that his wife was lying beside him. But every morning he found the space empty. Such a desperate anguish came over him then that it seemed to him that he had left one nightmare only to fall into another: A daylight nightmare, a conscious nightmare which kept its grip on him without pity and like the night one repeated itself. Over and over.

Hector would get up from the bed raging. He replaced the emptiness with violent and unstable thoughts. In his moment of need, after doing his duty as a soldier, after risking his life for the cause, she had abandoned him. *Why*? Her duty was no less than his. She was his wife. The Spaniard could fend for himself. Had he not done enough for the Spaniard? She was taking revenge for the Three Rowans folk. Damn her to hell. It was his estate. Everything here was his. How he managed it was no concern of hers, but she meddled, she thought she knew better than him, damn her, damn her, damn her.

The only thing that appeared to calm Hector somewhat and distract him from his angry thoughts was the laudanum. When he took the laudanum he entered a soporific, dream-like state which kept at bay the violence of his emotions while allowing his mind to drift into fantasies that could be peculiar but were mostly benign and in which he sometimes had difficulty distinguishing the real from the imaginary. The difficult moments came when the effects of the drug began to wear off. Then his headaches would return, with all his fears, including the fear that he would run out of laudanum. But this is where Lachlan came to his aid. After Lachlan returned from his selling trip it was just a matter of days before he took to calling on Hector, often staying overnight in the same bed that de la Rueda had used, and acting to all intents and purposes as Hector's factor. He it was now, when Hector was indisposed, who began to deal with cottars' and tenants' requests, whether to do with land, tools, cattle, or payment. Few cared for his manner, and they all knew about the Three Rowans folk, but there was not much they could do about anything and so they had to put up with him. And when Hector was down to the last of his laudanum, it was Lachlan who at once offered to fetch more.

'I will go myself. I will be back before nightfall.'

Lachlan encouraged Hector to swallow what little in the bottle remained. Leaving him in his bed, under the care of Mairi, he saddled a pony and set off on the eleven mile journey to MacQueen's.

Much of the path was flattish, for it passed fields and settlements, so Lachlan was at MacQueen's by early afternoon. The physician's house was an attractive place, surrounded by a profusion of rose and honeysuckle bushes. Lachlan found

MacQueen himself in the garden behind the house, his hunched back protruding among the vegetables, herbs, and medicinal plants he liked to grow. Not far from his side was an earthenware flagon, for MacQueen drank whisky in small quantities from the moment he woke up until he went to bed. Never more than mildly drunk, he was also never entirely sober. Although there was no particular bond of friendship between the two men, MacQueen was a long and steady customer of Lachlan's. As a result it was not long before Lachlan was on his way back to Hector's with three bottles of laudanum.

But on the journey Lachlan decided to stop at his own house first, which required only a short detour. It was evening when he arrived and because it was not raining and there were no midges the family and the animals were occupying the space outside. Forbia was milking the cow. Her husband, Pol, was mending a creel, the youngest children were free to play, but fifteen-year-old Aileen was sitting on a low three legged chair before a spinning wheel.

After dismounting the pony with the usual clumsy swing of his short legs, Lachlan immediately fixed his attention on his niece, who had momentarily stopped spinning and instead, after hiking her skirt above her knees, was intent on extracting a tick from the soft flesh of her thigh. Over the years Lachlan had watched Aileen grow. Of his sister's three daughters the one that had most caught his attention was the eldest, but Forbia had kept a strict eye on her and she was now gone to a local ghillie. The other daughter was not yet twelve, so in the last couple of years it had been Aileen that Lachlan mostly observed. Lachlan could see that Aileen was not particularly striking, nor did it seem to him that she was particularly alert. More the opposite; there was to her a certain carelessness of manner, a lack of sharpness, that made Lachlan believe it would not be so difficult for him to have his way with her. That so far he had not was because, as with her older sister, Lachlan had Forbia to overcome. The mere thought of Forbia's wrath, should she find out, was enough to deter Lachlan. But this did not mean that he did not think about it. He had observed closely how Aileen's skinny frame had grown soft curves that were pressing against her clothes. More than her mother, the girl resembled her father. Like him she was dark and small boned. Her eyes were brown, like her father's, and what Lachlan had seen of her skin appeared to him smooth and unblemished. He had often thought of running his hands over her skin and of being the first between her unsullied legs.

He thought of it again, but dismissed the thought and went up to Forbia.

'Well? Have you spoken to her?'

Forbia straightened up. 'No. But I will speak to her this evening. It will be easier if you are not in the way.'

'I will be at Hector's, then. Make it soon.'

Forbia lifted the one-handled milk cogg from the ground and looked her brother in the eye. 'This is all your scheme, Lachlan, so make sure it does not fail.'

Lachlan glanced over to where Aileen was sitting. She had pulled down her skirt and was staring at her mother and him. She was not Shona. She had not Shona's green eyes or her fire or her wit, but she was young, pliant, smooth warm flesh, and Hector was a sick man.

'Hector will be a lucky,' said Lachlan. 'But you make sure she is comely when she comes.'

There was a pitted limestone rock near the hobbled cow. Still holding the cogg, Forbia reached in with her free hand, scooped up a little milk and poured it into a hole in the rock, for, unlike her brother, she was superstitious.

'The best result would be if Hector marries her,' she said.

Lachlan watched his sister walk to the house. Her last words had made it plain what she expected of him. For a moment it scared him. He wondered if he was not taking on something too big? It was still possible to abandon his scheme. He could stop here, but he knew even as he contemplated it that he was not going to. The urge to dominate was too potent.

When Lachlan rode up to Hector's the sky was dark. Before entering the house he unsaddled the pony and led it to the brook to drink. Inside the house meanwhile Hector was in a poor state. Although the weather had stayed mild, he was sitting hunched over the hearth, wrapped in a plaid and shivering. His gut was in a knot, his head throbbed, he could not get warm, and there appeared to be no escape from the angst that assailed him. Like a cornered rat he felt a violent urge to lash out and free himself, but it was his own mind holding him at bay and he could see no way out. His familiar self was nowhere to be found. *A spell has been put on me. I am losing sight of myself. This cannot go on. Nothing has meaning to me now. Mairi over there, what meaning does she have for me? This house, what meaning does it have? All that has meaning are these pains in my body. I must be rid of them. I am in torment. How am I to be consoled? Where is my wife? Where is Lachlan with my medicine? What can be keeping him?*

And then, just as Hector was thinking this, Lachlan swaggered into the common room, unannounced, as if already so entitled. Mairi, who was near Hector attending to Margaret, was angered by the impudence but was in no position to protest. Hector on the other hand was so relieved as to ignore it.

'Have you the medicine?'

Lachlan held out the bottle but did not pass it to him. He looked on with a sneer as he obliged Hector to rise from his chair and remove the bottle from his hand.

Hector no longer bothered to use a spoon. He shuffled to the kitchen for a knife, peeled away the seal, pulled the cork and took a swig. He was tempted to take a second swig but resisted, not knowing that Lachlan had arrived with two more bottles. Quite soon he felt the knot in his stomach go away and his limbs stopped shaking, though his headache remained undiminished.

'Put mother to bed now will you please, Mairi. And then go to bed yourself. I will keep company with Lachlan.'

Mairi did as she was bid. While leading Margaret away she gave Lachlan a hostile look but he made to ignore her. *You will be gone from here soon, hag. Fear not.*

Earlier in the day, when Hector had been feeling less desperate, he had thought of management matters to discuss with Lachlan, but now he could not remember what they were. The desire to talk of such matters was gone. It did not seem important. Nothing seemed important.

'Any news today while I have been away?' asked Lachlan, pulling up a chair and sitting down by Hector.

'What news are you thinking of?'

'Well, your wife. Has she sent word at all?'

'She is with her brother.'

'I know that.' Lachlan nodded. 'But no other word?'

'What about?'

'Well, the Spaniard...'

Hector found himself becoming annoyed, but it was more a mental annoyance for the laudanum was blunting the rawness of his emotions.

'What about him?'

'Is he with her?'

'To help him escape. Why do you ask?'

'I heard different,' said Lachlan after a moment. 'Of course, it is idle gossip. Folk will say anything just to make conversation. In my travels I come across it all the time.'

Hector watched the peat smoulder in the fireplace under the cauldron. Suddenly he wanted to pick it up with his bare hands; a pain to block out the anguished fear that even the laudanum could not vanquish.

'What is it you have been told?'

Lachlan shrugged his muscular shoulders and pulled his thick lips down.

'Idle gossip. Do not trouble yourself with it.'

'What? What is it?' Hector's voice rose.

'They are a pair. That is what I heard.'

Hector jumped up. The fear was flooding him now. He felt himself drowning, but this feeling, while not stymied, was mitigated by the effect of the laudanum. The peculiar impression came to him that it was all happening not to himself so much as to a stranger inhabiting his body.

'My wife and the Spaniard they are a pair did you say? *A pair*!'

Hector glared down at Lachlan, fists clenched.

'It is just gossip.'

'I *rescued* the Spaniard. You were there. Did you not see me rescue the Spaniard?'

'I did,' Lachlan lied. 'He owes you his life'.

'He does! He does!' Hector sat down again but unable to remain still, one foot tapping the floor while he repeatedly banged his fist into the palm of his other hand. 'I will go there myself. I will take men there and kill them both! And you will help me. We will kill them!'

'But there is nothing we know for certain. And they are well protected. Douglas Glas has the sept at his back.'

'A pair you say. *A pair*! I save the Spaniard's life and this is how he repays me. They will not get away with it. I will find a way, I swear!'

'I will find out what more I can. It will take some days. Then we can decide.'

'Who told you?'

'Robertson, the innkeeper in Glenelg. There is not much that can go past him. I heard it from his own mouth.'

Hector was momentarily confused. He knew that Lachlan had been away but it was not clear in his mind when that had been precisely. The days and nights were all becoming an undifferentiated jumble.

'And what did he say?'

'They are fornicating.'

The thought was like a storm in Hector's head.

'The whore! I will kill her!'

Hector stood up again, His mind reeled with abrupt and lurid visions of Shona giving herself to the Spaniard's pleasure. He saw her clothes undone, her white legs open, her breasts exposed; he saw the Spaniard's hands on her body and his bare arse pumping between her legs and he could not bear it. Looking around wildly he saw the laudanum where he had put it down on the sideboard in the kitchen and going over he picked up the bottle and took another swig.

Lachlan snickered.

'She was never any good to you,' he said when Hector returned, clutching the bottle.

Hector sat down again without replying. The agitation was contained by a growing heaviness in his muscles. And his thoughts were drifting.

'Look how she tried to take my cattle for blackmail. It is a good arrangement we have for the Three Rowans tack. And there will be more, Hector. You and I, we can help each other prosper. Ach, you are better off without her. All she wants to do is interfere and lose you money.'

Hector's eyelids began to droop. He could hear laughter, a woman's laughter. 'Who is that?' he heard himself mutter and opened his eyes, looking around, but only Lachlan was there.

'My wife laughs at me. I am betrayed.'

'She is no good. We will find a way to get at her, you have my word. And in the meantime you can take your comfort from another. A virgin. Unsullied. Young. Do you want her?'

Hector found himself in an undefined space that was soft and warm. Colours surrounded him. He did not feel frightened. He liked it there. Even his headache did not feel so bad. He hardly had a headache at all. *Perhaps I will stay here for a while.* When Lachlan spoke to him again he did not hear him.

Lachlan stood up and went to the bedroom, where Mairi was finishing putting Margaret to bed.

'Come and give me a hand,' he said. 'Hector has fallen asleep in his chair.'

Mairi followed Lachlan back into the common room. They each got to one side of him and started lifting him by his arms. Hector opened his eyes but they had a blank unseeing expression and they soon closed again. With his arms over their shoulders they helped him into the bedroom and onto the bed.

'I am in charge here now,' Lachlan told Mairi, standing in the doorway as he was about to leave. 'Do not make trouble or I will have you removed.'

Mairi said nothing. She was afraid.

Two days later Aileen appeared. She came up to the house on her own, but her father stood on the far side of the brook watching her. Pol was conflicted. She was his daughter and she was young. Too young. What he would have wanted was for her to stay at home for another couple of years and then find herself a ghillie her own age to settle with. But these were uncertain times. Families had to stick together. If it was what her uncle and her mother had decided between them he could not change it. They had the power. He himself had no means to oppose them even had he wanted to. And of wanting to he was not sure. Pol thought his daughter could do worse than become the mistress of a rich man.

Pol watched her standing at the door in a new skirt and red and green arisaid, her hair braided and held in place by a wide band. She was there a while; a couple of times she turned to look back at him. He wondered if she had knocked, but then the door opened and a moment later she went in.

Lachlan, dressed in jacket and trews, was sitting talking to two men when Mairi brought her into the common room. The men were cottars of Hector's and they had farm matters to discuss. Lachlan, acting as Hector's factor, brought the discussion to a close. After the men had gone he took Aileen into Hector's study. There he stood back and appraised Aileen with a lascivious and unabashed gaze. She was washed. Her cheeks were rosy and fresh. Her clothes becoming. She looked about her but asked no questions. Her manner was as he had always known it to be, quiet and malleable.

Lachlan liked it that way. It made him think again of ravishing her but as always the image of Forbia intruded.

'Has your mother told you why you are here?'

'I am to live here and do as you say.'

'And if I say there is a man here I want you to lie with, what then?'

'That too. Mother said I was to lie with a man in his bed.'

Lachlan took another look at his niece. He was baffled by her. The matter seemed to be of such little importance to her that he could not tell if she did not understand what was being demanded of her or if she understood it only too well.

'Tonight late I will show you to his room. You will remove all your clothes and lie with him. And you will let him do what it pleases him to do with you.'

Aileen looked at Lachlan with her bland brown eyes and simpered. All her fifteen years she had lived without questioning. She could reason and she had feelings, but a kind of lethargy seemed to dominate her. Nothing in her life had so far occurred to rouse her from the underlying befuddlement at her core. Even now, all her uncle's project did was to make her wonder what the man was like and whether it would tickle when he put his thing inside her.

Hector was floating in the air. It was such a pleasant sensation that euphoria bubbled up inside him and he laughed. He was lying on his back laughing when the heavy embroidered curtain at the edge of his bed was pushed aside and a small naked figure slipped in beside him and pulled the blanket of fine wool that half covered him over herself. Hector was not aware of her. It was all air around him still and he was floating in it. But gradually the heat of her skin near his made itself felt, passing into his body and changing the quality of his dream so that the air he was floating in became visible as something soft, solid, smooth, very much like skin. He could not say how that was possible but he had an impression now of a body close to his own and very soon he found his fingers reaching out, touching what was clearly human flesh. Shona. It was his wife.

Hector's eyes opened but he was confused, he did not know if he was awake or asleep. Beside him he saw the shape of a small female figure under the blanket but it was not Shona, it was not his wife, he did not know who she was or even if she was real. His eyes closed again. Whether he slept or not he did not know but he could feel the presence beside him. His hand reached out. Smooth, soft, warm flesh. Something to hold. Something to keep the darkness from rising up.

TWENTY FOUR

'It is arranged,' said Douglas.

Shona, sitting on a low chair, looked up from the plunger she was pushing in the wooden butter churn.

'He is to be taken to Corran.' Douglas stood in front of the hearth and brushed the rain off his plaid.

'Who tells you?'

'Sleepy Macphail. He is down by the shore now loading timber. Our guest is helping.'

'Is the message from our sister?'

'From Peter. They have a place where he can hide, an empty shieling. He can wait there until someone comes for him. Then he will be taken to the Rough Bounds, but whereabouts I do not know.'

'When?'

'When what?'

'To Corran. When is he to go?'

'Sleepy is due back next week. He will slip our guest on board then. What happens after is no longer up to me.'

'Who is paying Sleepy?

'Do not worry about that. The man and I have dealings. I will take care of it.'

'I suppose Peter will be keeping quiet as to the plans afoot for the lords.'

Douglas nodded. 'But if Tullibardine and the others arrive in the Rough Bounds we should hear about it soon enough from our sister. In any case the militia will not get to them there, or the army. Out at sea is another matter; that is where they will be at their weakest.'

Shona started pushing the plunger on the churn once more. Douglas served himself a bowl of ale, conversed briefly with his wife, then went out again. All morning Shona helped her sister-in-law with chores. After making butter she went to the burn and, since the rain had stopped, scrubbed clean all the wooden containers and utensils used for dairy products. Then one of Douglas' cottars appeared with a pony bearing two full creels of fish fresh from the sea. Shona and the two eldest of her brother's children were soon at work inside the house gutting, salting and layering the fish in a barrel.

While thus occupied, Shona was ruminating, wondering what she was going to do when the Spaniard left. It was near three weeks since they had conversed in the cavern. At first, afterwards, Shona had wanted to unburden herself on paper and explain to the Spaniard all the things about her life and situation she had been unable to explain to him properly in person. A couple more times she had gone for French lessons and for periods she had sat at her brother's table with pencil and paper and the French dictionary. But while she could formulate sentences in French to explain many of the things she was yearning to say she could never finish the letter in her mind, not for lack of skill, but because she was uncertain suddenly of what she was wanting the outcome for herself to be. That she must endeavour to put his mind at ease was not in doubt. But what would she take from it herself? Secretly there were moments when she saw herself going with him, leaving the country altogether and putting herself at the mercy of the unknown. The glimpse of a great adventure then opened up before her, a notion that filled her with trepidation and made her heart flutter. But thinking and deciding were not the same. Besides the fear there was a sense of duty. As much as she persuaded herself that all her feelings for Hector were gone she could not say the same for kin, friends, servants, and the tenants and cottars on the estate who in one way or another had links to her. Thoughts of them tugged at her to make her stay, and while it was true that she had not changed Hector's mind up to now, was it so certain that she never would? Had she the right to stop trying? And was it so certain, also, that relations between them were forever beyond repair? Perhaps there was a way back after all, somehow, across the morass that separated them? Miracles did happen. God could bless her with children. Hector might yet change his ways in a manner she could adapt to. But if she renounced her life here and the Spaniard were persuaded to take her with him, it would have to be forever. She could not imagine how it would be possible for her to return from such a total severance of her present circumstance. Thus torn, divided by two contrary urges, she found no way of addressing de la Rueda in a manner that left everything clear, either for de la Rueda or herself. The truth was that beyond the yearning of her body, and her wish to ease de la Rueda's conscience, she needed to know just how fully she desired to join her fate to his before she could put it down on paper. So she wrote parts of the letter out, but prevaricated, and left it unfinished while she struggled painfully, despairingly even, to work out her path.

As for de la Rueda, he laboured at things physical. Every morning he woke up afflicted. To some extent, with their talk in the cavern, Shona had made him understand that their union had not been so clear a betrayal as he had at first believed. Her husband, it appeared, in her judgement at least, was not so honourable a man as he had assumed. This is what she had tried to tell him. The marriage was not good. She had not given herself to him without reason. And she had promised him a letter, to make him understand more clearly. But the drowning heaviness he felt in his soul remained. He did not blame her, she had her reasons, but he could not so easily absolve himself. For all those years, ever since he had seen her portrait, he had carried the image of her in his mind like a talisman. She had appeared to him in dreams, in battle, at moments when he had felt himself close to death. She had saved him. Or so he had believed, for now he had to wonder if actually it had not been the Devil's scheme all along to use her as a decoy? Everything in his moral self seemed to him now suspicious, as though he could no longer trust himself to act in the way he wished to act, to be the person he wished to be. He felt stained inside, corrupted, morally adrift, but it did not prevent him from wanting her, from thinking of her, from waiting for her. All he knew to do to get away from dwelling on his situation was to throw himself into physical labour. Never one in the past to willingly leave a warm bed, now he got up almost the moment he opened his eyes, as if the bed itself were in flames. Once dressed he was soon out of the barn ready to do all and any work Douglas could provide for him. Virtually all of it was to do with the sawing, felling, and transportation of timber to the shore. Some jobs he could do alone; most he did alongside others. It was hard, dangerous work, and men were impressed with de la Rueda's willingness to labour all day in all conditions. They were respectful towards him, always polite in their gestures, and while there was no possibility of engaging in conversation, he was able to pick up here and there the odd word of their language. When the day was over de la Rueda was so exhausted he could hold a scarce thought in his mind. He was aware of Shona, her presence at the table in Douglas' house and at other moments, but he had no strength to dwell on her. He wished only to eat and rest. As soon as he lay down on the bed in the barn he was asleep. It was later, often in the middle of the night, that he awoke weighed down by the despair in his soul that all day long he had managed to avoid.

So time passed until the day before Sleepy Macphail was due to arrive. In the afternoon Shona helped her sister-in-law and a servant, a cottar woman from a nearby house, prepare a meal more elaborate than usual as a farewell gesture for their guest. As she plucked one of two ducks that had been slain and did various other chores, all the while she was dwelling on her predicament, trying to make up her mind, and as much as it distressed her she was attempting to persuade herself that she had no choice but to let the Spaniard depart from here without her. *I have come far enough. Later I will finish the letter. I will give it to him and then may he go with God to the Rough Bounds and his own country.*

But when Douglas appeared in the afternoon, all at once and without being able to prevent it, Shona heard herself saying, 'I have been thinking; I will go with the Spaniard to our sister's. I would like to see our sister again.'

Both Douglas and Kirstine looked at her in surprise.

'It was not so long ago that Rhona was at our uncle's funeral,' observed Douglas, a frown appearing on his otherwise flushed and good-humoured face.

'My mind is made up. I will go nevertheless.'

All women could be stubborn, Douglas knew. His own wife would sometimes not budge when she had a notion fixed. But the stubbornness in Shona was fierce. He had encountered it often enough when they were children to know that he had little appetite to battle against it now as an adult. Still, Rhona could not be the whole reason why she would want to go. And if that was only a part of the reason what was the rest? *The Spaniard. It had to be the Spaniard.*

'Well, I know better than to try and talk you out of it. Are you thinking of asking Neil to go with you?'

'I am not. But I want to ask you to take Neil and John back if that is what they wish.'

'Would they not be better off where they are?'

Shona took a deep breath.

'Hector is my husband, but I no longer care for him.'

'We have guessed that. One way or another you have been telling us so since you arrived, and before that even.'

'We have suspected it for a couple of years now,' Kirstine agreed.

'I cannot trust him. He will have little regard for Neil or Old John's well-being if I should not care to live with him again. Hector puts profit above all else, but you know about all this.'

'The times are changing, Shona. It is everywhere the same. Hector is no different from many another landlord.'

'But it is not my way, Douglas. And not yours; at least I hope not.'

Douglas turned his face away. Kirstine saw the passing look of distress but kept silent.

'I do not know how much longer we can carry on here as we are,' said Douglas. 'Timber is slow to replenish and when we run short I may have to put sheep on some of the arable myself. But well, we will not turn them away. Neil is kin and Old John was our father's man.'

'I will tell them. They can decide for themselves when I know better what I am doing.'

Douglas gave a laugh in spite of himself. 'And when might that be?'

'I will dwell upon it when I am at our sister's. Meanwhile Neil and Old John must do as they wish. The boat will have to return to Hector in any case.'

'He may be displeased if it returns to him without you.'

He can keep company with the Devil then.

When de la Rueda came in for dinner he did not know that it was a farewell meal. But he could see straight away that it was not like other evenings for the table was laid with the best crockery, the children were a little cleaner than usual, and both Shona and Kirstine had added fresh embellishments to their attire. Douglas soon had his best quaich out, made of silver and carved wood, and was filling it with whisky. After being together for these last few weeks the two men had established a simplified mode of communication consisting of gestures with the occasional Gaelic, French or Latin word thrown in that seemed to work well enough. But Douglas did not have the means to broach the subject that was on his mind, and as for de la Rueda, it was as much as he could manage to pretend Shona was not the sole focus of his attention. He was afraid to look at her, even more to speak to her.

'Do you not think we should inform our guest of the situation?' Douglas said eventually as they were sitting down at the table.

Shona waited until de la Rueda had been served: duck with rosemary, cheese, and a little kale accompanied by a mug of ale.

'*Monsieur*, tomorrow you go. Boat. You go boat.'

De la Rueda was taken aback. His departure was something he was always anticipating, but now as he raised his eyes to Shona his emotions surged in turmoil. *Where? To my own country? But without you. Is that what I want? Or would I rather damnation? Lord Jesus save me.*

'Where, M*adame?*' de la Rueda spoke with difficulty. 'Where is the boat taking me?'

'A different house. My sister…' Shona could not find the word. 'My sister she does. She do for you.'

'Arrange? Did your sister arrange it?'

'*Oui.* My sister arrange. I go on boat...to my sister… with you.' Shona spoke the last words quickly, looking down at her food, but almost at once she looked up again.

And de la Rueda was alive again. His heart thumped. Almost he smiled. *Damned, dishonoured, but alive. My life is not my own. I cannot save it.*

'And Spain?' he asked. 'Are there arrangements?'

'Douglas, our guest wishes to know if there are arrangements for his journey home?'

'I think not just yet. There should be once the lords start arriving, although it will be a while before a ship can be purchased.'

'My brother cannot say, *Monsieur.* We wait for arrange boat to… country yours.'

After the food Douglas brought out the quaich once more. The men imbibed larger quantities than the women or children but all had a taste or more of whisky. Then de la Rueda stood up, bowed, and took his leave. A child was sent to fetch the servant woman who had gone back to her house and family not a hundred yards away. When she came in she was given what was the left of the two ducks and some cheese. A scrap was given to the dog. After that everyone, except Shona, retired to bed. For a while Shona sat in front of the hearth, then she got up and went to the table where, with a lamp and the dictionary, she tried to finish the letter to de la Rueda. But a sudden impetuous change of mind came to her. Wrapping the arisaid around her, she left the house and stepped the few yards to the malting barn. Without knocking she pushed the door open. De la Rueda lay on his bed under a blanket, but he was dressed and not asleep. He heard the door open and turned his head. She stopped by the door, a shadowy figure under the hood of the arisaid. Straight away de la Rueda sat up. For just a moment longer Shona hesitated, then she came over to him with her quick, slightly pigeon-toed steps.

'I do not love husband,' she said. 'I cannot live with him. No dishonour you. *I choose.* Is me. I choose *you.* I am free woman.'

She pulled the hood of the arisaid away and without a kertch to cover her head she stood before him with her long hair loose and her eyes glowing in the penumbra and her breasts taut against the fabric of her shirt.

God save me. De la Rueda lifted his arms and reached for her.

'This is where I turn back,' said the innkeeper.

They had come to a stream and the three men had dismounted while the ponies sipped at the water that flowed gurgling in between bracken and over dark stones.

'Tell me again,' said Lachlan.

'Straight on. After a mile or so there is a pile of rocks from olden times. Turn uphill there, through the birch trees, you will see it.'

'And there is no one else staying. You are certain of this?'

'That is the information I have.'

It was one of the things that most worried Lachlan, that there could be one or more others in the shieling besides the whore and the Spaniard, for it was not clear the means by which the whore was to join her sister in the Rough Bounds. Whether by boat or on foot he did not know. The innkeeper could only send a post boy with the information he had received himself, which, so Lachlan understood, had come from the informant's wife on Skye, and it was that the Spaniard and the whore were in days to be put on Sleepy Machpail's boat and taken to Corran, there to await transport into the Rough Bounds where lived the whore's sister. That was all he knew, and he had arrived with his brother-in-law as soon as he was able, staying out of sight as much as he could. So far fate had favoured him by getting the whore here, for just as well he could have lost her had she gone somewhere else, further afield. In fact, while the possibility of getting rid of her had settled in his mind he had not actually expected an opportunity of such convenience to present itself. But it was all very dangerous. He could take nothing for given. Almost he had been on the point of calling it off when he had tried and failed to get Hector tied in. Neither bullying or flattery had succeeded. And as much as Hector was poking his niece, and for all the laudanum he was taking down, he would not say what Lachlan desired him to say. Hector had sworn and made threats in the heat of the moment but nothing more. He had not agreed that Lachlan should arrange it, he had not sat down with him to plan it. Still, as things stood, if he and Pol were not caught but it was discovered, he could hope to put the blame on Hector regardless. He could make it appear that it was all Hector's plan to avenge himself on his wife and he could deflect his own participation. But if those two were not alone, if there were others come from the whore's brother or, more likely, her sister, and he were caught or even clearly seen it would be very difficult for him to make a case. A living witness would change all. Lachlan did not fancy his chances against the Glas and Macdonald of Arisaig clans without a foil in between.

The innkeeper turned his pony around and mounted the saddle. Although there was little light it was enough for the pony to embark on the return journey of twelve or so miles.

'I am not here and I never came here,' the innkeeper muttered to Lachlan as the pony moved off.

After the other ponies had drunk they were hobbled, then Lachlan took off his plaid, for the evening was warm, and in shirt and trews he readjusted across his muscular chest the belts that held his two pistols and ammunition pouch and powder horn. Then he eased his broadsword up and down in its scabbard and touched the hilt of his dirk.

'Check the haversack again, Pol.'

The small man opened the canvas haversack. A strong smell of pine resin wafted up. The pitch soaked cloth wads were as they should be. 'It is all there.'

'Is the tinderbox dry?'

Pol opened the tinderbox. 'It is.'

'Let us go then.'

The two men crossed the stream and began marching over the heath. The brooding sky to the west, over the sea, was stained with red and yellow. The hills immediately above and around them were empty. The nearest settlement, which they had managed to avoid, was several miles away. The last thing Lachlan wanted was to encounter another living soul. After they had been walking a little while a small knoll appeared with lichen-covered stones and rock slabs scattered on its summit – all that remained of a pagan site. Here Lachlan stopped. He motioned for Pol to stay put and then stepping as quietly as he knew how, he went around the knoll and obliquely up a slope to a copse of birch and hazel trees. Bending low he stepped in among the trees and after a few yards he could peer out of them onto a slightly sloping heath that bordered a hazel forest and where less than a hundred yards from him stood a small stone hut with a roof of thatched bracken. There was no indication of life; not even smoke from a fire. Was there nobody? Well, he would chance it anyway. If there was nobody it did not matter.

The two of them reclined on a rough mattress of heather, side by side, the plaid and arisaid converted into blankets, and their backs cushioned with more heather against the stone wall.

'What is like?' asked Shona. 'Is big land. Yours. You have?'

'It is different to here,' de la Rueda said. 'But yes. It is big enough.'

'How many cows?'

'Not so many. It cannot be like here; too many wolves and bears.'

Shona did not understand.

'*Loups,*' she repeated. 'What is?'

De la Rueda grinned, opened his mouth and made howling sounds.

Wolves. Her green eyes opened wide. Although she had never heard a wolf howl it was rumoured that one had been killed not so many years back in Sutherland.

'Where live you… is *loups*?'

'Many. They eat cows. Eat sheep. Eat goats. Eat people.' De la Rueda held up his hands and scrunched his fingers as he brought them down and playfully, all at once, began tickling her. Shona wriggled and laughed. De la Rueda kissed her, chuckling, and then leaned back again against the wall.

'What… to eat, grows?'

'On my land?'

'*Oui.*'

'Many things. Wheat. Potatoes. Maize. Fruit. Grapes for wine. Apples, pears, cherries...'

Shona only understood some of the words. But it did not matter. She had a sense that he was talking abundance.

'You will like it,' he said. 'In my country it is warmer; more sun, a lot more sun. And we are together now. It had to be. It was fate.'

Shona's hand found his under the blanket. She was comforted. She liked the feel of his hand wrapped around hers and their bodies pressed side by side. What the future held for them she did not know, but she would not turn back now. Her life with Hector was over. She was with Alejandro, she would live with him in Spain and every day she would pray to God to have mercy on them. Why should they be condemned? Hector had not deserved her love. God would know. God could see everything, He could look into their souls and see that they were without blame, that it was love that had brought them together, a love she had not had for Hector, had never felt for him. How could God not forgive them for wanting to be happy?

De la Rueda was also thinking of their lives ahead. He was not so sure as Shona that their union was without sin. Hector remained always in the back of his mind, an uncomfortable accusatory presence disposed to haunt his conscience and make his feelings towards Shona less clear. But he did not doubt that he loved her like he had loved no other woman before and believed he could never so love again. And it gave him hope. He had not completed his service, but he could buy his way out of the army. He would retire with Shona to his estate. If God willed it, they would have children. He would be a good father, a good man to Shona, and he would seek God's favour. He would work hard, go to Mass, be fair and honest with all those who depended on him. De la Rueda could imagine how time might go by, how in spite of the stain to his honour he might find contentment and peace with the woman he loved.

There was a sudden crackling sound.

For just an instant de la Rueda was nonplussed, then he jumped up. But even as he did so the crackling sound was spreading above his head in the low roof. Yellow flames appeared. And smoke. De la Rueda grabbed his sheathed sword and almost in the same motion his other arm reached over and seized hold of Shona, pulling her to her feet. The flames exploded inches above their heads and smoke swirled. They both knew they had but moments before they were burnt alive. De la Rueda unsheathed the sword. Looking at Shona, he threw out his arms. 'You run! Run! Understand? Run!' With one shoulder he rammed the wooden door open and without hesitating he seized Shona and pushed her out, shouting again, 'Run!' A shot sounded as Shona began to run, but Lachlan, standing by the door, had not fired straight. Even as he was pressing the trigger de la Rueda's sword had lashed out from behind Shona into empty space, missing Lachlan but not before deflecting his aim just enough so that the bullet no more than grazed her arm. Then de la Rueda was upon him. Although Lachlan's spare hand held a dirk he had no time to stab de la Rueda before their bodies closed and de la Rueda was inside his guard. Lachan was strong but de la Rueda held him close with his free arm around his waist while his sword arm lashed at his legs. Lachlan felt his legs collapsing. He struggled violently but fell backwards onto the ground. Looking up, he saw de la Rueda standing hunched above him with the orange and black blaze of the roof behind and de la Rueda's arm raised to bring his sword down. Then de la Rueda felt a thud, a shattering inside his chest, in his heart. The crackling sound of the fire so nearby masked the musket shot that came from the copse, but de la Rueda knew he had been shot. Shona, from the edge of the hazel wood, heard the shot clearly. She stopped and looked back and saw de la Rueda lurching, stumbling, waiving his sword to bring it down on the prone man she at once recognized to be Lachlan. But instead of striking Lachlan, de la Rueda turned away and looked straight at Shona.

I see you. My time is over but yours is yet to be. Fly now. Save yourself.

De la Rueda raised his eyes to heaven as they clouded over and he felt his soul leave him, expanding into infinite space at the moment the sword fell from his hand and his body dropped to the earth.

Lachlan was alive but could not rise to his feet. An artery in his leg was severed and blood was pumping out, a pool of it gathering on the ground around him. Pol watched, crouched on the ground behind the trunk of a birch tree. He waited to see if Lachlan would get to his feet, for he did not dare show himself while Shona was there to see him.

Shona also held back. But not for long. *I am ready. We will die together.* She ran back and dropped to her knees beside de la Rueda, praying to find him alive. His eyes were open and there appeared to be the shadow of a smile on his bearded face. He looked peaceful, but he was gone from her.

Pol still watched. He saw Shona kneeling over the Spaniard and a yard or two away from her he saw Lachlan's body make an abrupt effort, as though to rise from the stain of blood, then fall back, twitch, and become still. Shona looked over his body towards the copse. Pol was well hidden. She would not see him crouched behind the birch trees. Quietly he reached into his ammunition pouch for another cartridge and he was about to bite into the paper so as to start loading the musket when he changed his mind. What was the point? If not already dead Lachlan would soon be so. It was for Forbia to take charge now and make the decisions. Pol would not take the risk for an outcome that for him had become suddenly unpredictable.

Quietly he rose to his feet, and bending low, musket in hand, began to retreat.

Pol had not gone four steps when he changed his mind again. His daughter was with the laird now. They were together. A couple. He could not let Shona live. *She will destroy us all. She must die. I must kill her.* Pol turned about and once again he reached for a cartridge, but this time he stepped wrongly. There was a cracking sound under his foot. And when he looked up he saw Shona, as still as a doe, her head straight and her big eyes fixed in his direction. Then she jumped up and began to run.

The dense hazel trees were close by. She threw herself into the first narrow gap she saw. Low branches smashed against her. A tugging at her heel made her yelp, fearing it was his hand, but it was her foot slipping. Pol was five yards and more behind her, gasping as he threw down his musket, which would be of no use to him here.

It was not a thicket she knew. She crouched low, squeezing and twisting under the hard branches as she flailed to push aside the thinner ones. Her heart beat in her ears and in between the beats she could hear him behind her as he struggled with the branches himself. Pol wanted to kill her but it was not so much fear of dying that was impelling her escape. It was more of not finding the means to kill him first. He was only a small man, but he was a man; stronger, wiry, and armed.

He was upon her. She heard his wheezing breath and felt her skirt being pulled back. Bringing her hand down she yanked the cloth with all her strength while at the same time twisting her body away. In so doing she turned just enough to find herself staring into Pol's small savage eyes as he tried to hold her back with one hand while drawing a dirk with the other. But two firm branches and several lesser ones stood between them. Before Pol could fully remove the dirk, Shona had buried her teeth into his hand, biting hard while again she yanked at her skirt. It came free and instantly she fled under a low arch of branches. Pol, grunting, scrambled sideways to get past the branches in his way. It was a matter of seconds but long enough for Shona to gain a distance of several yards. At the end of the arch the ground fell away sharply. A cluster of tall fissured limestone rocks stood among the trees on the slope. Without hesitating she dived almost head first around the side of them. Landing on her knees she picked herself up and darted around a hazel tree and behind a second stack of rocks. Here she dared glance back, saw no one, and noticed that beside her the stack was split by a deep cleft with a lesser rock partially obscuring it. Fear was urging her body to run again, but behind the fear a more implacable rage asserted itself. Scrambling over the rock she squeezed into the cleft and ducked low.

Pol had arrived too late at the stacks to see which way she had gone. Clutching the dirk, he swiftly circled the first stack and then moved to the second. His eyes darted this way and that as he went around it. Though he noticed the cleft he saw nothing in it; he passed it by, descending to yet another outcrop on steeper ground, closer to the shore. Shona had heard him going by. Almost as soon as he was gone she raised her head from behind the rock and climbed out. She realized now she had the advantage. It was her chance to escape. Leaving the rock she started to climb the slope to gain distance when, looking to her right, she noticed that the heavy thicket there would conceal her but also, if she went to the edge, it would give her a view of the shoreline below. Making as little sound as possible and almost on her hands and knees, she moved into the thicket.

Now crouching behind a tree on the very edge of the thicket she peered below her and almost at once she spotted Pol in his grubby plaid, blue bonnet on his head, dirk in hand, emerging onto the swampy bank above the shore itself. Shona watched him stop and look about him and then back up at the thicket. He was undecided but after a moment he started heading toward the ground directly beneath Shona. All along it, at the edge of the curving shoreline there were stacks of rock. One of these was directly below her. It projected from a narrow strip of bog and rocks and had a flat top. The stony shoreline was some three yards below it. Shona thought quickly. It was dangerous but rage governed her. She did not care for life or safety. Leaving the hazel thicket, she stopped to claw a rock from the boggy ground. Holding the rock in both hands, she flattened herself down on her belly on top of the stack. Moments passed. She heard Pol before she saw him. The scraping sound of his feet was just audible above the hum of the breeze and the sea. She drew her knees in, sat up quietly, and tightened her grip on the rock. Pol was moving now around the side of the stack. Although she could not see him she had a sense that he was below her. She took a breath, jumped to her feet, and stepped to the edge of the stack. He was below her, two yards down and half a yard to her left.

Pol was starting to raise his head when she jumped. He had no time to avoid her. She landed on his head and they crashed to the ground. She was still holding the rock. After an instant when she did not know quite what was happening she felt him moving under her, struggling. She pulled her body aside, saw his balding head, without the bonnet now, and brought the rock down. Once. And then again. He made no more sound than a grunt. He stopped moving. But still she lifted the rock and brought it down, smashing Pol's skull, blood splattering her. Again and again she brought the rock down, howling with grief and rage.

EPILOGUE

It was the first time Shona had emerged on the deck since the storm had abated early in the morning. After the dank turmoil in her quarters, she breathed in the fresh sea air with relief. Above her the sun shone down from a sky of such intense blue as she had not seen before. But it was October. The breeze that came from the sea was cold and Shona wrapped the arisaid tightly around her as she stood by the rail, the ship creaking and gently rolling under her feet. Presently gulls appeared overhead. In the far distance across a sea that had become mercifully benign, a long thin outline of land was visible. Shona thought it must be France and at once she was both hopeful and sad.

'It will not be long now, Shona.'

She had not noticed the man approach. But he stopped by her side now. He was wrapped up in a fine quality plaid; a tall, vaguely effeminate figure with a powdered, snub nosed face framed by a long white peruke.

'It will not be, your lordship.'

'It is not our own country, of course.' The Marquis of Tullibardine lamented, trying to quell a feeling of bitter disappointment, for the loss of the battle festered in his mind like a wound.

When Shona remained silent the marquis clapped his hands and made himself bring up a weak smile. 'We must put a brave face on it, however. And much goes on in Paris to keep one amused. I hope you will find it agreeable and myself not too mean an employer.'

'Thank you. I am in your debt.'

'As I am in yours.'

The marquis did not elaborate. But Shona knew he was referring to the arrangements accomplished by her sister's husband and others to conceal him in the Rough Bounds and to purchase his passage out of the country. As for Shona, she in turn was obliged to the marquis for offering to take her on as his housekeeper. It was the start of a new life for her; one that just a few months ago she would never have dreamed of. *I will live to see what happens, and I will try to make the best of it.* But deep within she was broken. She grieved for Alejandro, she grieved for her Spanish captain. Without him the new life was not the one she had anticipated.

Except for one thing. She had missed three periods. She was all but certain she was with child. Alejandro's child. A flicker of gold from out of the darkness.

END